WIRES CROSSED

By BETH FANTASKEY

Illustrated by ONEILLJONES

CLARION BOOKS
Imprints of HarperCollins Publishers

Clarion Books is an imprint of HarperCollins Publishers.
HarperAlley is an imprint of HarperCollins Publishers.

Wires Crossed
Text copyright © 2024 by Beth Fantaskey
Illustrations copyright © 2024 by ONeillJones

Library of Congress Control Number: 2023937008
ISBN 978-0-35-839544-7 — ISBN 978-0-35-839621-5 (pbk.)

The illustrations in this book were created with an ancient Wacom Cintiq 13HD
in Clip Studio Paint with the help of entirely too much coffee.
Typography by Phil Caminiti and Alice Wang

24 25 26 27 28 GPS 10 9 8 7 6 5 4 3 2 1
First Edition

WIRES CROSSED

For Paige, Mei, and Hope —B.F.

For R.A.D. Always, forever,
no matter what —O.N.J.

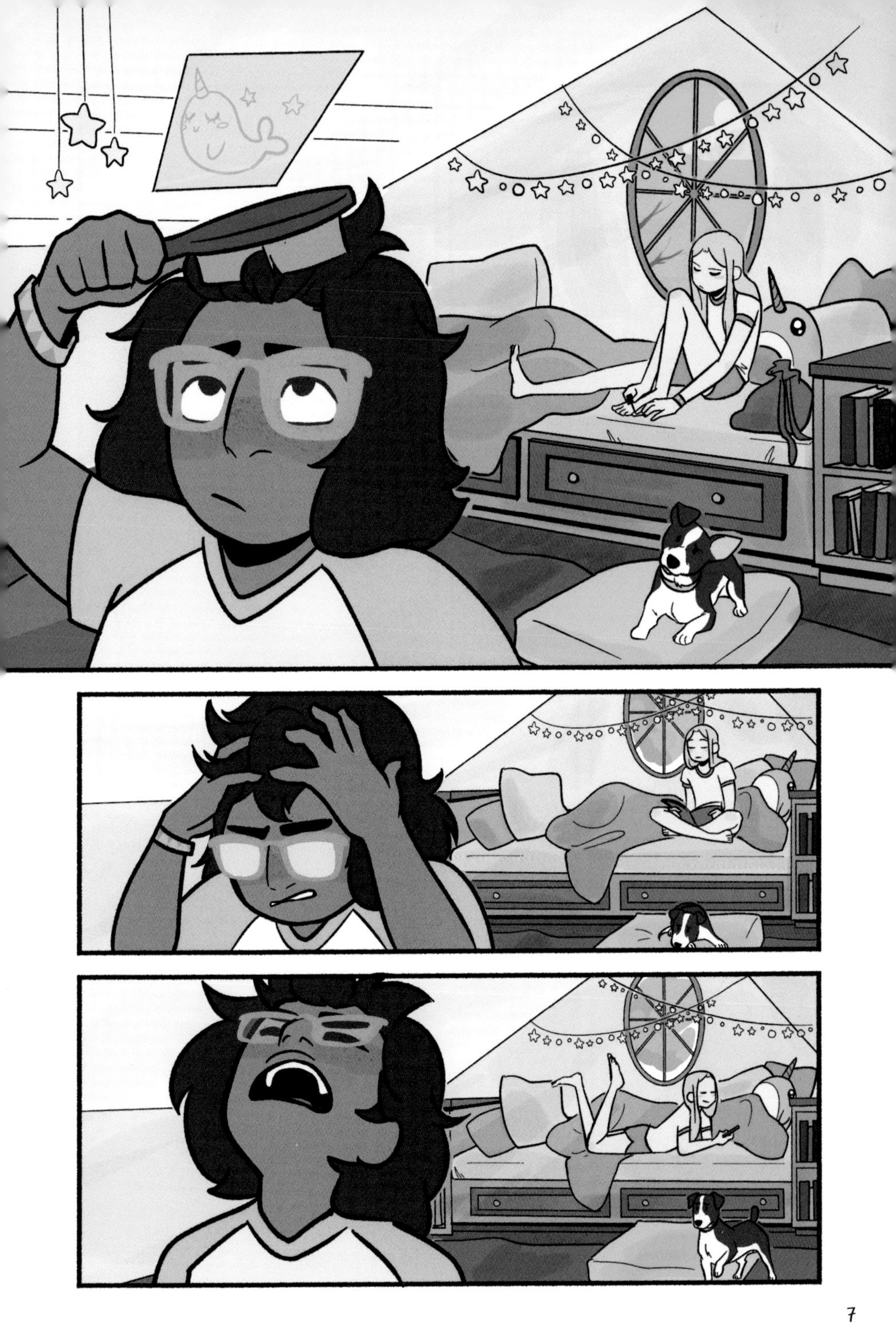

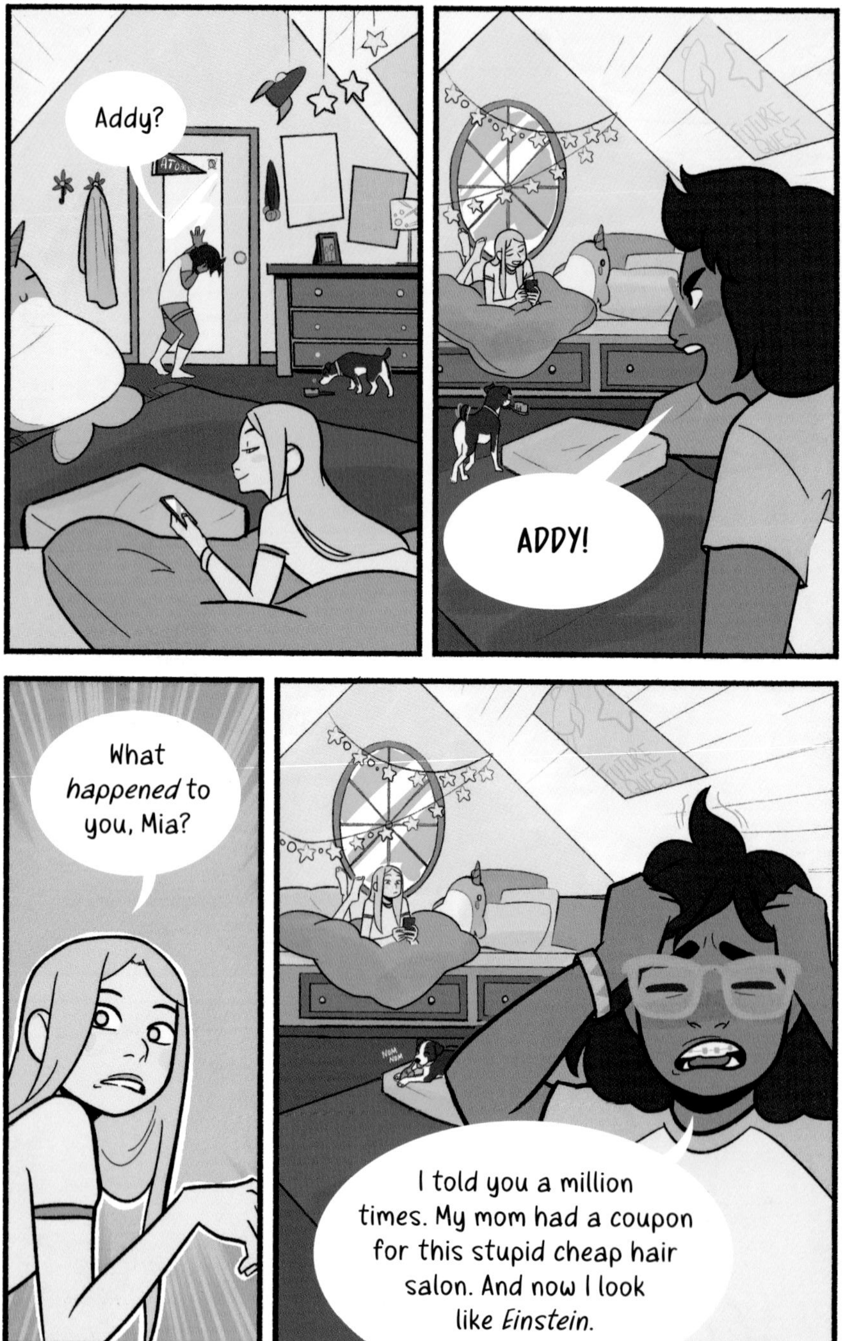
Addy?
ADDY!
What *happened* to you, Mia?
NOM NOM
I told you a million times. My mom had a coupon for this stupid cheap hair salon. And now I look like *Einstein*.

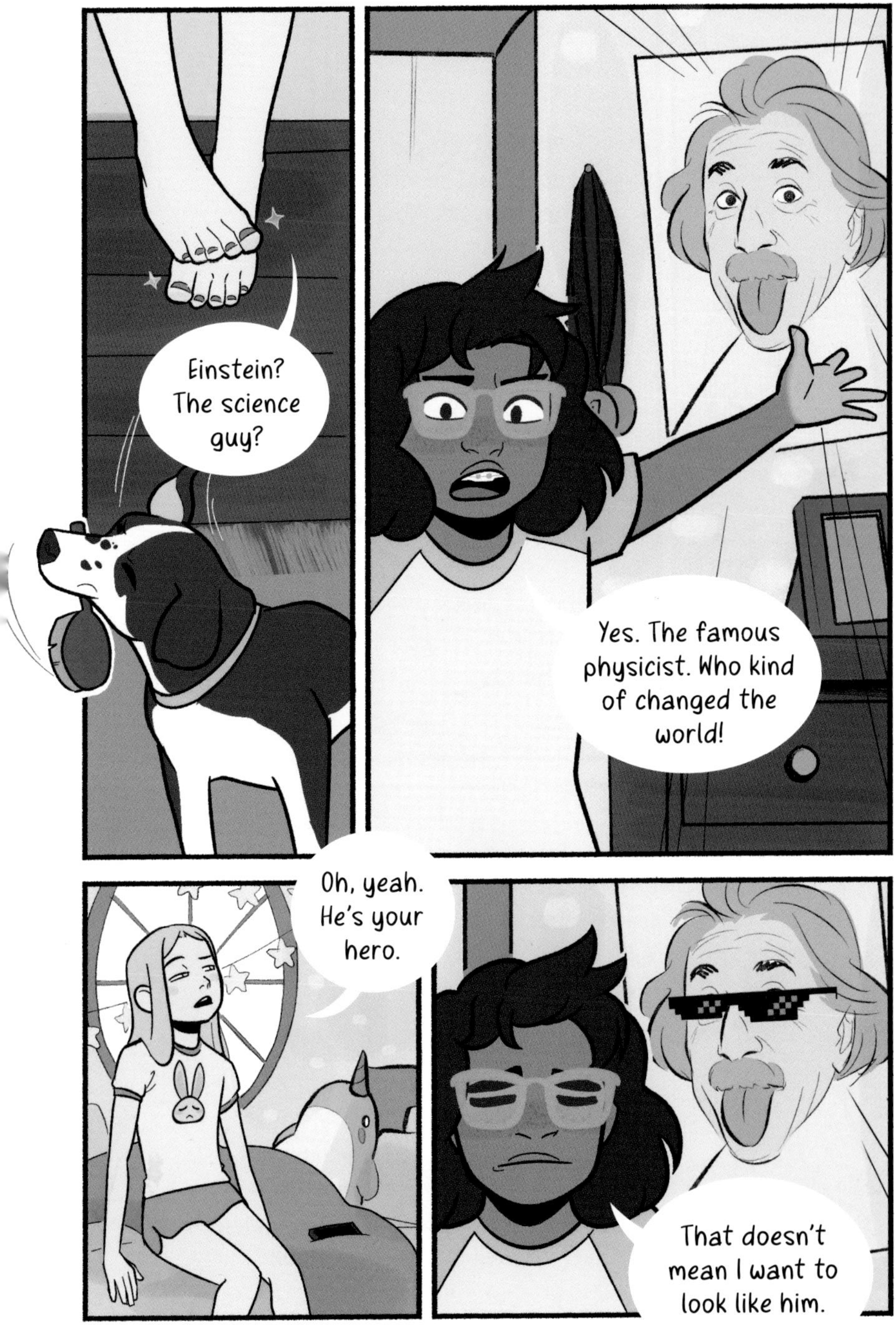
Einstein? The science guy?
Yes. The famous physicist. Who kind of changed the world!
Oh, yeah. He's your hero.
That doesn't mean I want to look like him.

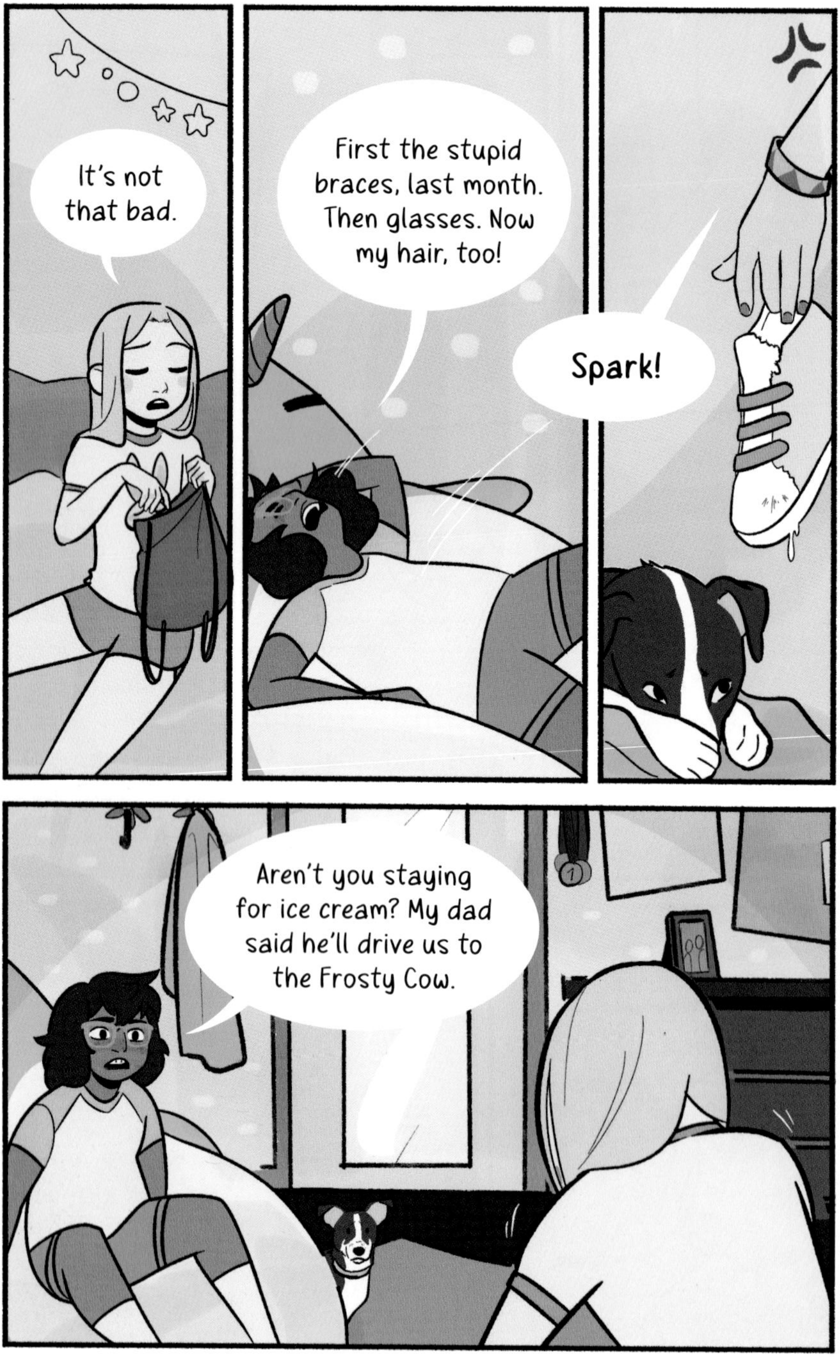
It's not that bad.
First the stupid braces, last month. Then glasses. Now my hair, too!
Spark!
Aren't you staying for ice cream? My dad said he'll drive us to the Frosty Cow.

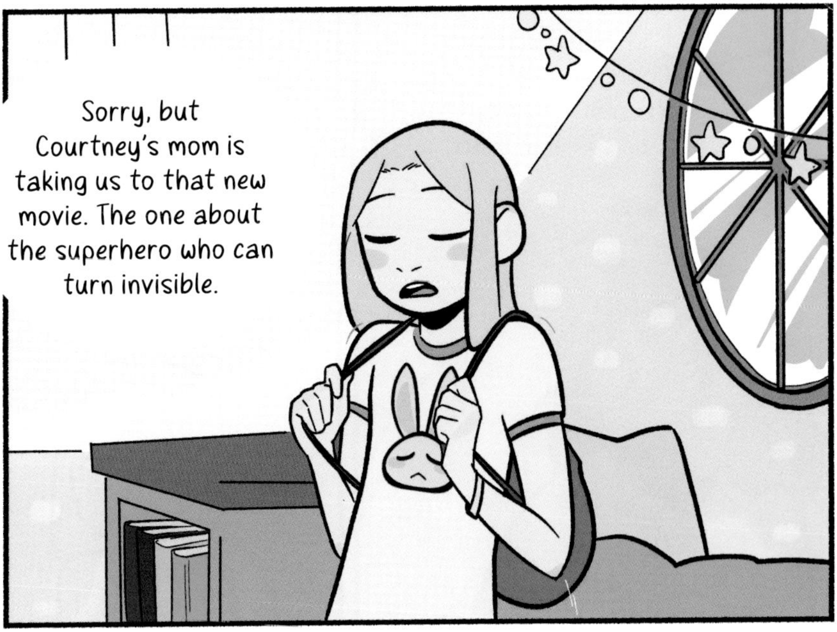
Sorry, but Courtney's mom is taking us to that new movie. The one about the superhero who can turn invisible.

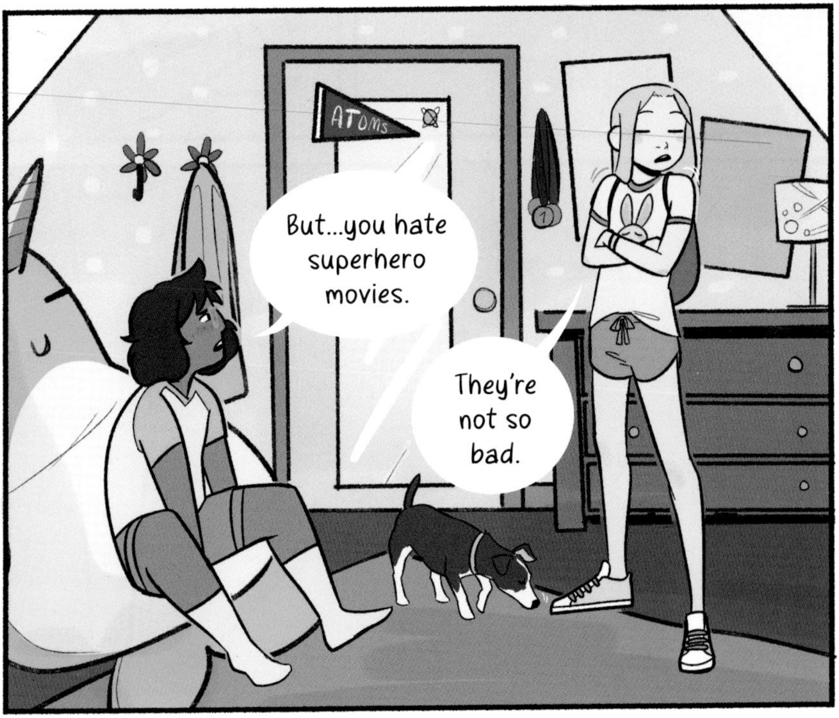
ATOMS
But...you hate superhero movies.
They're not so bad.

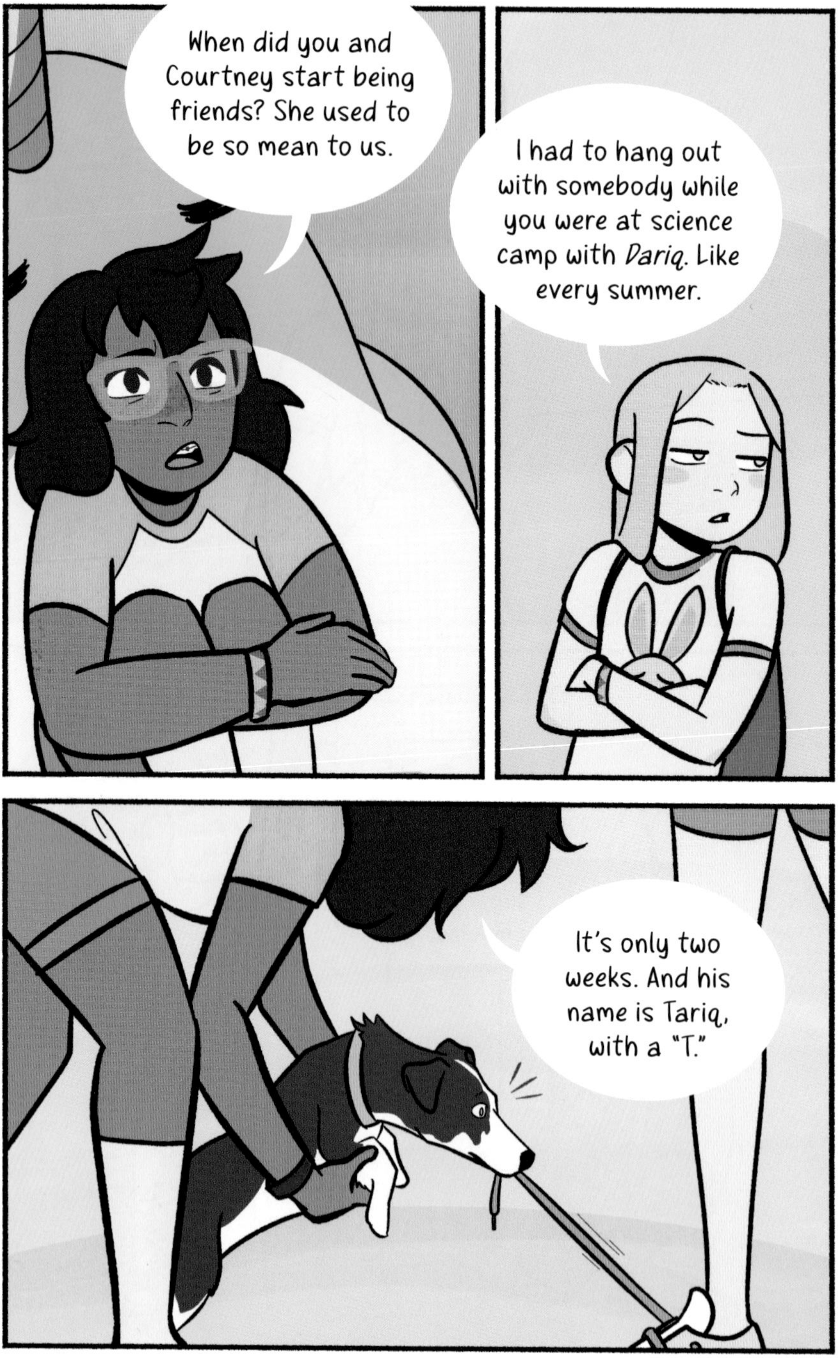
When did you and Courtney start being friends? She used to be so mean to us.
I had to hang out with somebody while you were at science camp with *Dariq*. Like every summer.
It's only two weeks. And his name is Tariq, with a "T."

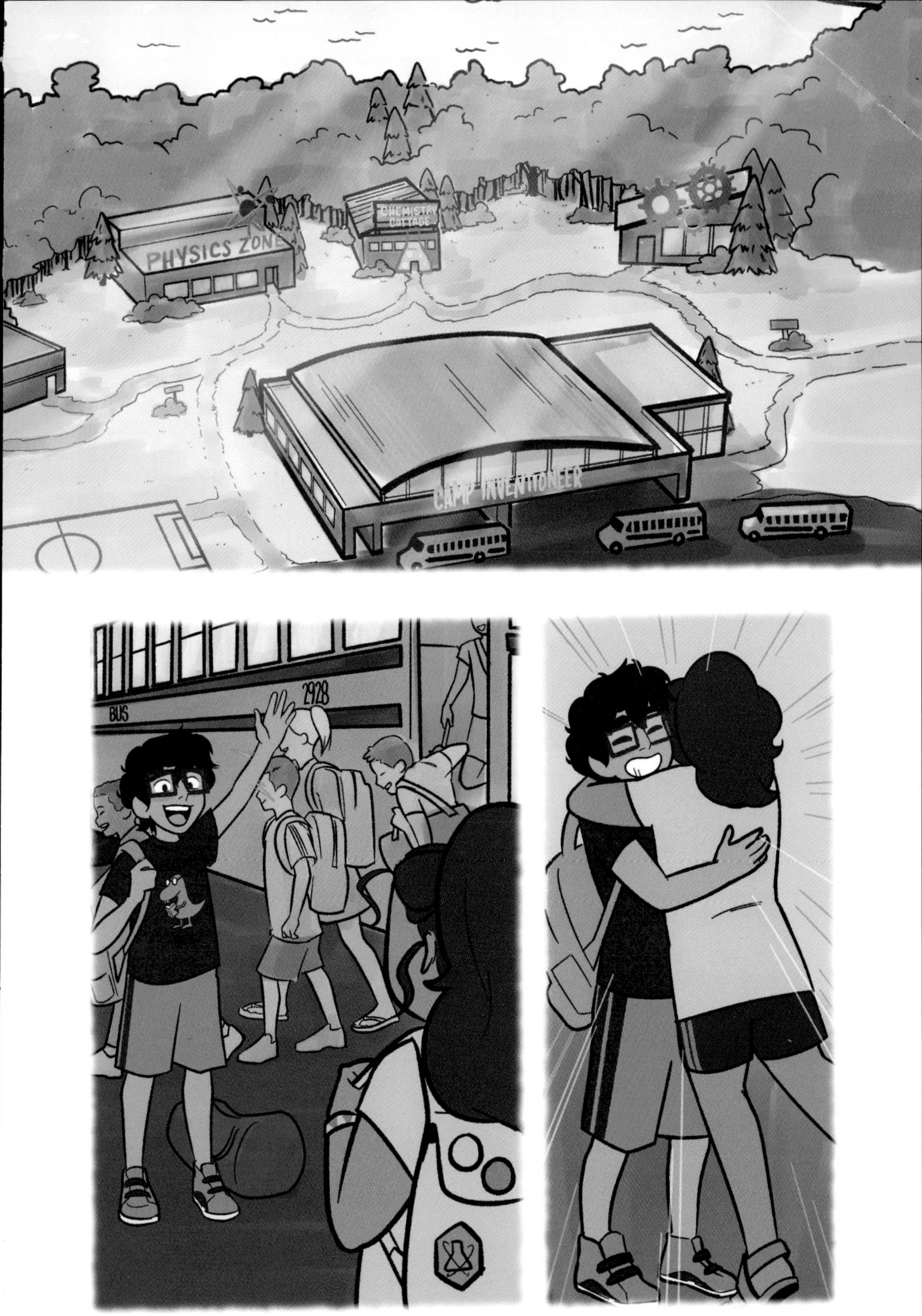
PHYSICS ZONE
CHEMISTRY COTTAGE
CAMP INVENTIONEER
2928
BUS

SEE YOU
NEXT YEAR
0110101 01101001
0110001 !!

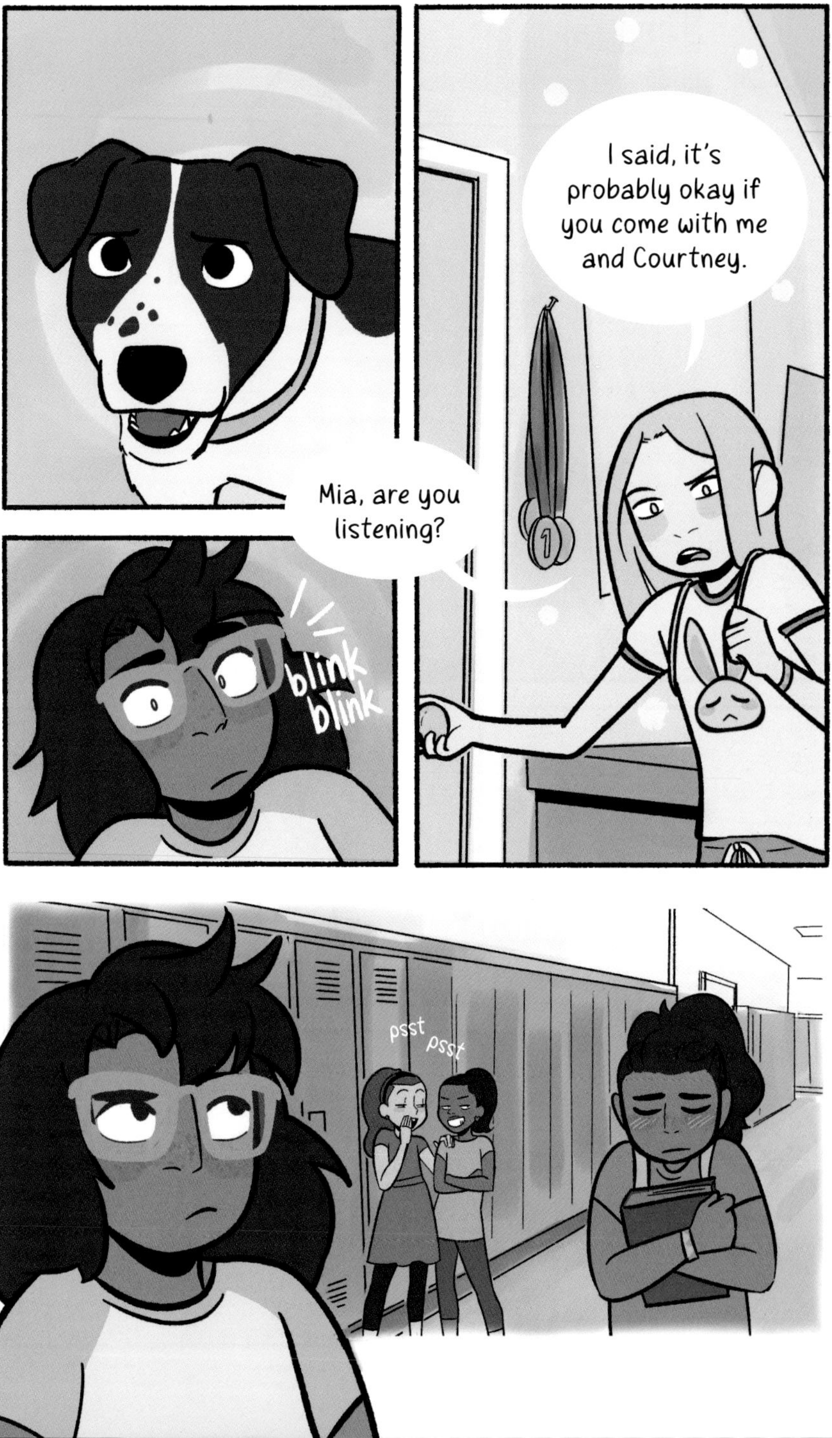
I said, it's probably okay if you come with me and Courtney.
Mia, are you listening?
blink blink
psst psst

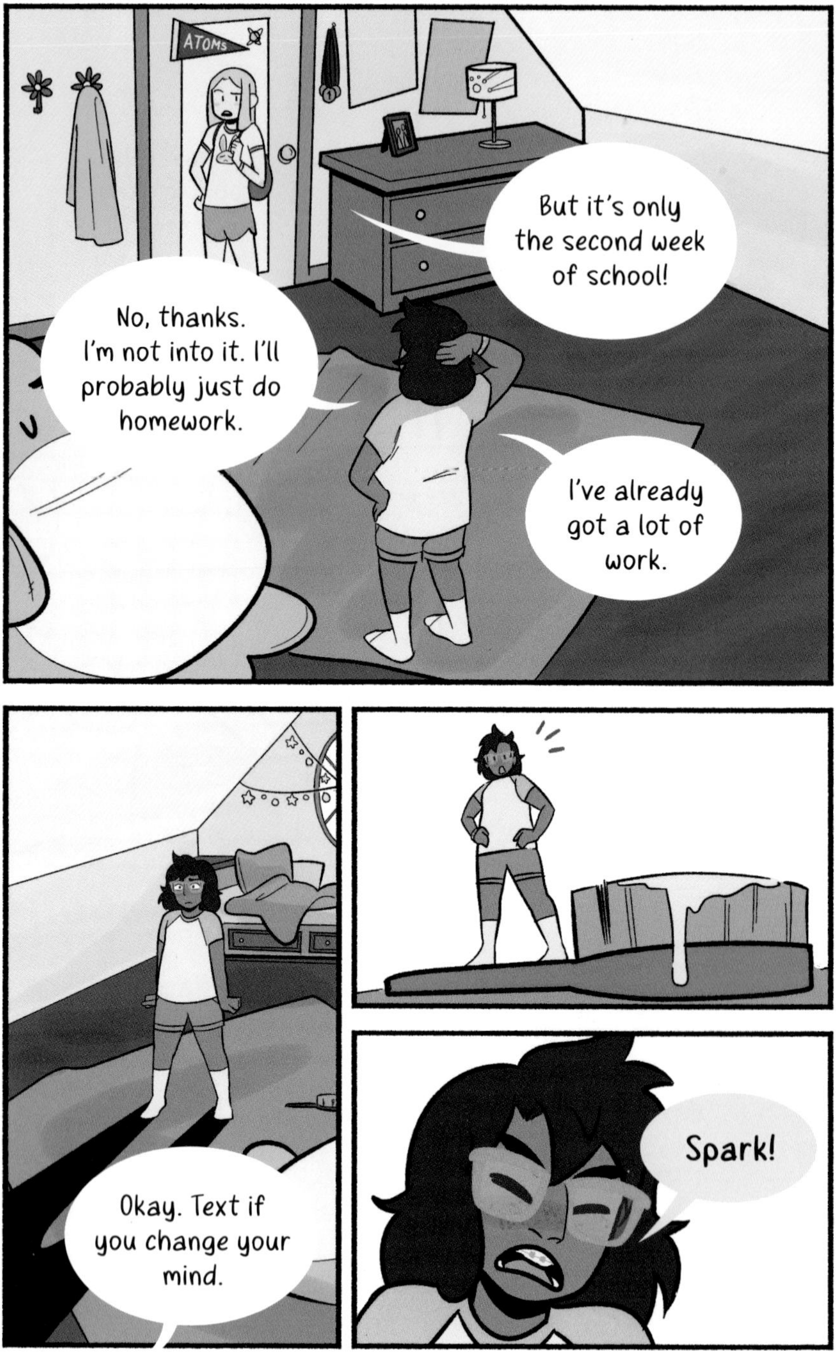
ATOMS
No, thanks. I'm not into it. I'll probably just do homework.
But it's only the second week of school!
I've already got a lot of work.
Okay. Text if you change your mind.
Spark!

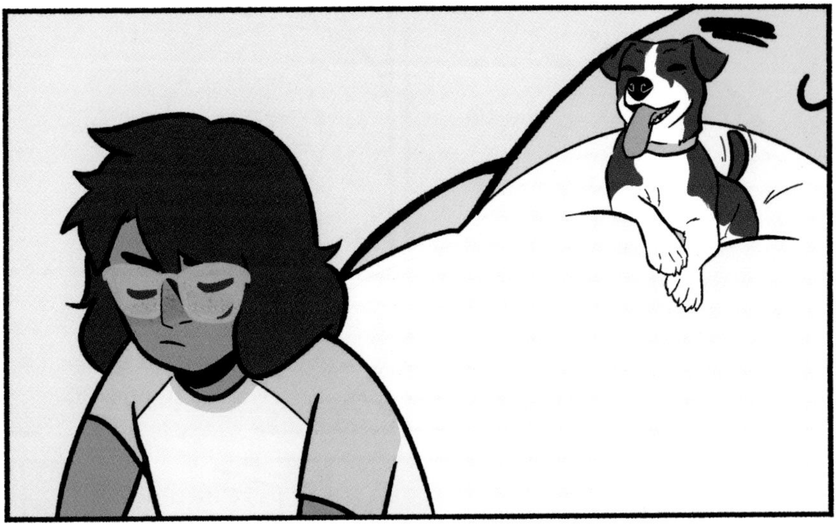

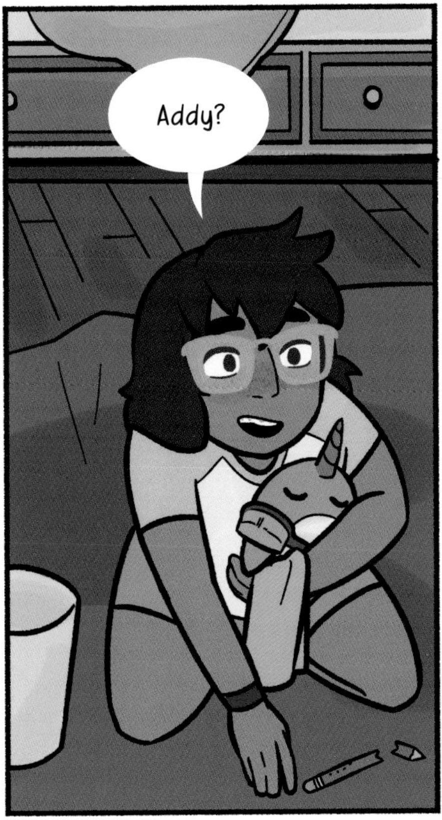
Addy?

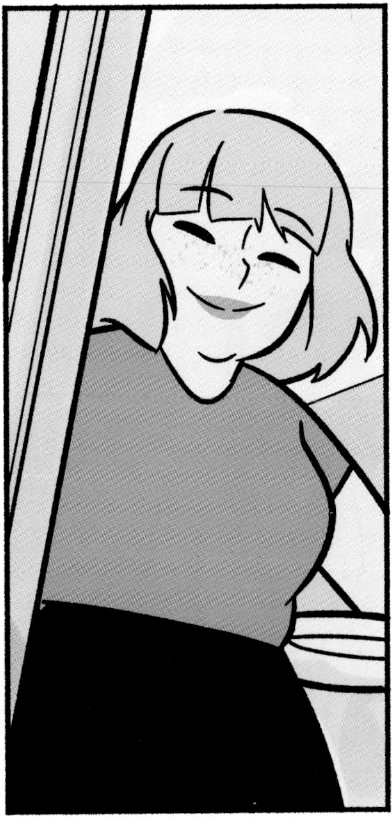

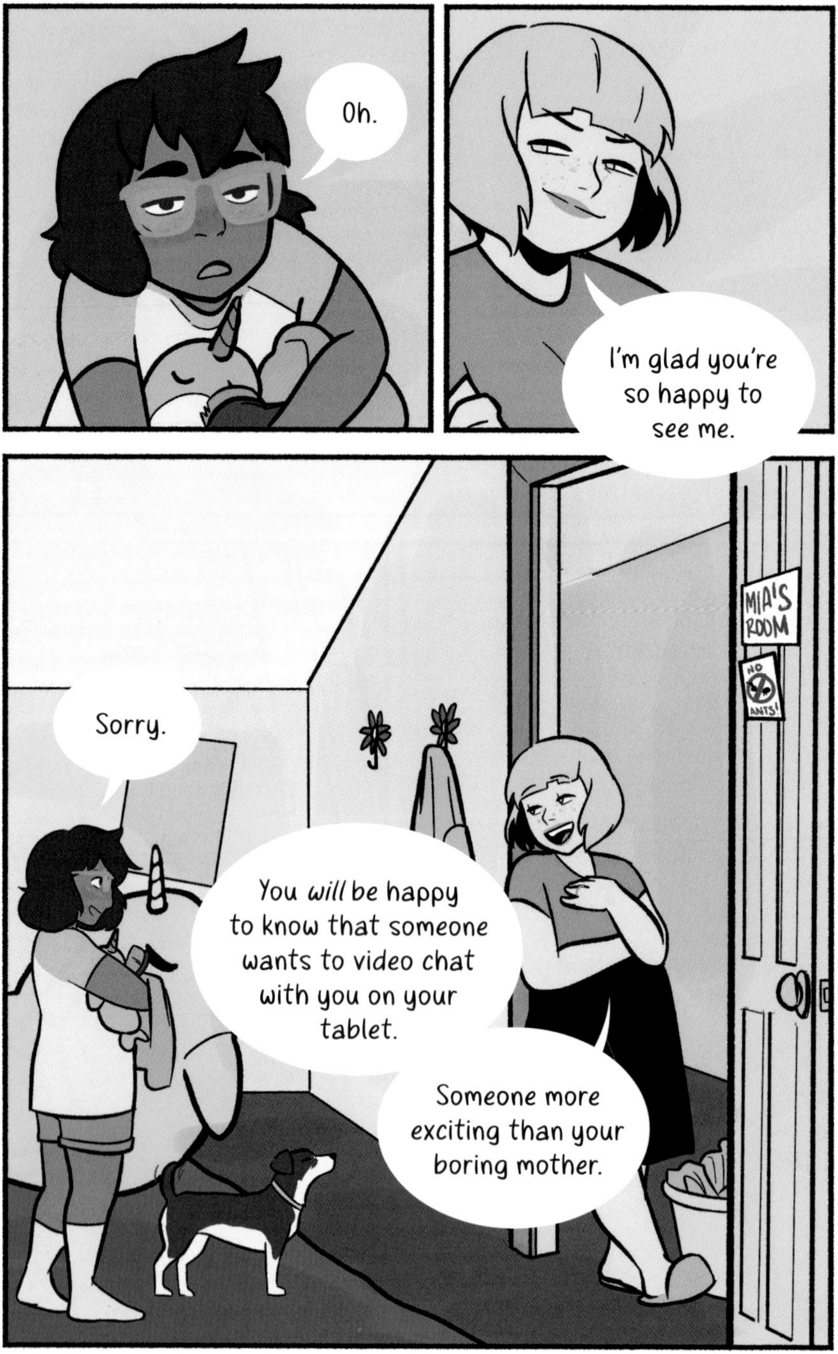
Oh.
I'm glad you're so happy to see me.
MIA'S ROOM
NO ANTS!
Sorry.
You *will* be happy to know that someone wants to video chat with you on your tablet.
Someone more exciting than your boring mother.

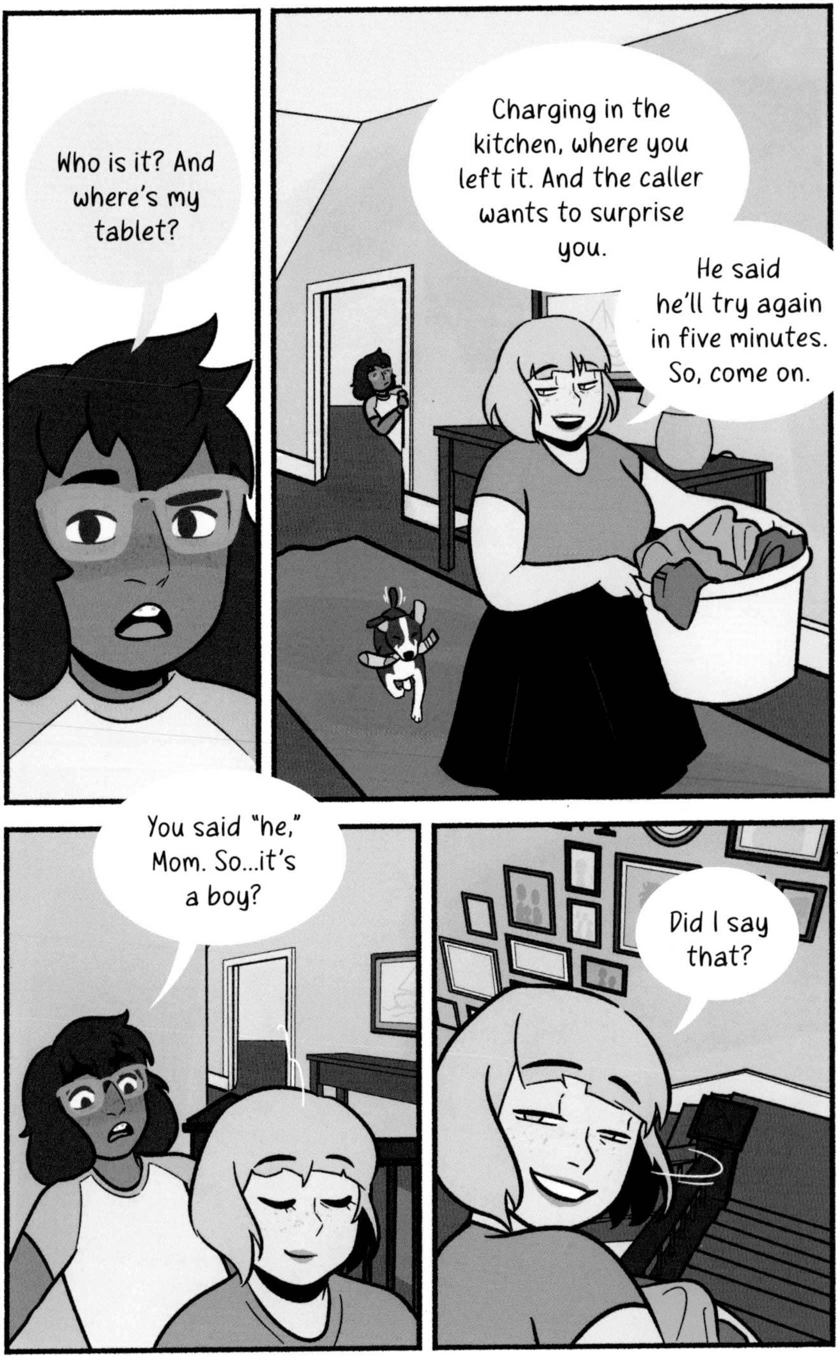
Who is it? And where's my tablet?
Charging in the kitchen, where you left it. And the caller wants to surprise you.
He said he'll try again in five minutes. So, come on.
You said "he," Mom. So...it's a boy?
Did I say that?

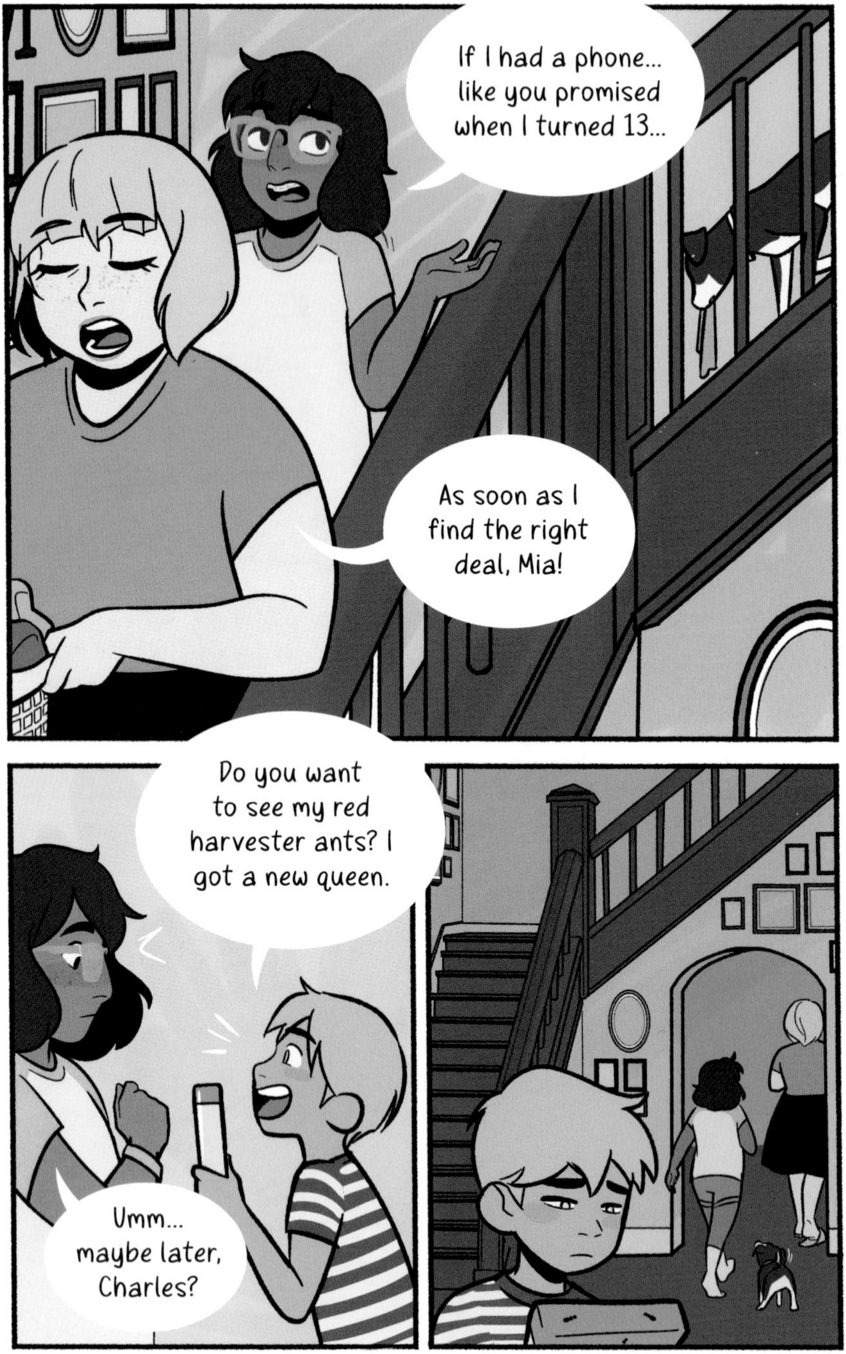
If I had a phone... like you promised when I turned 13...
As soon as I find the right deal, Mia!
Do you want to see my red harvester ants? I got a new queen.
Umm... maybe later, Charles?

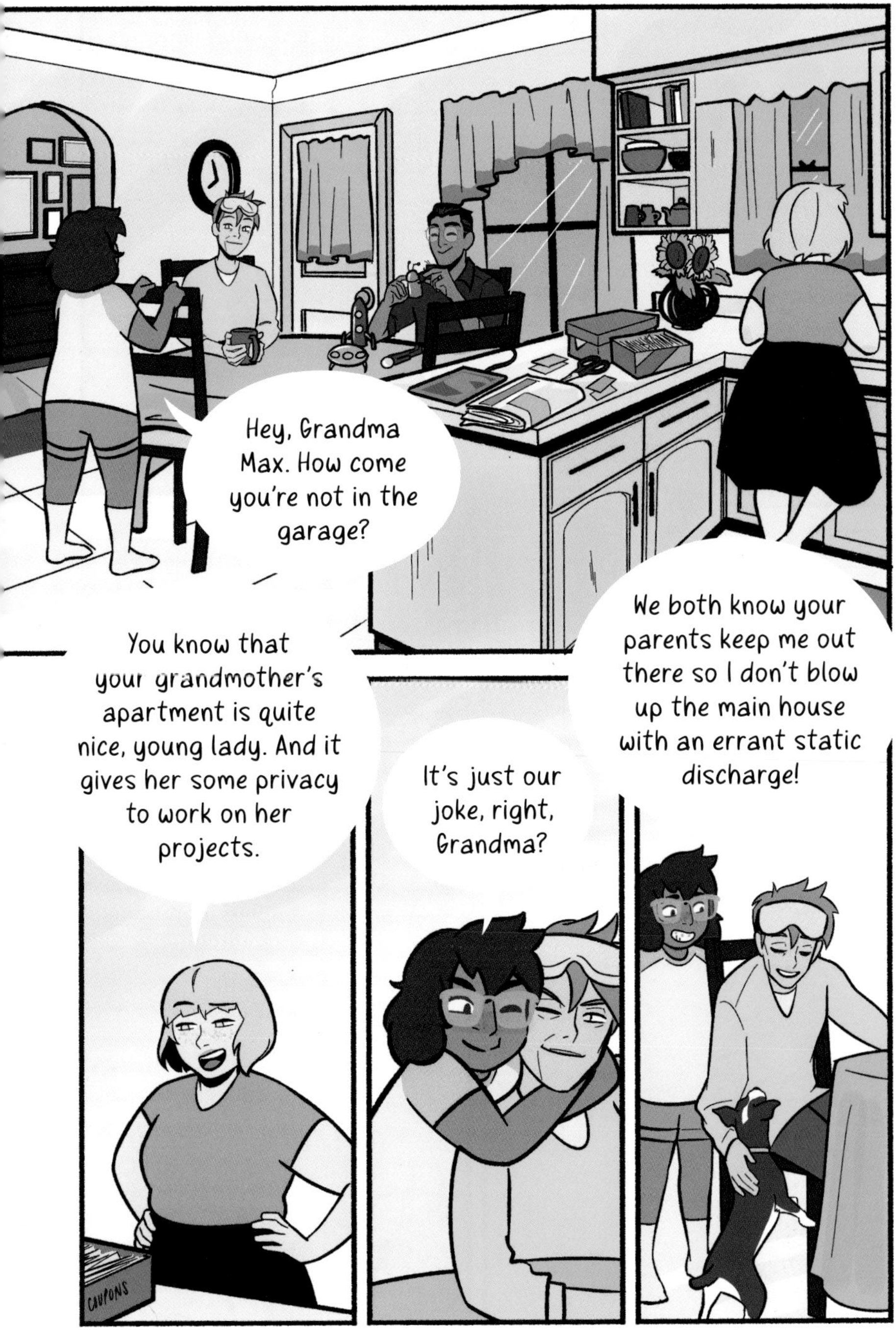
Hey, Grandma Max. How come you're not in the garage?
You know that your grandmother's apartment is quite nice, young lady. And it gives her some privacy to work on her projects.
It's just our joke, right, Grandma?
We both know your parents keep me out there so I don't blow up the main house with an errant static discharge!
COUPONS

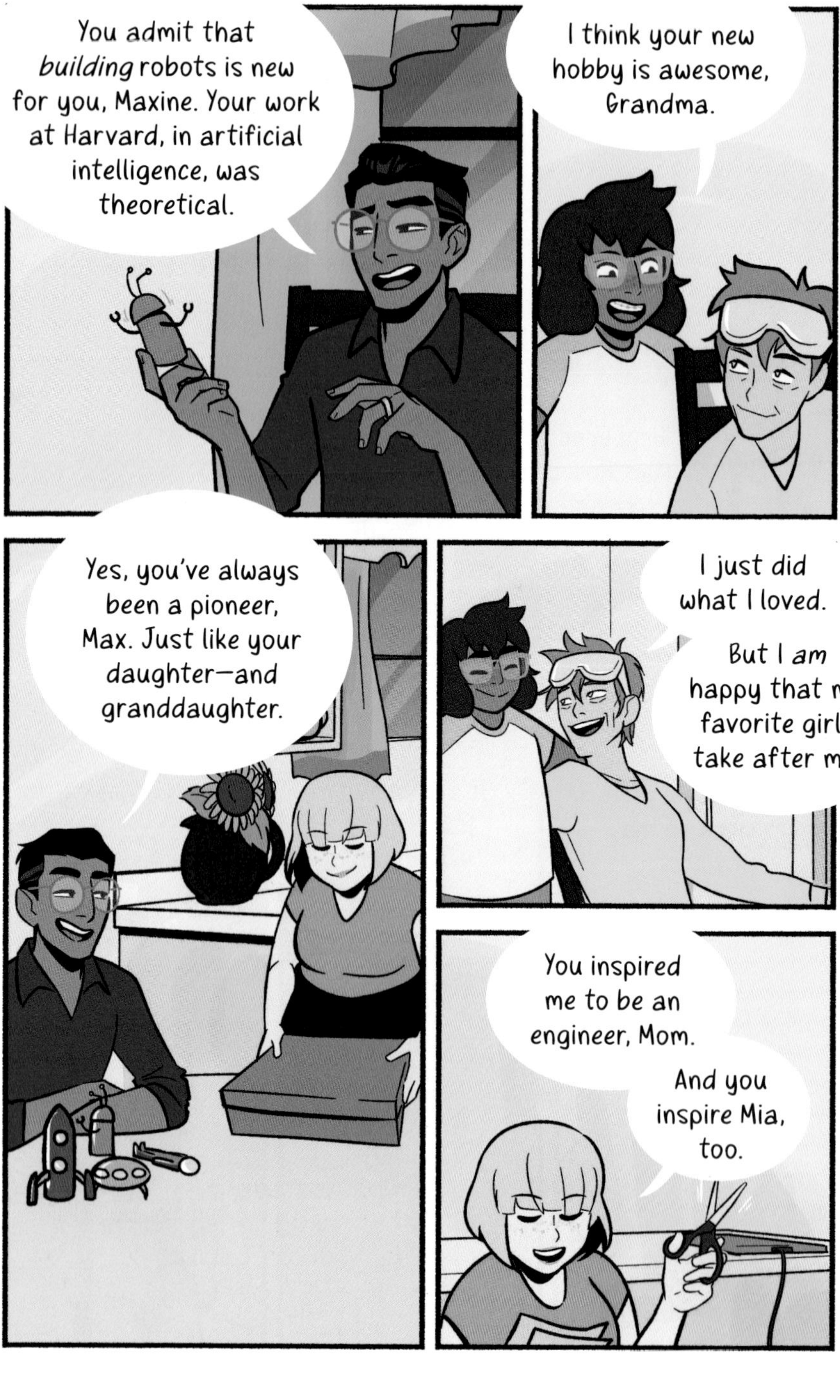
You admit that *building* robots is new for you, Maxine. Your work at Harvard, in artificial intelligence, was theoretical.
I think your new hobby is awesome, Grandma.
Yes, you've always been a pioneer, Max. Just like your daughter—and granddaughter.
I just did what I loved.
But I *am* happy that my favorite girls take after me.
You inspired me to be an engineer, Mom.
And you inspire Mia, too.

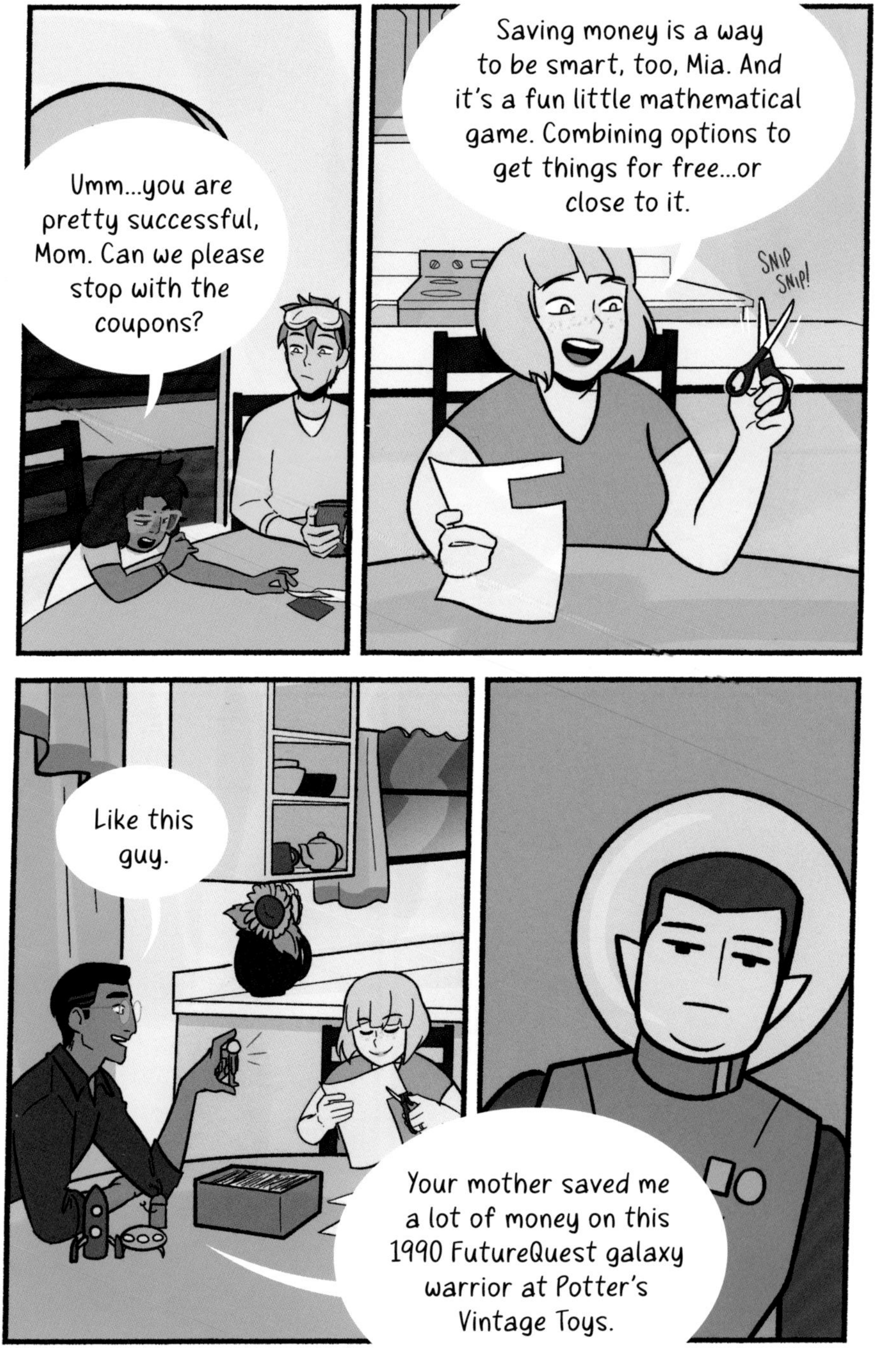
Umm...you are pretty successful, Mom. Can we please stop with the coupons?
Saving money is a way to be smart, too, Mia. And it's a fun little mathematical game. Combining options to get things for free...or close to it.
SNIP SNIP!
Like this guy.
Your mother saved me a lot of money on this 1990 FutureQuest galaxy warrior at Potter's Vintage Toys.

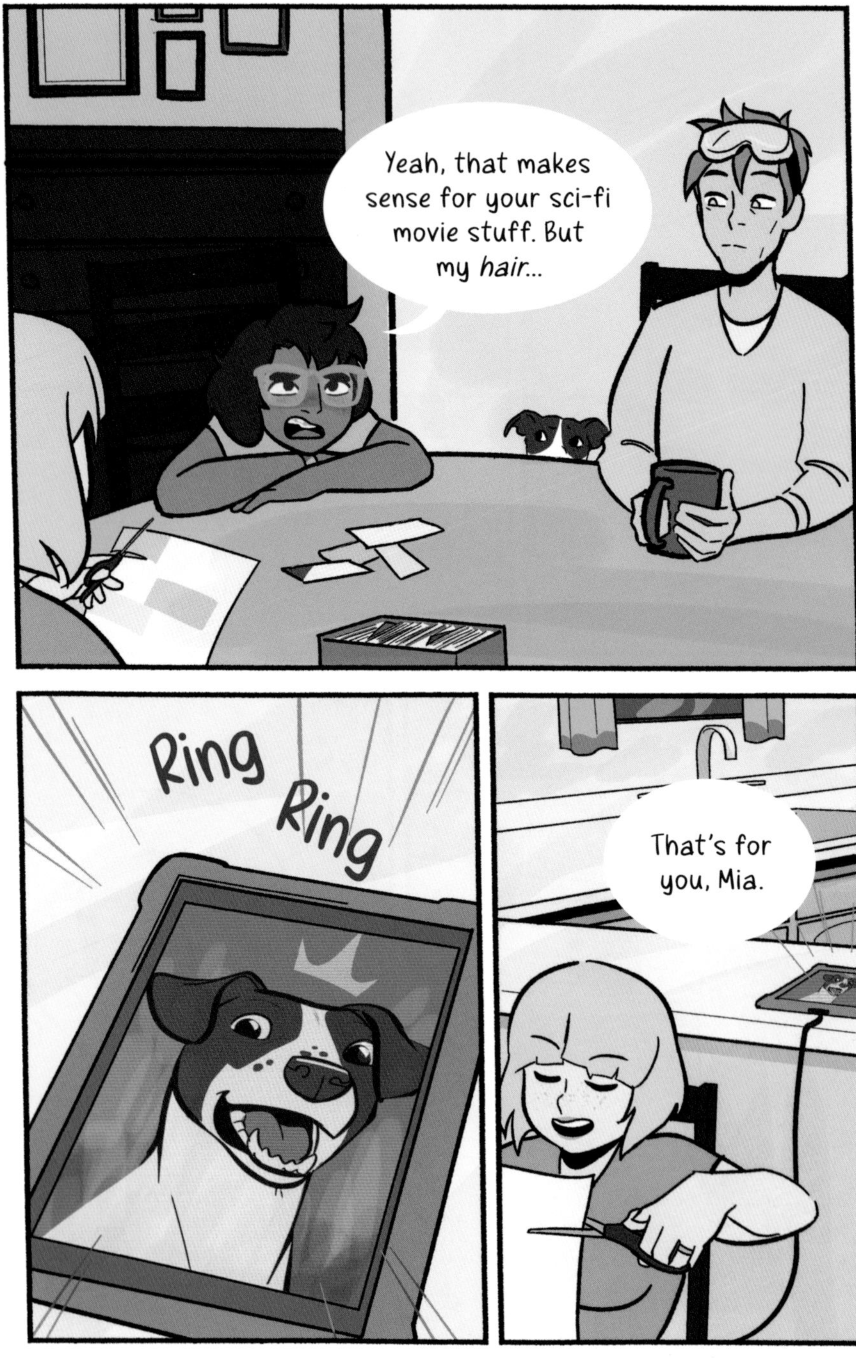
Yeah, that makes sense for your sci-fi movie stuff. But my *hair*...
Ring
Ring
That's for you, Mia.

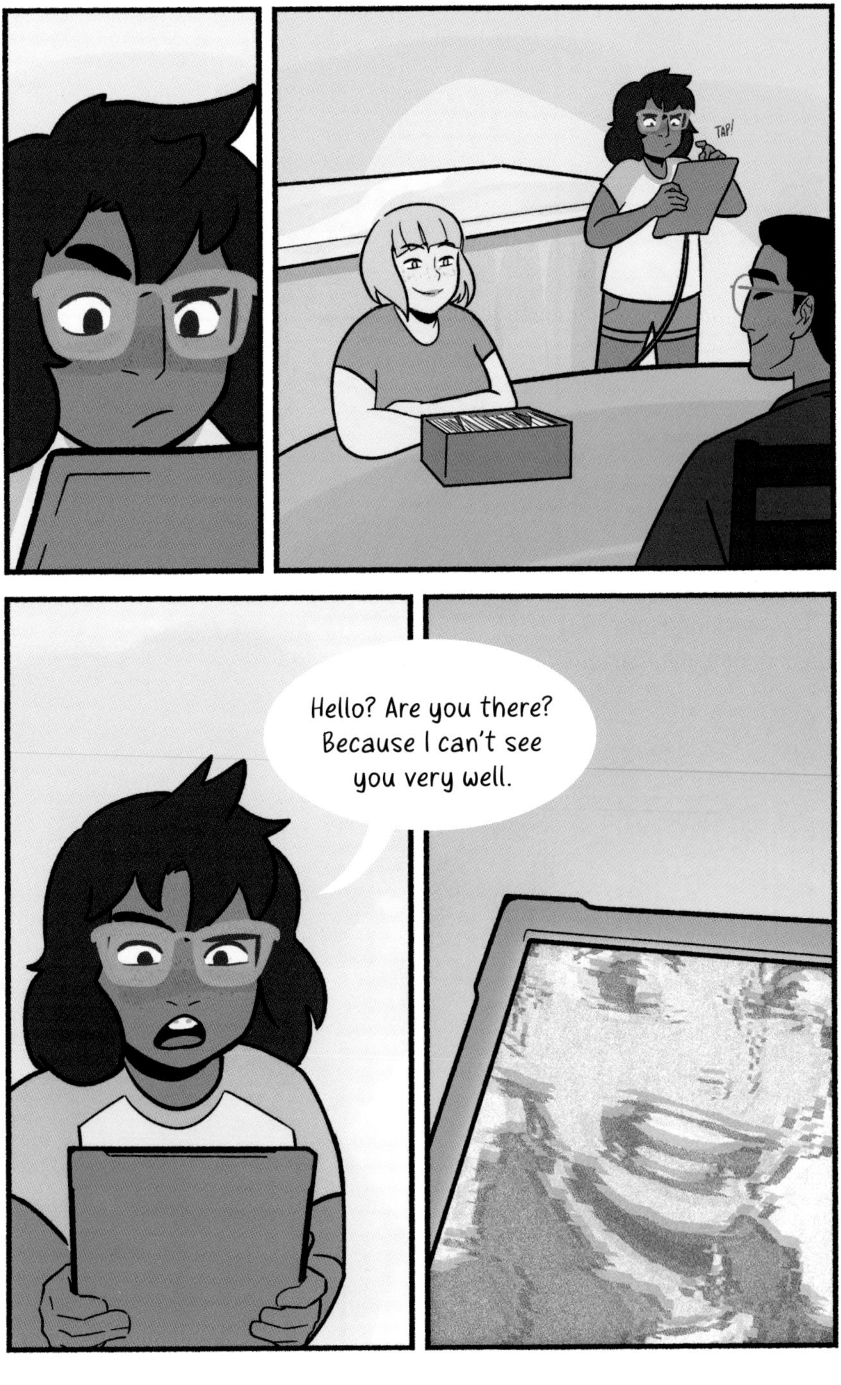
TAP!
Hello? Are you there? Because I can't see you very well.

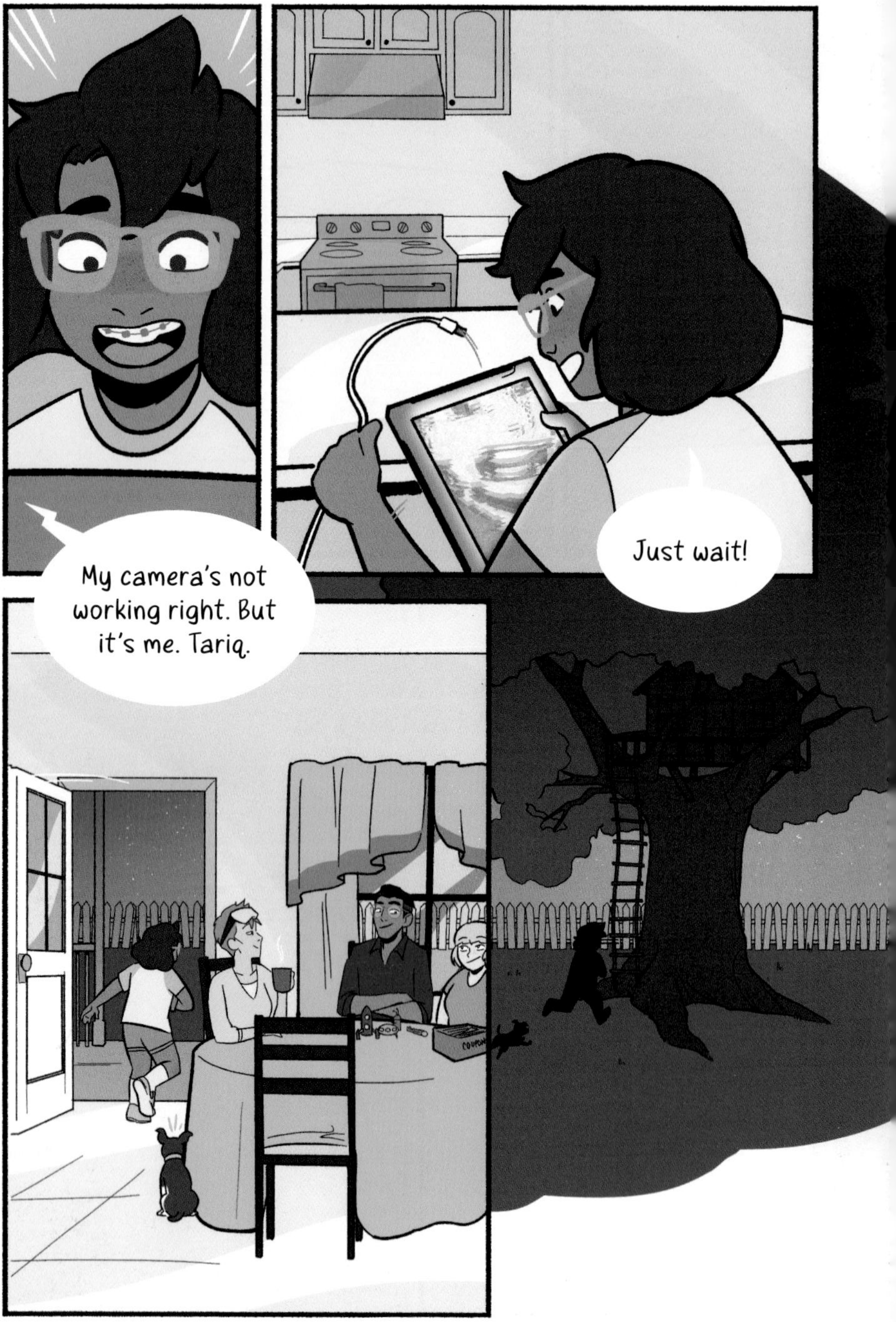
My camera's not working right. But it's me. Tariq.
Just wait!

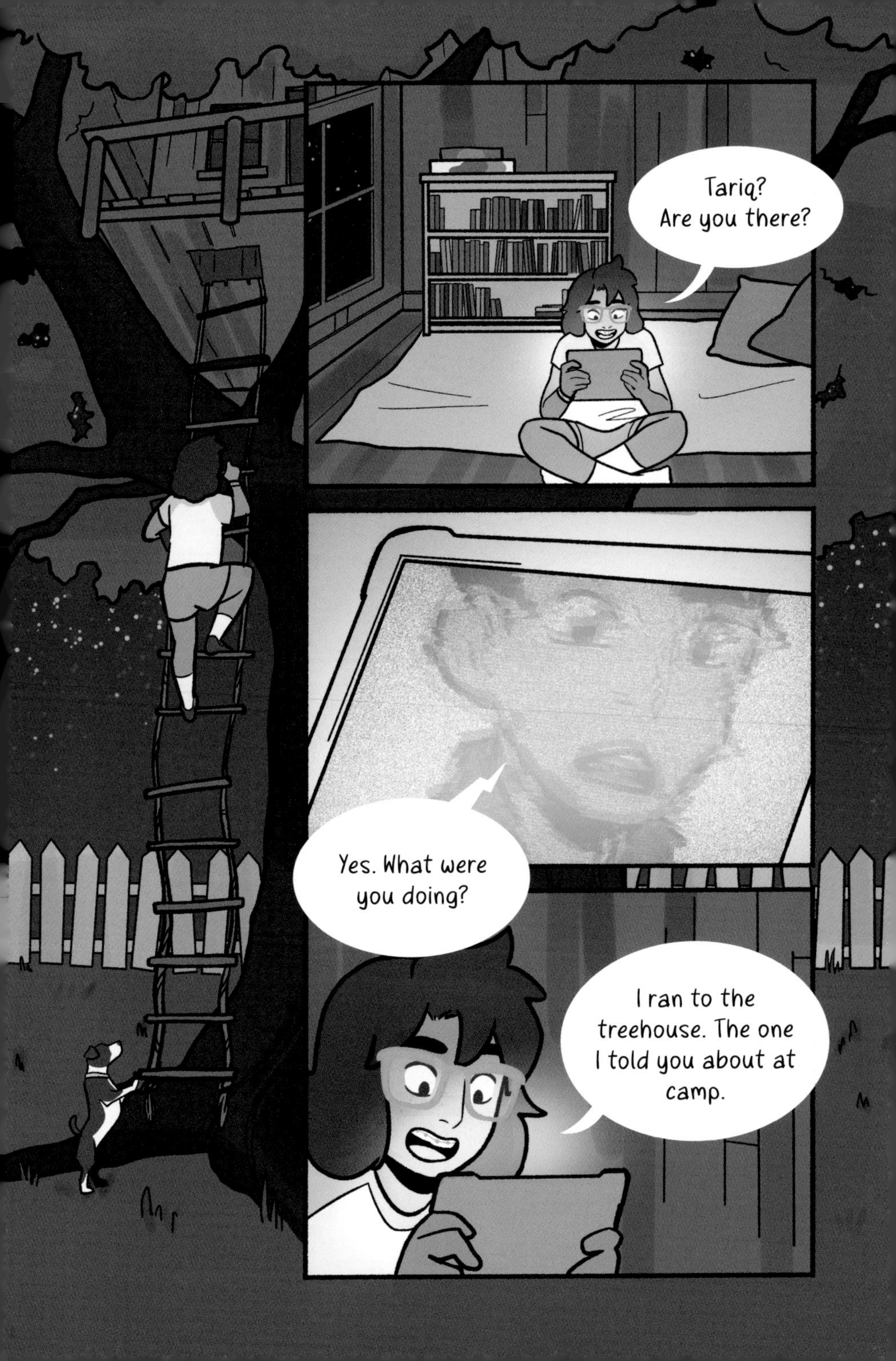
Tariq?
Are you there?
Yes. What were you doing?
I ran to the treehouse. The one I told you about at camp.

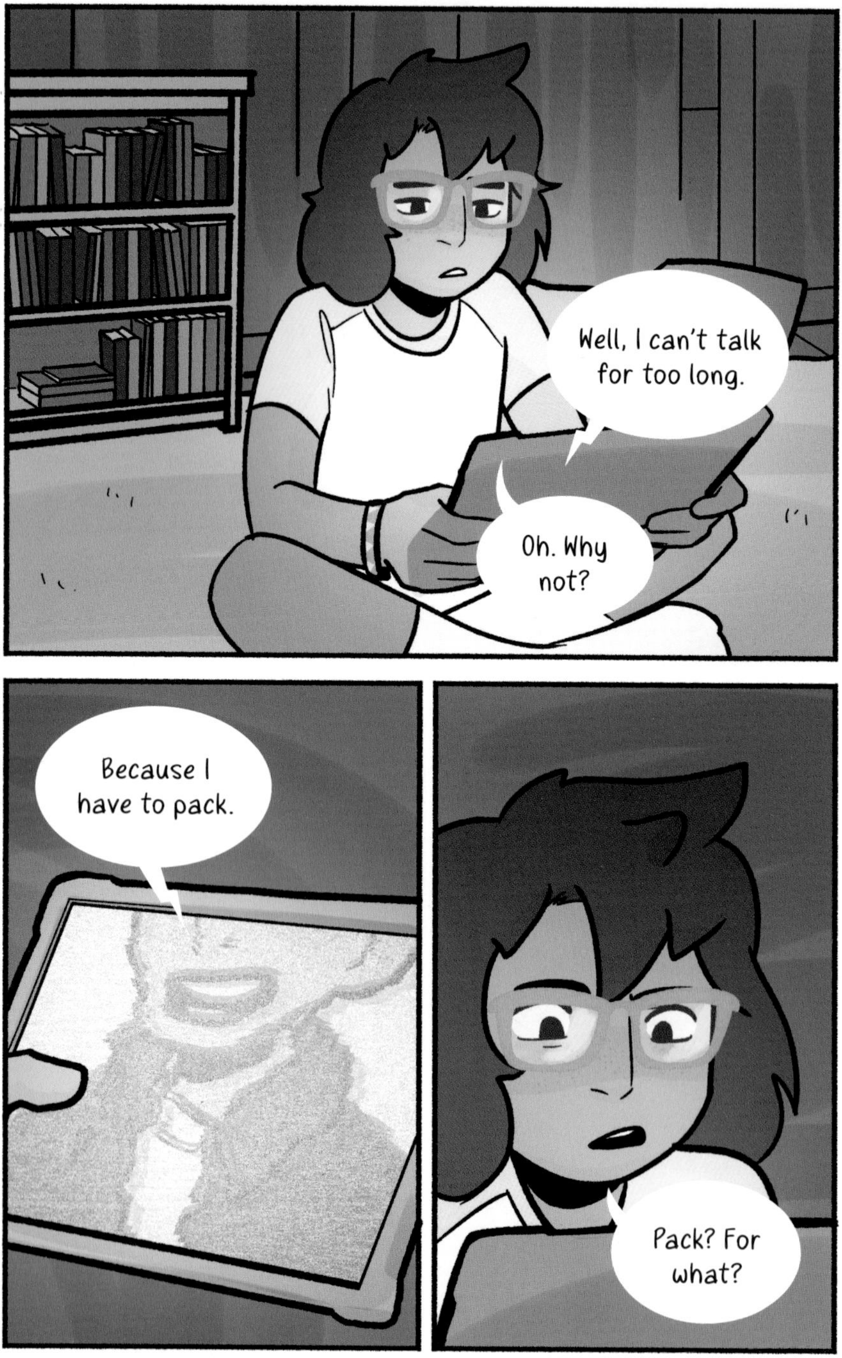
Well, I can't talk for too long.
Oh. Why not?
Because I have to pack.
Pack? For what?

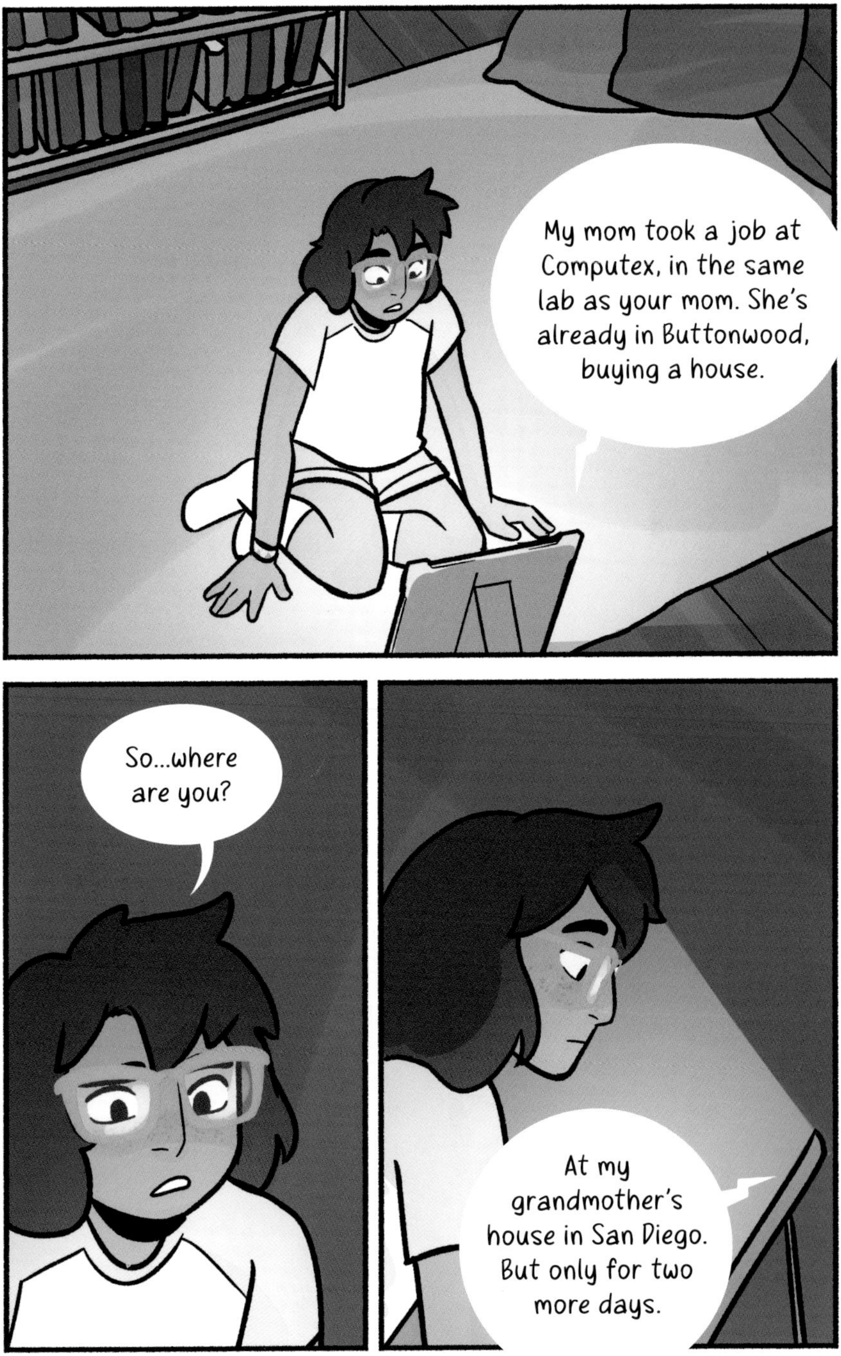
My mom took a job at Computex, in the same lab as your mom. She's already in Buttonwood, buying a house.
So...where are you?
At my grandmother's house in San Diego. But only for two more days.

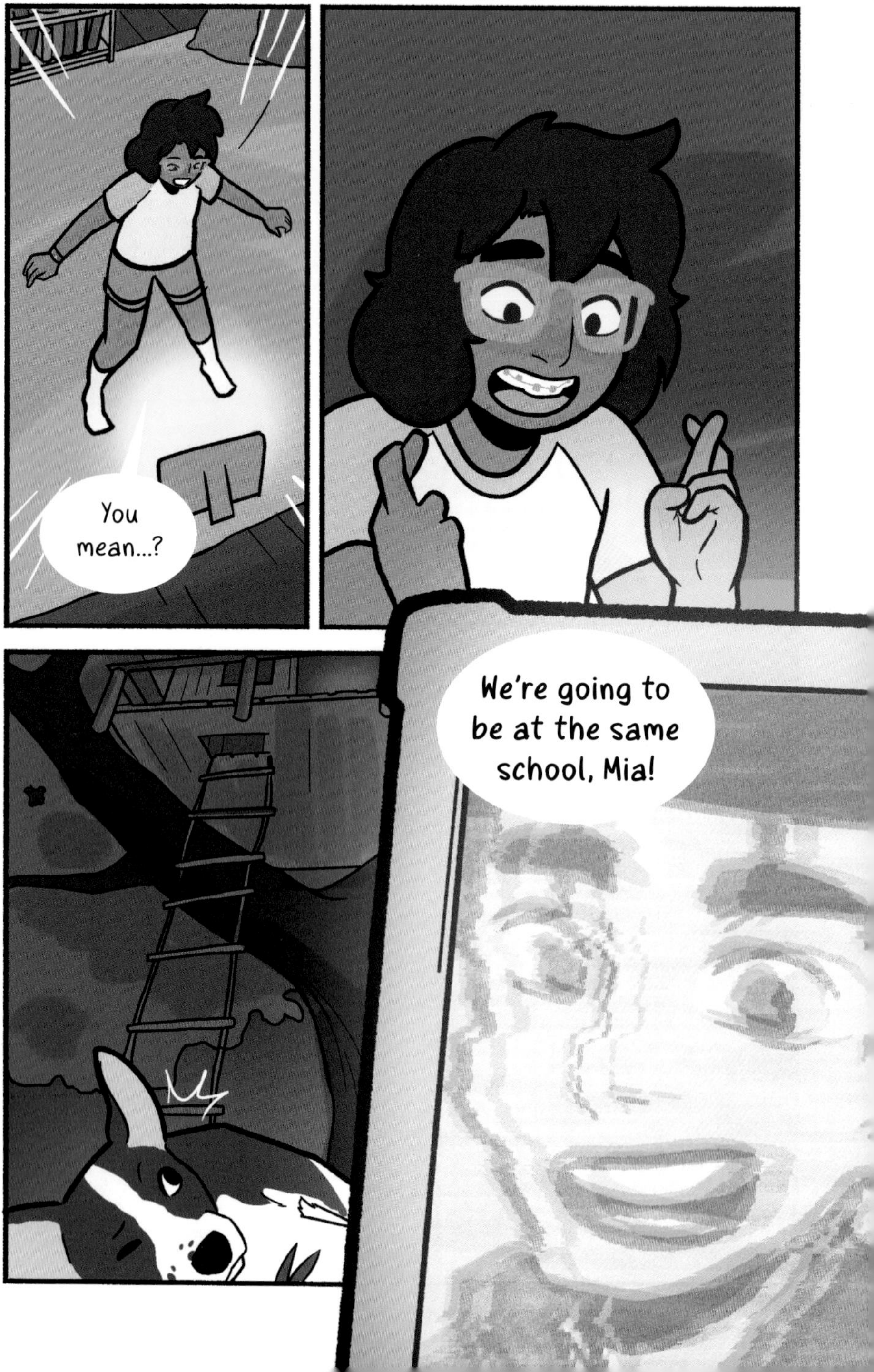
You mean...?
We're going to be at the same school, Mia!

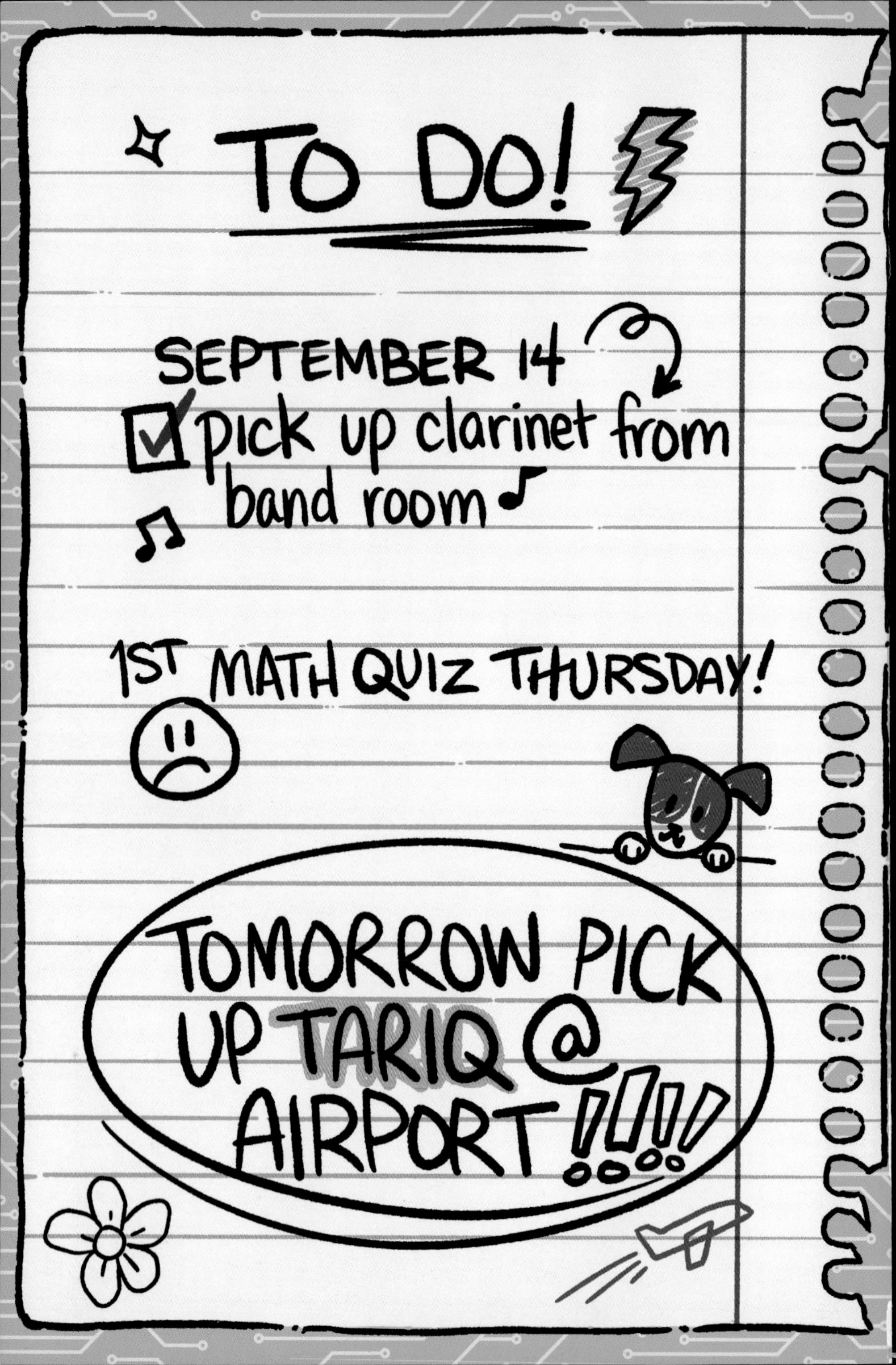
TO DO!
SEPTEMBER 14
pick up clarinet from band room
1ST MATH QUIZ THURSDAY!
TOMORROW PICK UP TARIQ @ AIRPORT!!!!!

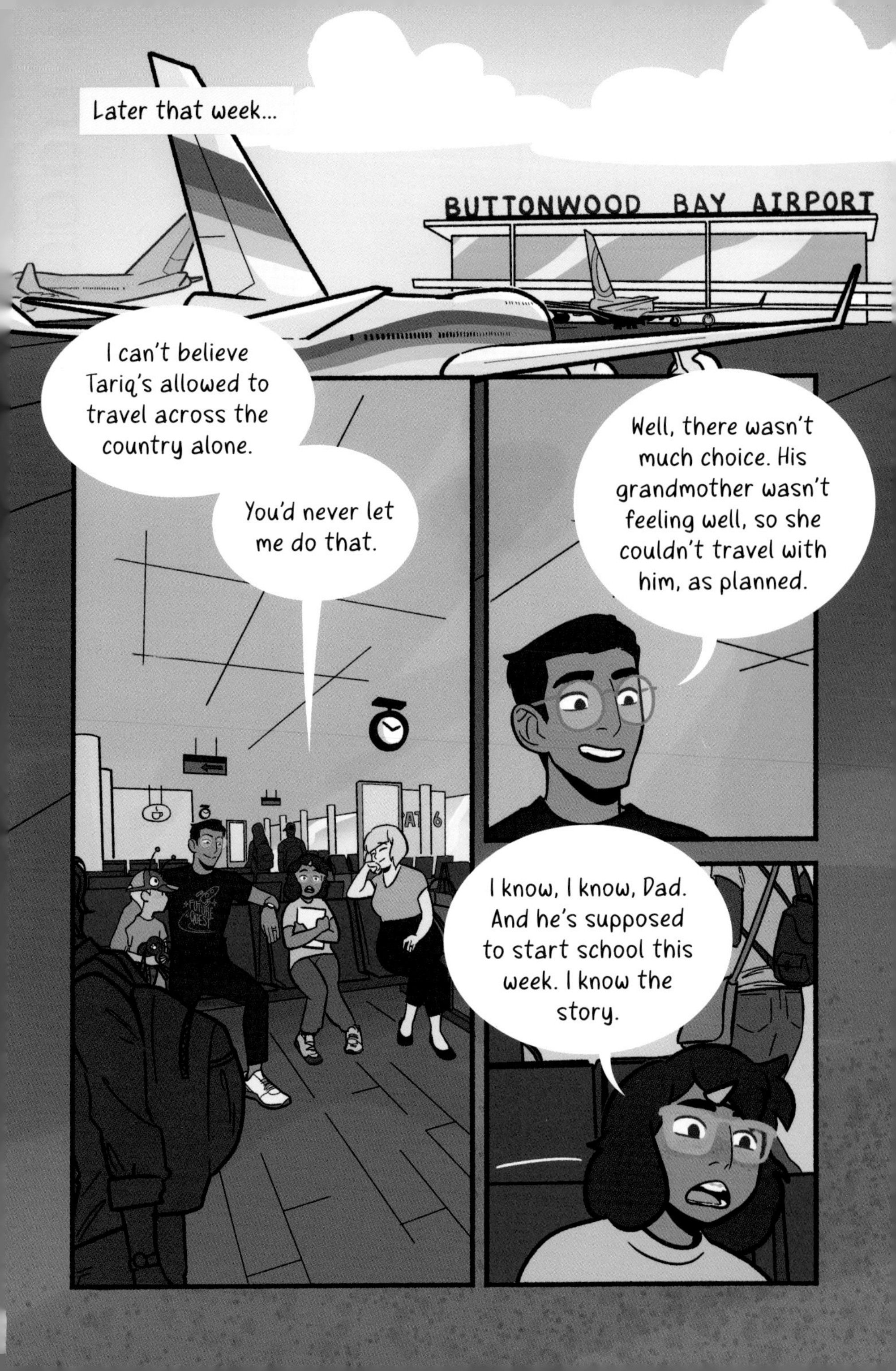
Later that week...
BUTTONWOOD BAY AIRPORT
I can't believe Tariq's allowed to travel across the country alone.
You'd never let me do that.
Well, there wasn't much choice. His grandmother wasn't feeling well, so she couldn't travel with him, as planned.
I know, I know, Dad. And he's supposed to start school this week. I know the story.

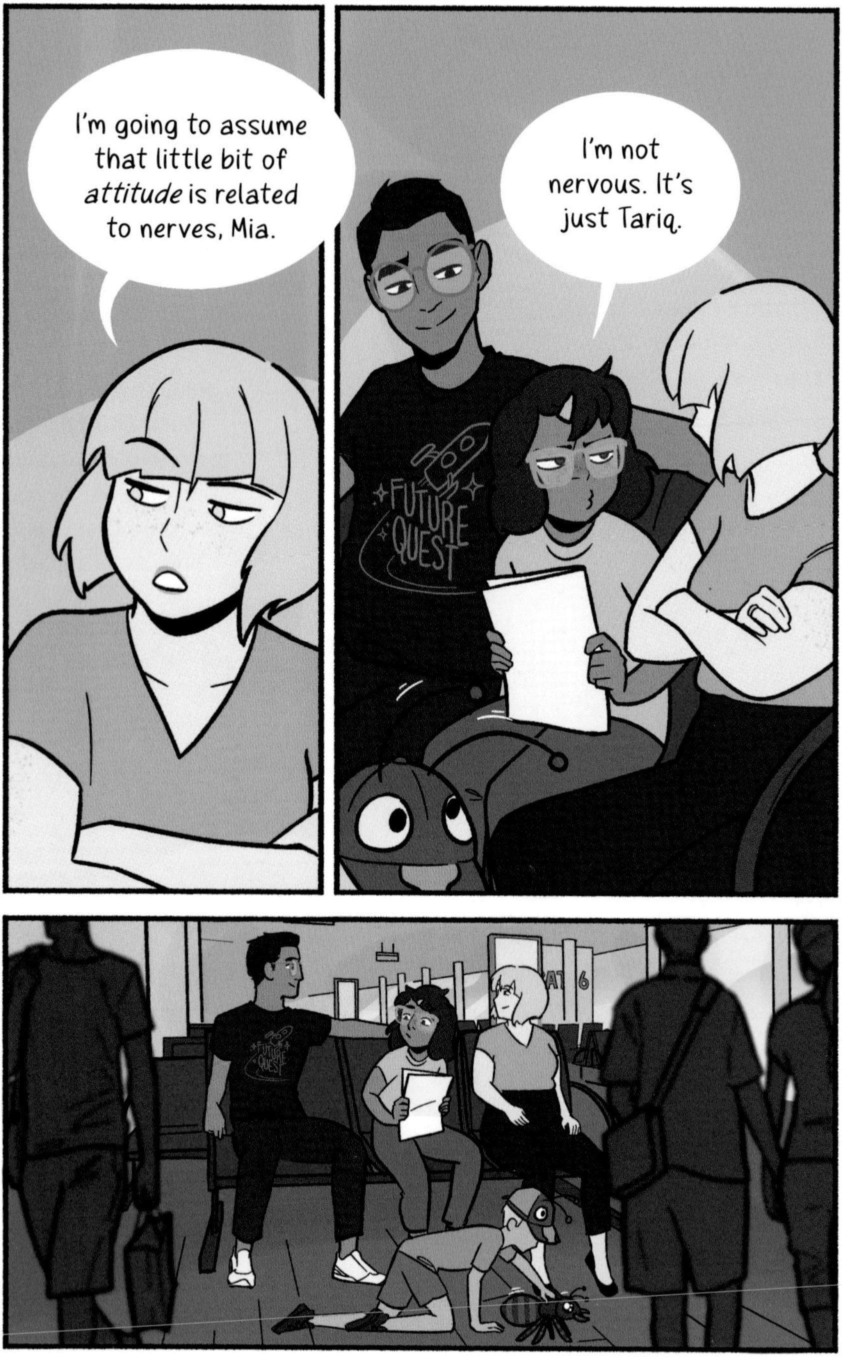
I'm going to assume that little bit of *attitude* is related to nerves, Mia.
I'm not nervous. It's just Tariq.
FUTURE QUEST
FUTURE QUEST
GAT 6

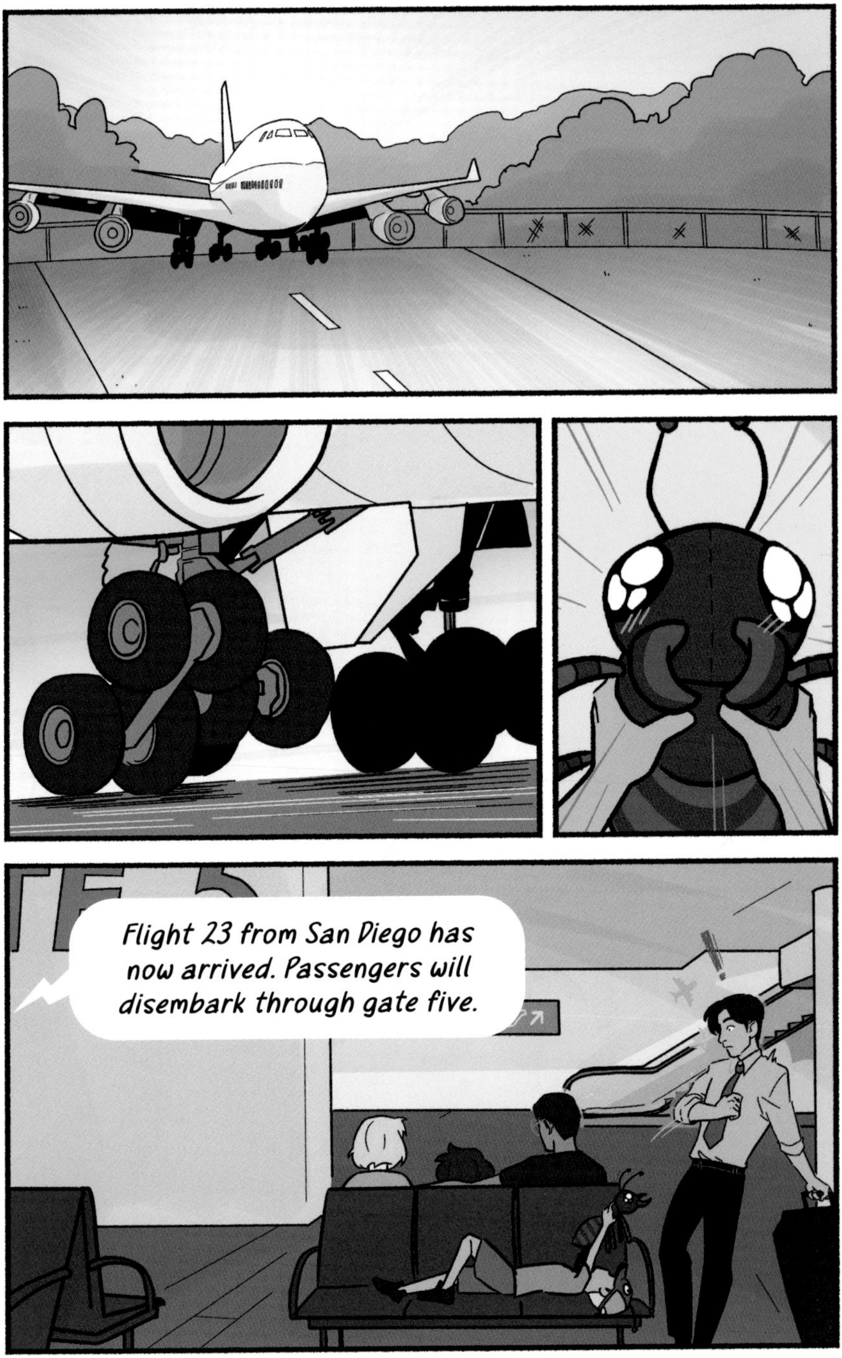
Flight 23 from San Diego has now arrived. Passengers will disembark through gate five.

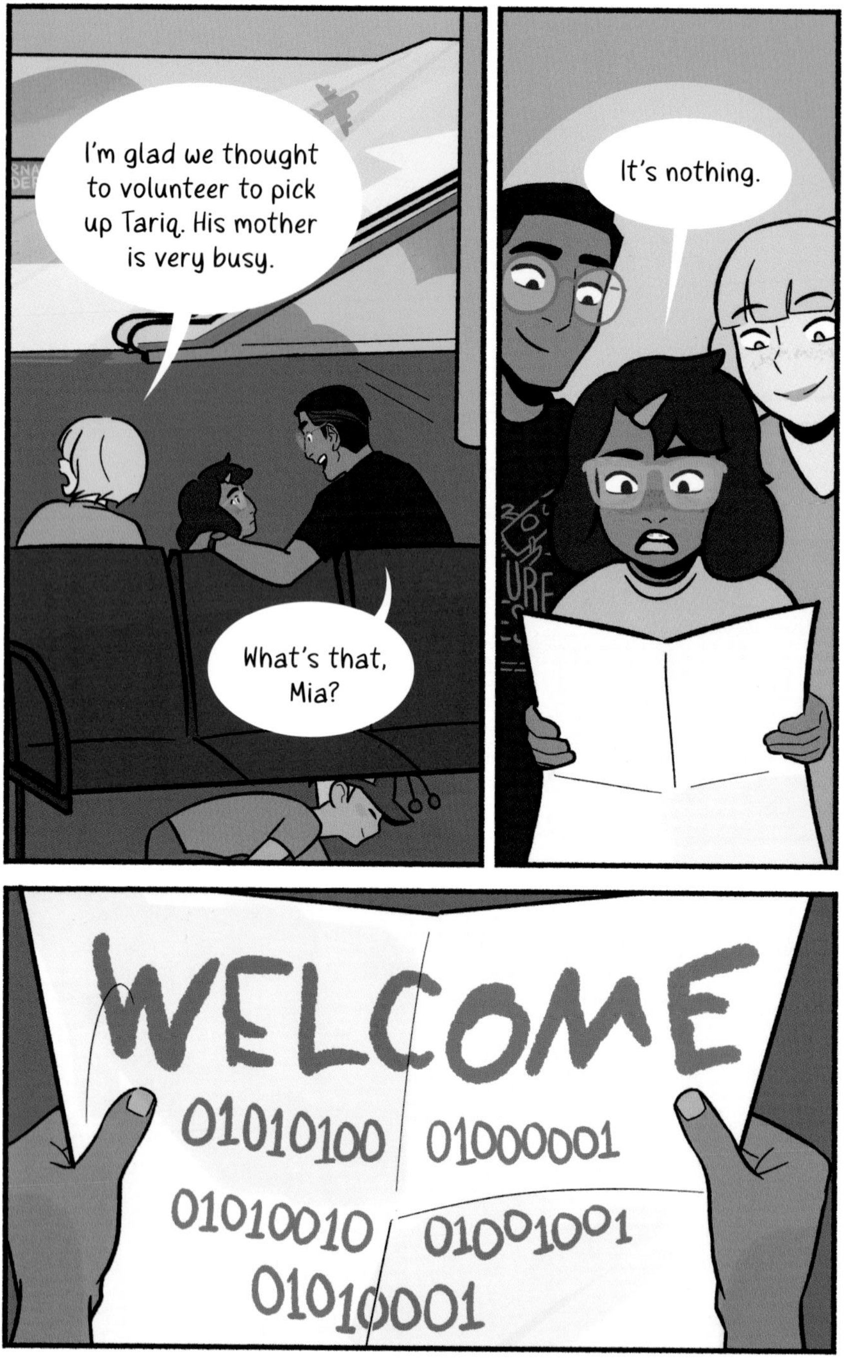
I'm glad we thought to volunteer to pick up Tariq. His mother is very busy.
What's that, Mia?
It's nothing.
WELCOME
01010100 01000001
01010010 01001001
01010001

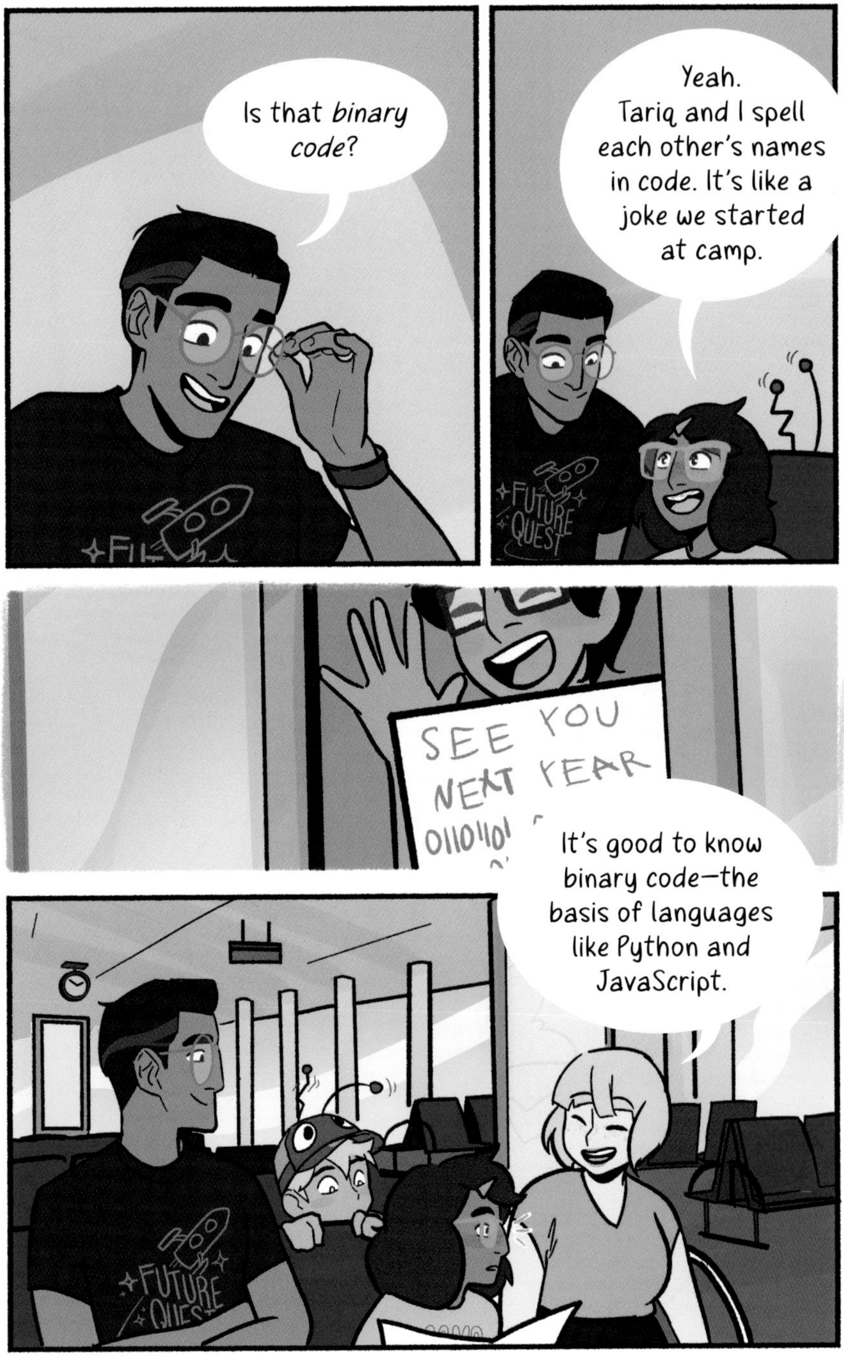
Is that *binary code*?
Yeah. Tariq and I spell each other's names in code. It's like a joke we started at camp.
FUTURE QUEST
SEE YOU NEXT YEAR
It's good to know binary code—the basis of languages like Python and JavaScript.
FUTURE QUEST

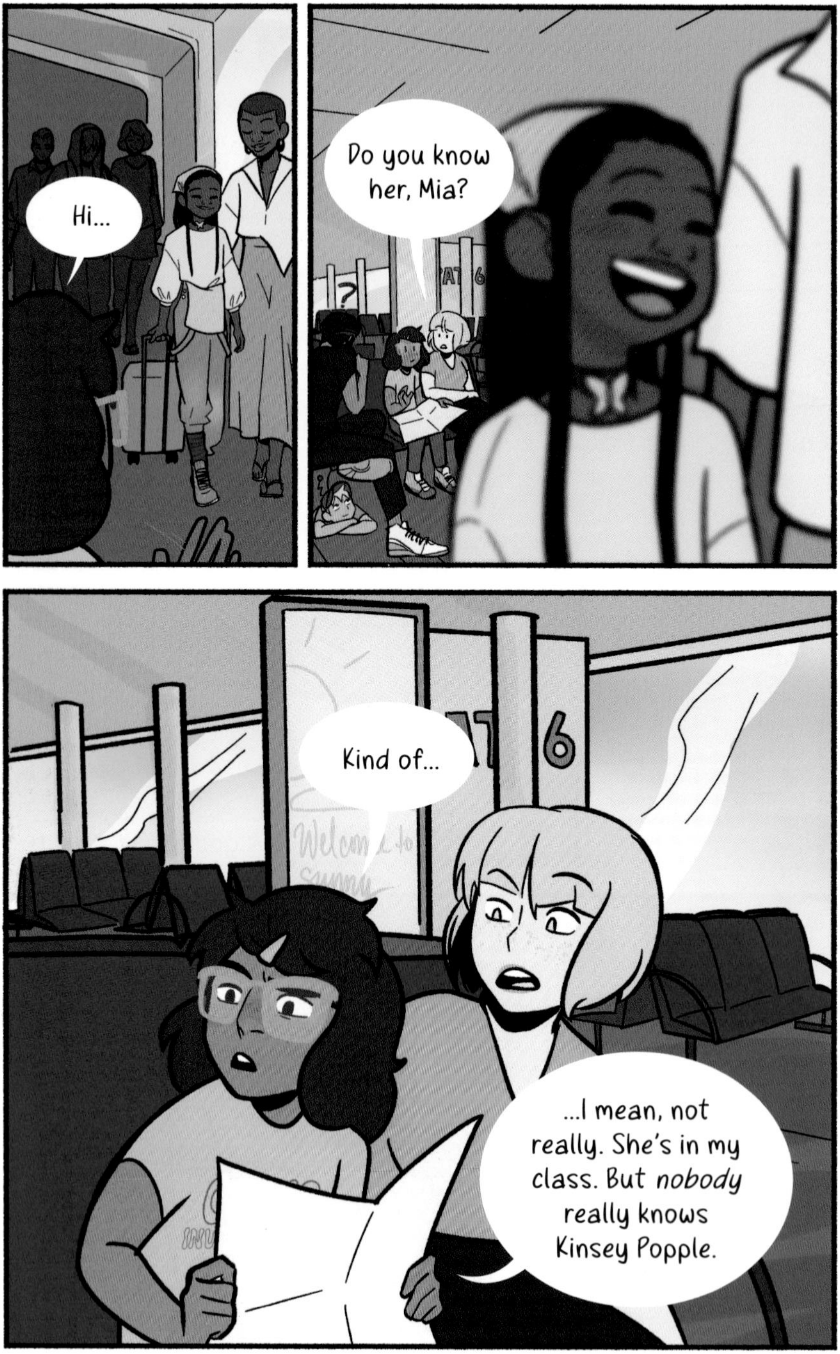
Hi...
Do you know her, Mia?
Kind of...
...I mean, not really. She's in my class. But *nobody* really knows Kinsey Popple.

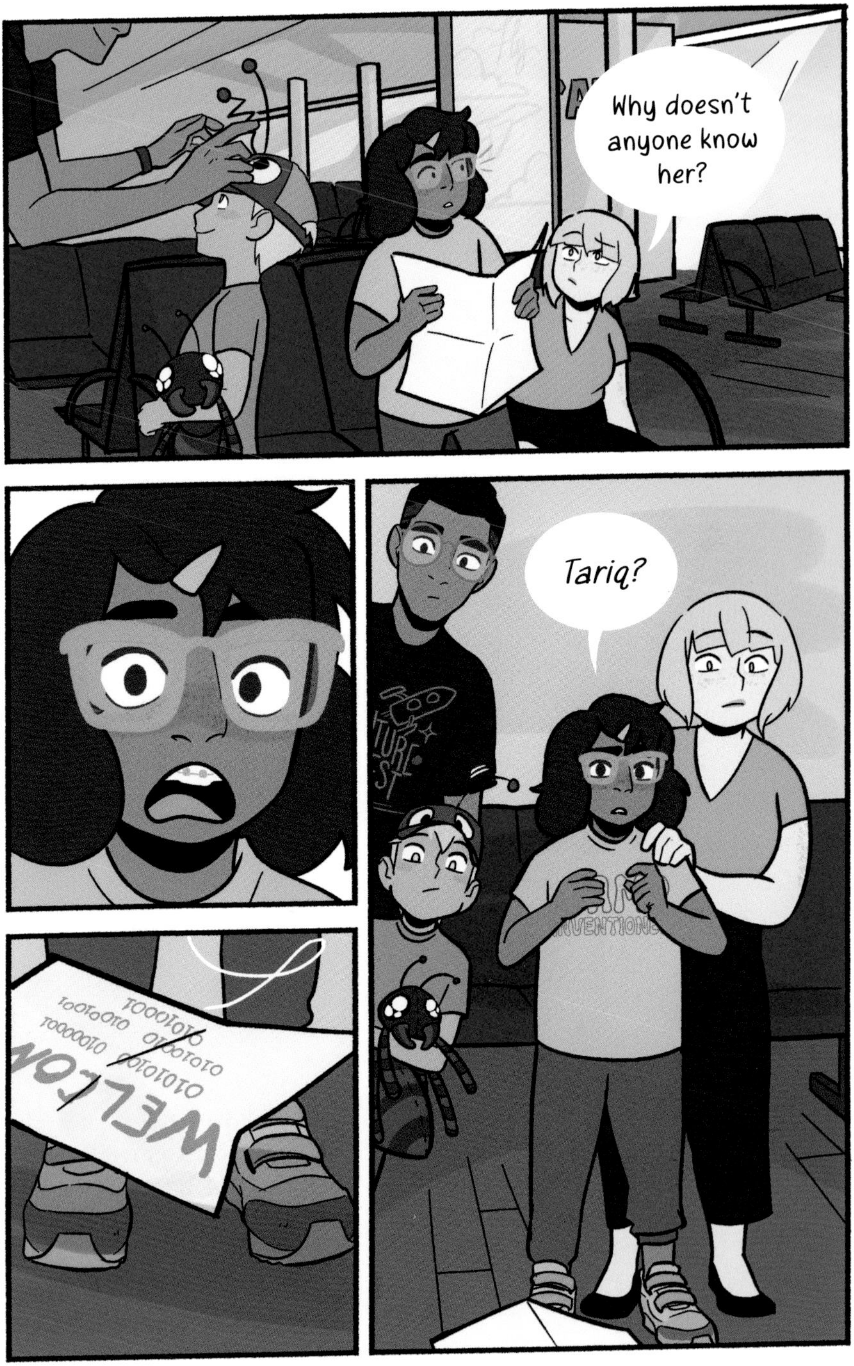
Why doesn't anyone know her?
Tariq?

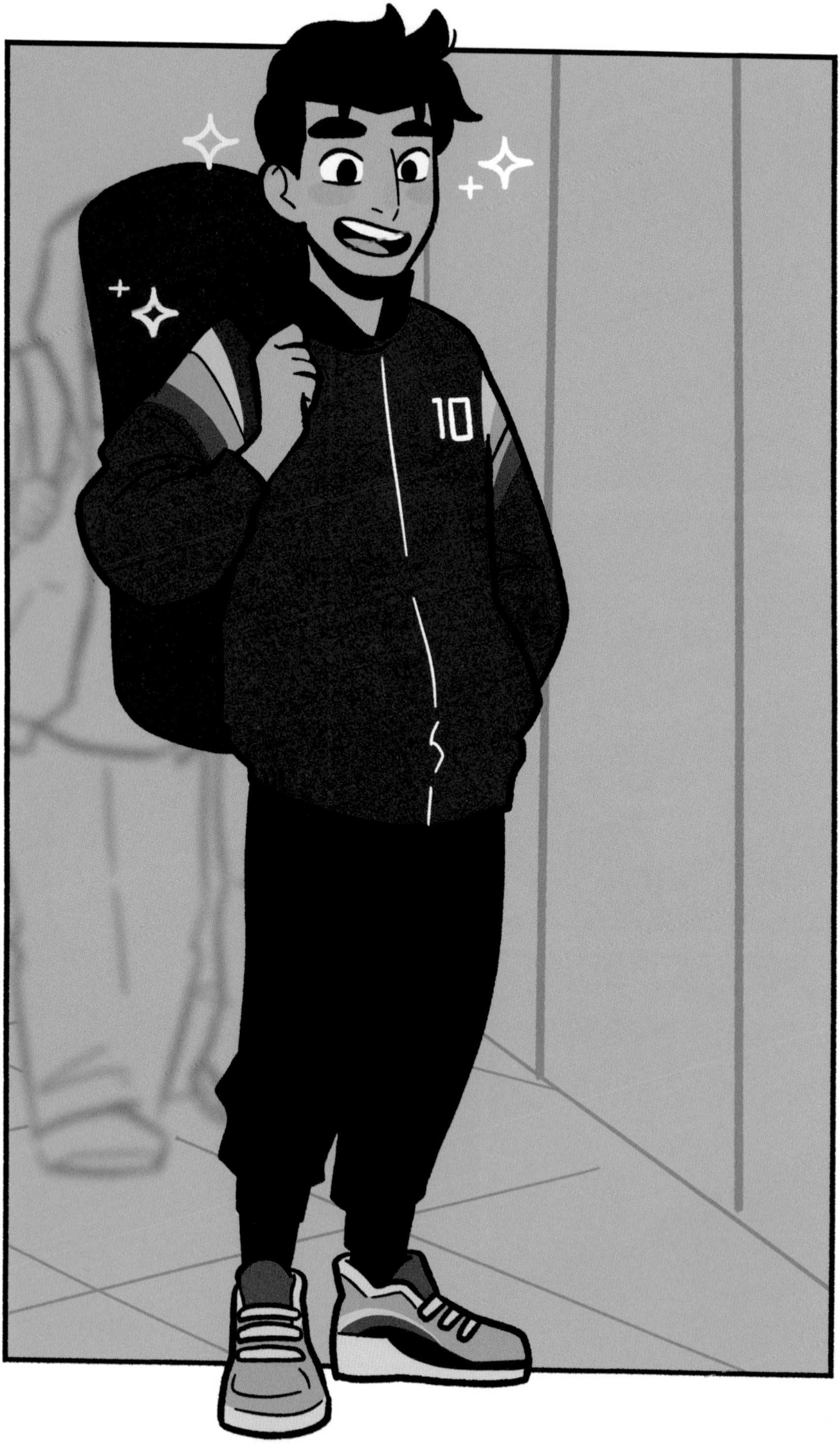
10

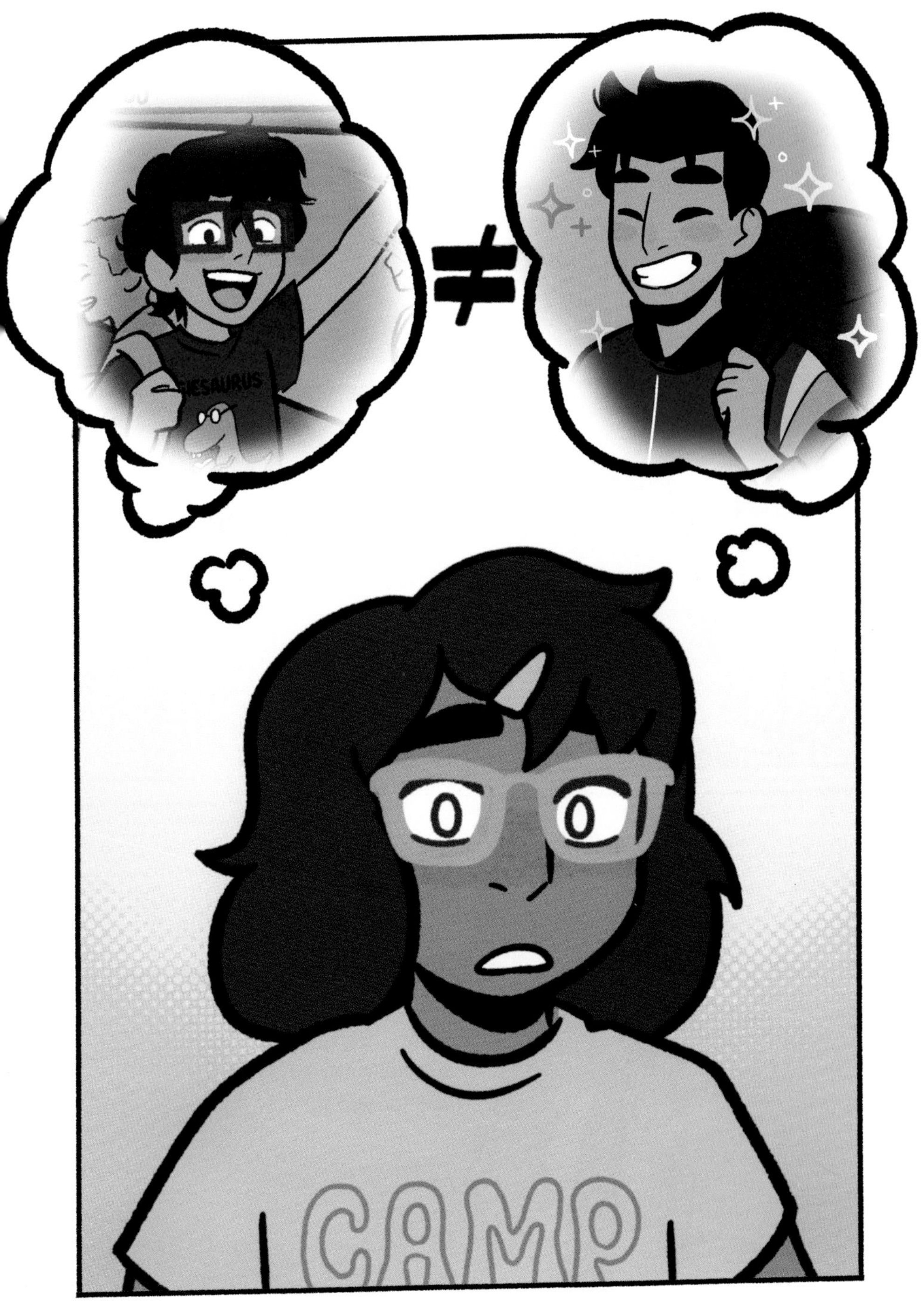
CAMP

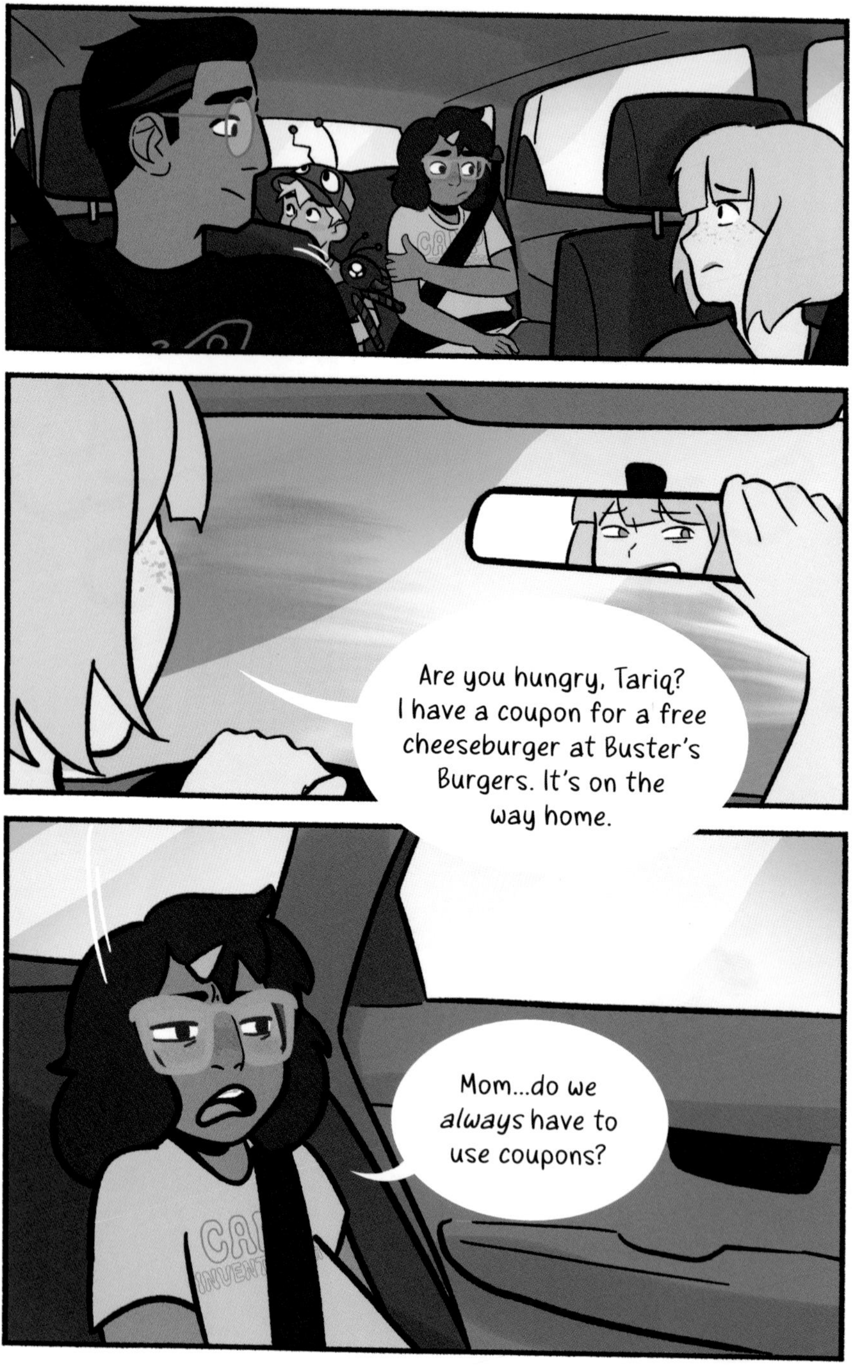
Are you hungry, Tariq? I have a coupon for a free cheeseburger at Buster's Burgers. It's on the way home.
Mom...do we *always* have to use coupons?

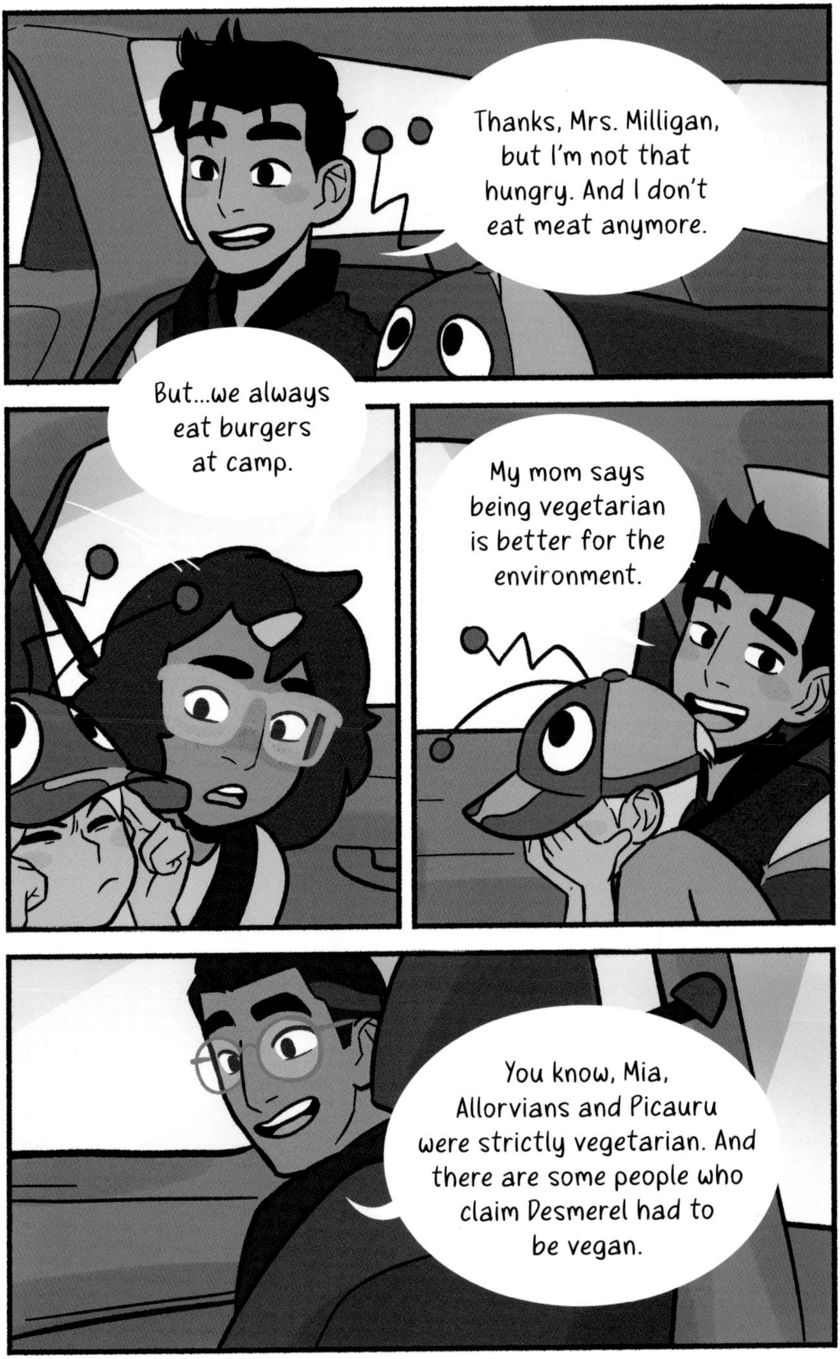
Thanks, Mrs. Milligan, but I'm not that hungry. And I don't eat meat anymore.
But...we always eat burgers at camp.
My mom says being vegetarian is better for the environment.
You know, Mia, Allorvians and Picauru were strictly vegetarian. And there are some people who claim Desmerel had to be vegan.

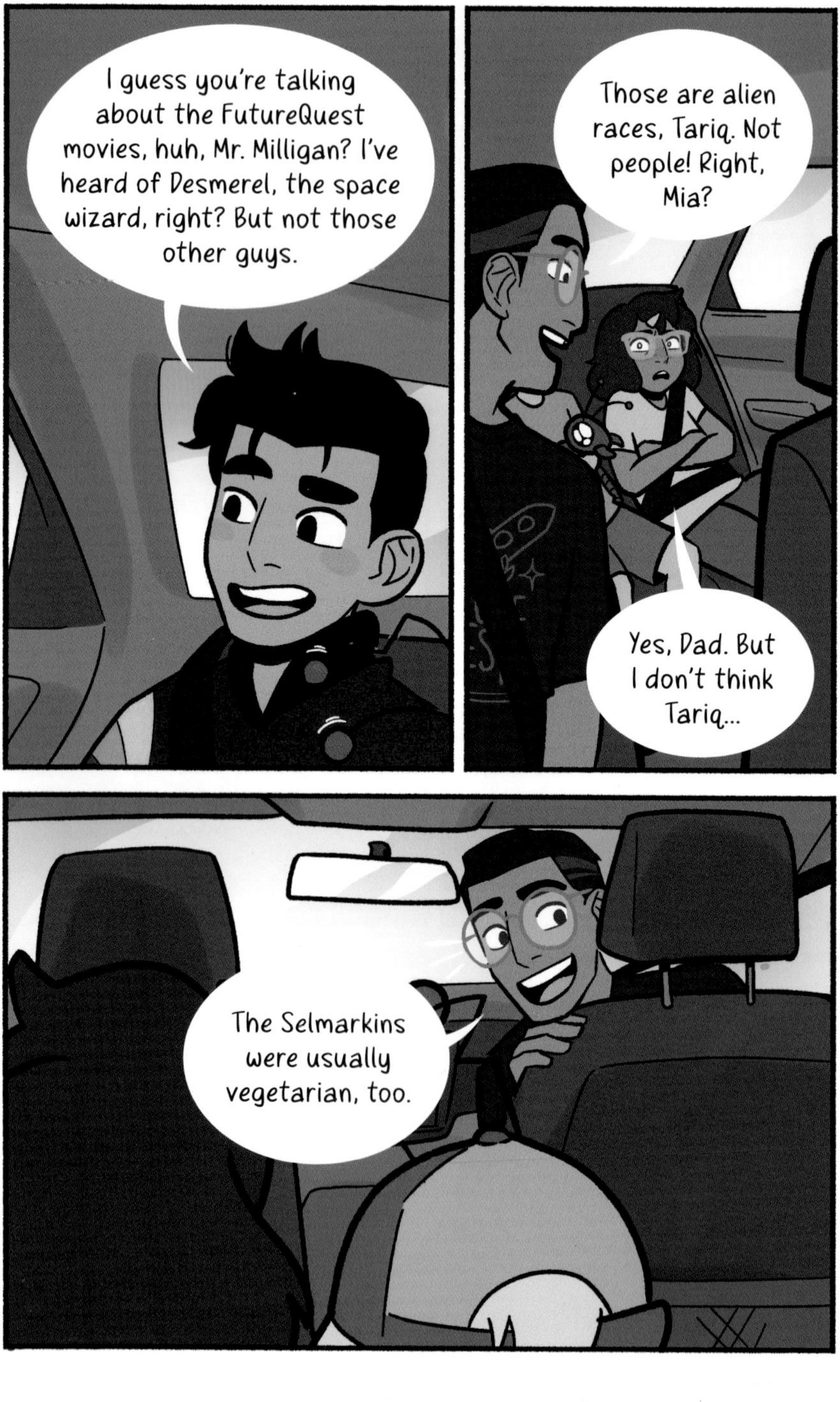
I guess you're talking about the FutureQuest movies, huh, Mr. Milligan? I've heard of Desmerel, the space wizard, right? But not those other guys.
Those are alien races, Tariq. Not people! Right, Mia?
Yes, Dad. But I don't think Tariq...
The Selmarkins were usually vegetarian, too.

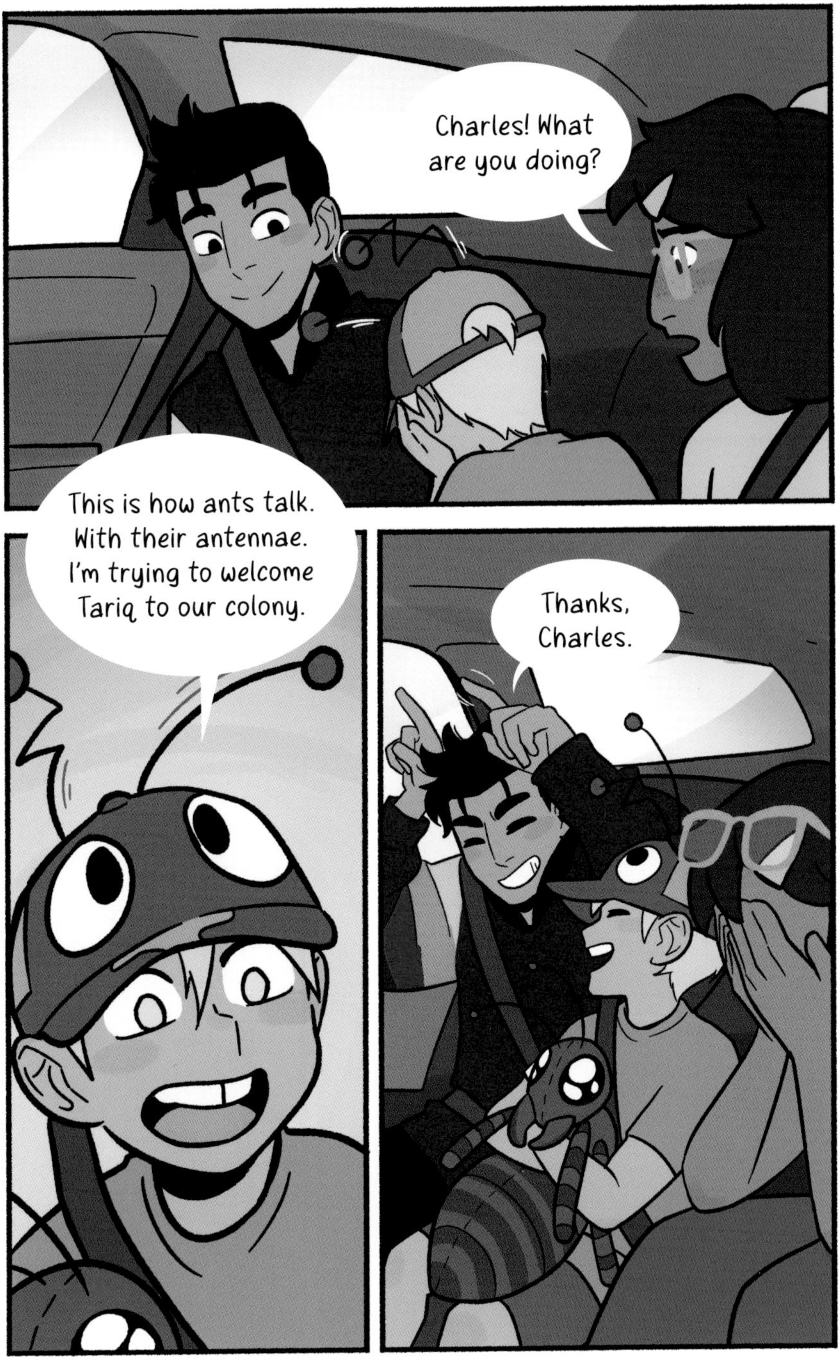
Charles! What are you doing?
This is how ants talk. With their antennae. I'm trying to welcome Tariq to our colony.
Thanks, Charles.

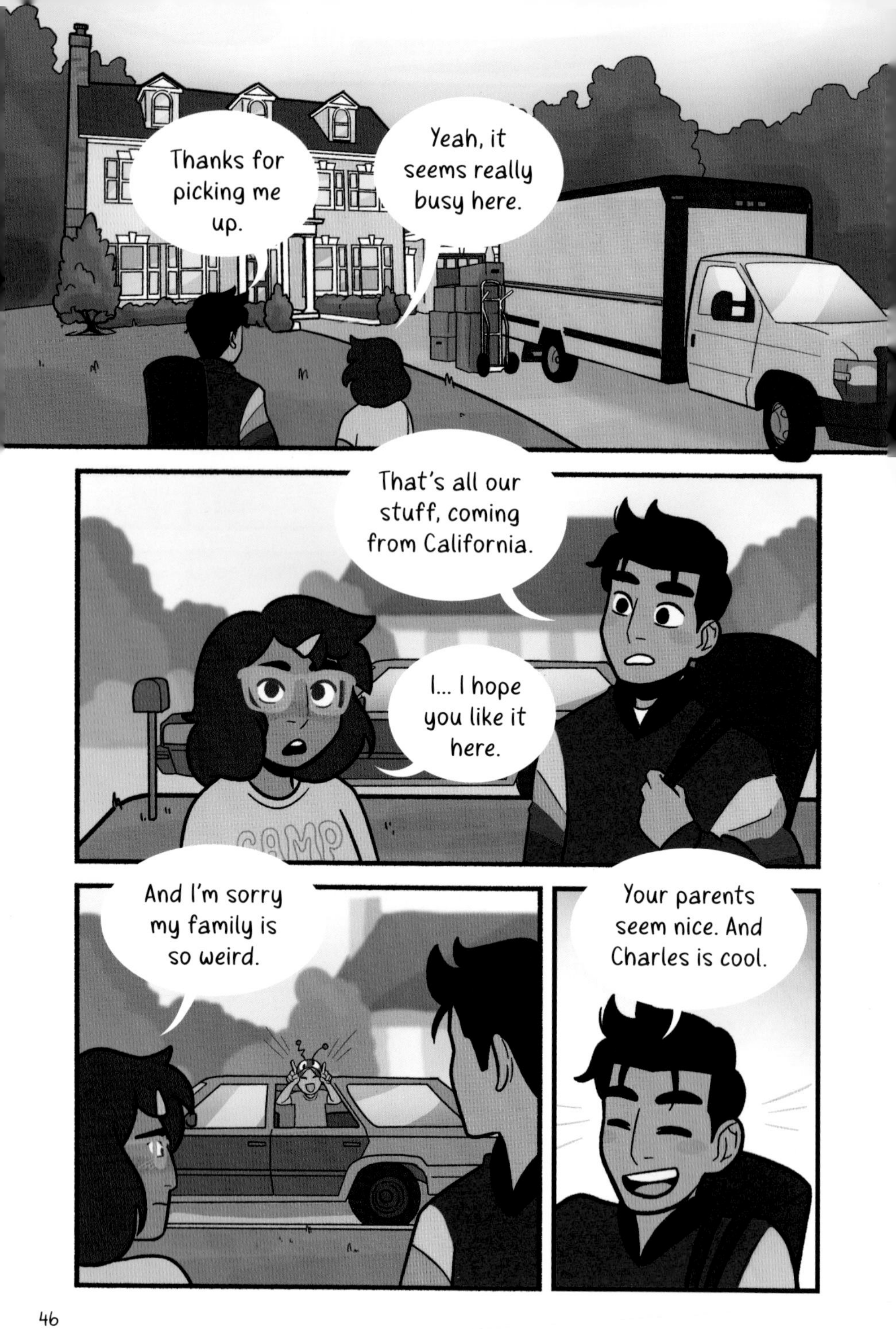
Thanks for picking me up.
Yeah, it seems really busy here.
That's all our stuff, coming from California.
I... I hope you like it here.
CAMP
And I'm sorry my family is so weird.
Your parents seem nice. And Charles is cool.

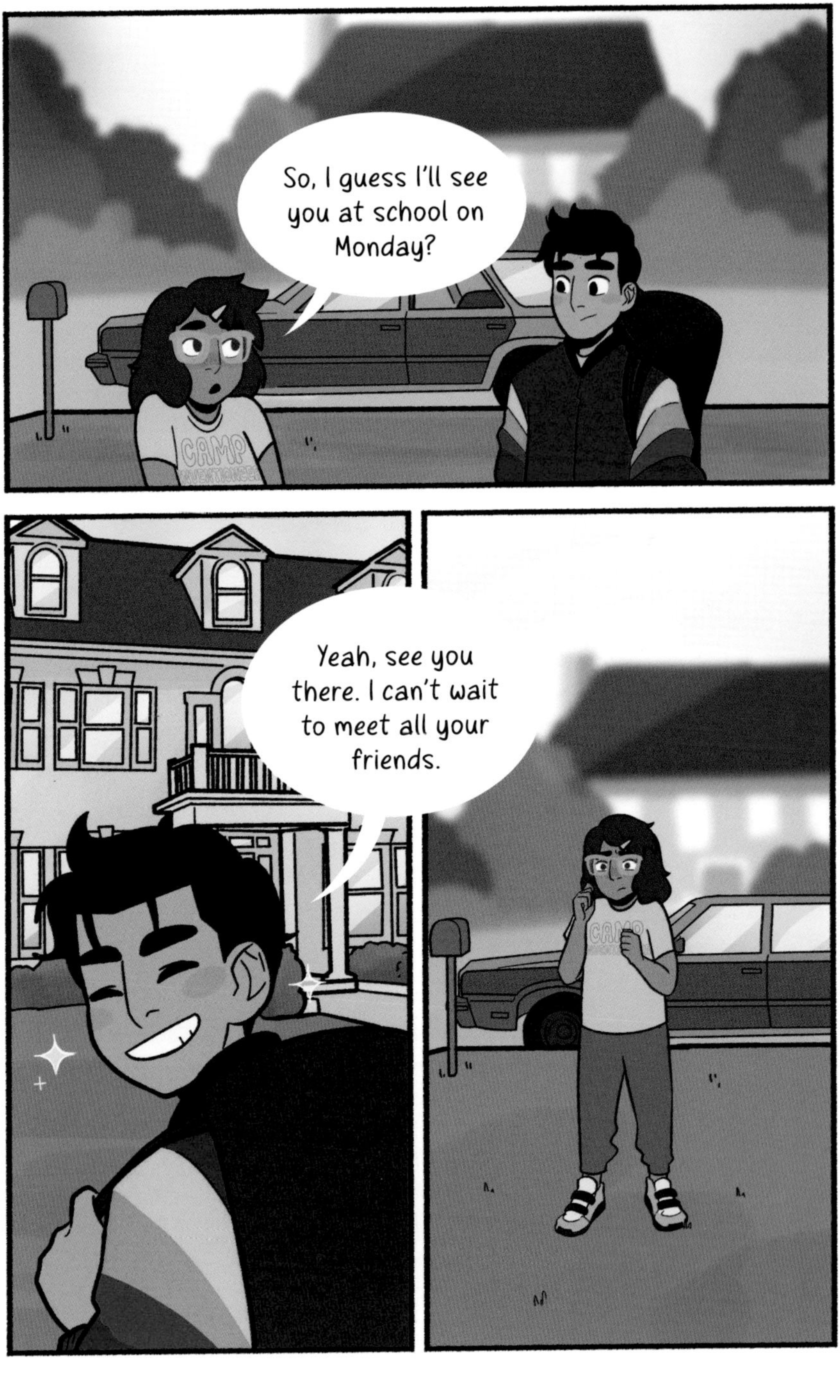
So, I guess I'll see you at school on Monday?
Yeah, see you there. I can't wait to meet all your friends.

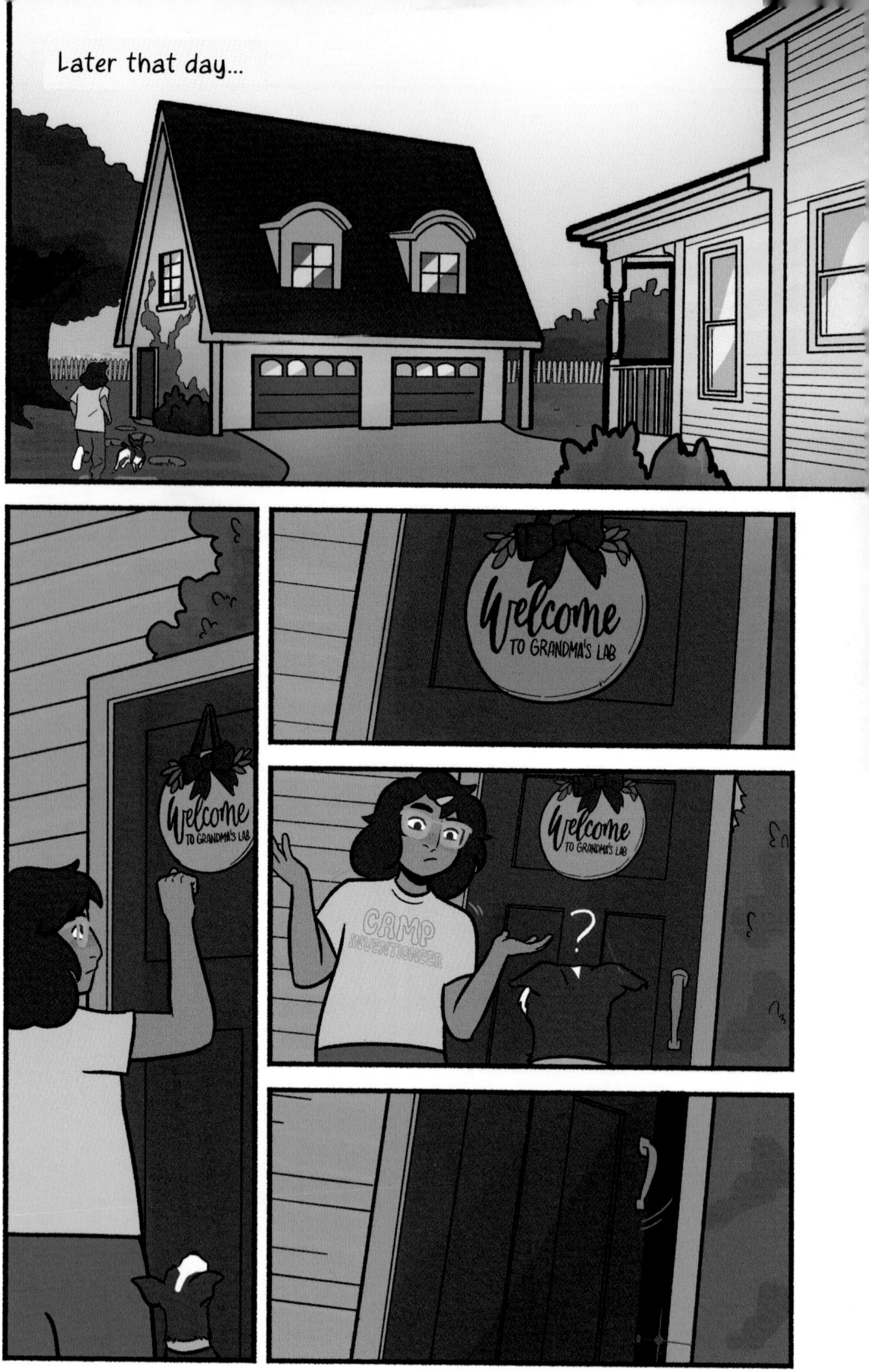
Later that day...
Welcome
TO GRANDMA'S LAB
Welcome
TO GRANDMA'S LAB
Welcome
TO GRANDMA'S LAB
CAMP
INVENTIONEER
?

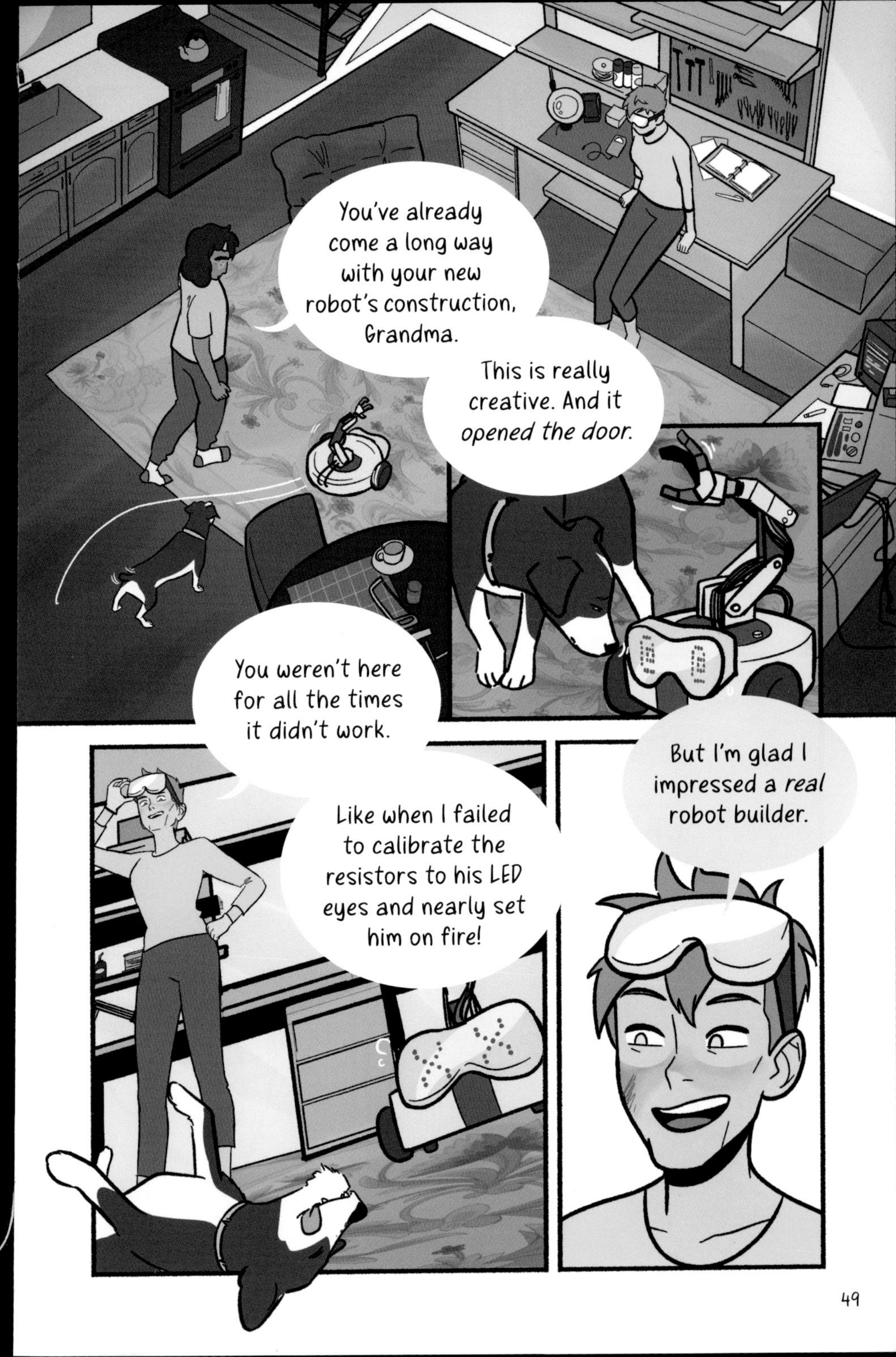
You've already come a long way with your new robot's construction, Grandma.
This is really creative. And it *opened the door.*
You weren't here for all the times it didn't work.
Like when I failed to calibrate the resistors to his LED eyes and nearly set him on fire!
But I'm glad I impressed a *real* robot builder.

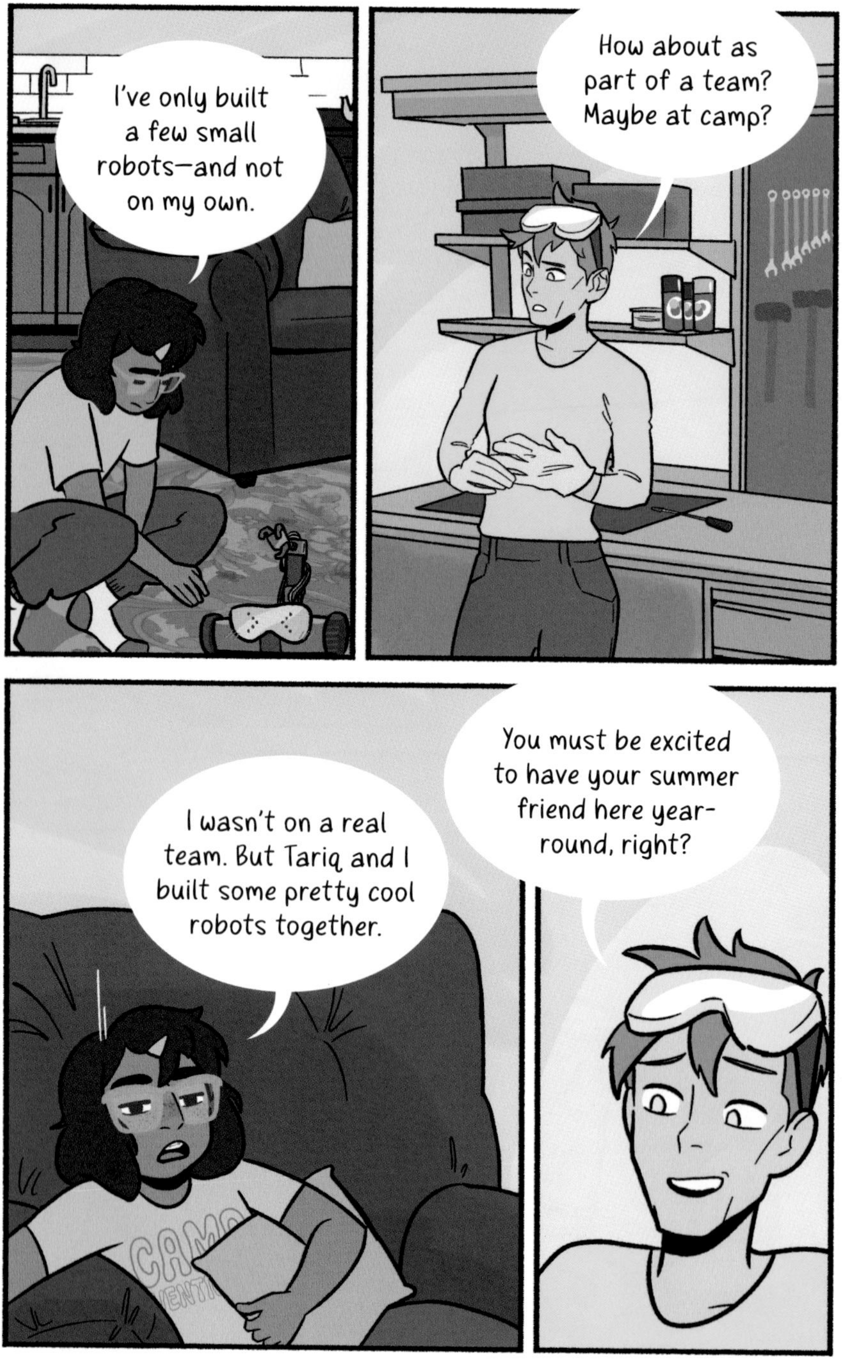
I've only built a few small robots—and not on my own.
How about as part of a team? Maybe at camp?
You must be excited to have your summer friend here year-round, right?
I wasn't on a real team. But Tariq and I built some pretty cool robots together.

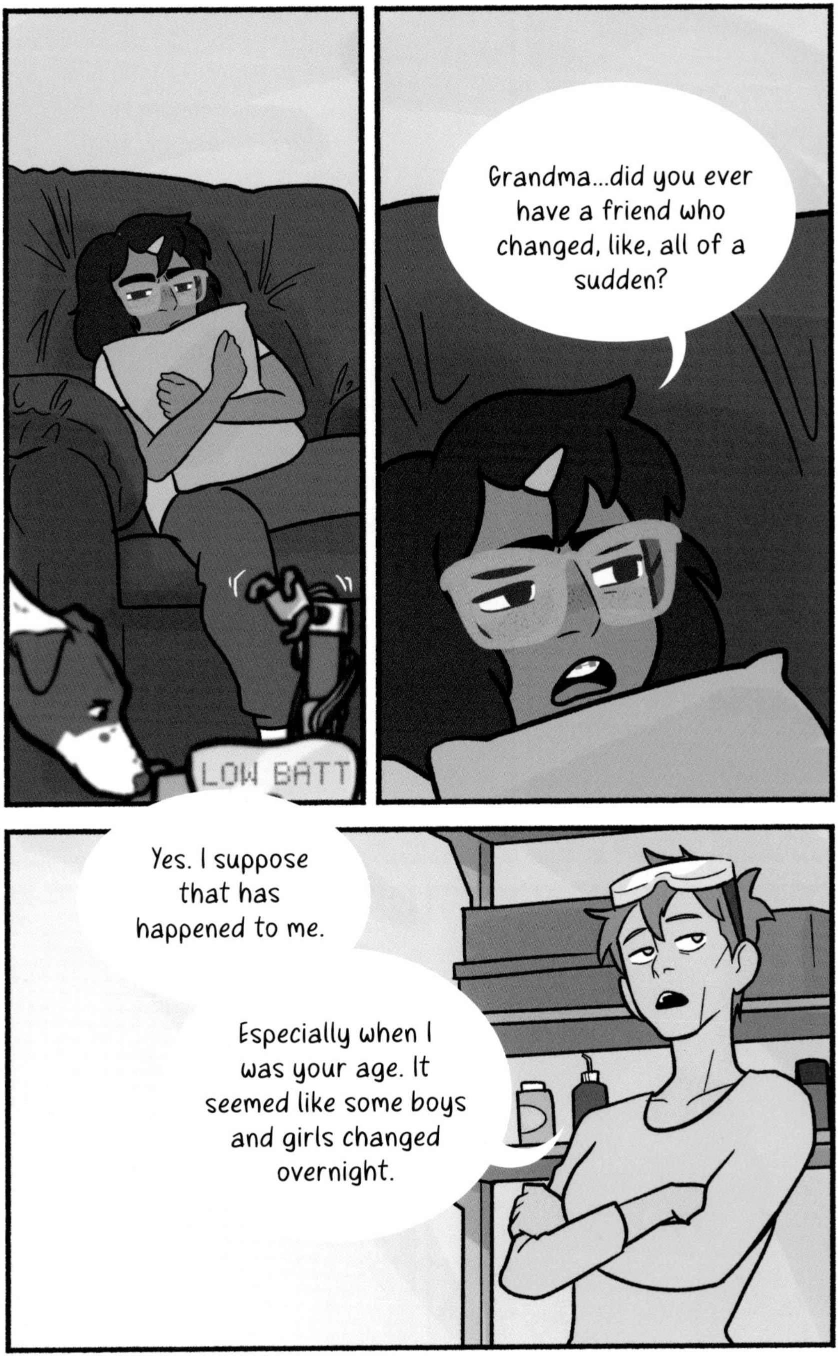

Grandma...did you ever have a friend who changed, like, all of a sudden?
LOW BATT
Yes. I suppose that has happened to me.
Especially when I was your age. It seemed like some boys and girls changed overnight.

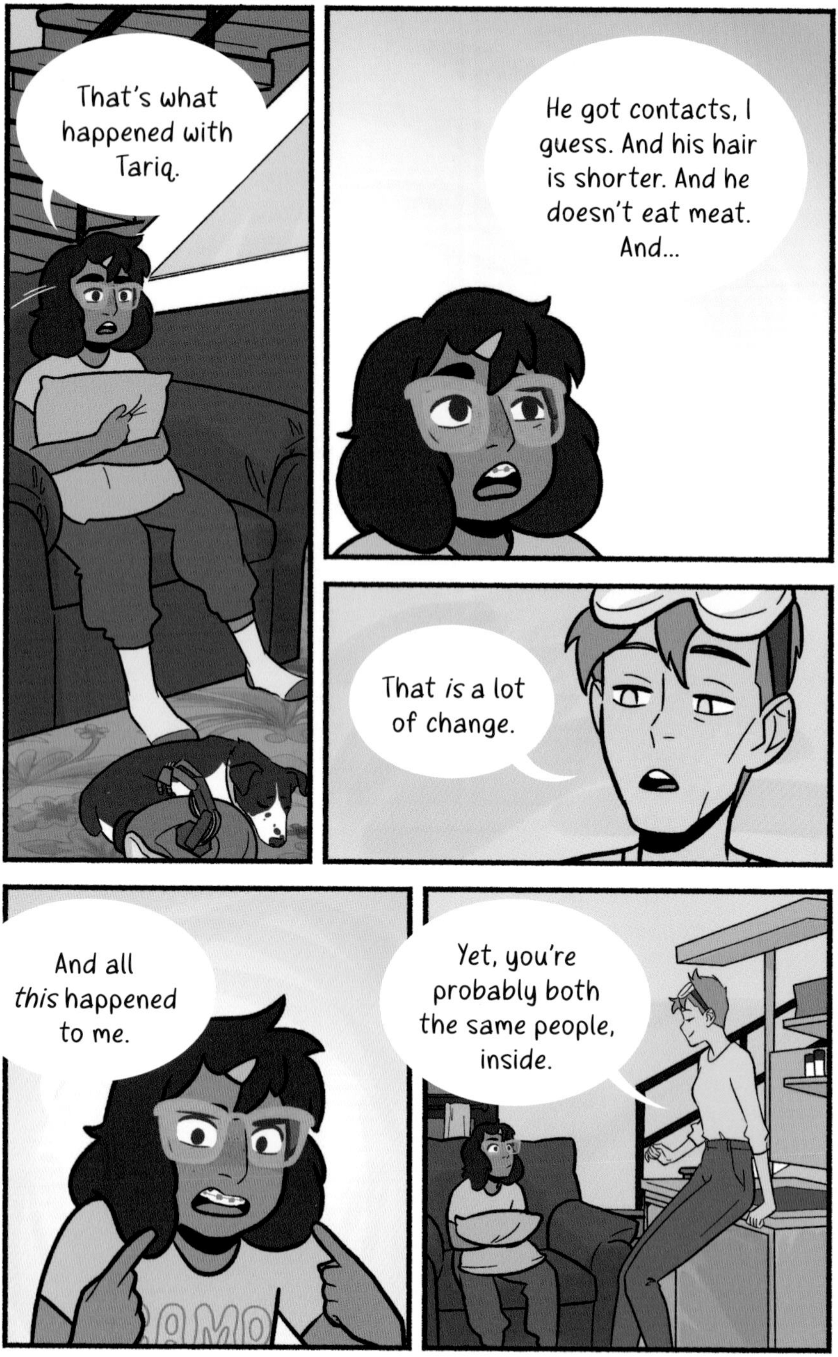
That's what happened with Tariq.
He got contacts, I guess. And his hair is shorter. And he doesn't eat meat. And...
That *is* a lot of change.
And all *this* happened to me.
Yet, you're probably both the same people, inside.

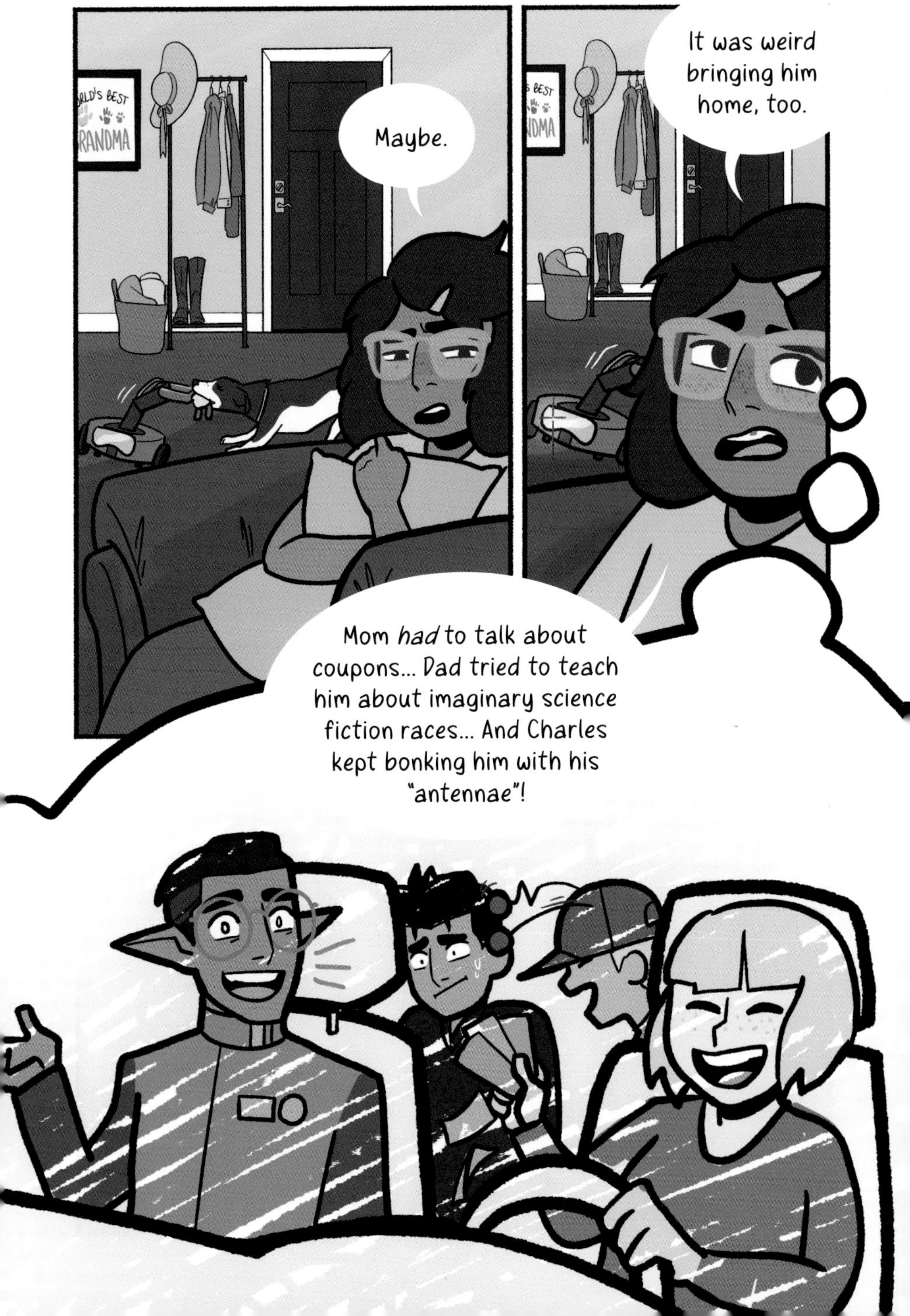
RLD'S BEST RANDMA
Maybe.
It was weird bringing him home, too.
Mom *had* to talk about coupons... Dad tried to teach him about imaginary science fiction races... And Charles kept bonking him with his "antennae"!

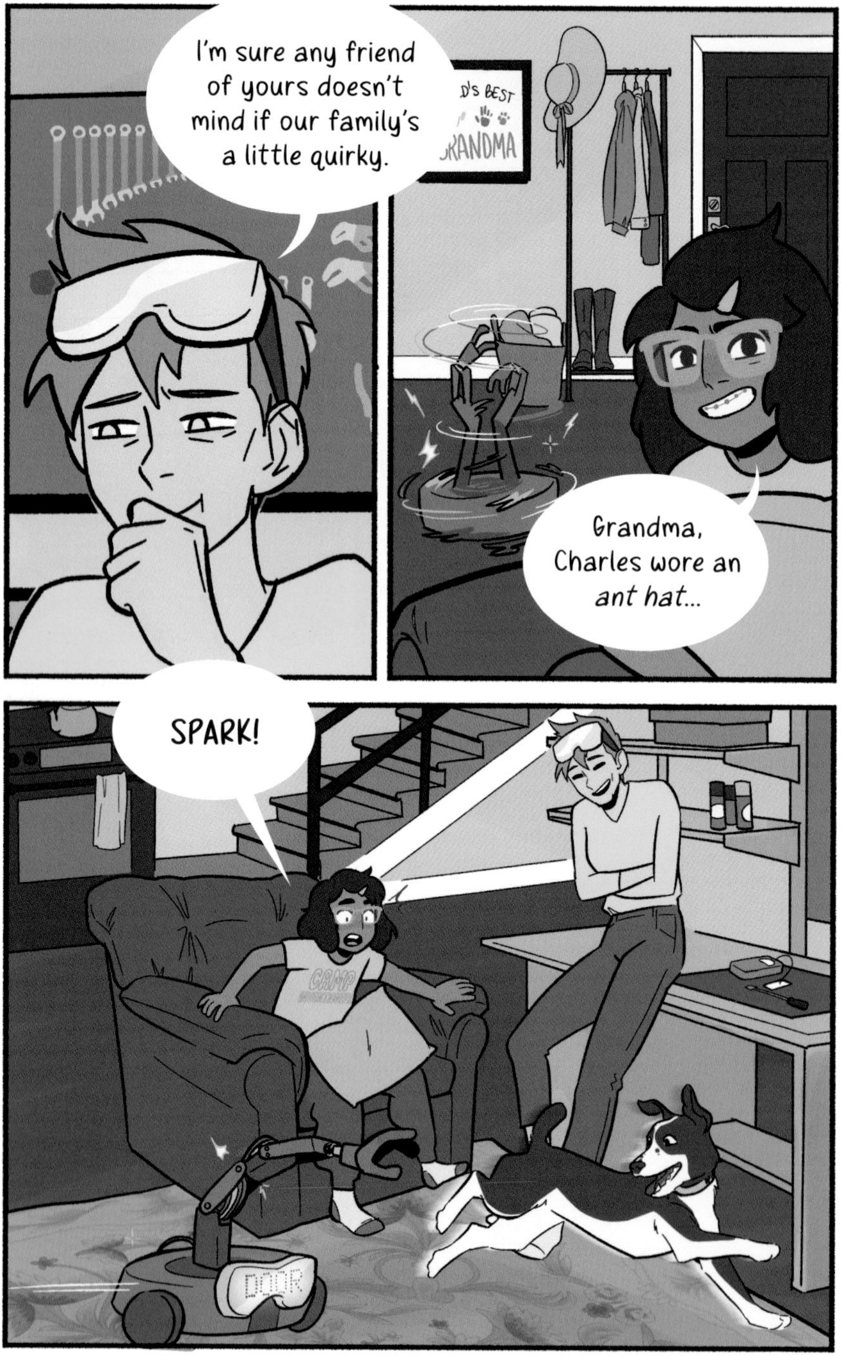
I'm sure any friend of yours doesn't mind if our family's a little quirky.
..D'S BEST ..RANDMA
Grandma, Charles wore an *ant hat*...
SPARK!
CAMP
DOOR

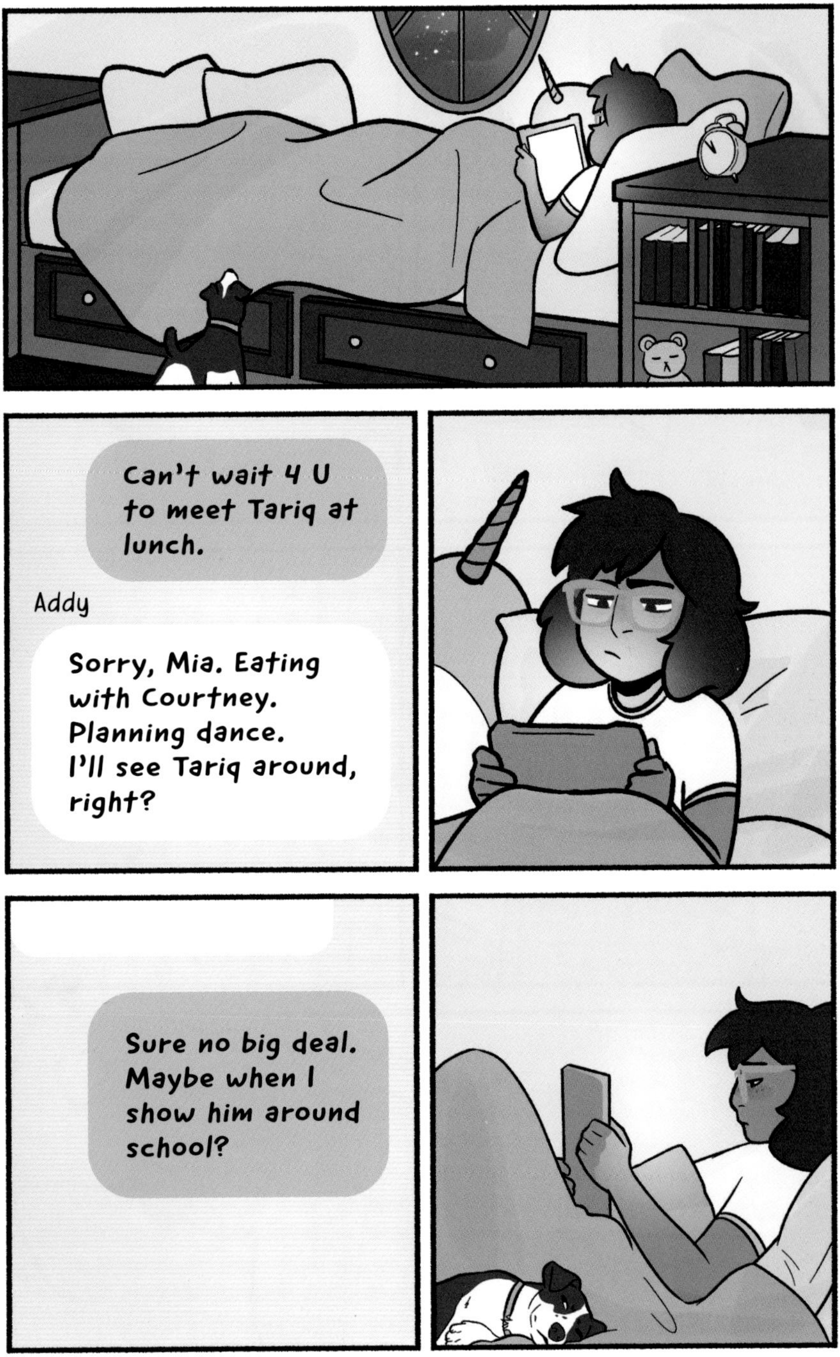
Can't wait 4 U to meet Tariq at lunch.
Addy
Sorry, Mia. Eating with Courtney. Planning dance. I'll see Tariq around, right?
Sure no big deal. Maybe when I show him around school?

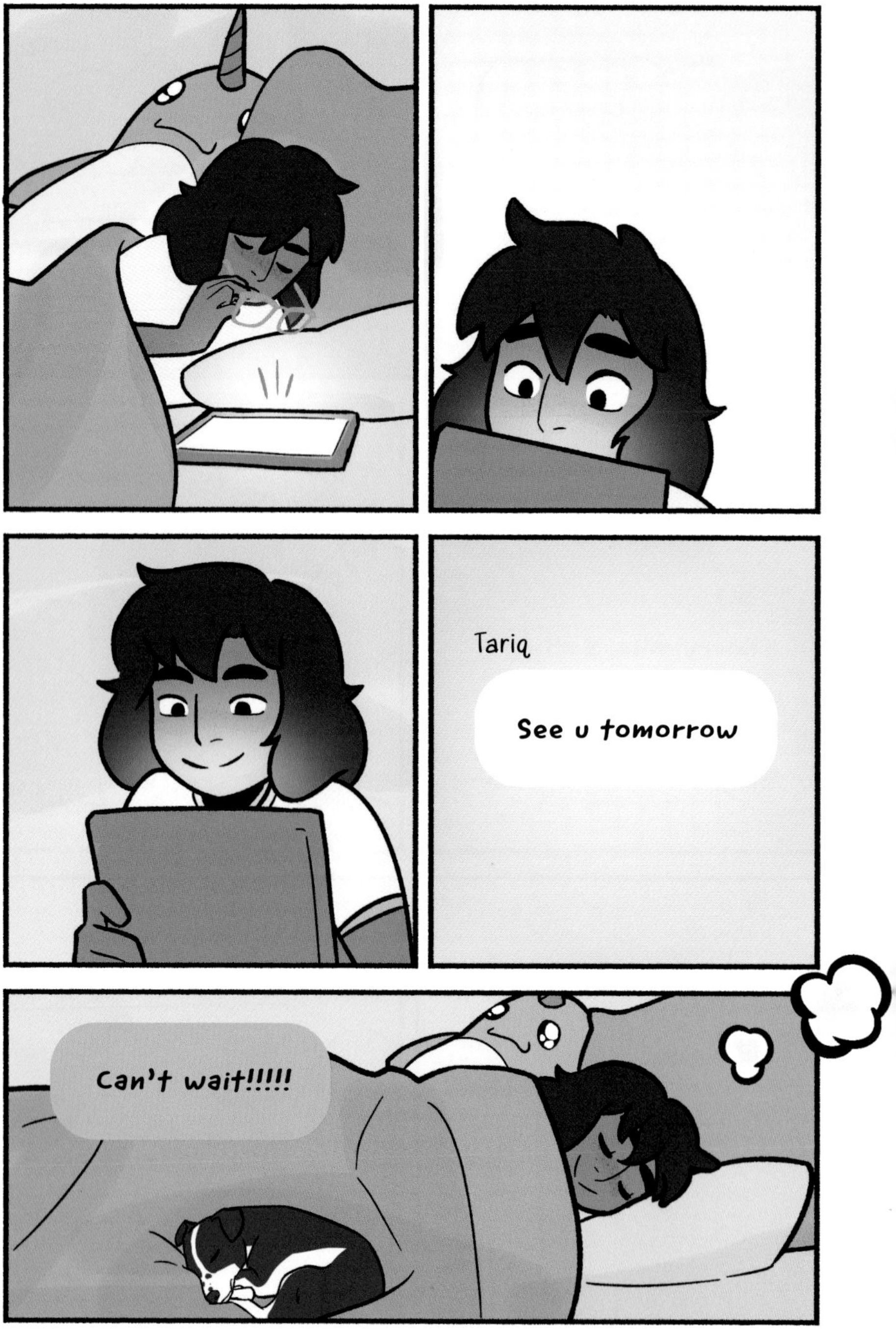
Tariq
See u tomorrow
Can't wait!!!!!

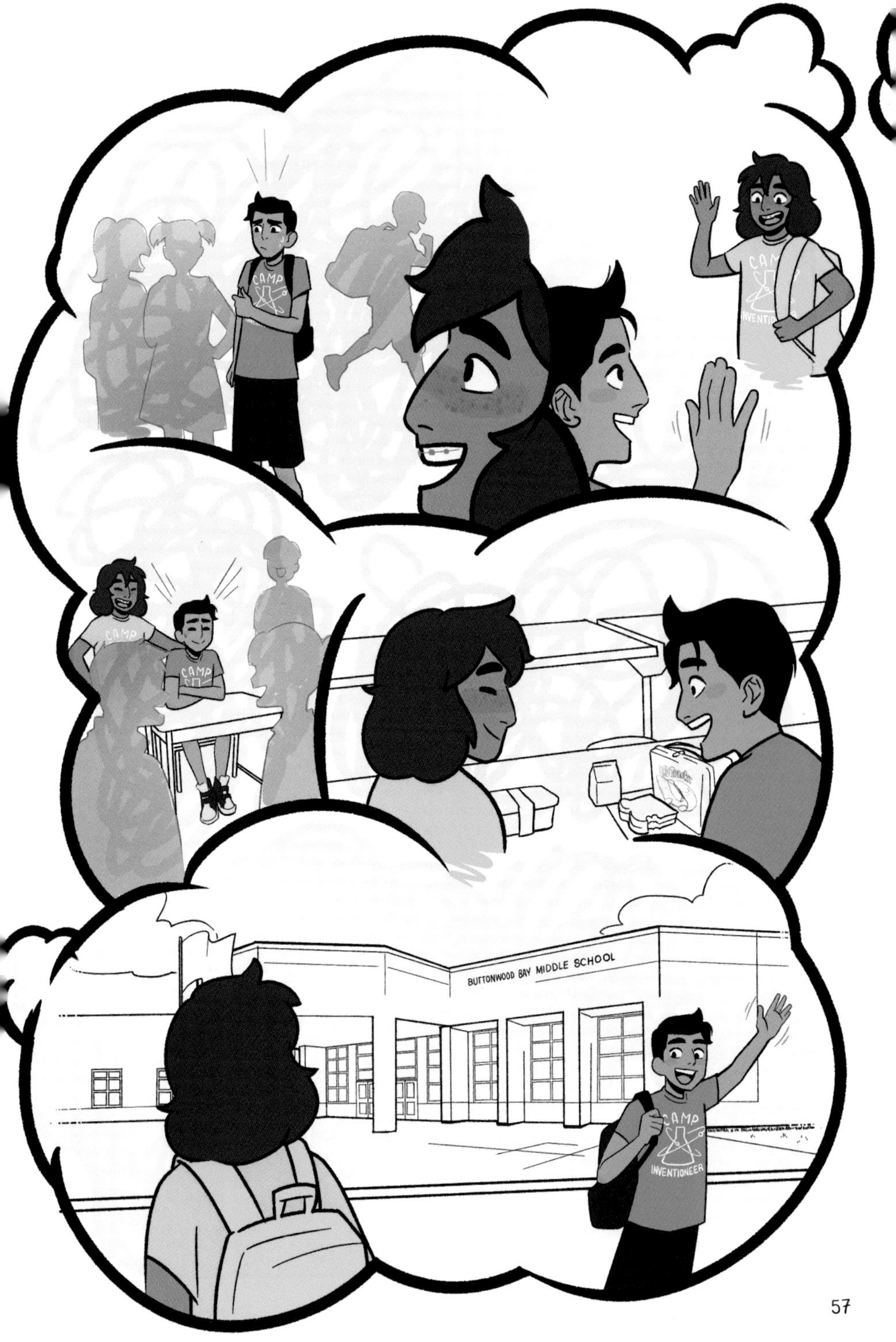
CAMP
CAMP INVENTIONEER
CAMP
CAMP
BUTTONWOOD BAY MIDDLE SCHOOL
CAMP INVENTIONEER

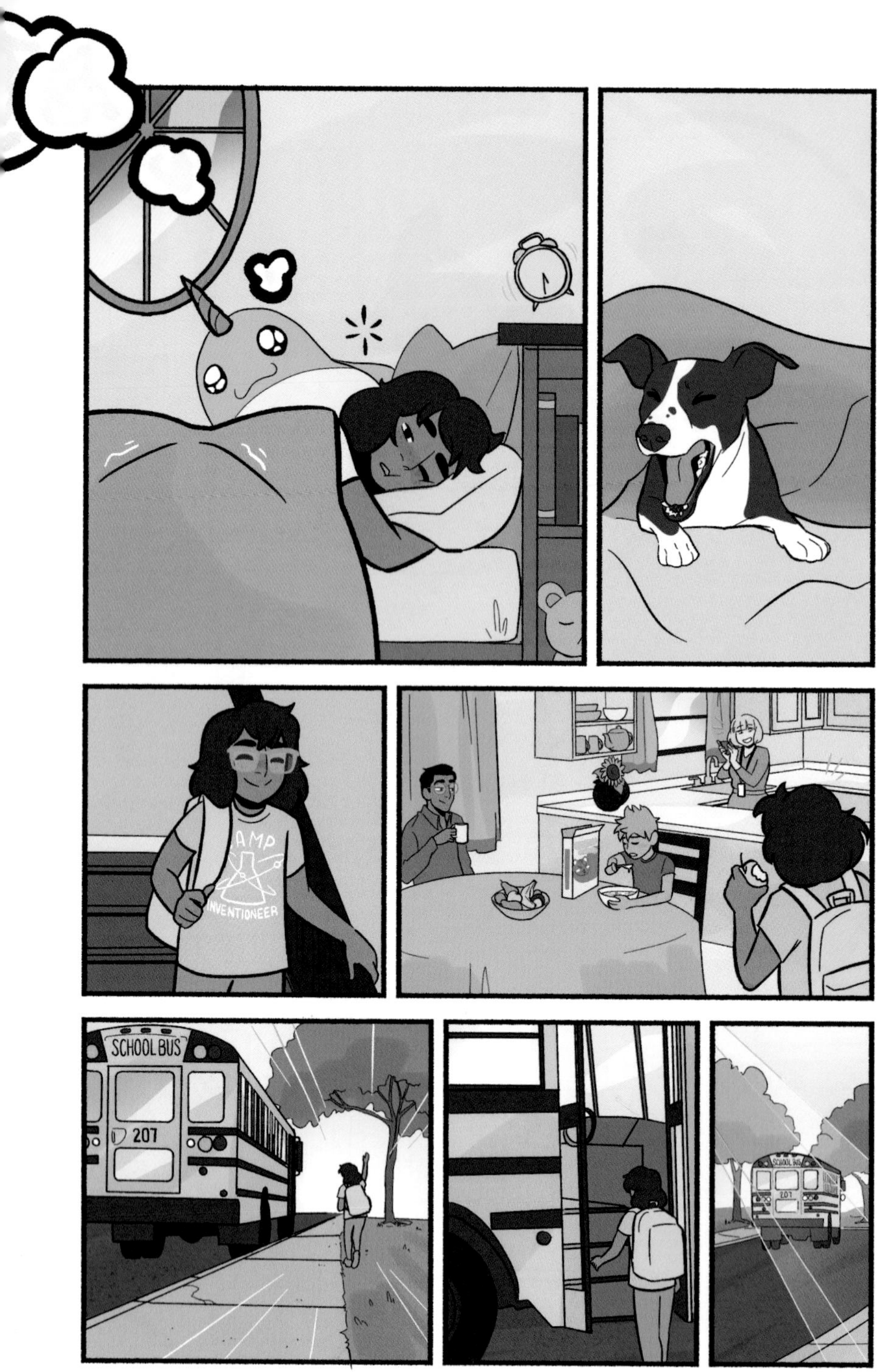
CAMP
INVENTIONEER
SCHOOL BUS
207
SCHOOL BUS
207

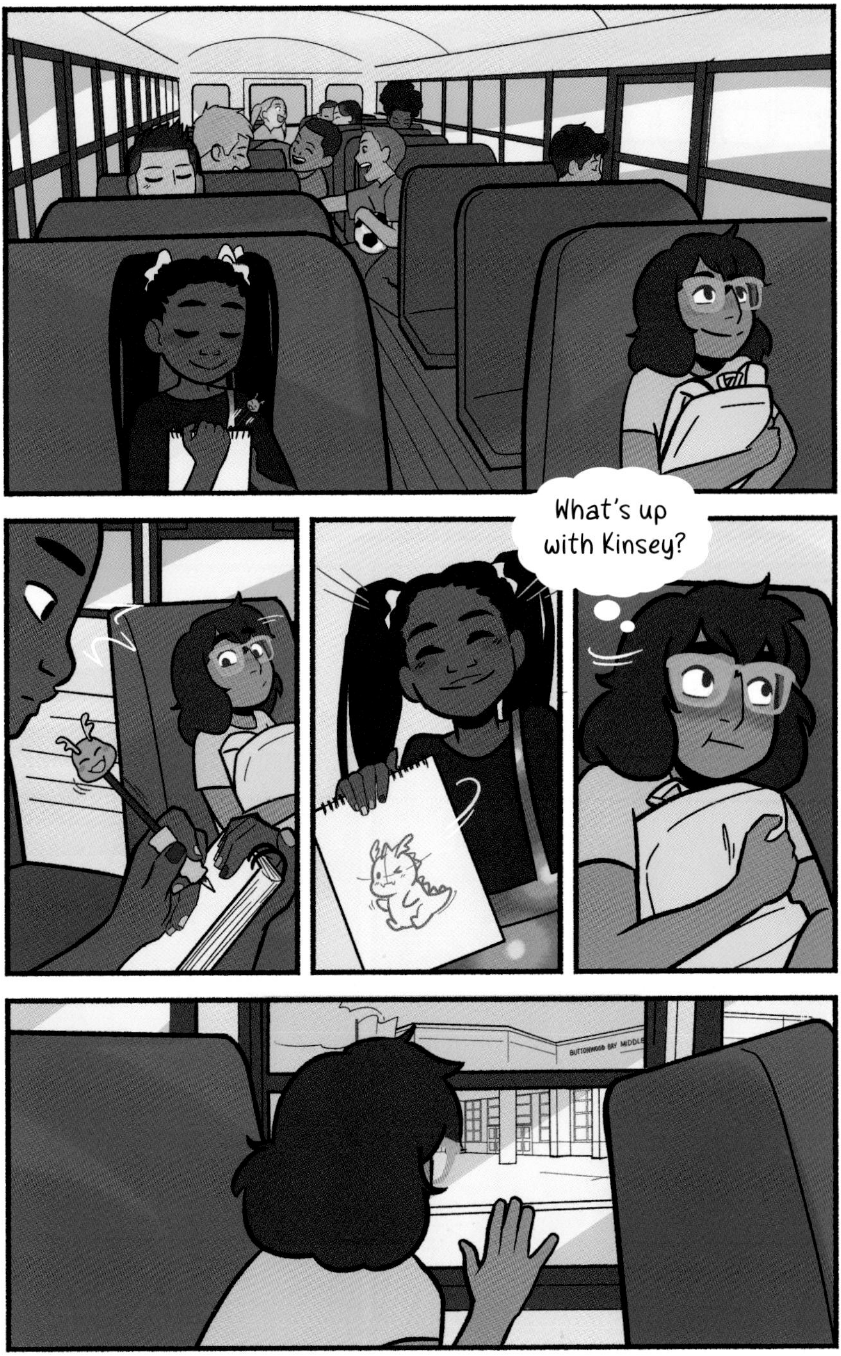
What's up with Kinsey?
BUTTONWOOD BAY MIDDLE

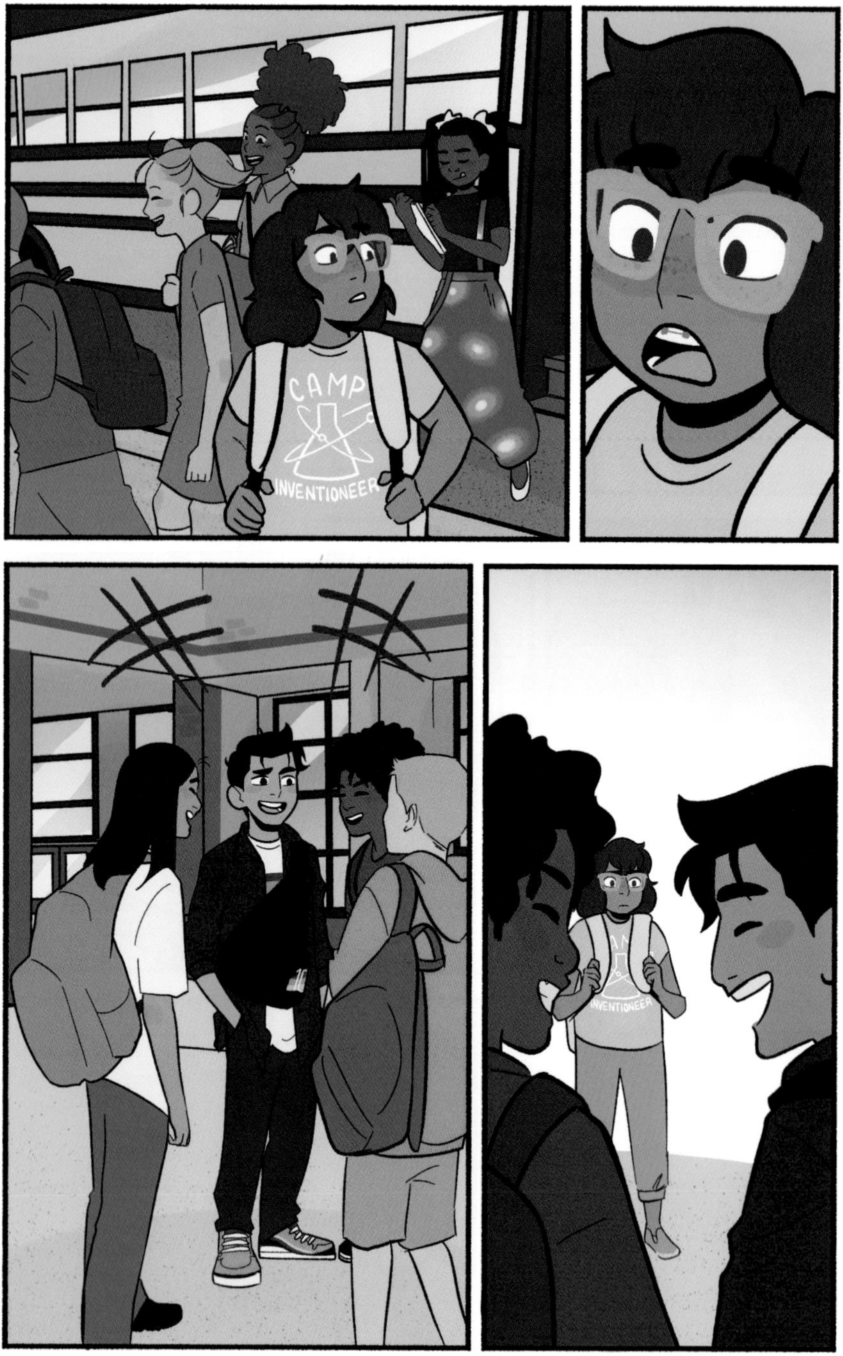
CAMP
INVENTIONEER
INVENTIONEER

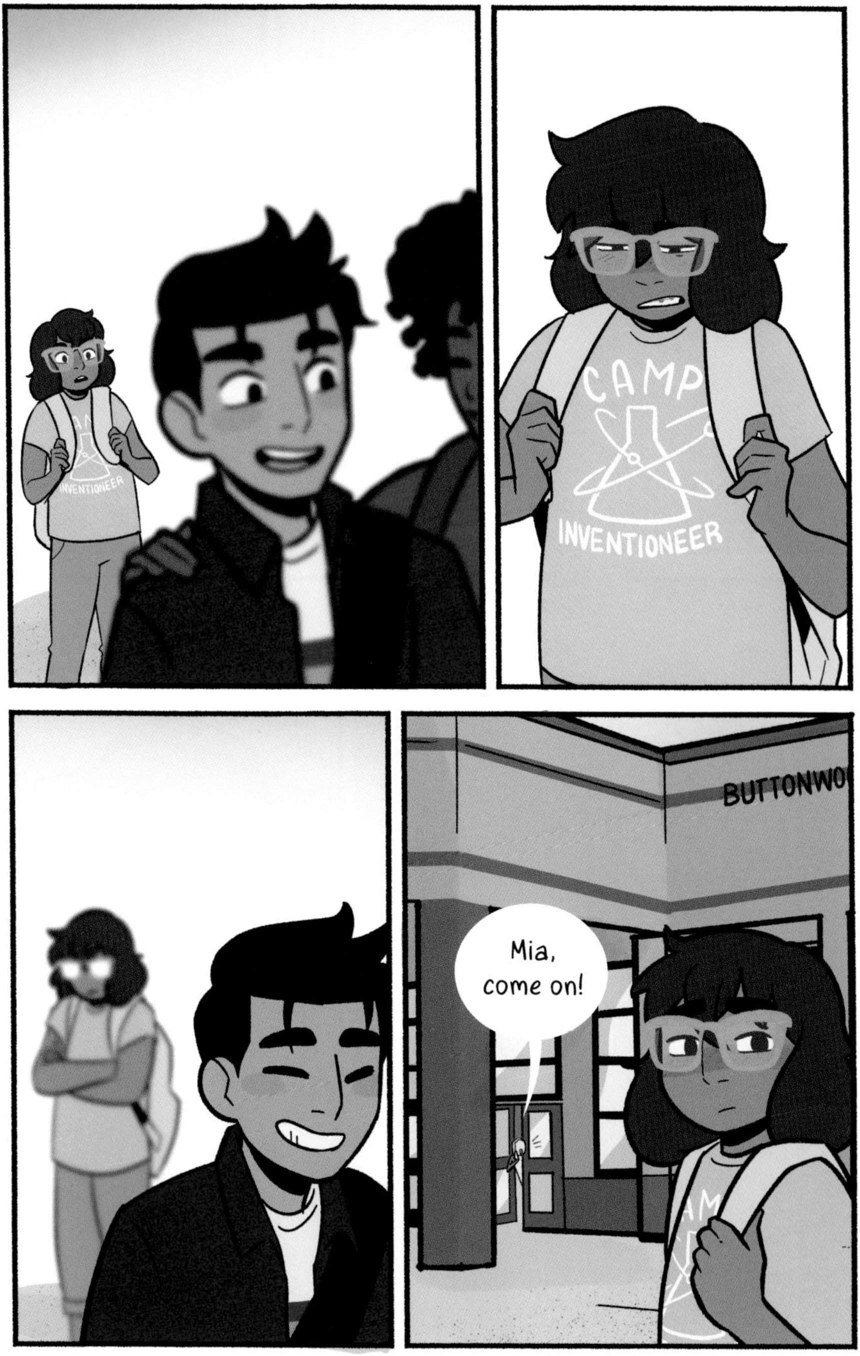
INVENTIONEER
CAMP
INVENTIONEER
BUTTONWO
Mia,
come on!

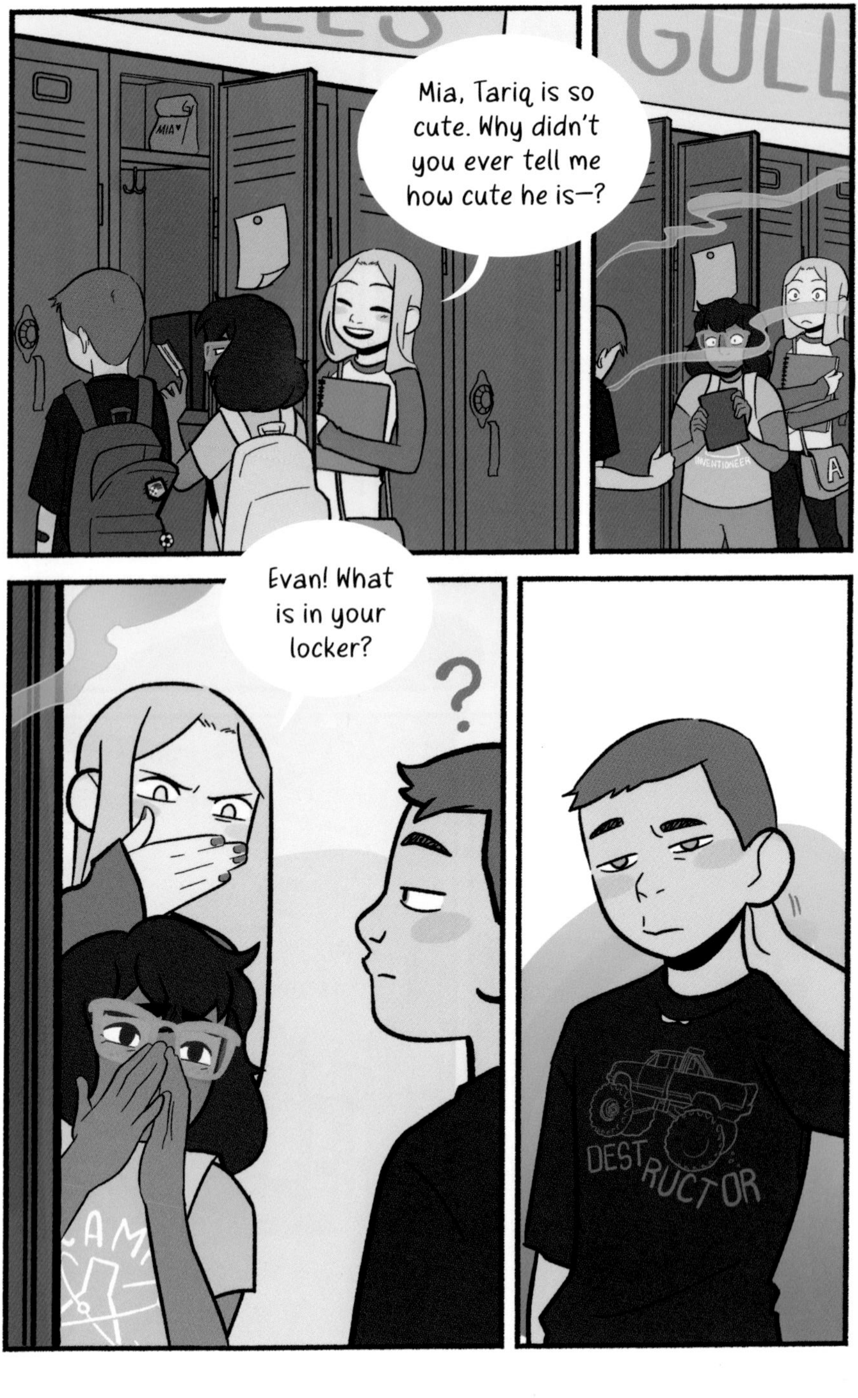
GULLS
GULL
MIA♥
Mia, Tariq is so cute. Why didn't you ever tell me how cute he is—?
INVENTIONEER
A
Evan! What is in your locker?
?
DESTRUCTOR

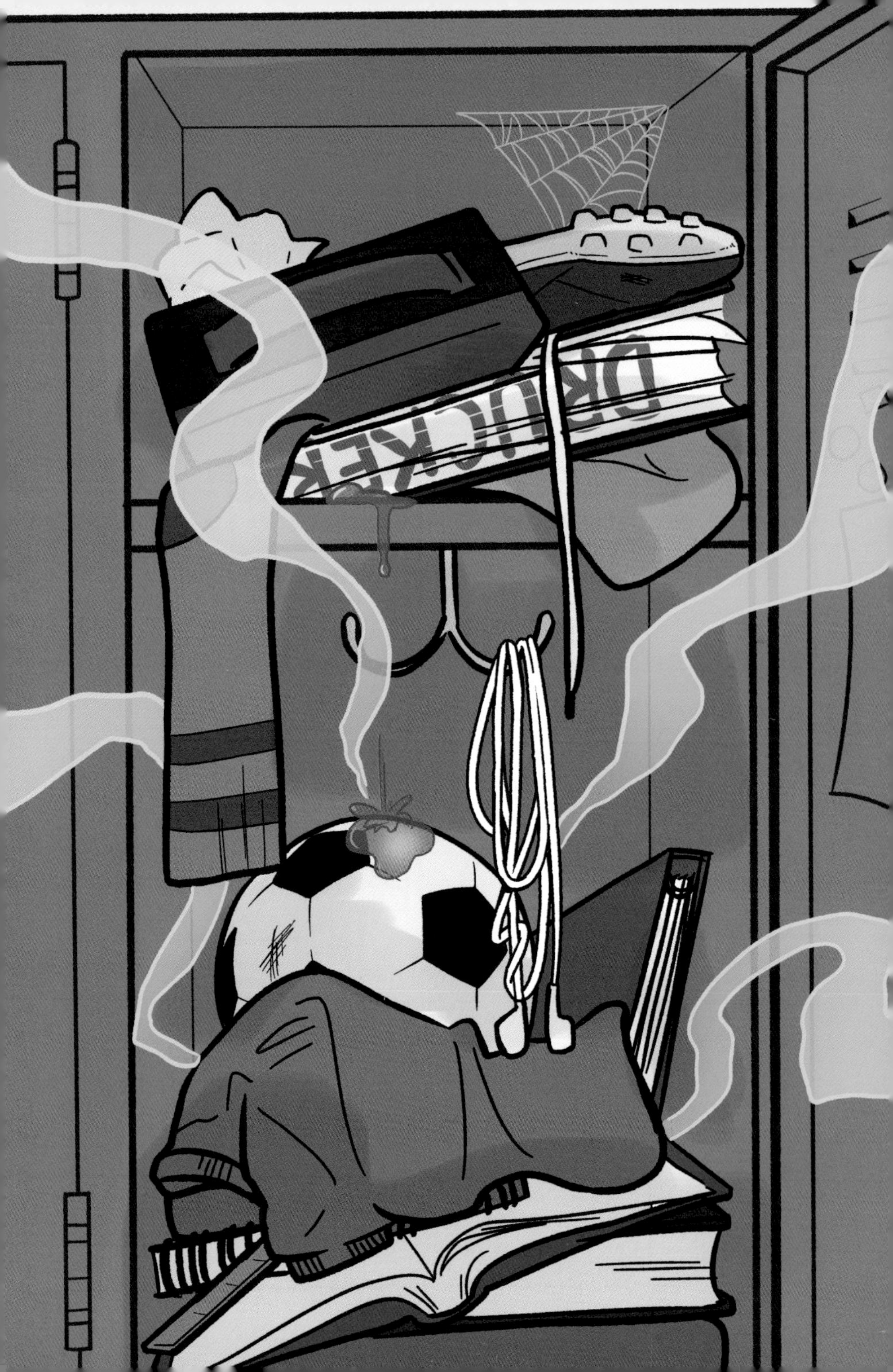
DRUCKER

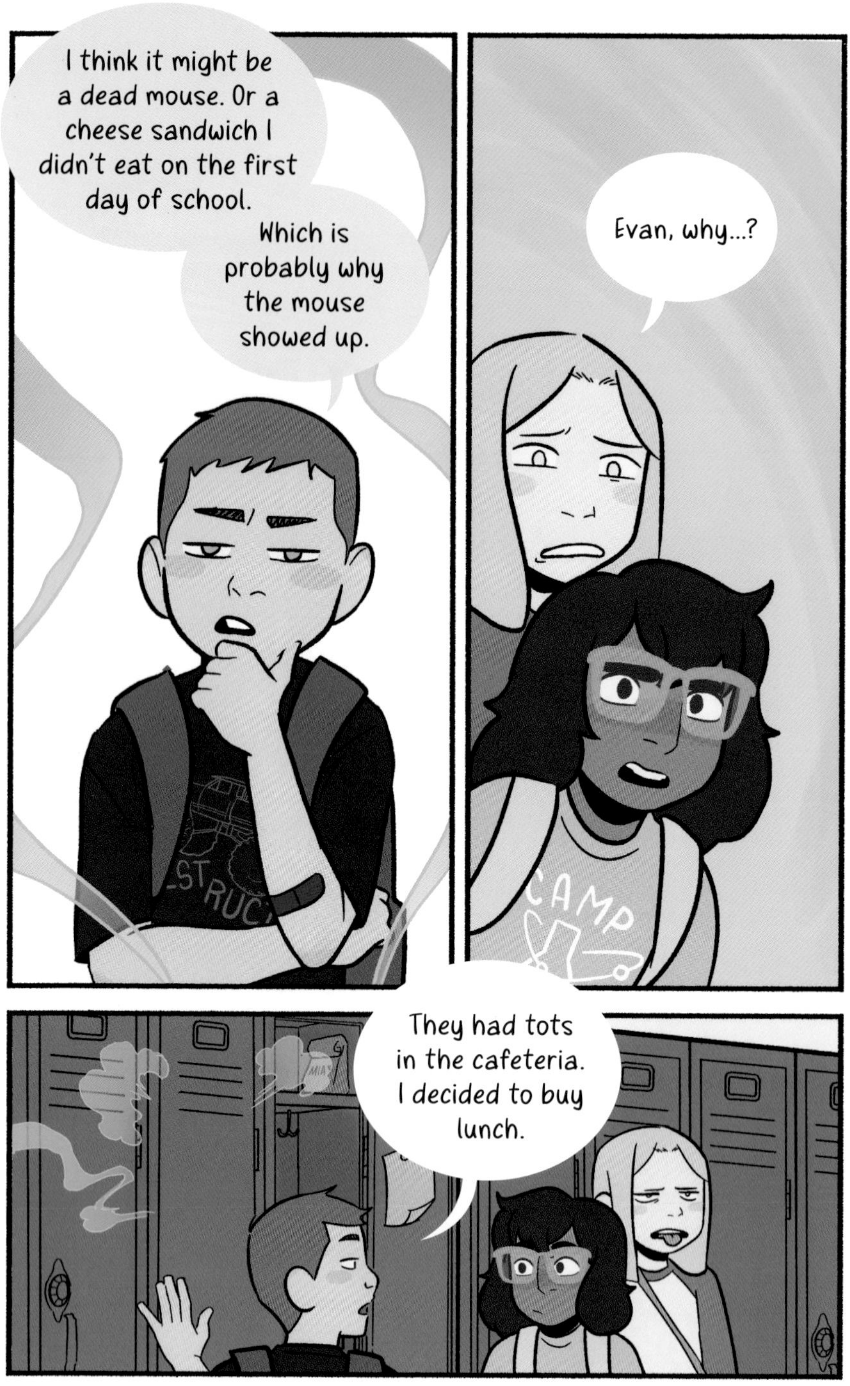
I think it might be a dead mouse. Or a cheese sandwich I didn't eat on the first day of school.
Which is probably why the mouse showed up.
Evan, why...?
They had tots in the cafeteria. I decided to buy lunch.

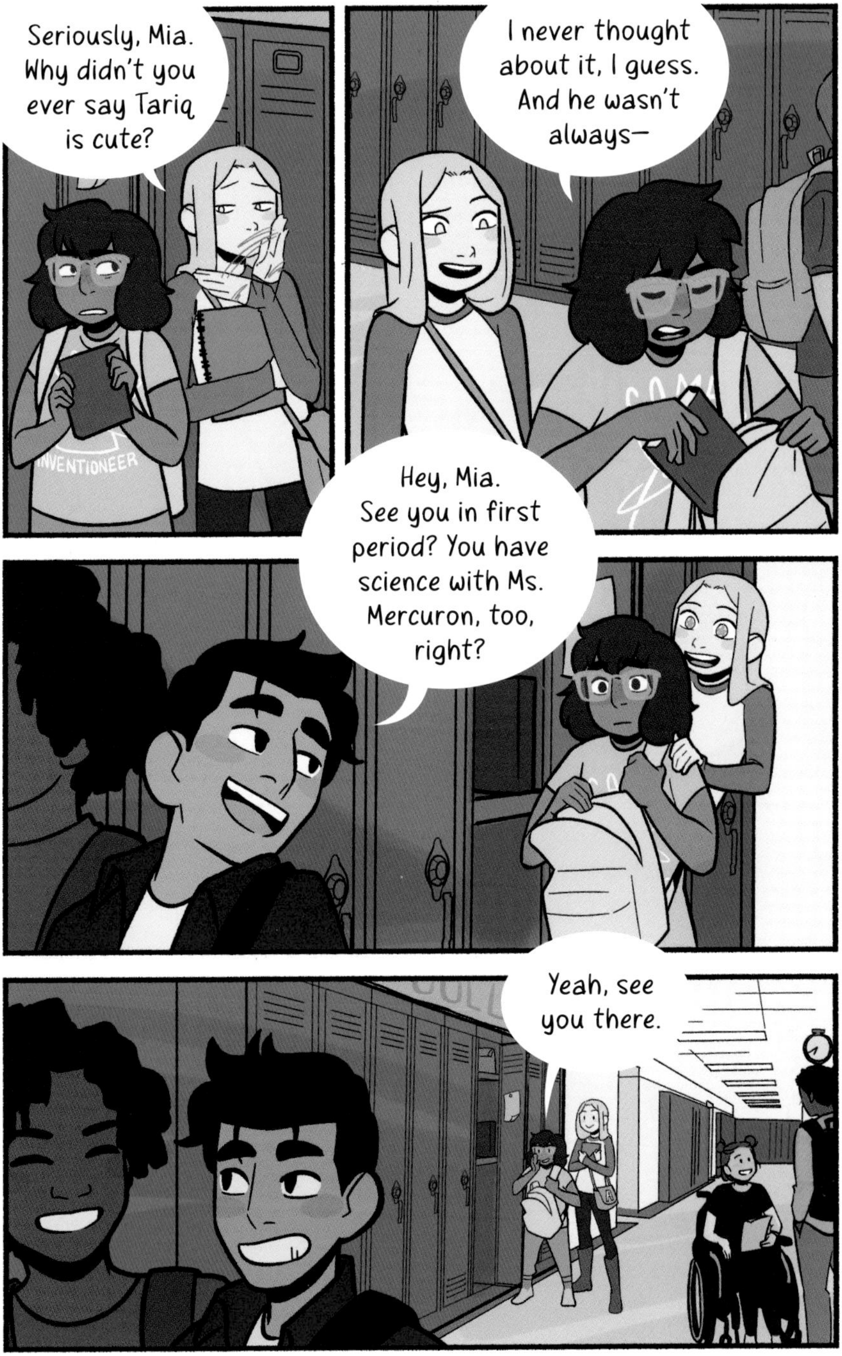

Seriously, Mia. Why didn't you ever say Tariq is cute?
I never thought about it, I guess. And he wasn't always—
INVENTIONEER
Hey, Mia. See you in first period? You have science with Ms. Mercuron, too, right?
Yeah, see you there.

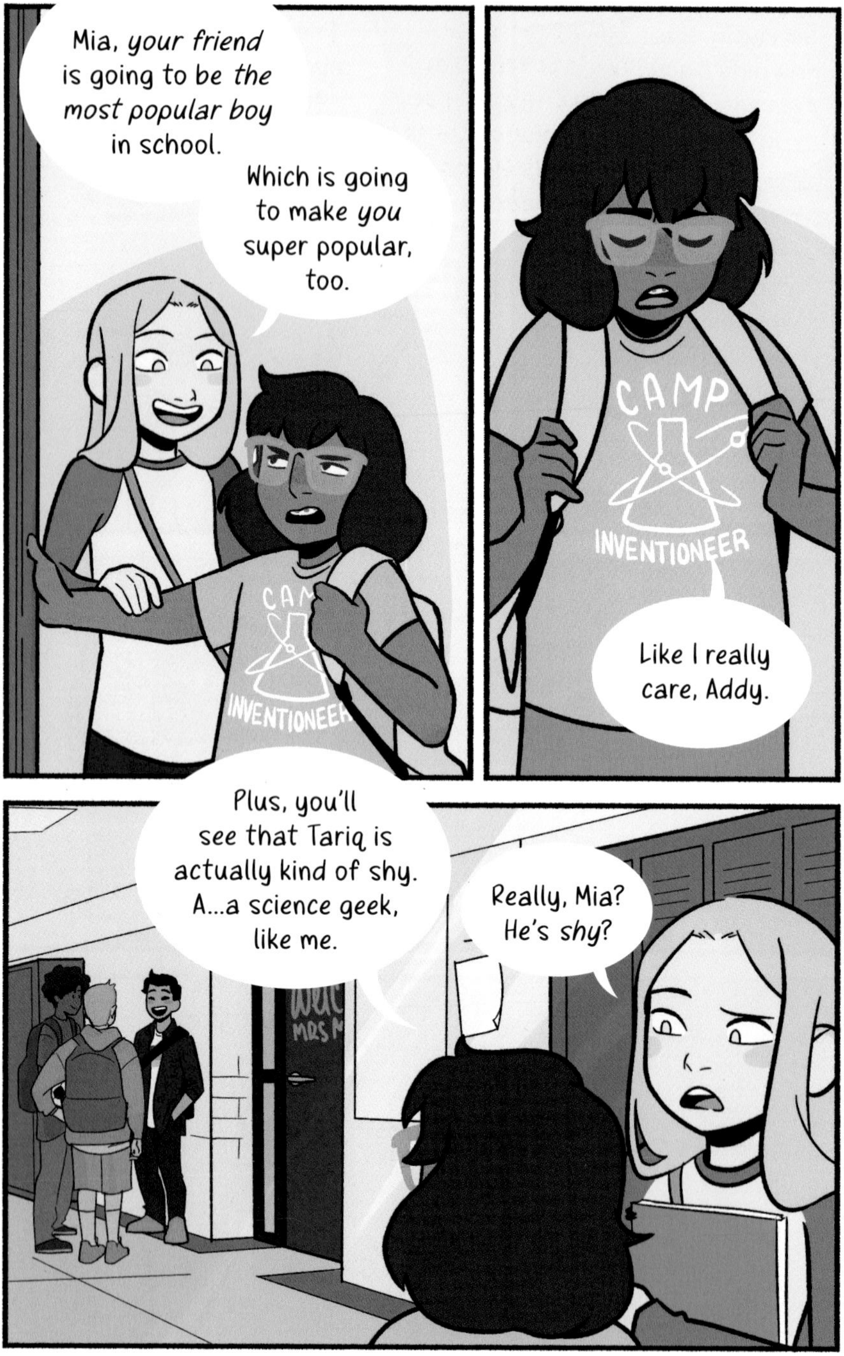
Mia, *your friend* is going to be *the most popular boy* in school.
Which is going to make *you* super popular, too.
CAMP
INVENTIONEER
CAMP
INVENTIONEER
Like I really care, Addy.
Plus, you'll see that Tariq is actually kind of shy. A...a science geek, like me.
Really, Mia? He's *shy*?

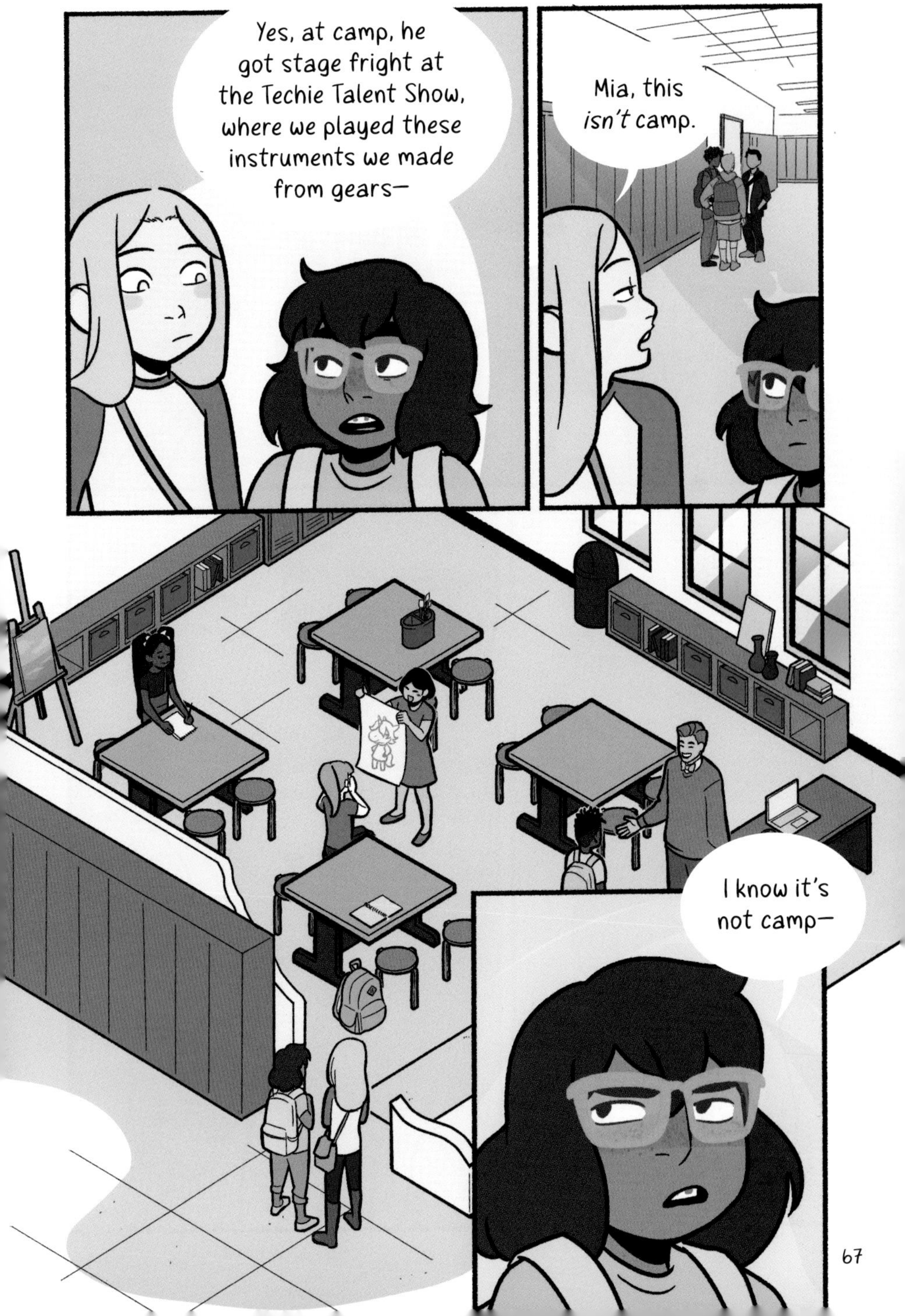
Yes, at camp, he got stage fright at the Techie Talent Show, where we played these instruments we made from gears—
Mia, this *isn't* camp.
I know it's not camp—

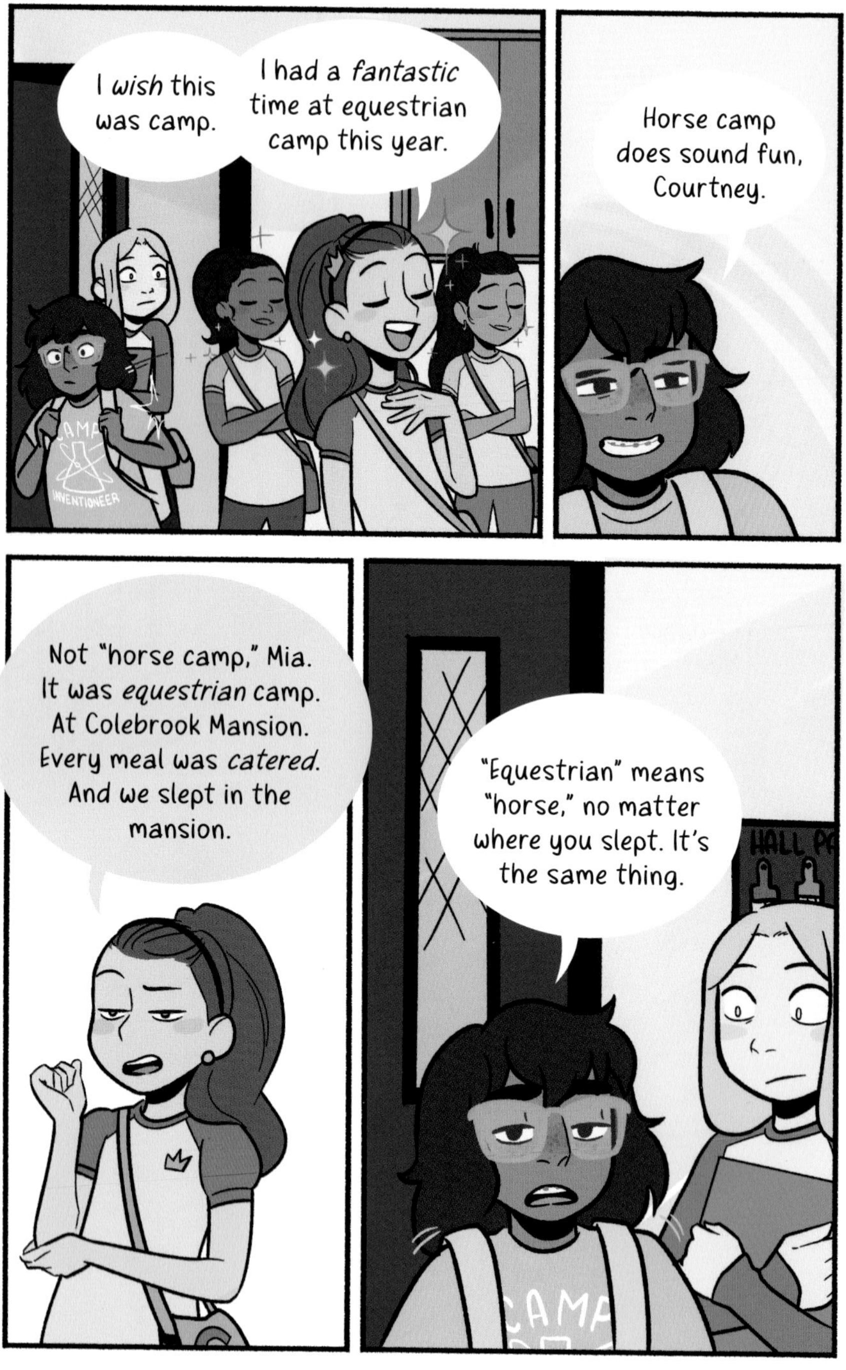
I *wish* this was camp.
I had a *fantastic* time at equestrian camp this year.
INVENTIONEER
Horse camp does sound fun, Courtney.
Not "horse camp," Mia. It was *equestrian* camp. At Colebrook Mansion. Every meal was *catered*. And we slept in the mansion.
"Equestrian" means "horse," no matter where you slept. It's the same thing.

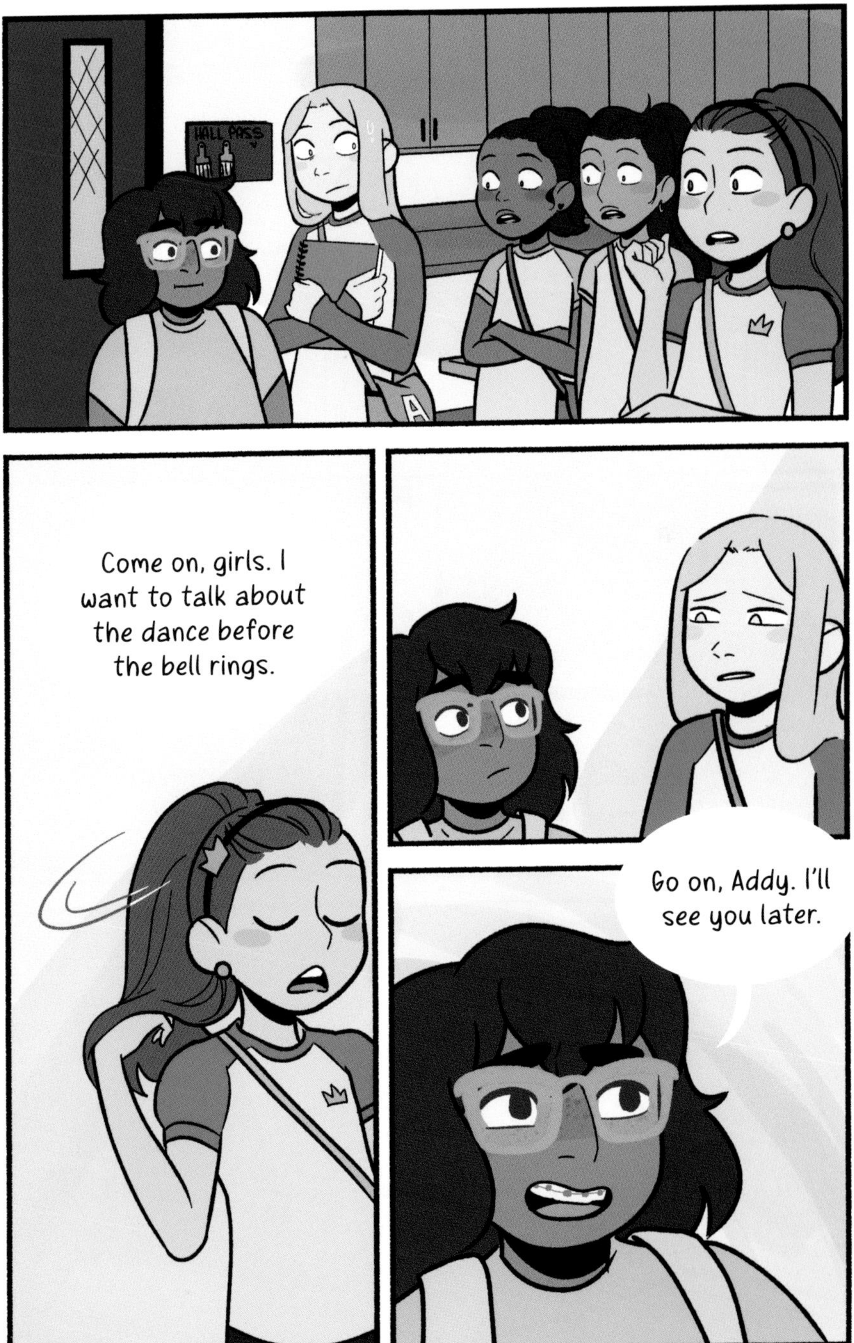
HALL PASS
Come on, girls. I want to talk about the dance before the bell rings.
Go on, Addy. I'll see you later.

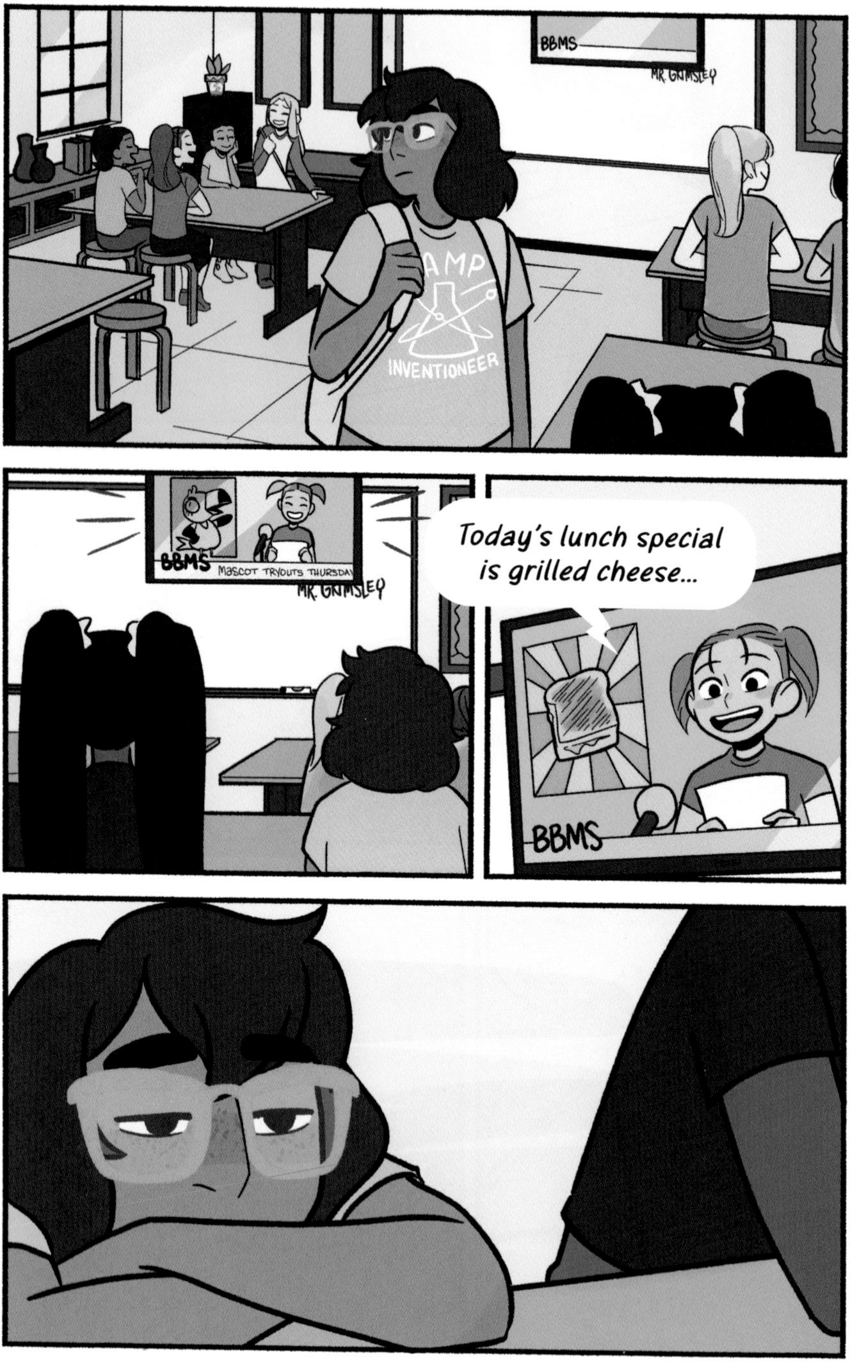
BBMS
MR. GRIMSLEY
INVENTIONEER
BBMS
MASCOT TRYOUTS THURSDAY
MR. GRIMSLEY
Today's lunch special is grilled cheese...
BBMS

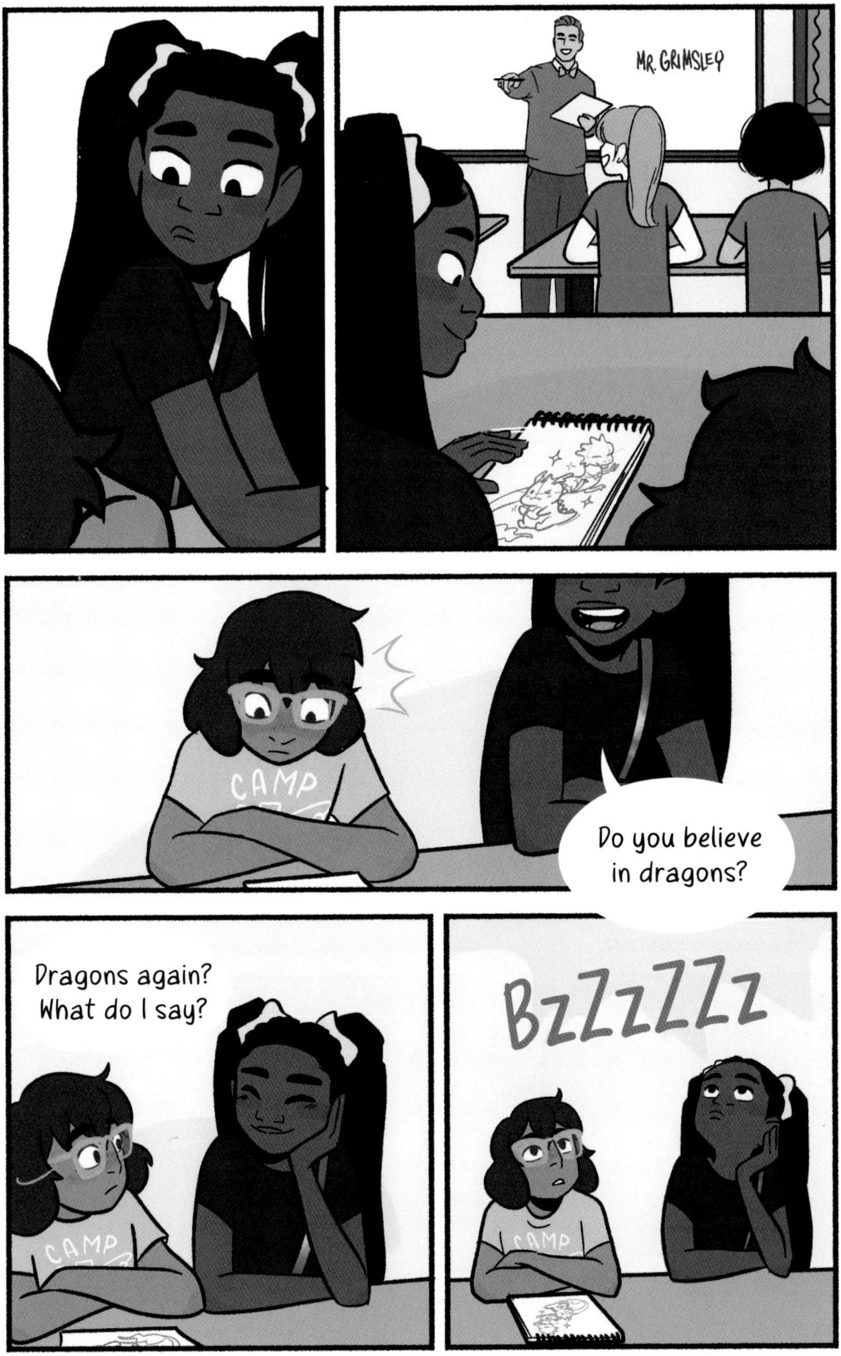
MR. GRIMSLEY
Do you believe in dragons?
Dragons again? What do I say?
BzZzZZz

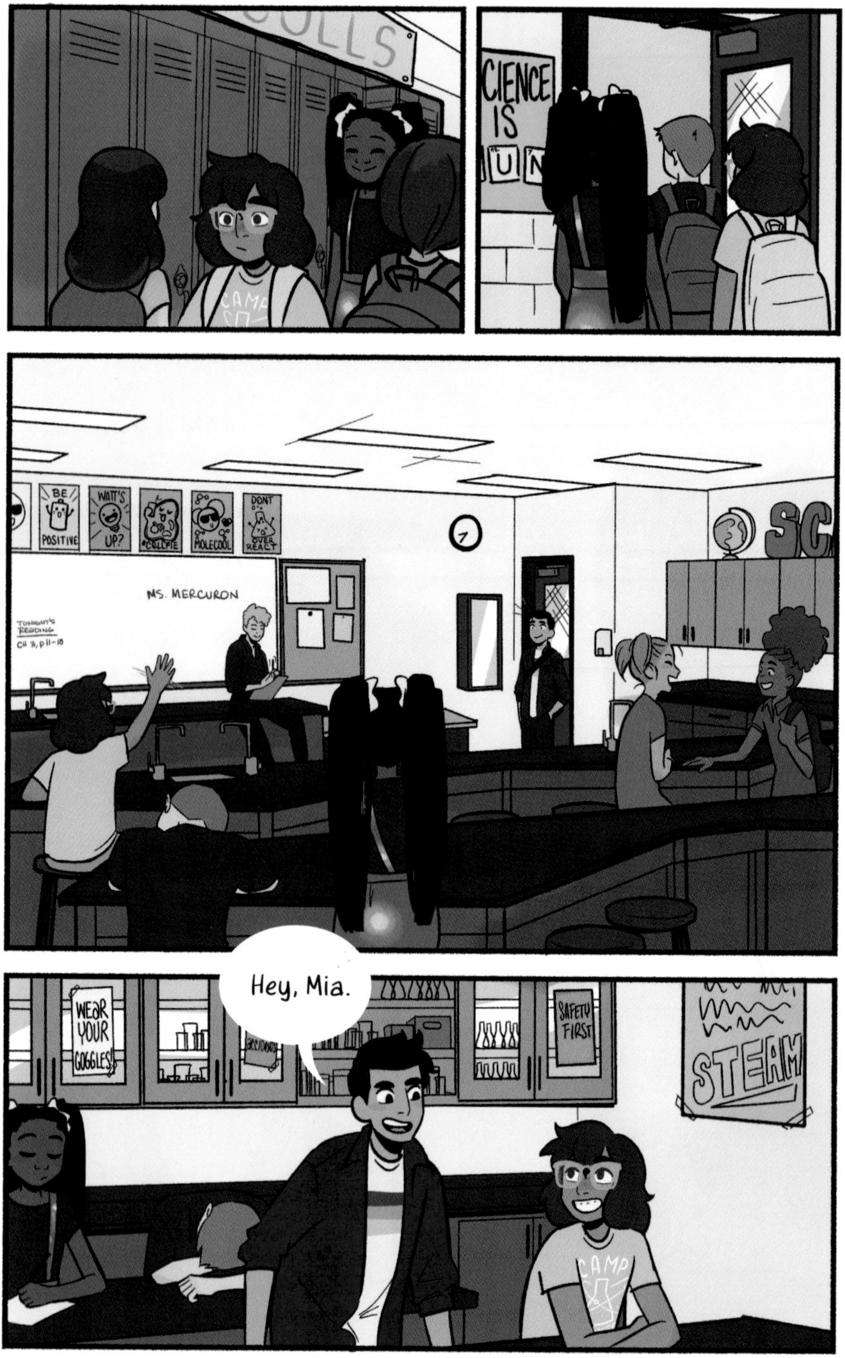
BE POSITIVE
WATT'S UP?
#CELLFIE
MOLECOOL
DONT OVER REACT
MS. MERCURON
Hey, Mia.
WEAR YOUR GOGGLES!
SAFETY FIRST
STEAM

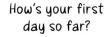
How's your first
day so far?

Great. Everybody
seems really cool.

You're going to like
this class. Ms. Mercuron
lets students who
really like science do
independent studies.

I'm starting a project
on engineering design
and thermodynamics.

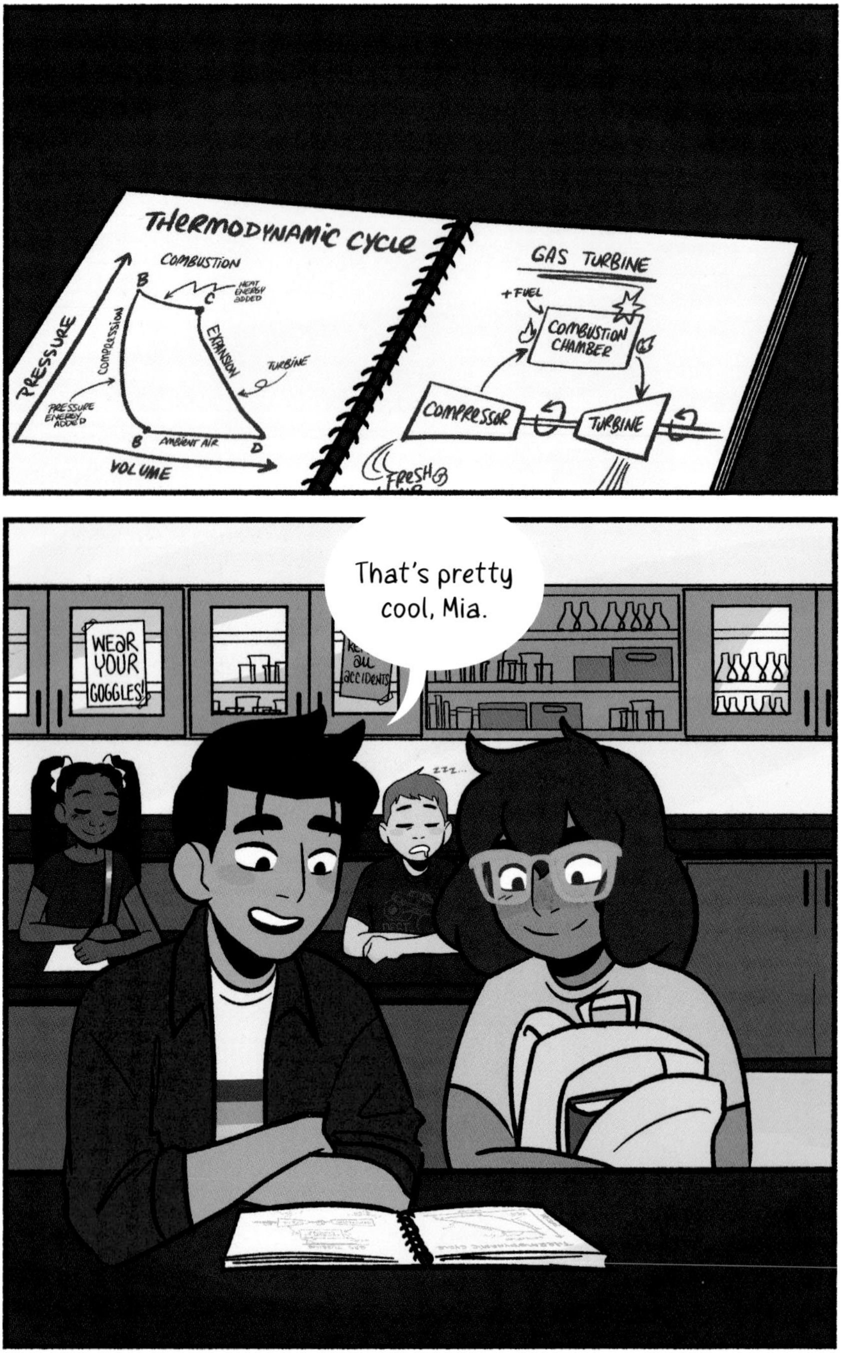
THERMODYNAMIC CYCLE
COMBUSTION
B
C
HEAT ENERGY ADDED
PRESSURE
COMPRESSION
EXPANSION
TURBINE
PRESSURE ENERGY ADDED
B
AMBIENT AIR
D
VOLUME
GAS TURBINE
+FUEL
COMBUSTION CHAMBER
COMPRESSOR
TURBINE
FRESH
That's pretty cool, Mia.
WEAR YOUR GOGGLES!
zzz...

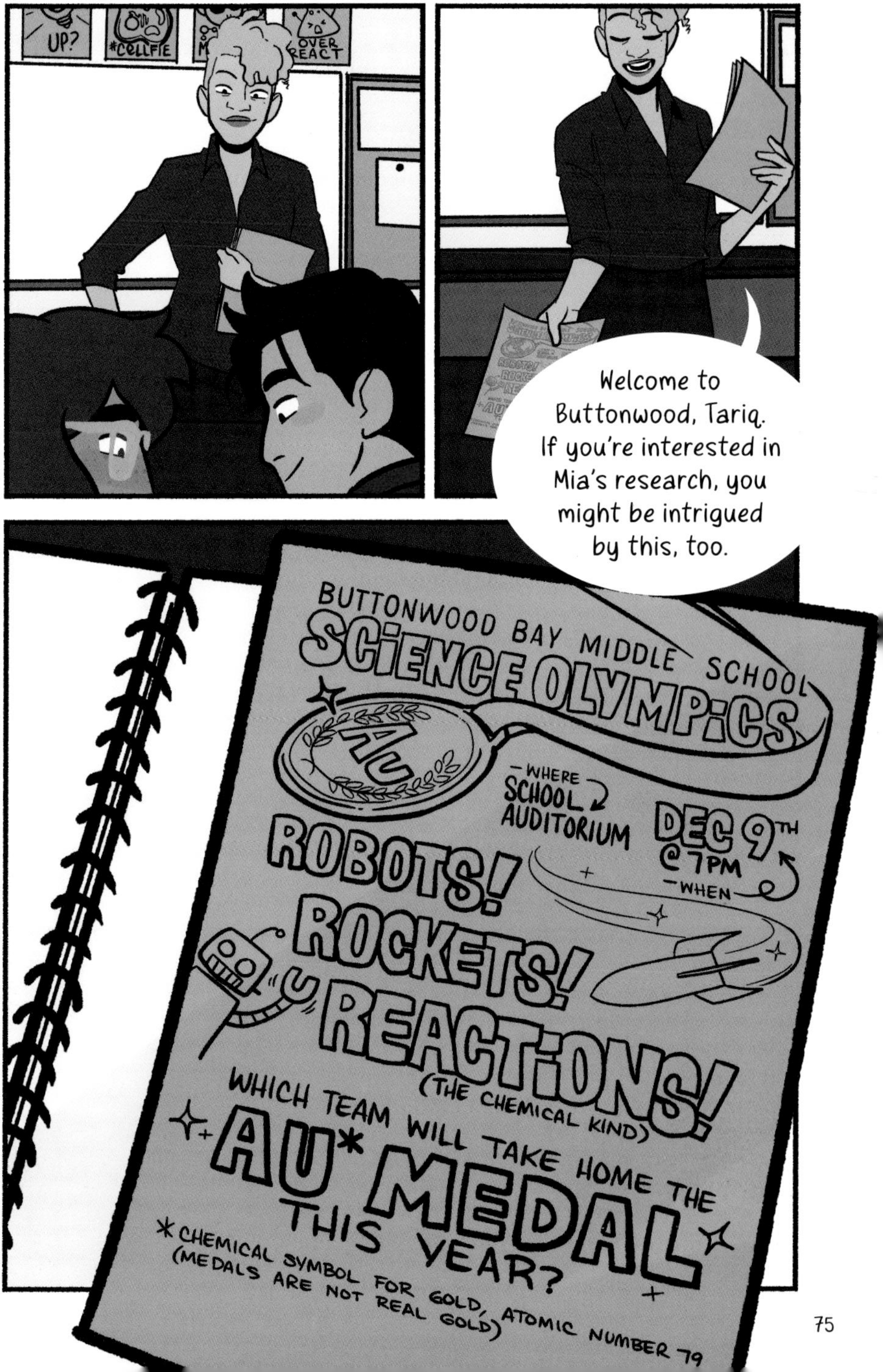
UP?
#CELLFIE
OVER REACT
Welcome to Buttonwood, Tariq. If you're interested in Mia's research, you might be intrigued by this, too.
BUTTONWOOD BAY MIDDLE SCHOOL
SCIENCE OLYMPICS
AU
-WHERE-
SCHOOL AUDITORIUM
DEC 9TH @7PM
-WHEN-
ROBOTS!
ROCKETS!
REACTIONS!
(THE CHEMICAL KIND)
WHICH TEAM WILL TAKE HOME THE
AU* MEDAL
THIS YEAR?
*CHEMICAL SYMBOL FOR GOLD, ATOMIC NUMBER 79
(MEDALS ARE NOT REAL GOLD)

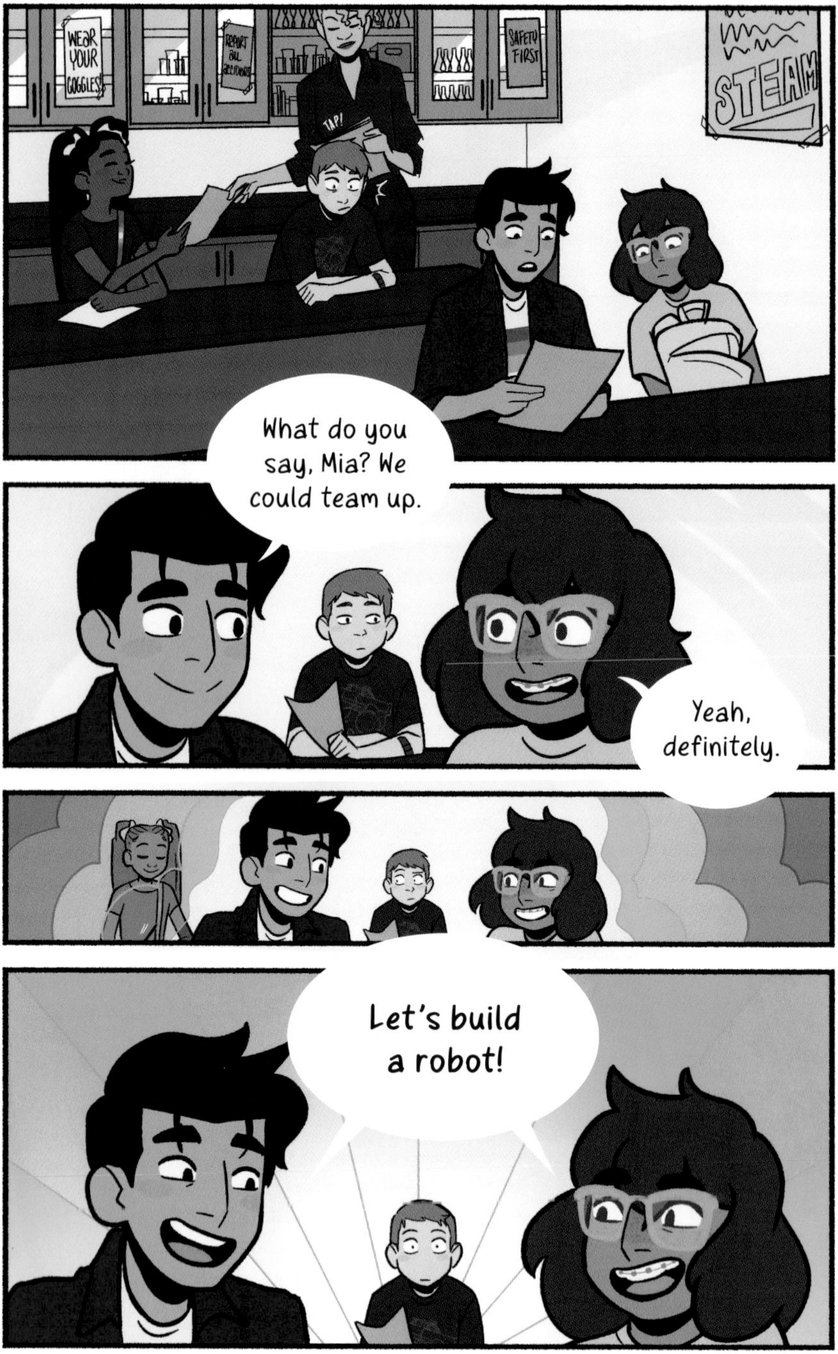
WEAR YOUR GOGGLES!
REPORT ALL ACCIDENTS
SAFETY FIRST
STEAM
TAP!
What do you say, Mia? We could team up.
Yeah, definitely.
Let's build a robot!

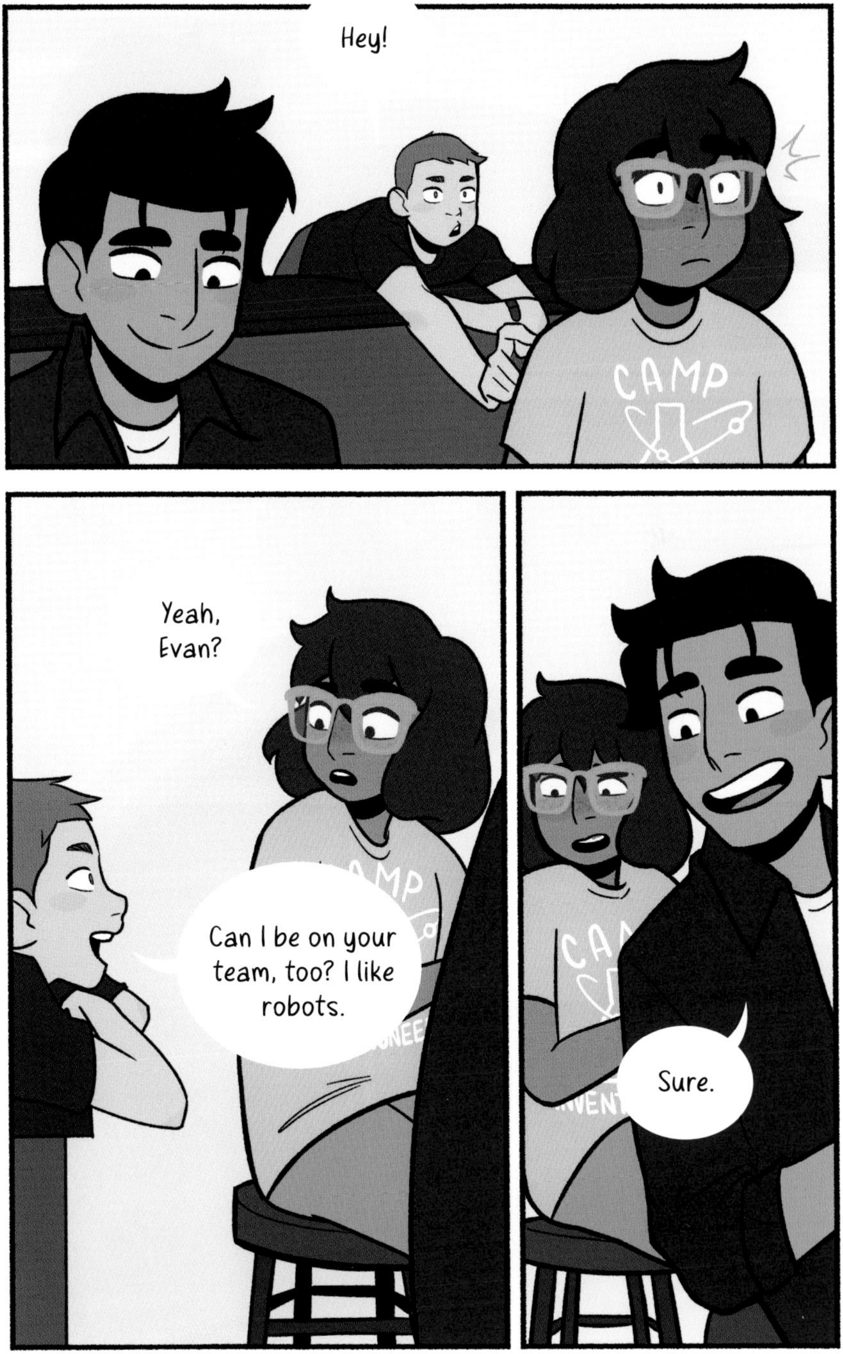
Hey!
Yeah, Evan?
Can I be on your team, too? I like robots.
Sure.

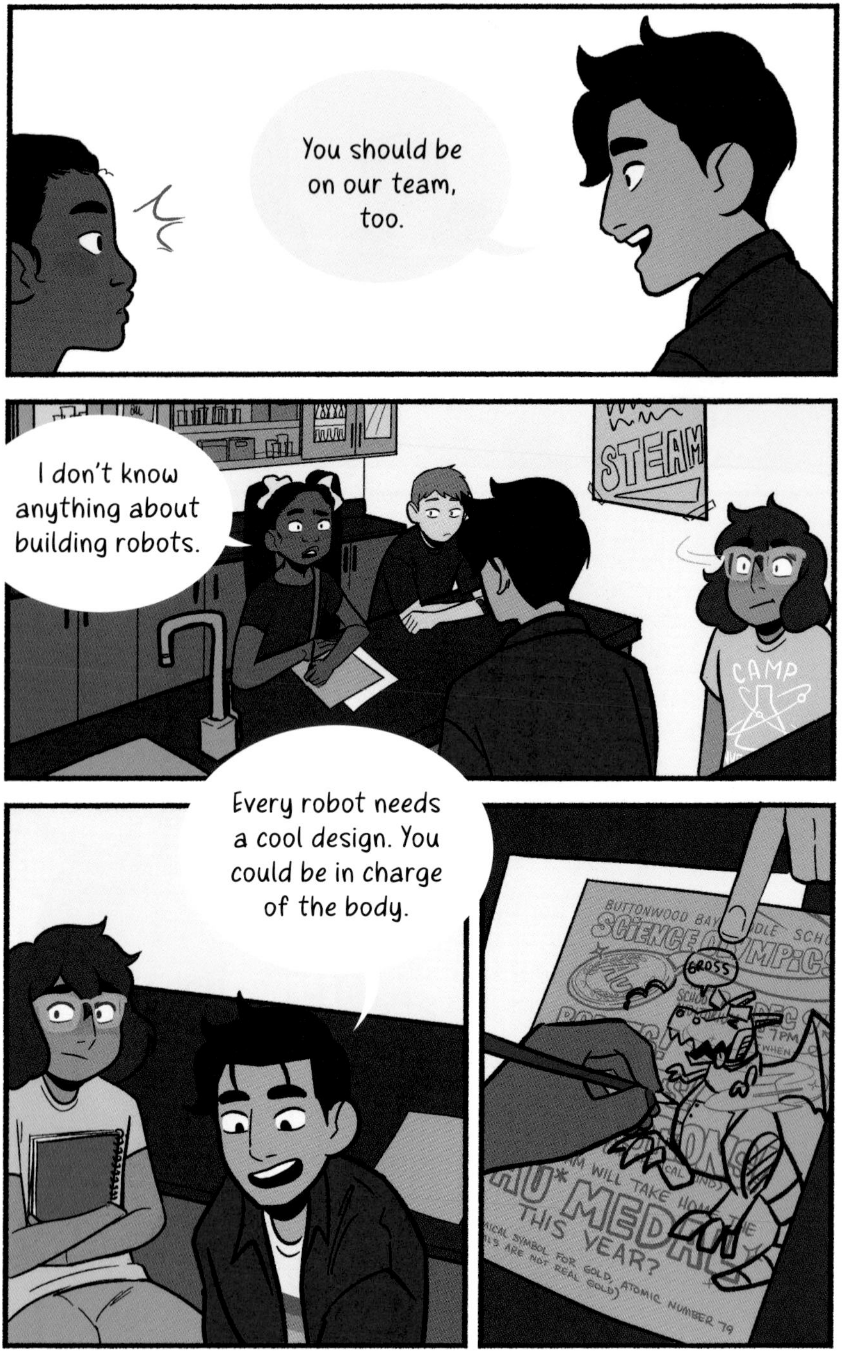
You should be on our team, too.
STEAM
I don't know anything about building robots.
CAMP
Every robot needs a cool design. You could be in charge of the body.
BUTTONWOOD BAY
GROSS
WILL TAKE HOME THE
THIS YEAR?
ATOMIC NUMBER 79

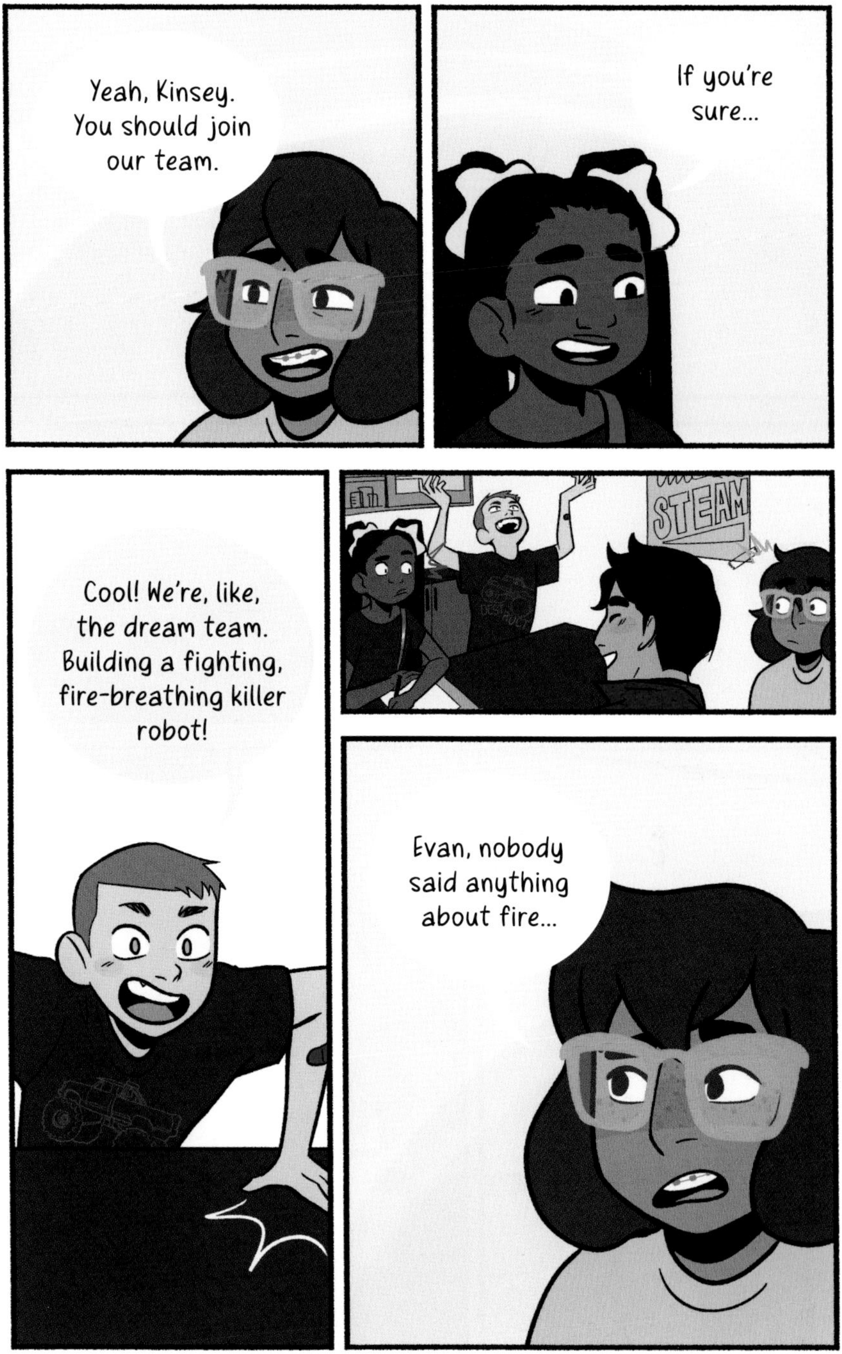
Yeah, Kinsey. You should join our team.
If you're sure...
Cool! We're, like, the dream team. Building a fighting, fire-breathing killer robot!
STEAM
Evan, nobody said anything about fire...

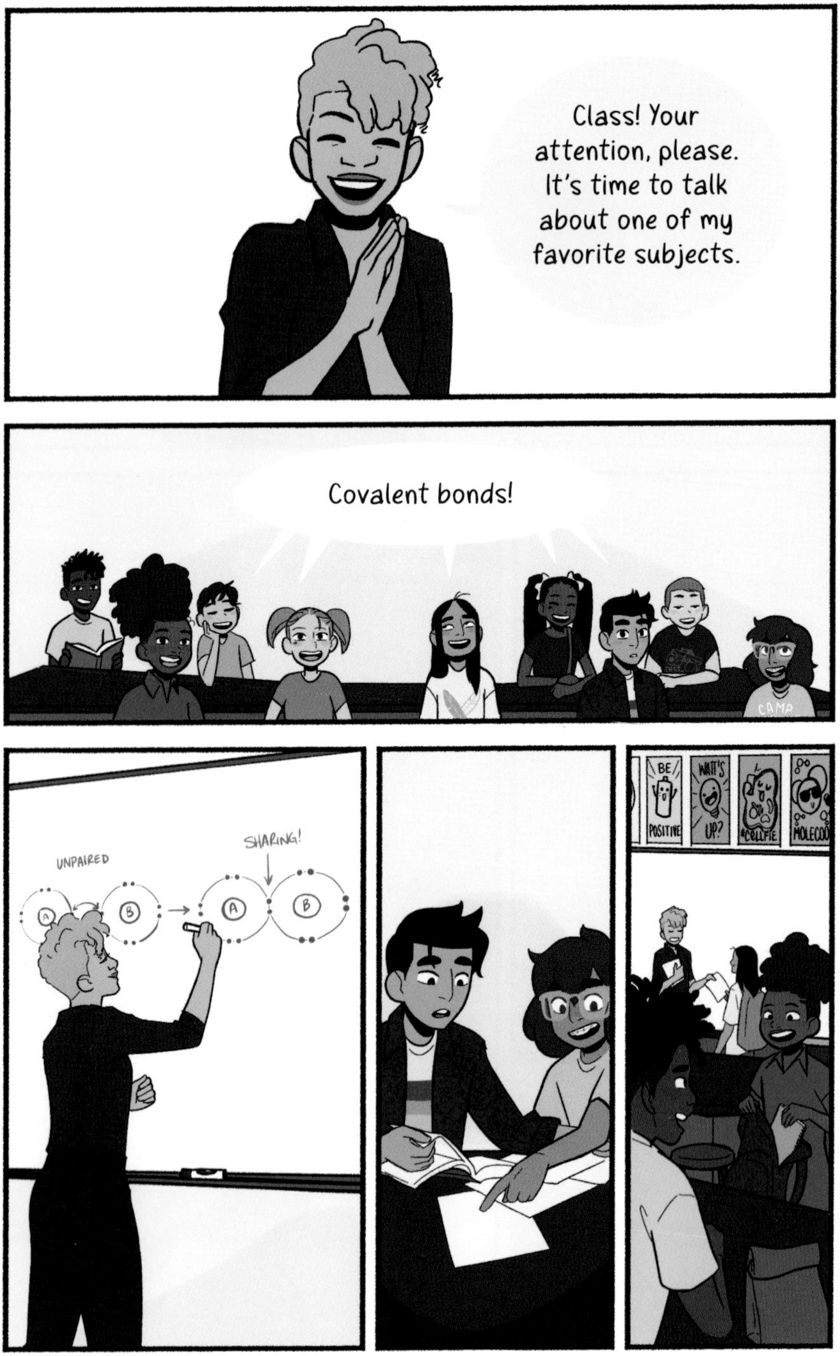
Class! Your attention, please. It's time to talk about one of my favorite subjects.
Covalent bonds!
UNPAIRED
SHARING!
A
B
A
B
BE
POSITIVE
WATT'S
UP?
#CELLFIE

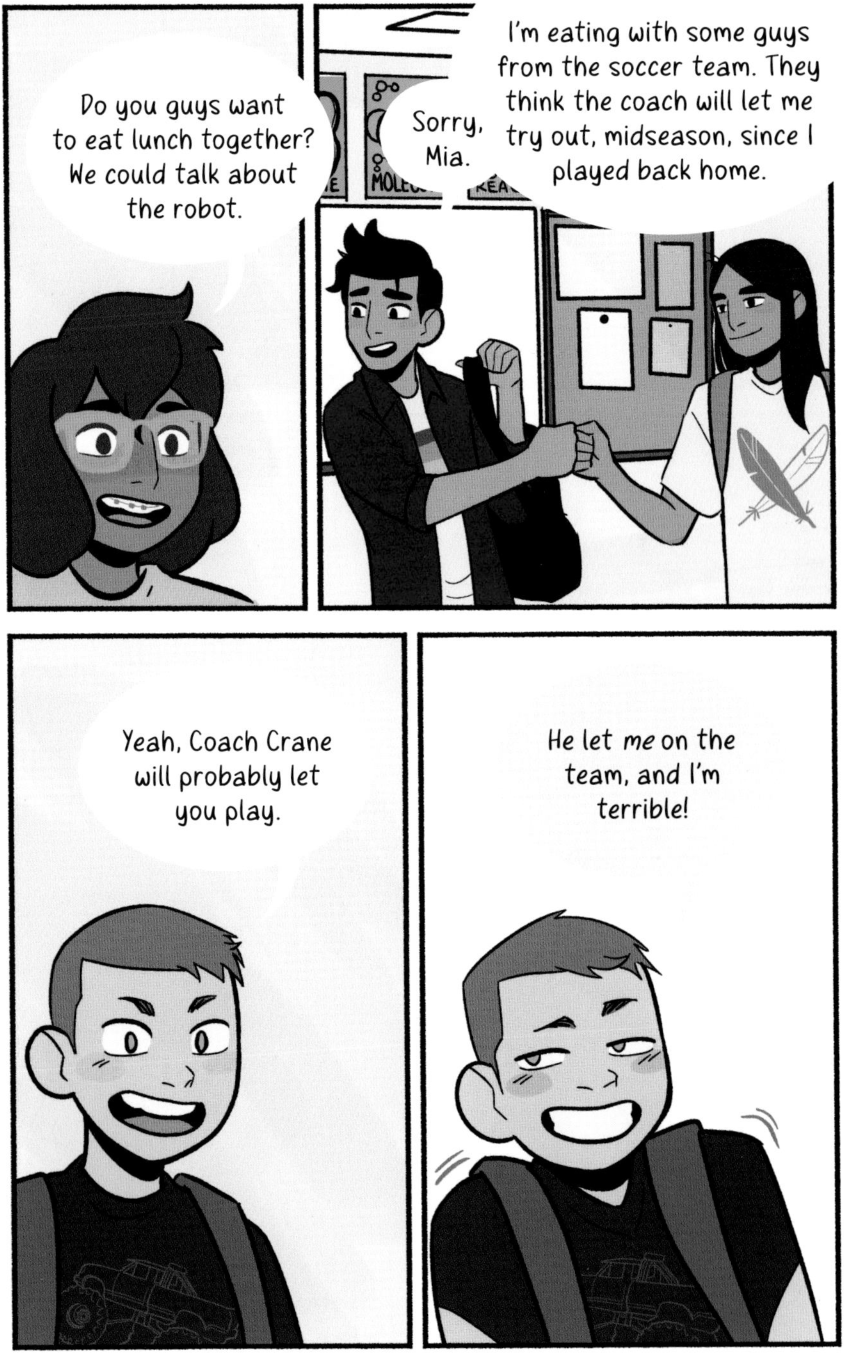
Do you guys want to eat lunch together? We could talk about the robot.
Sorry, Mia.
I'm eating with some guys from the soccer team. They think the coach will let me try out, midseason, since I played back home.
Yeah, Coach Crane will probably let you play.
He let *me* on the team, and I'm terrible!

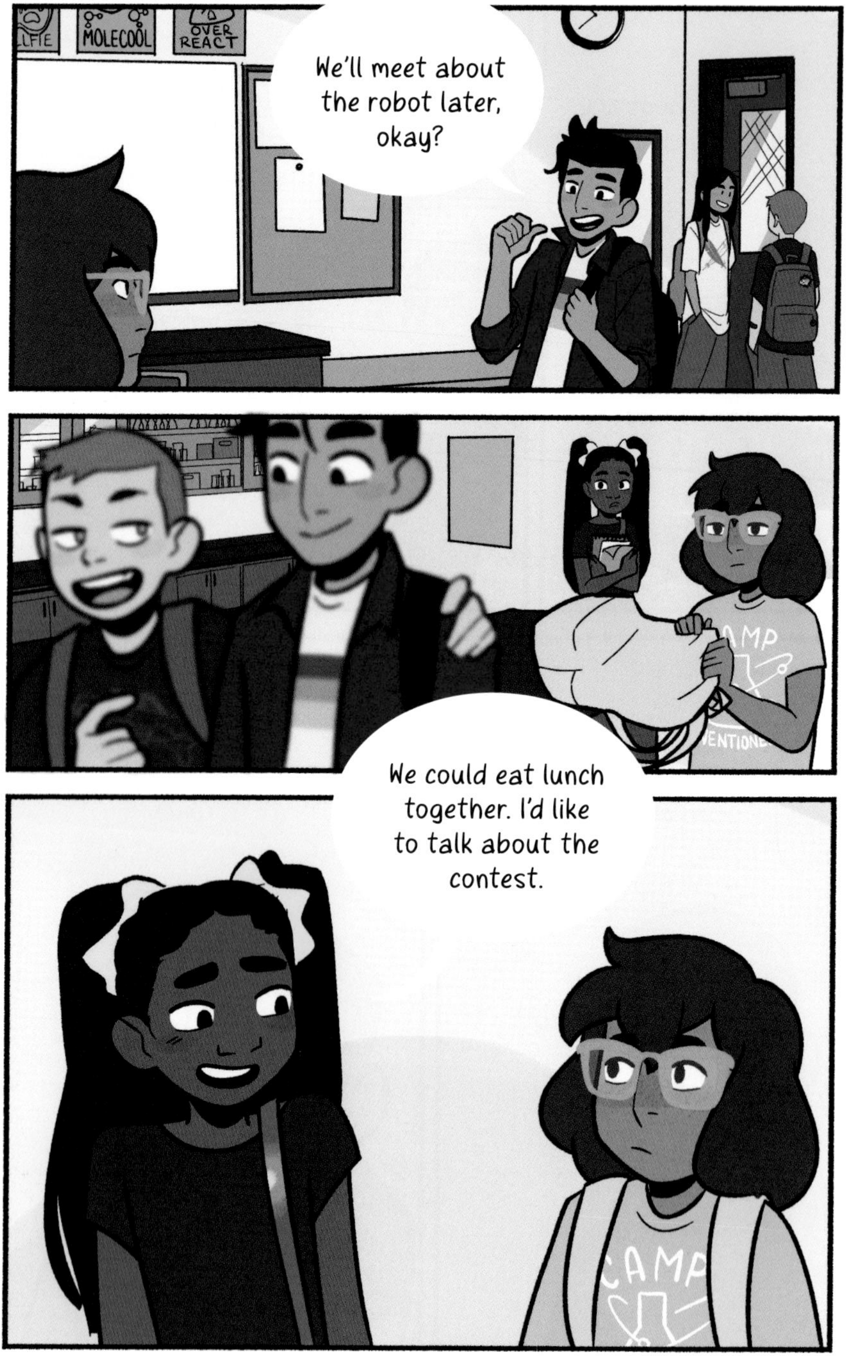
MOLECOOL
OVER REACT
We'll meet about the robot later, okay?
We could eat lunch together. I'd like to talk about the contest.

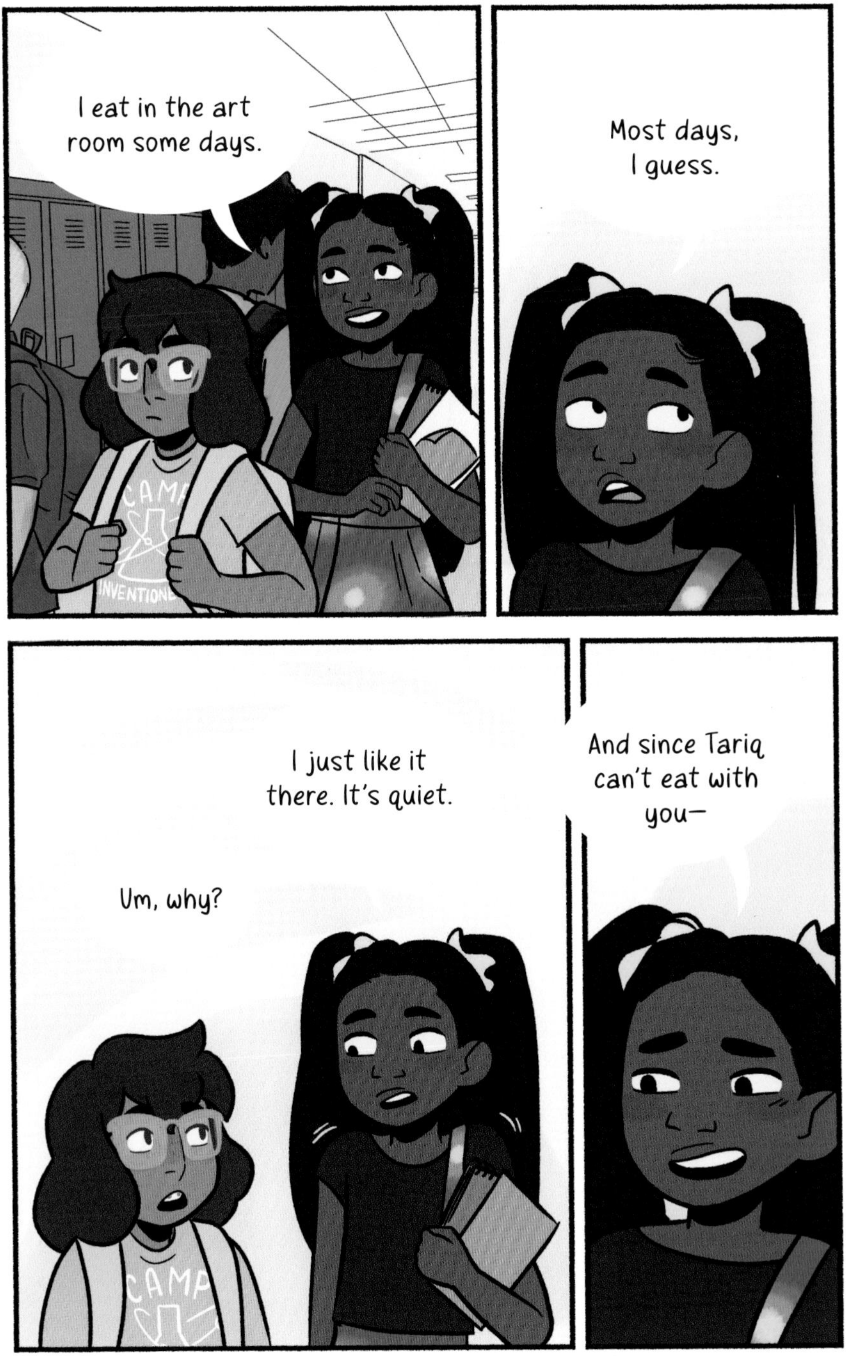
I eat in the art room some days.
CAMP INVENTIONE
Most days, I guess.
I just like it there. It's quiet.
Um, why?
CAMP
And since Tariq can't eat with you—

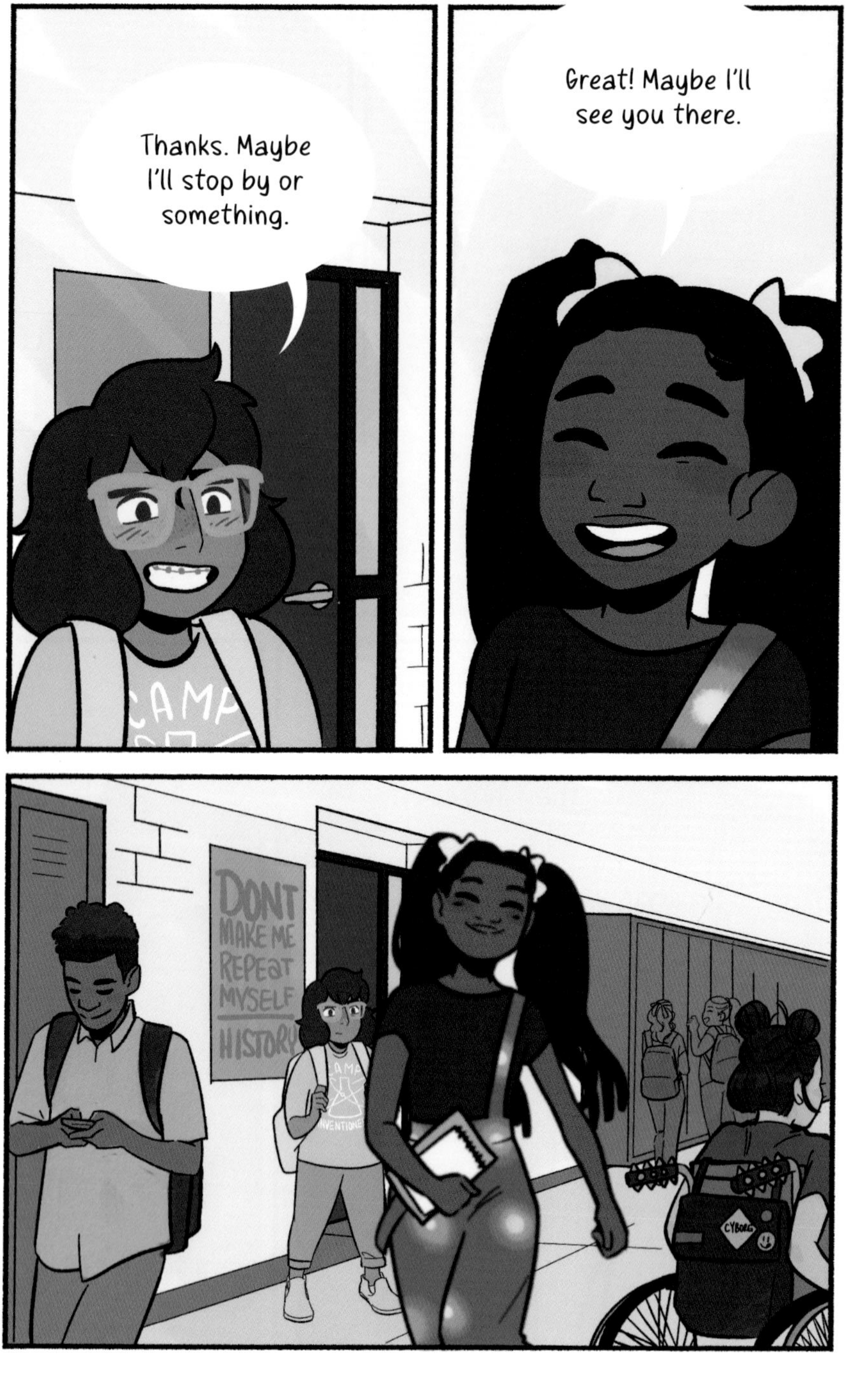
Thanks. Maybe I'll stop by or something.
Great! Maybe I'll see you there.
DONT MAKE ME REPEAT MYSELF
HISTORY
CYBORG

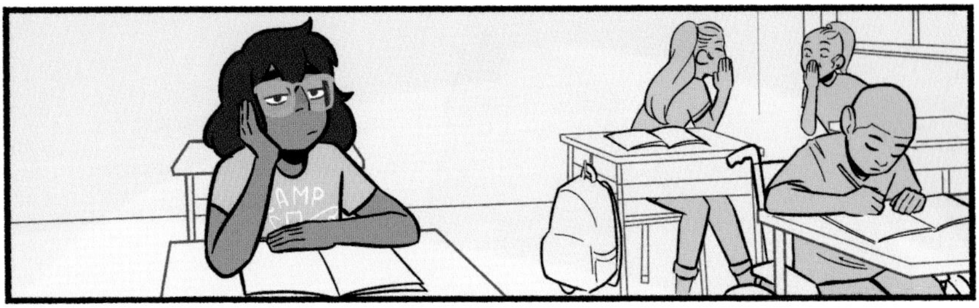

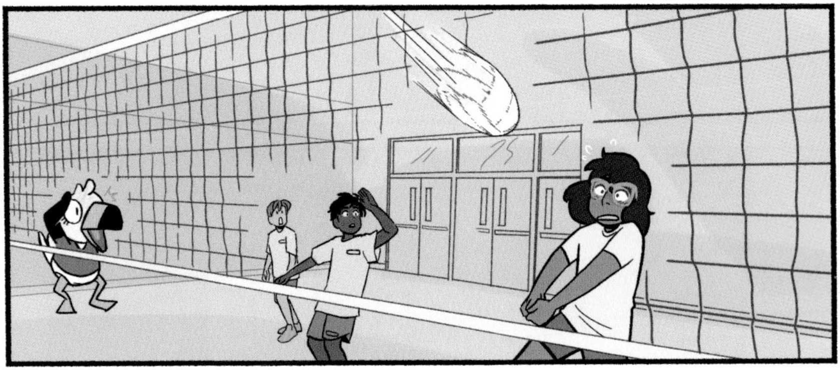

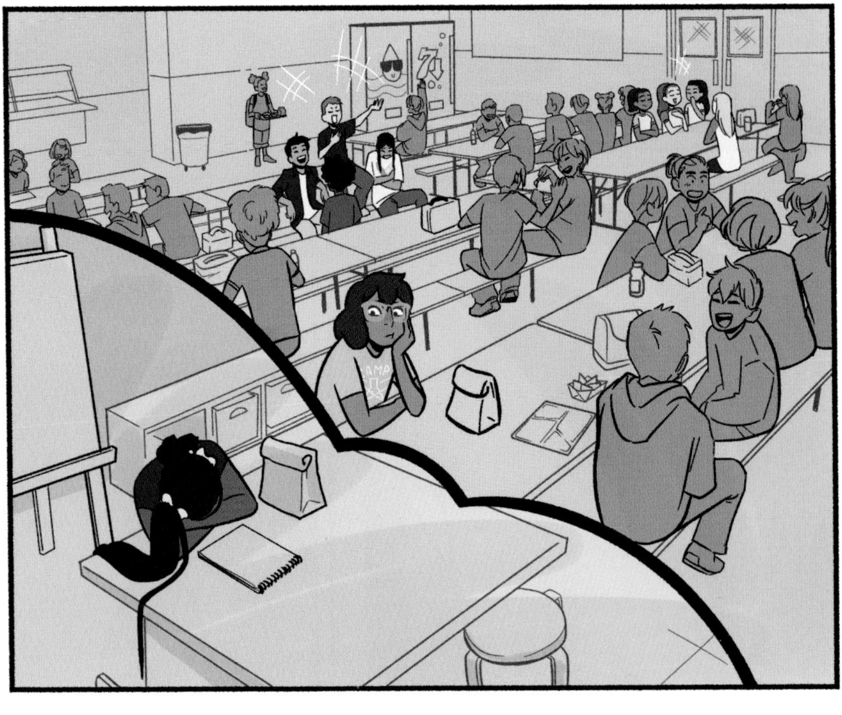

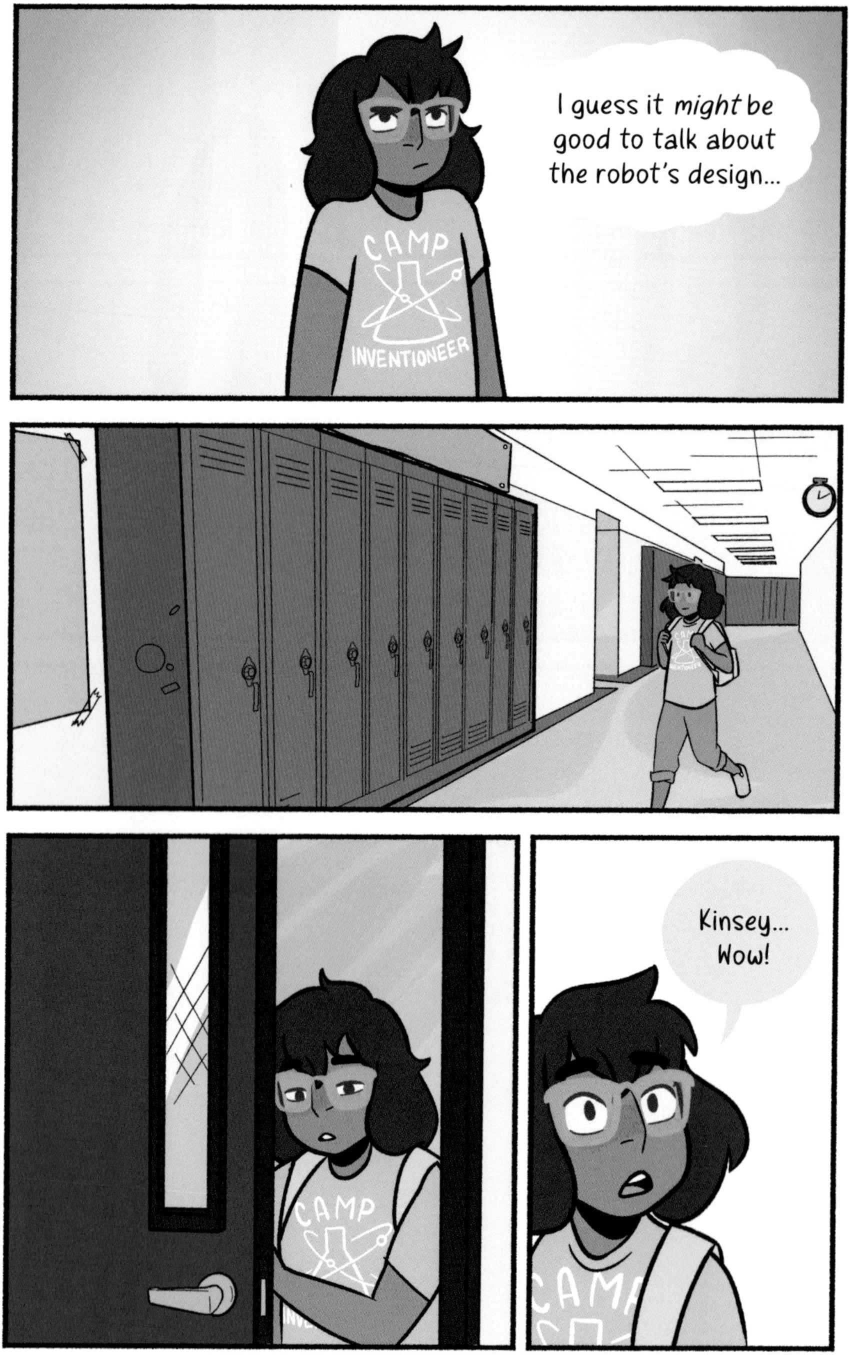
I guess it *might* be good to talk about the robot's design...
CAMP
INVENTIONEER
Kinsey... Wow!

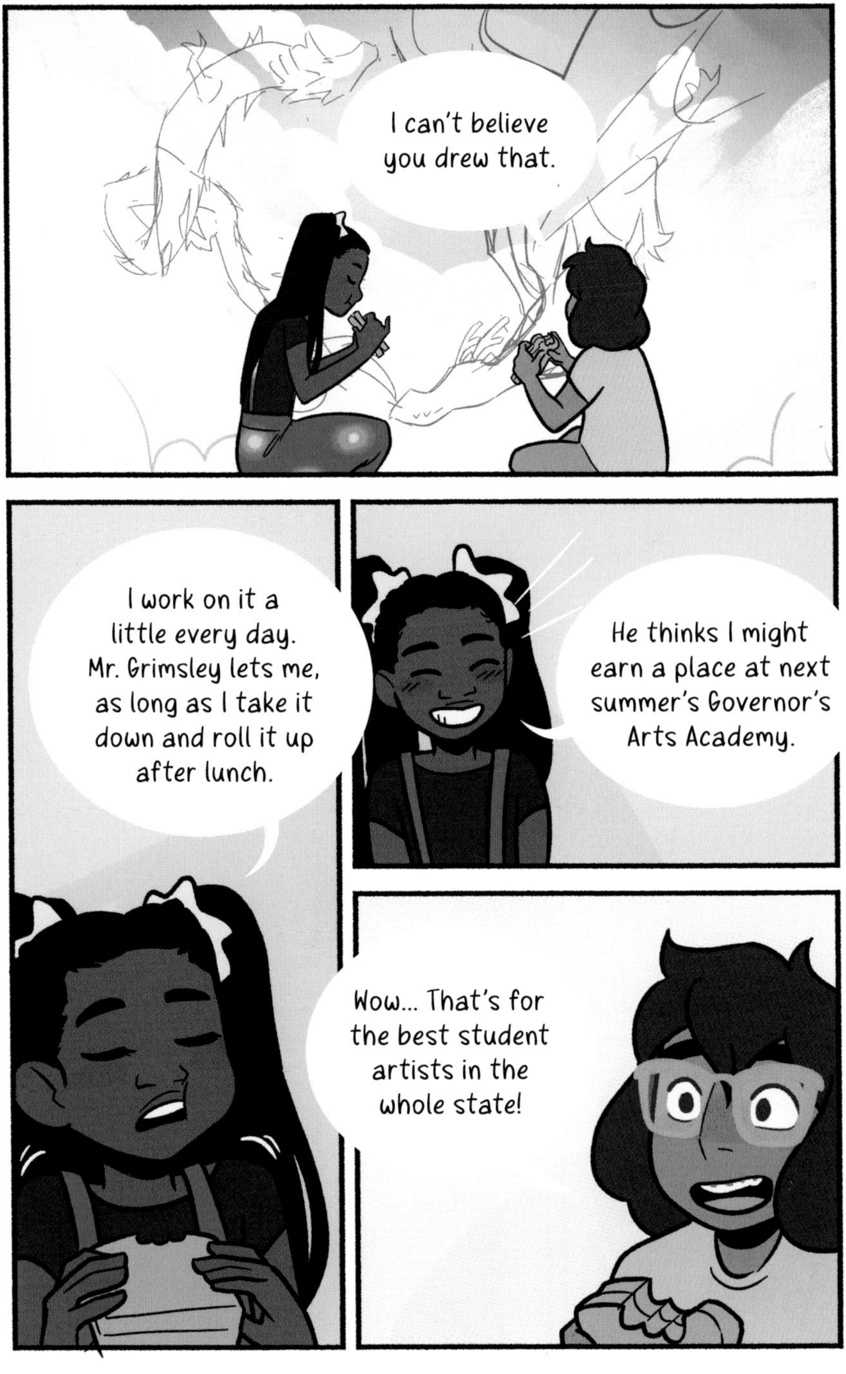
I can't believe you drew that.
I work on it a little every day. Mr. Grimsley lets me, as long as I take it down and roll it up after lunch.
He thinks I might earn a place at next summer's Governor's Arts Academy.
Wow... That's for the best student artists in the whole state!

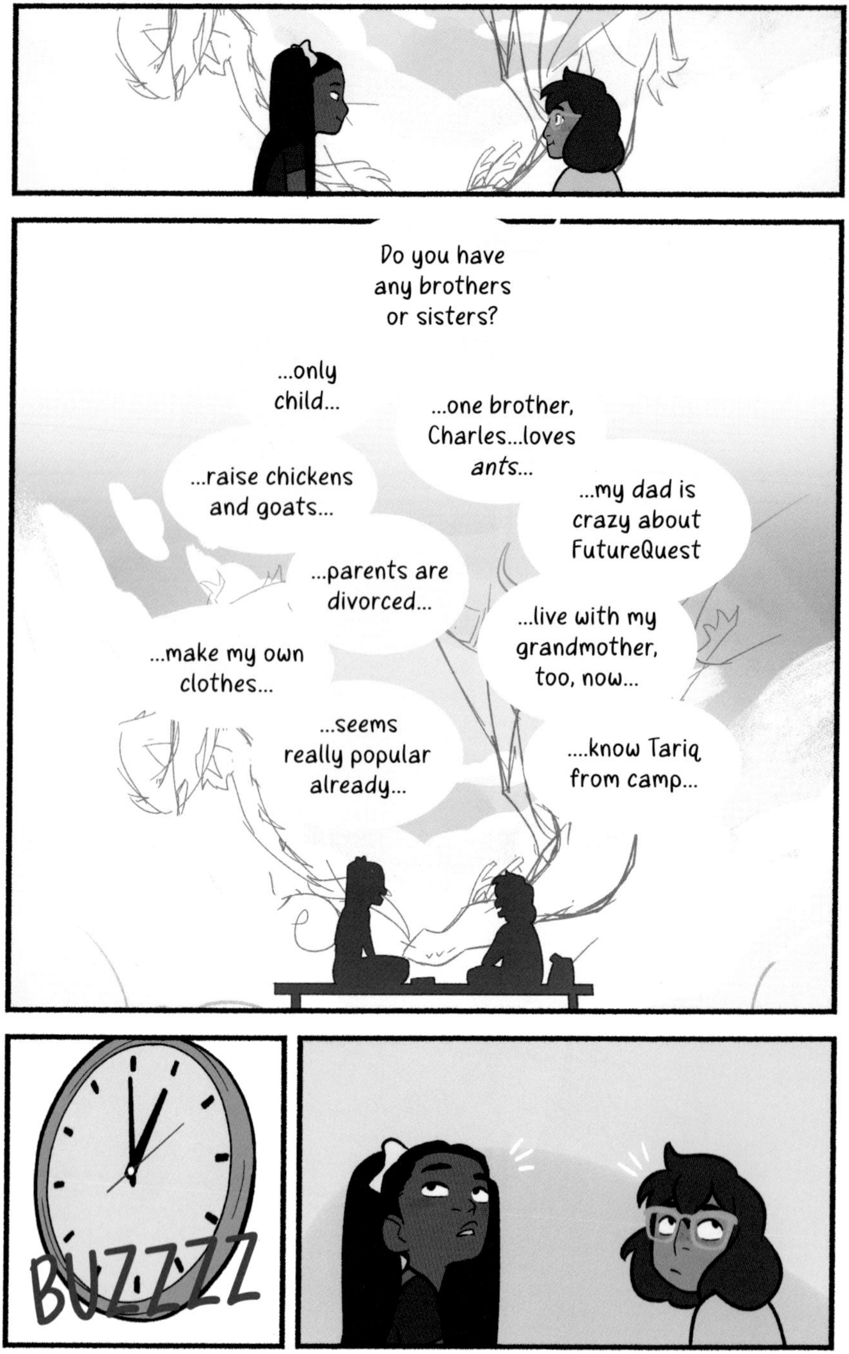
Do you have any brothers or sisters?
...only child...
...one brother, Charles...loves *ants*...
...raise chickens and goats...
...my dad is crazy about FutureQuest
...parents are divorced...
...live with my grandmother, too, now...
...make my own clothes...
...seems really popular already...
....know Tariq from camp...
BUZZZZ

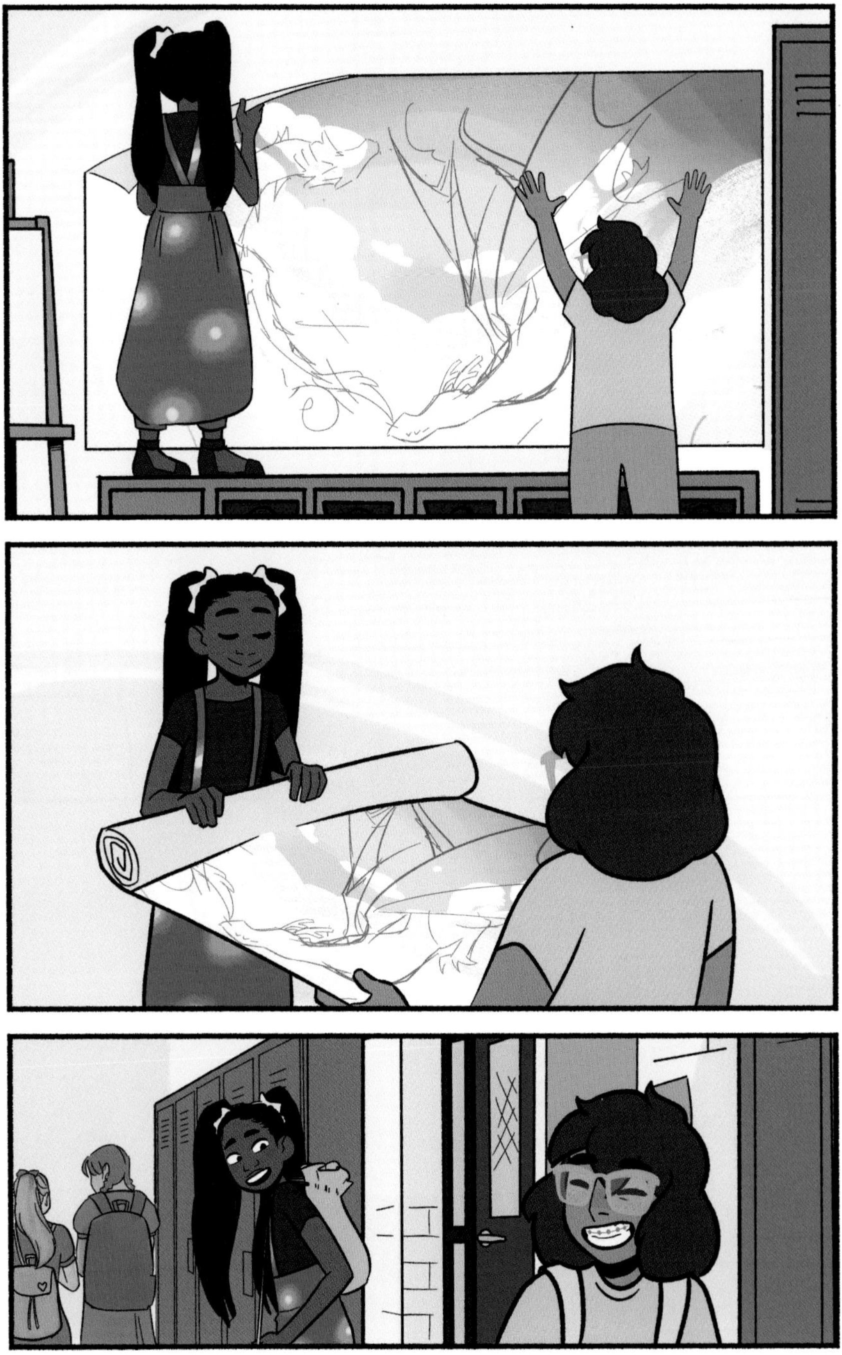

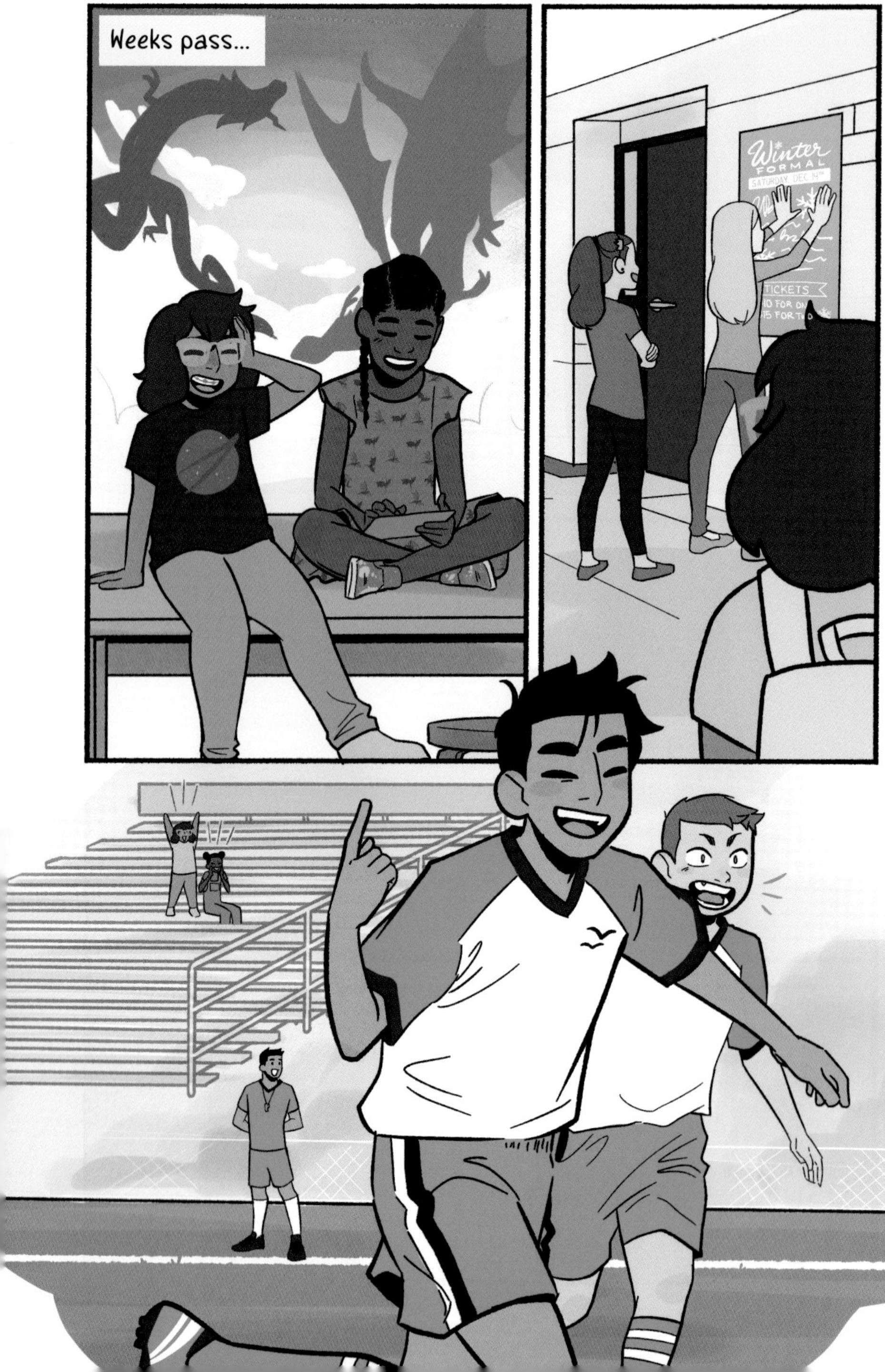
Weeks pass...
Winter
FORMAL
TICKETS

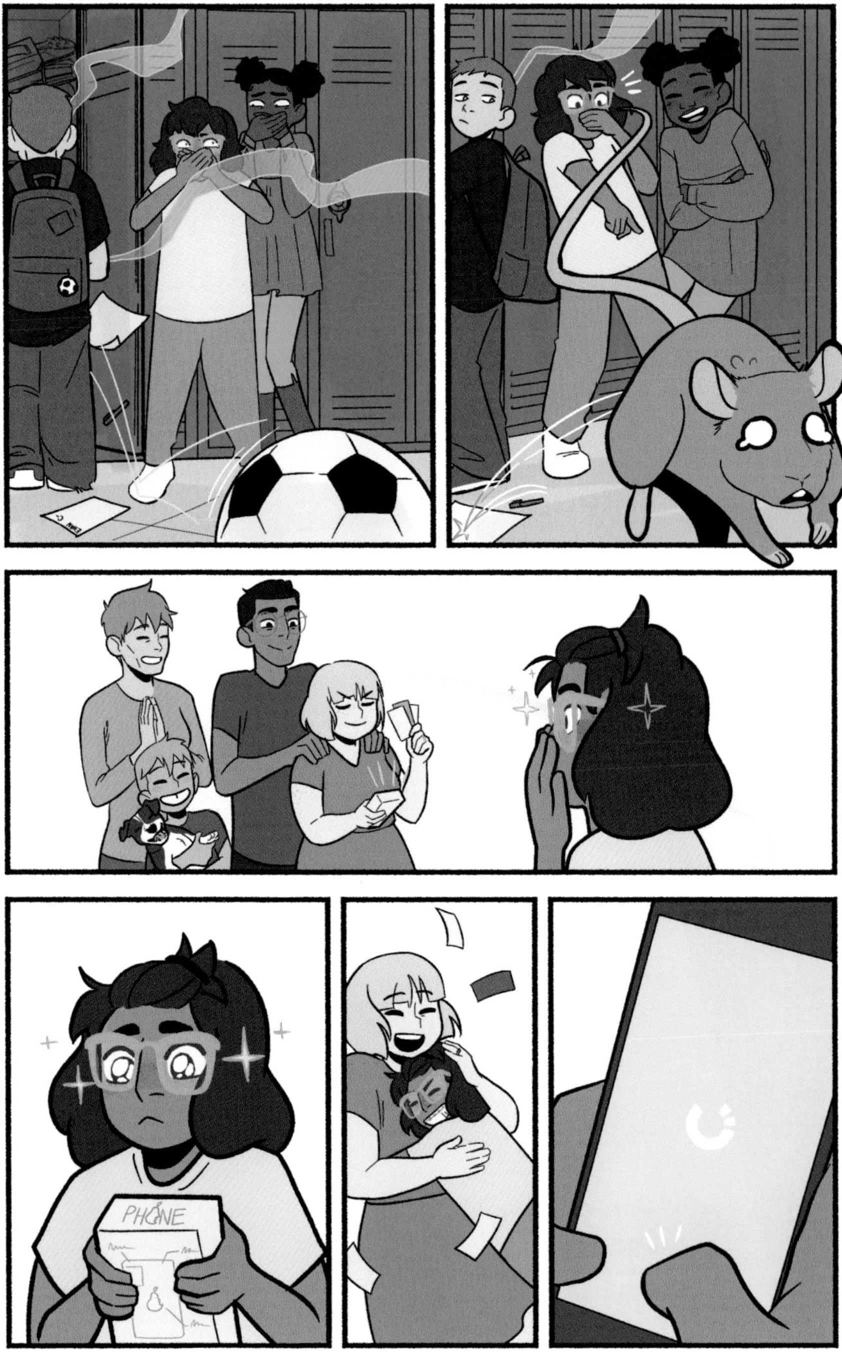
PHONE

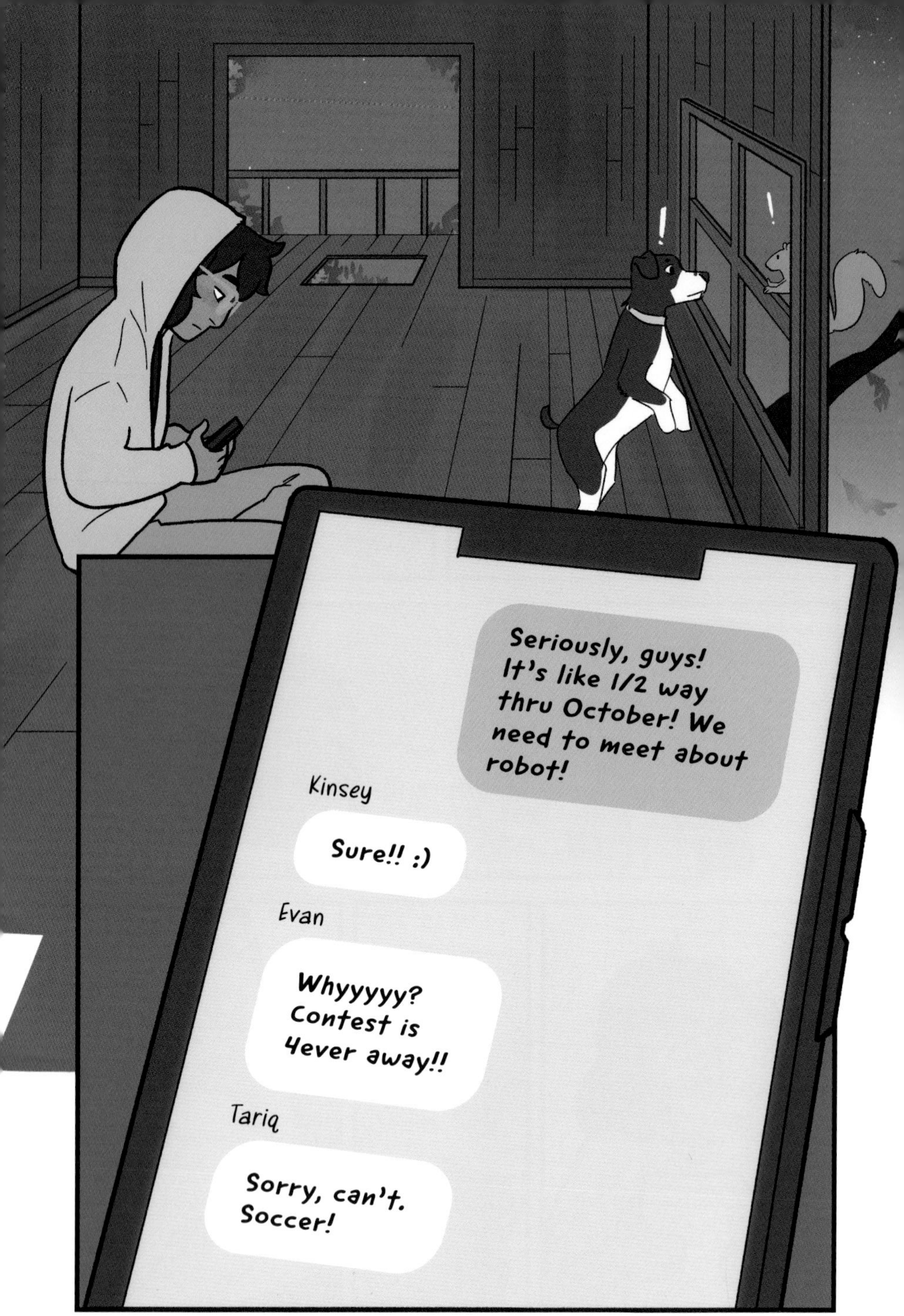
!
!
Seriously, guys! It's like 1/2 way thru October! We need to meet about robot!
Kinsey
Sure!! :)
Evan
Whyyyyy? Contest is 4ever away!!
Tariq
Sorry, can't. Soccer!

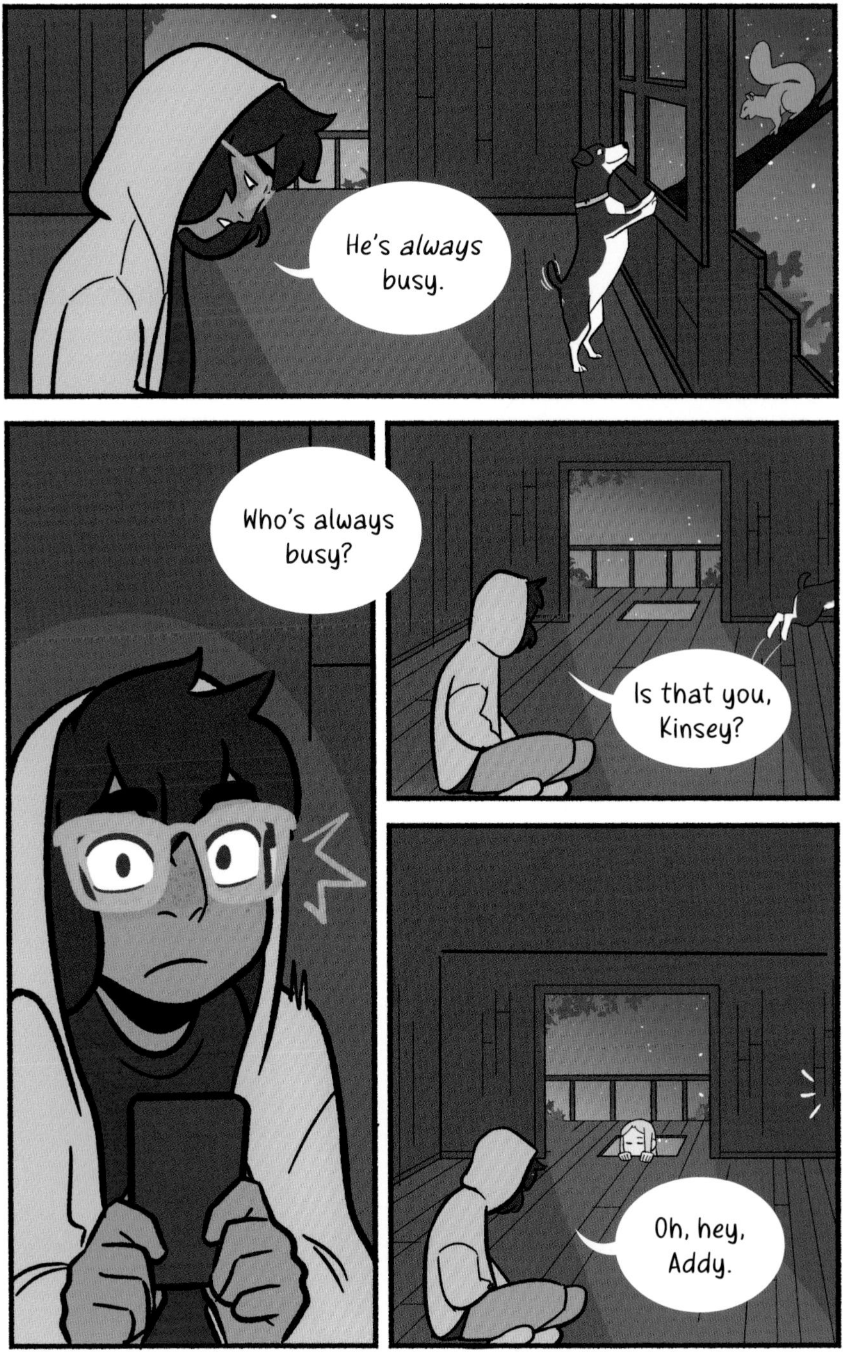
He's *always* busy.
Who's always busy?
Is that you, Kinsey?
Oh, hey, Addy.

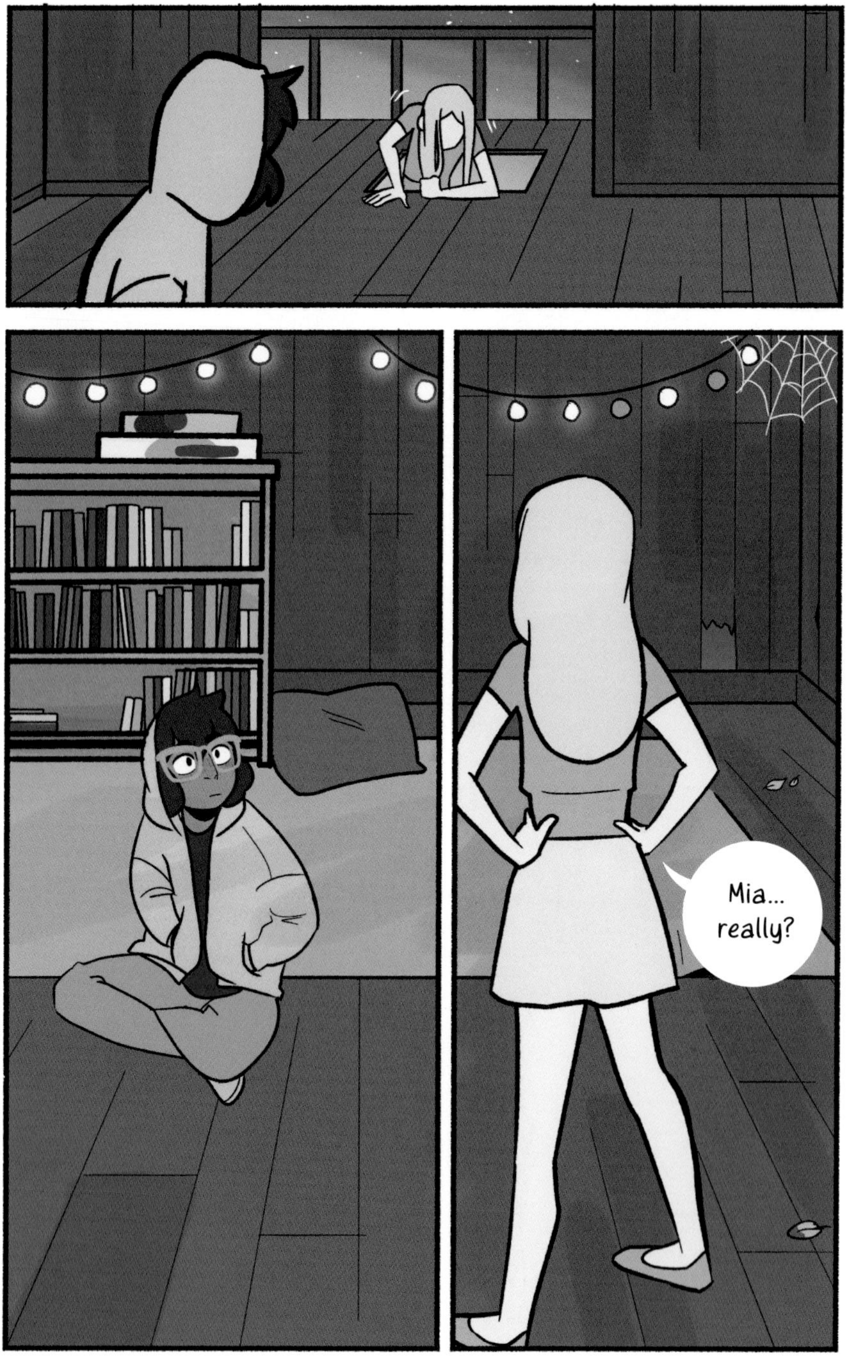
Mia...
really?

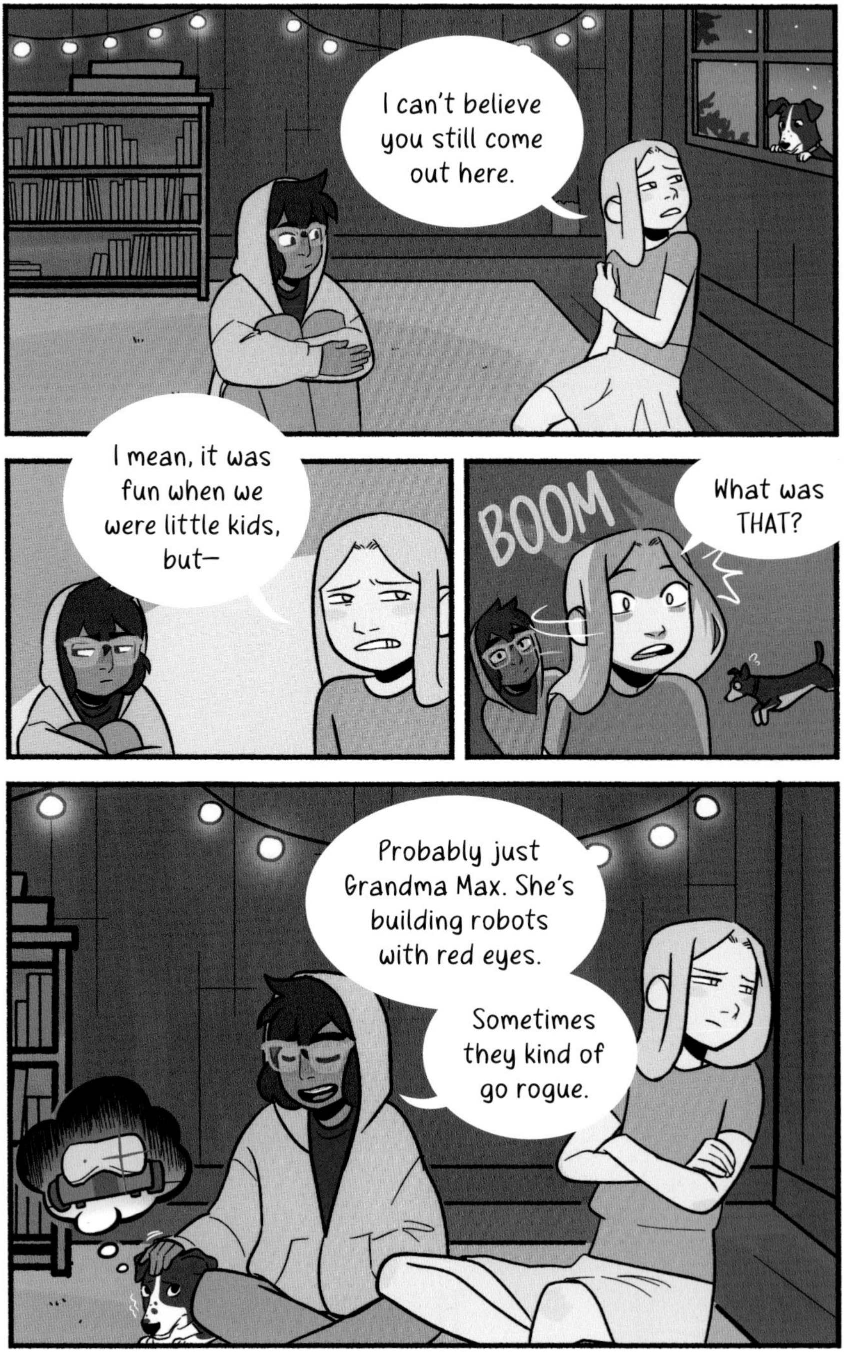
I can't believe you still come out here.
I mean, it was fun when we were little kids, but—
BOOM
What was THAT?
Probably just Grandma Max. She's building robots with red eyes.
Sometimes they kind of go rogue.

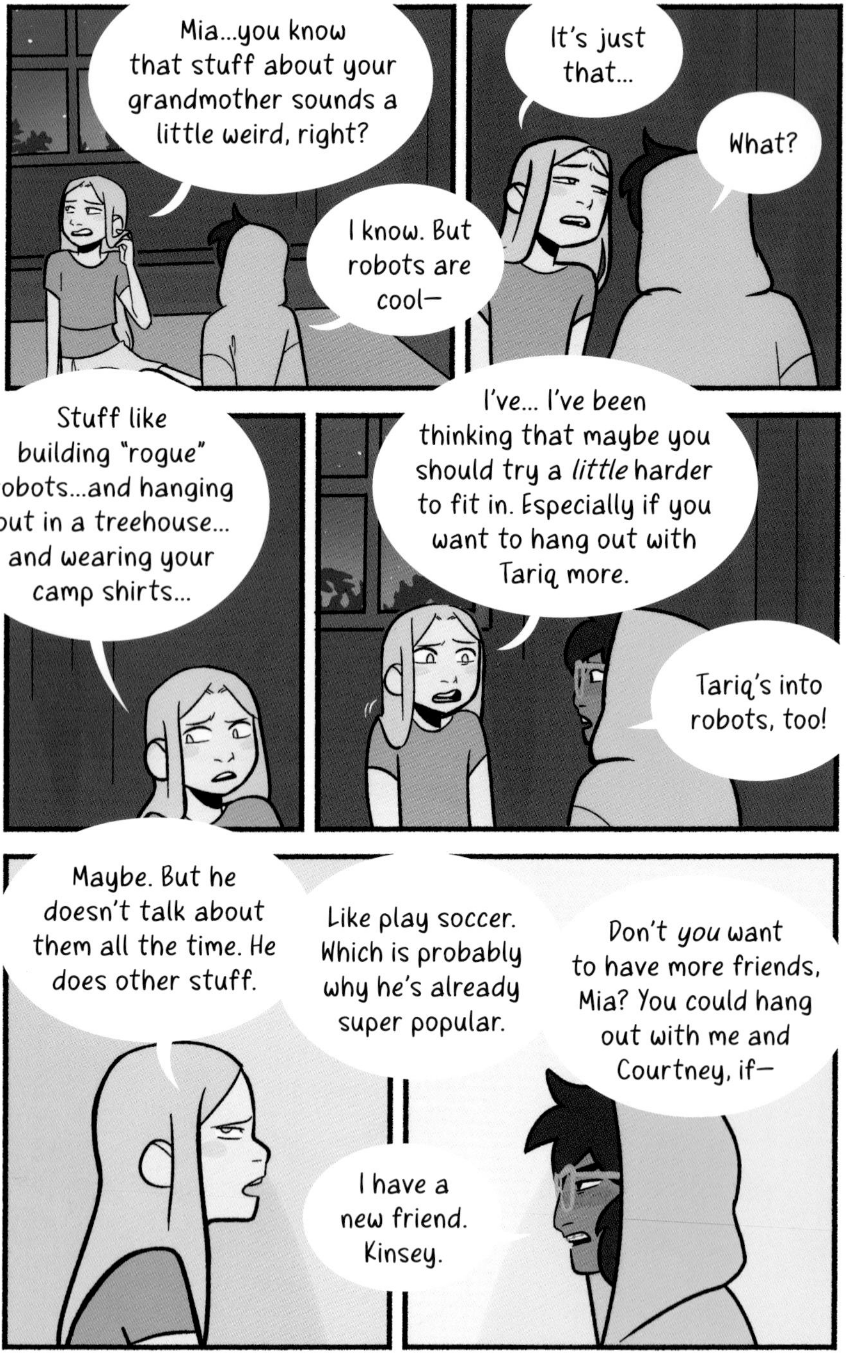
Mia...you know that stuff about your grandmother sounds a little weird, right?
I know. But robots are cool—
It's just that...
What?
Stuff like building "rogue" robots...and hanging out in a treehouse... and wearing your camp shirts...
I've... I've been thinking that maybe you should try a *little* harder to fit in. Especially if you want to hang out with Tariq more.
Tariq's into robots, too!
Maybe. But he doesn't talk about them all the time. He does other stuff.
Like play soccer. Which is probably why he's already super popular.
Don't *you* want to have more friends, Mia? You could hang out with me and Courtney, if—
I have a new friend. Kinsey.

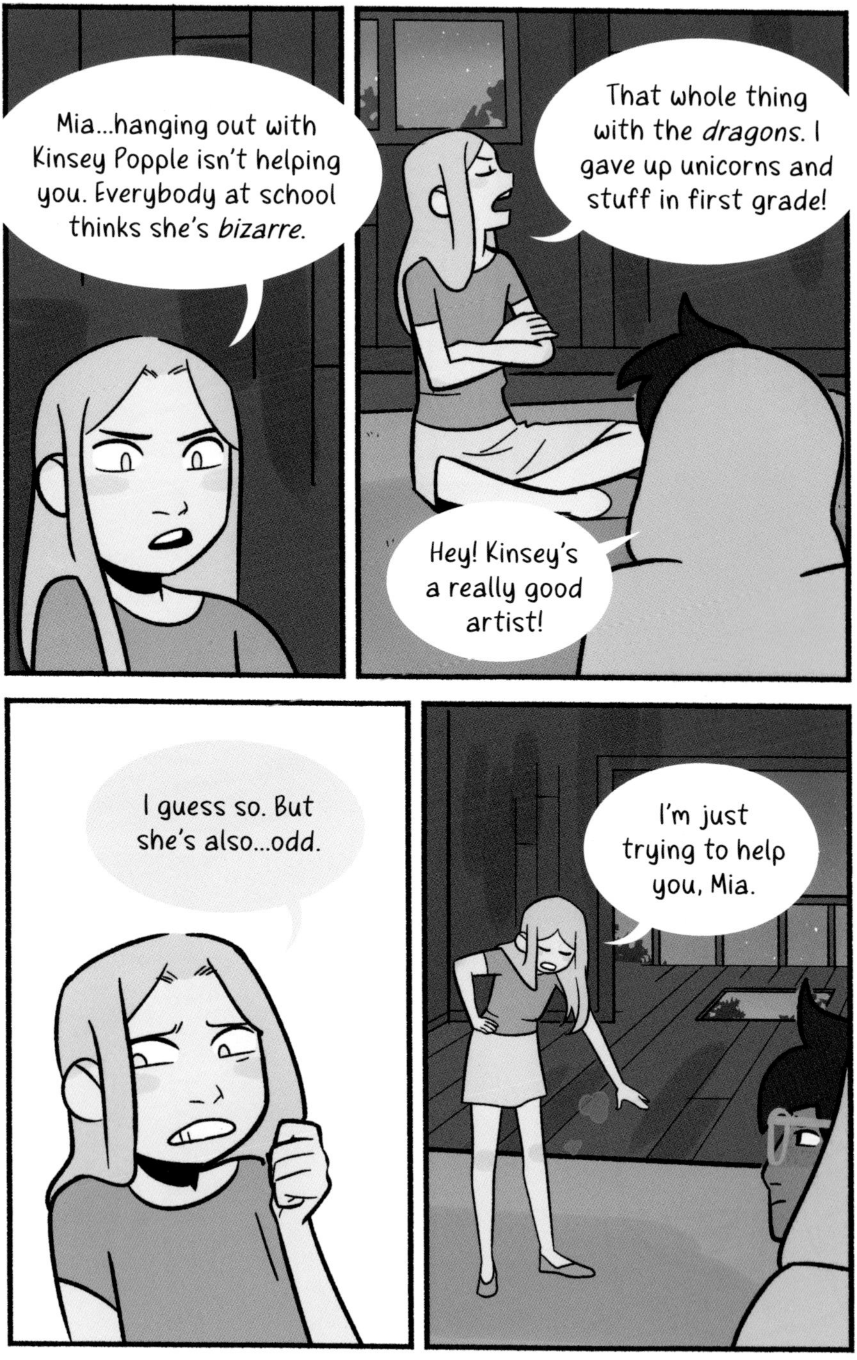
Mia...hanging out with Kinsey Popple isn't helping you. Everybody at school thinks she's *bizarre*.
That whole thing with the *dragons*. I gave up unicorns and stuff in first grade!
Hey! Kinsey's a really good artist!
I guess so. But she's also...odd.
I'm just trying to help you, Mia.

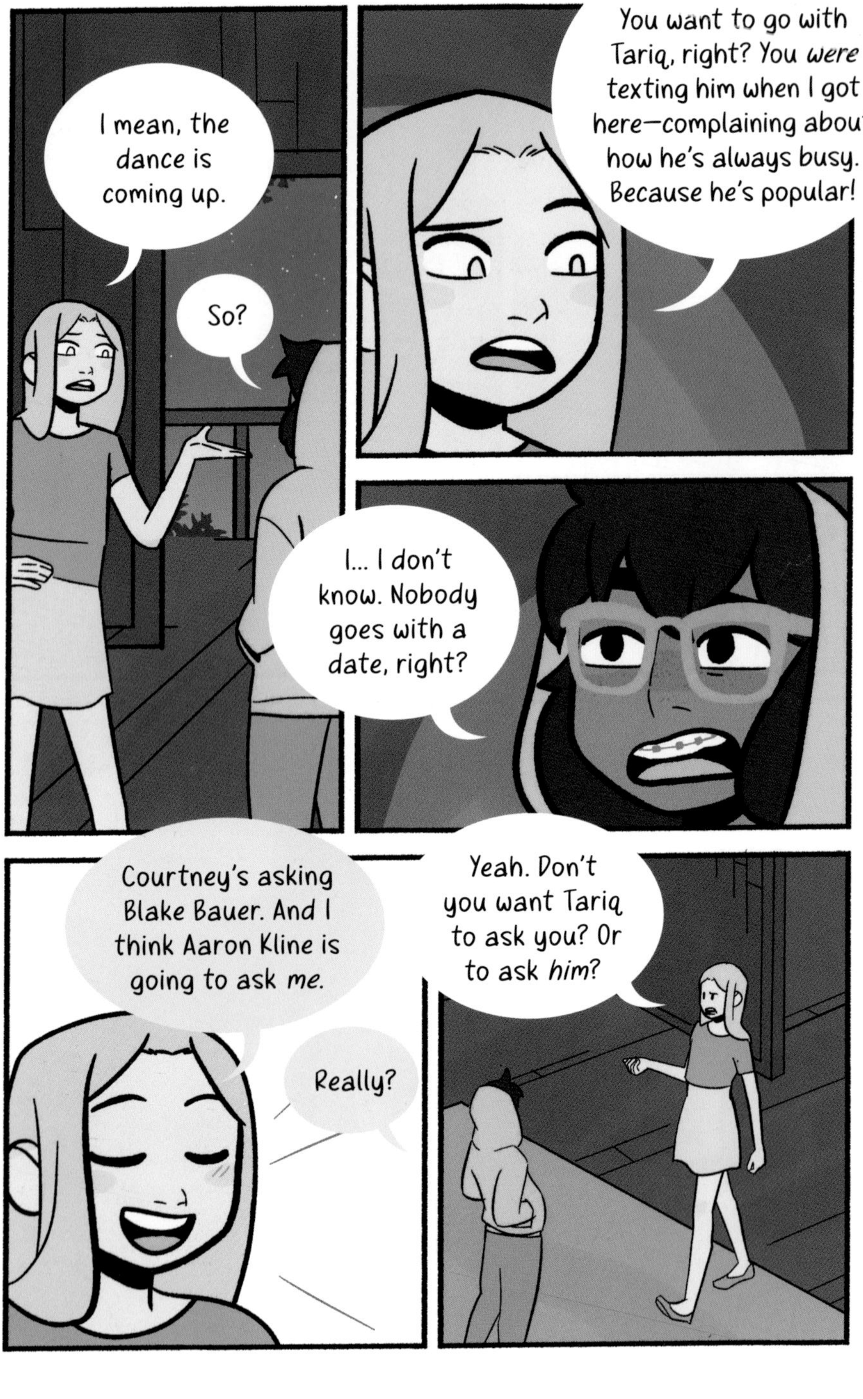
I mean, the dance is coming up.
So?
You want to go with Tariq, right? You *were* texting him when I got here—complaining about how he's always busy. Because he's popular!
I... I don't know. Nobody goes with a date, right?
Courtney's asking Blake Bauer. And I think Aaron Kline is going to ask *me*.
Really?
Yeah. Don't you want Tariq to ask you? Or to ask *him*?

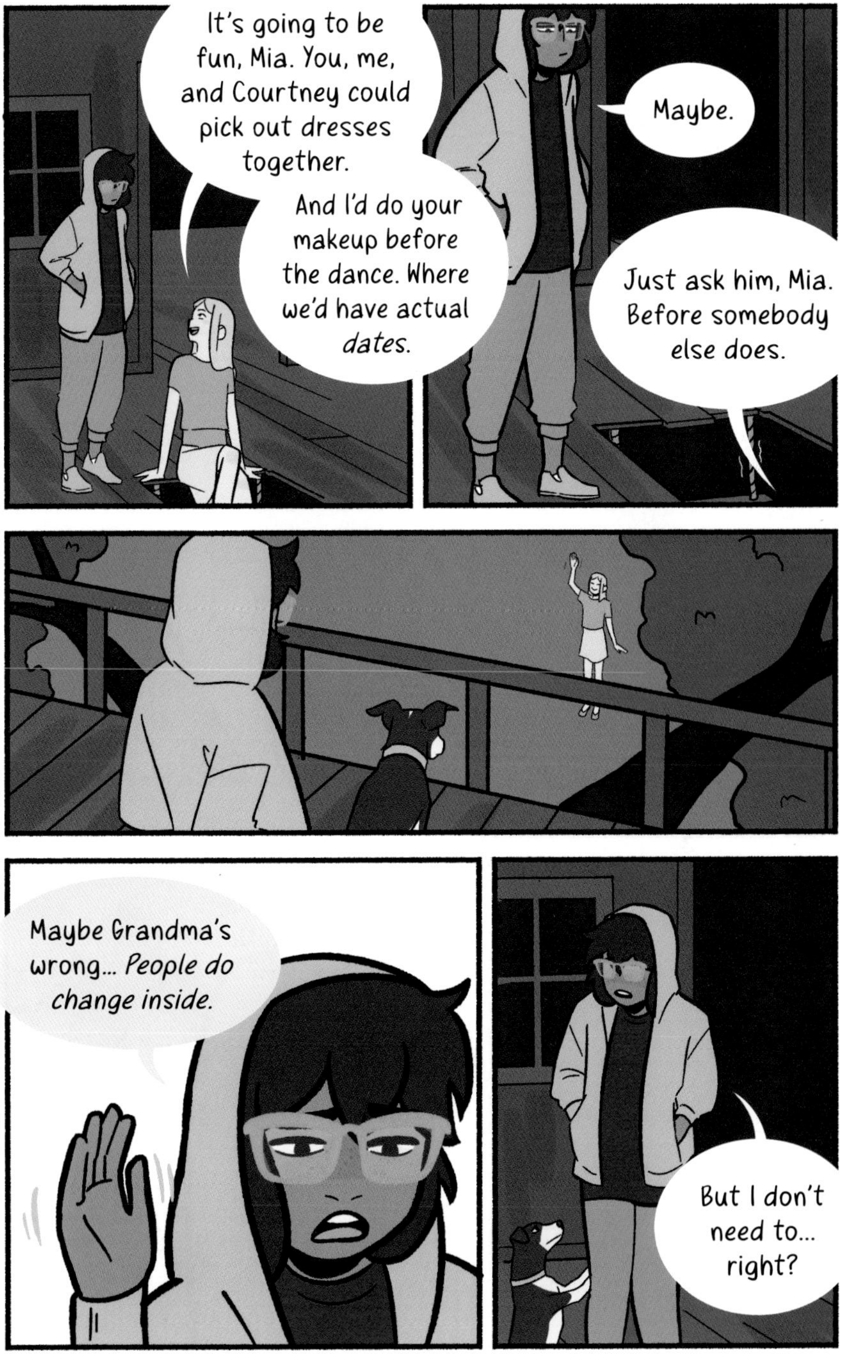
It's going to be fun, Mia. You, me, and Courtney could pick out dresses together.
And I'd do your makeup before the dance. Where we'd have actual *dates*.
Maybe.
Just ask him, Mia. Before somebody else does.
Maybe Grandma's wrong... *People do change inside.*
But I don't need to... right?

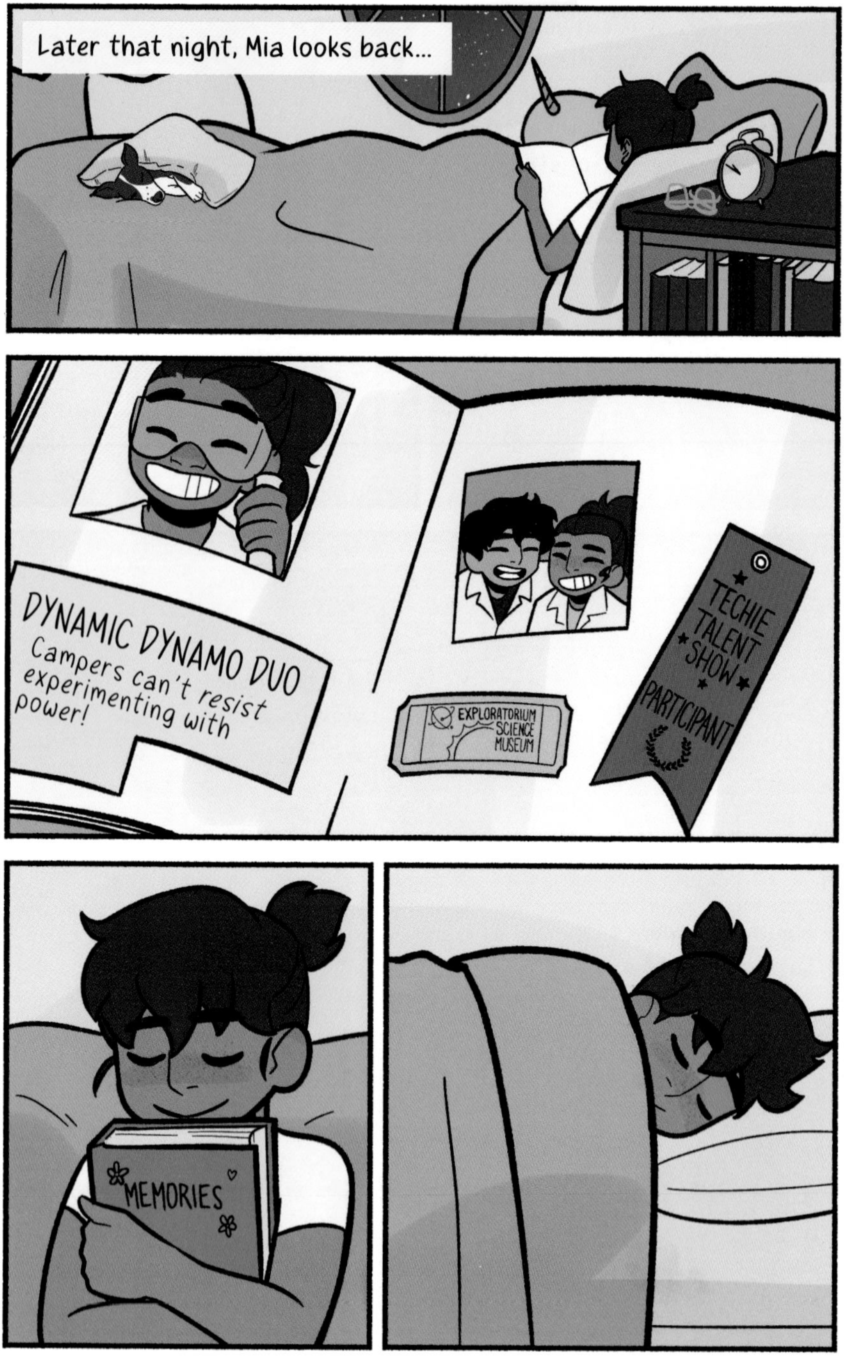

Later that night, Mia looks back...
DYNAMIC DYNAMO DUO
Campers can't resist experimenting with power!
EXPLORATORIUM SCIENCE MUSEUM
TECHIE TALENT SHOW
PARTICIPANT
MEMORIES

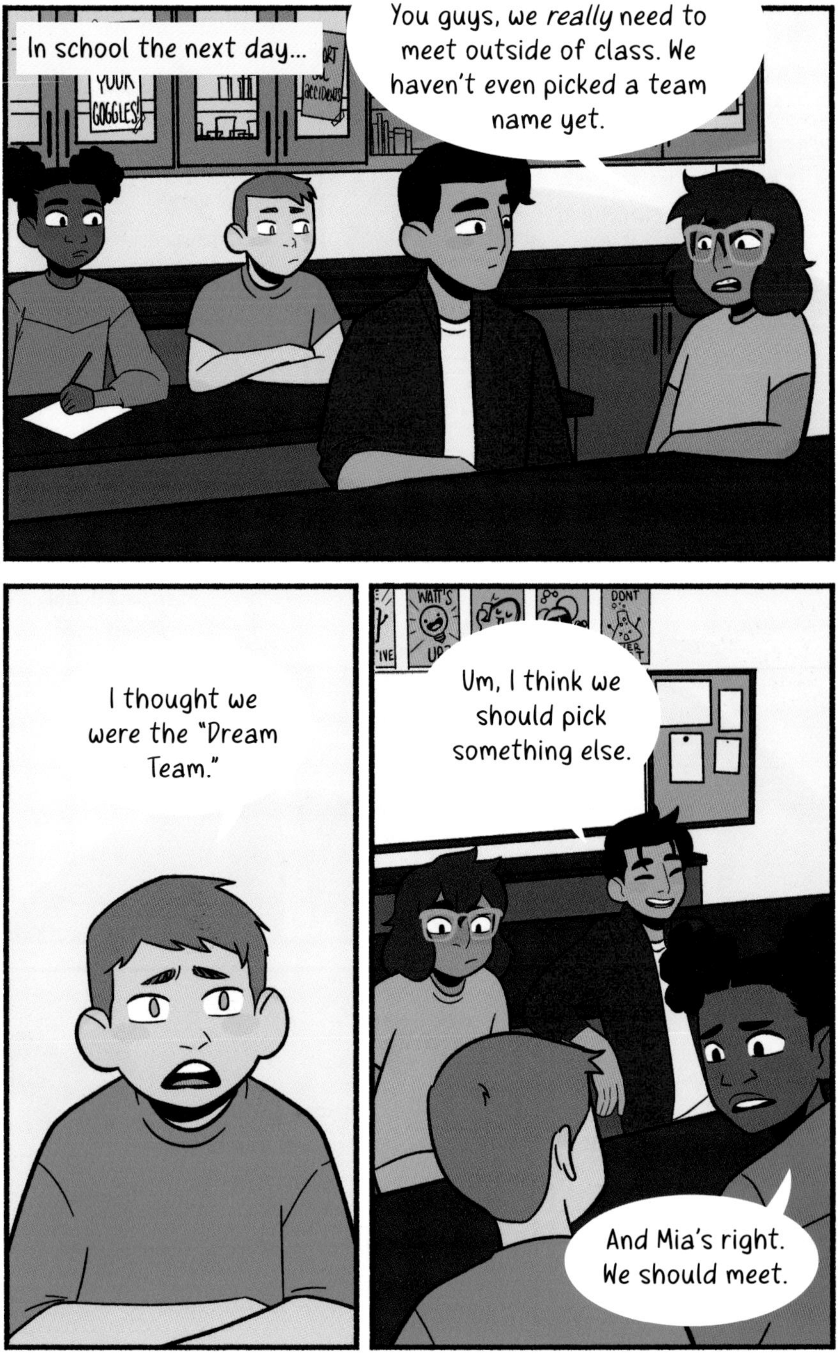
In school the next day...
You guys, we *really* need to meet outside of class. We haven't even picked a team name yet.
I thought we were the "Dream Team."
Um, I think we should pick something else.
And Mia's right. We should meet.

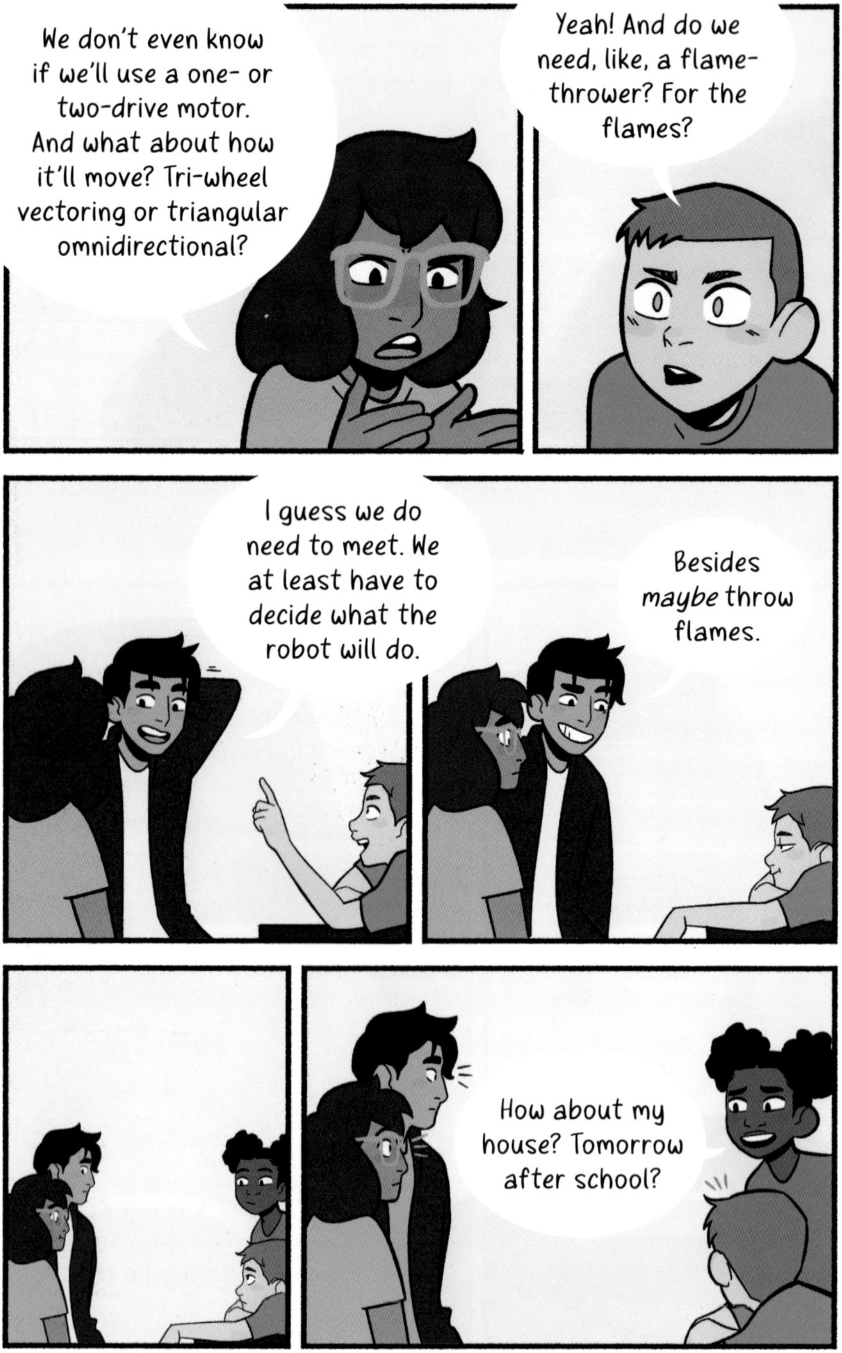
We don't even know if we'll use a one- or two-drive motor. And what about how it'll move? Tri-wheel vectoring or triangular omnidirectional?
Yeah! And do we need, like, a flame-thrower? For the flames?
I guess we do need to meet. We at least have to decide what the robot will do.
Besides *maybe* throw flames.
How about my house? Tomorrow after school?

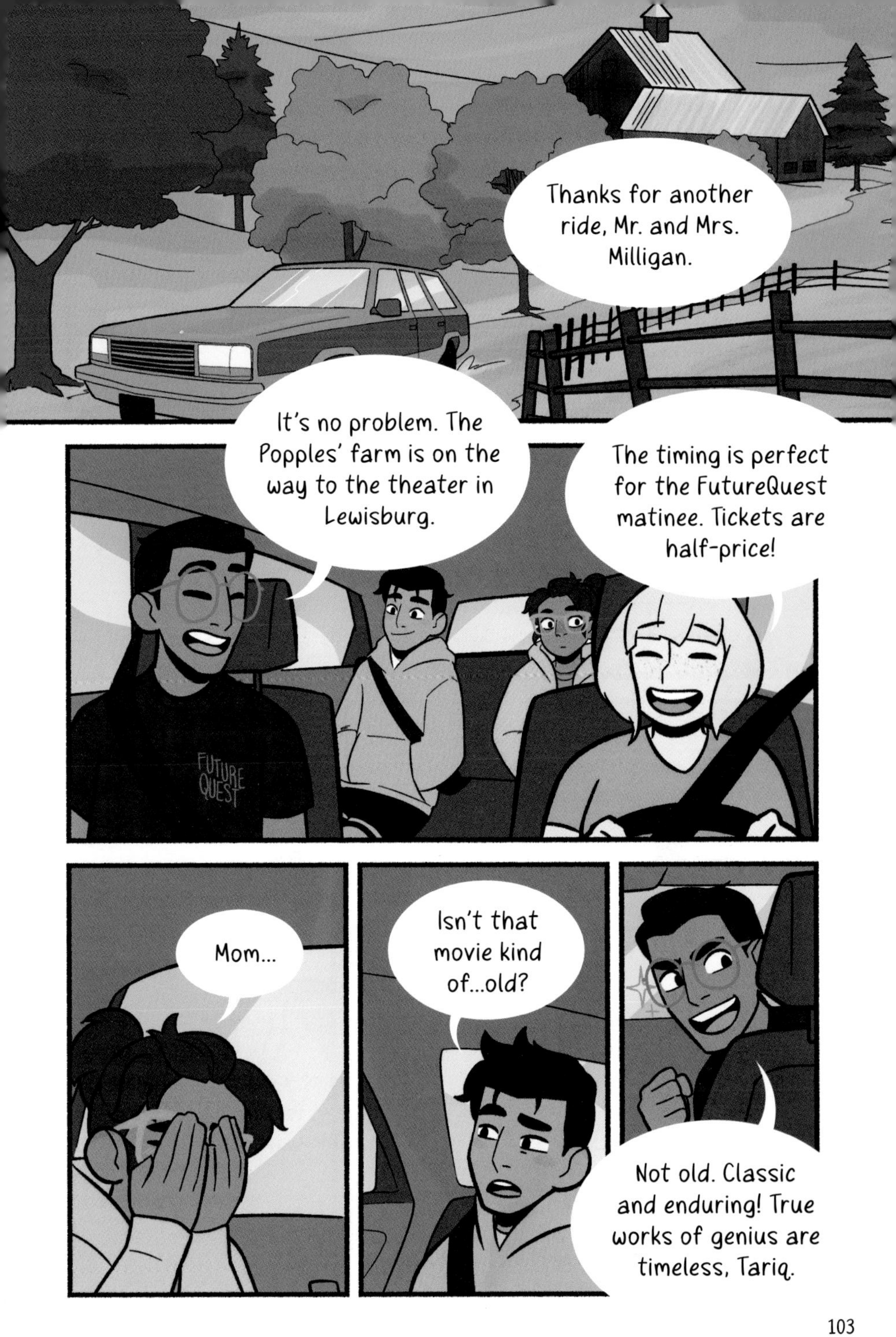
Thanks for another ride, Mr. and Mrs. Milligan.
It's no problem. The Popples' farm is on the way to the theater in Lewisburg.
The timing is perfect for the FutureQuest matinee. Tickets are half-price!
FUTURE QUEST
Mom...
Isn't that movie kind of...old?
Not old. Classic and enduring! True works of genius are timeless, Tariq.

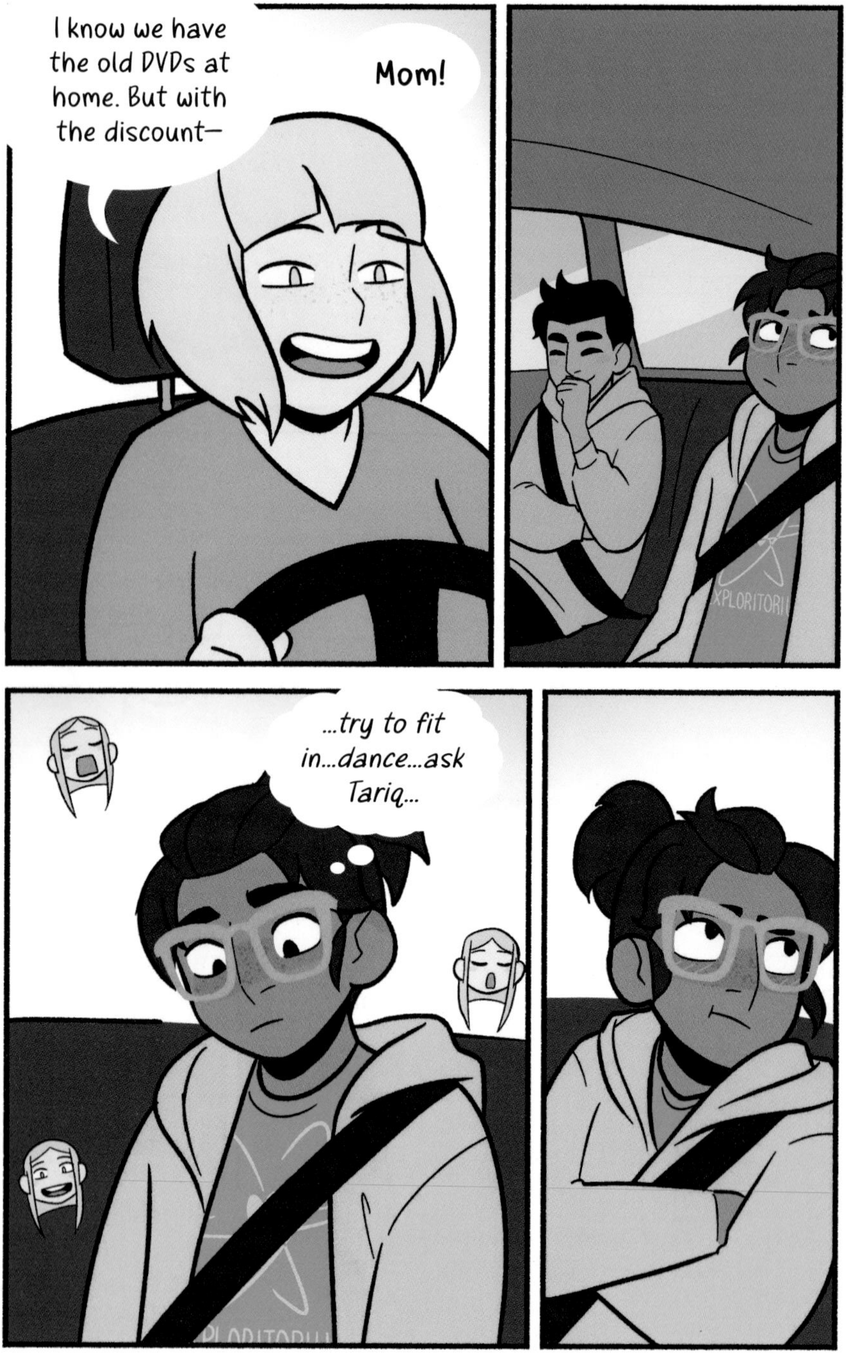
I know we have the old DVDs at home. But with the discount—
Mom!
...try to fit in...dance...ask Tariq...
XPLORITORI

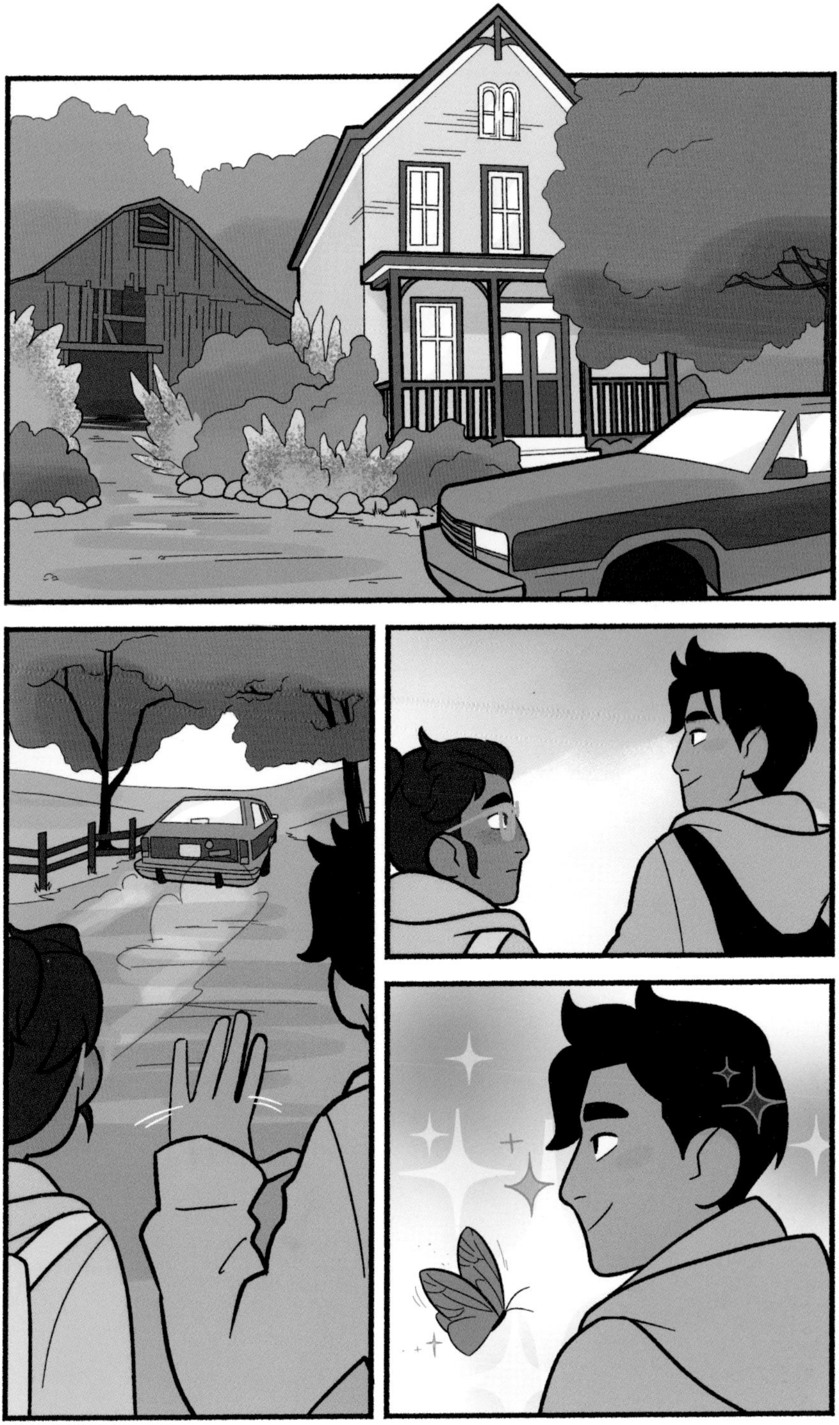

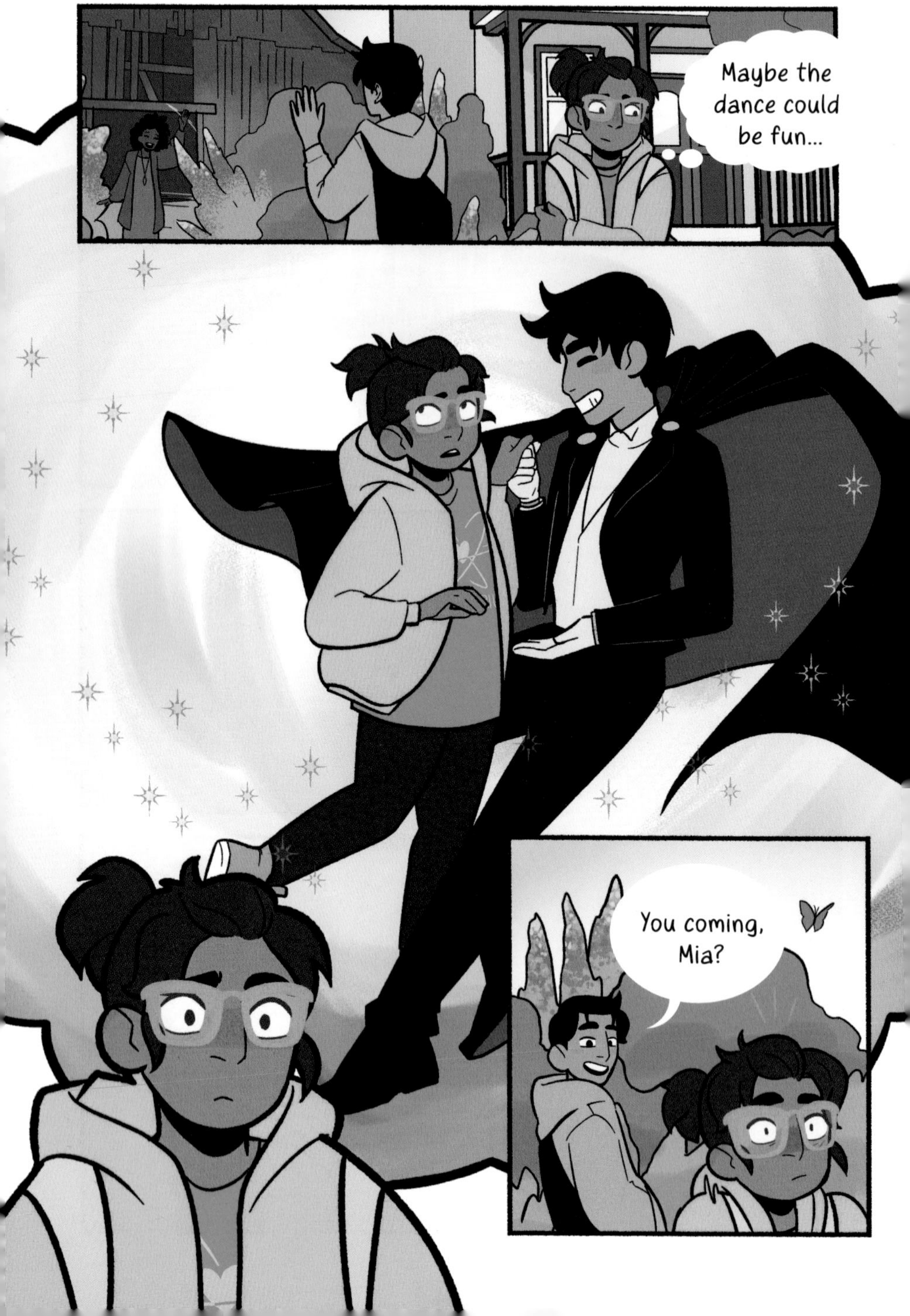
Maybe the dance could be fun...
You coming, Mia?

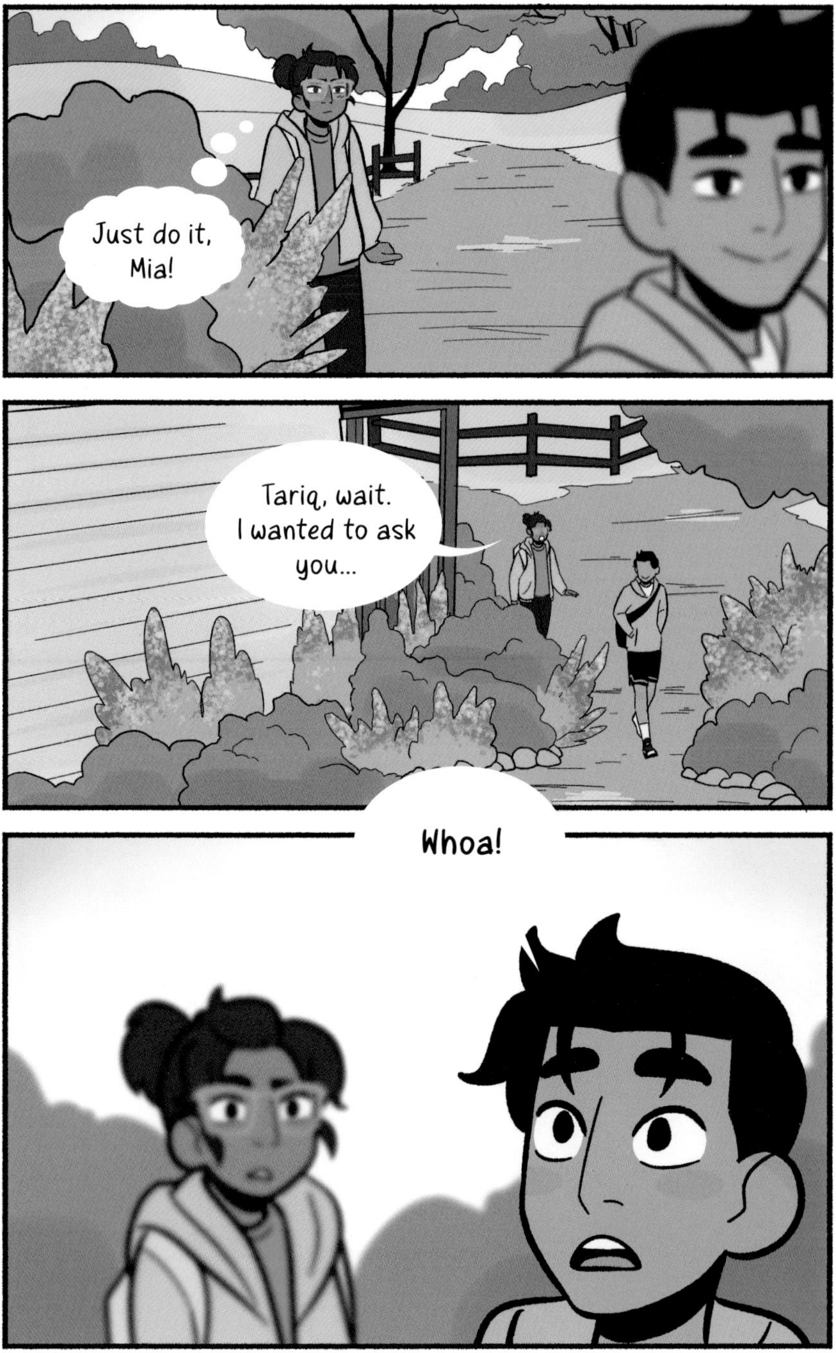
Just do it, Mia!
Tariq, wait. I wanted to ask you...
Whoa!

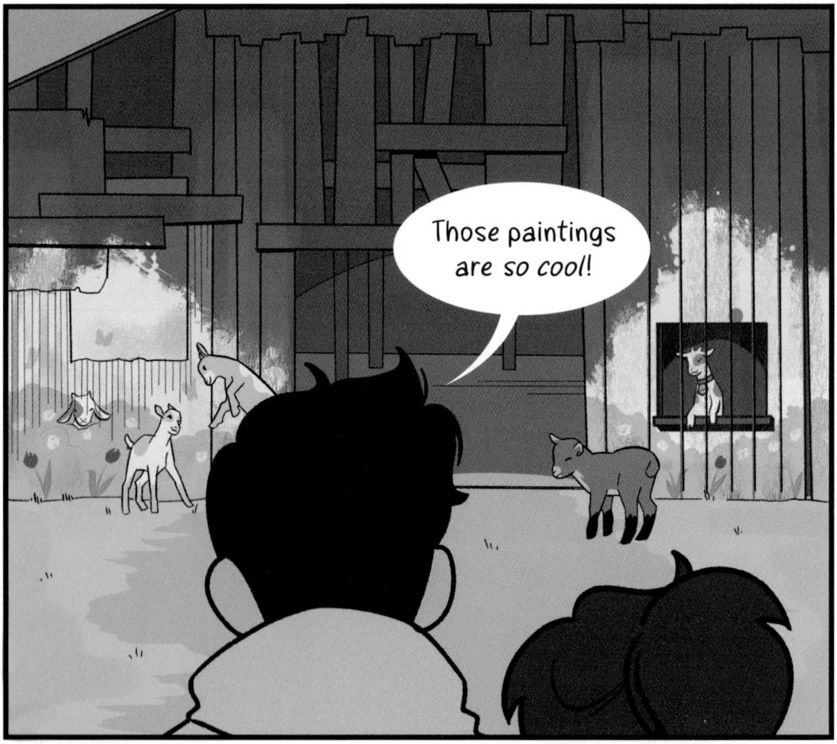
Those paintings are so *cool*!

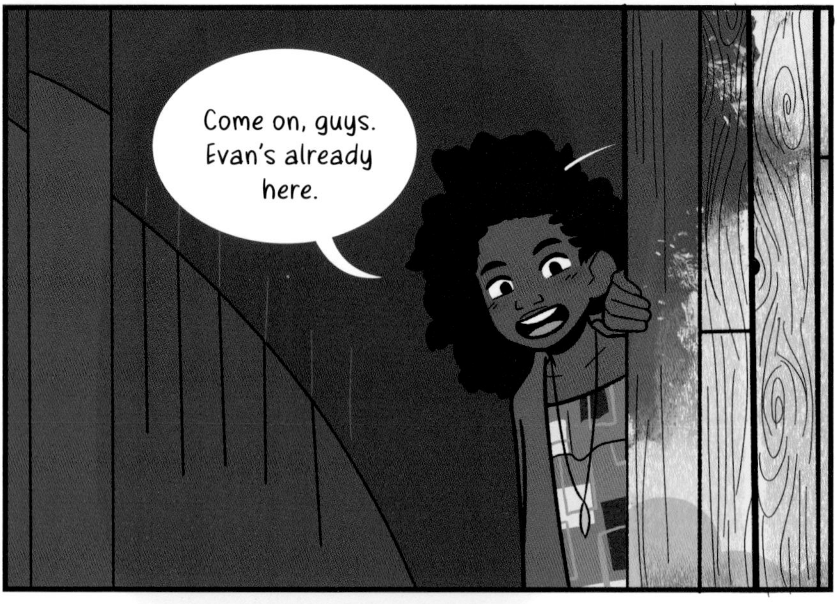
Come on, guys. Evan's already here.

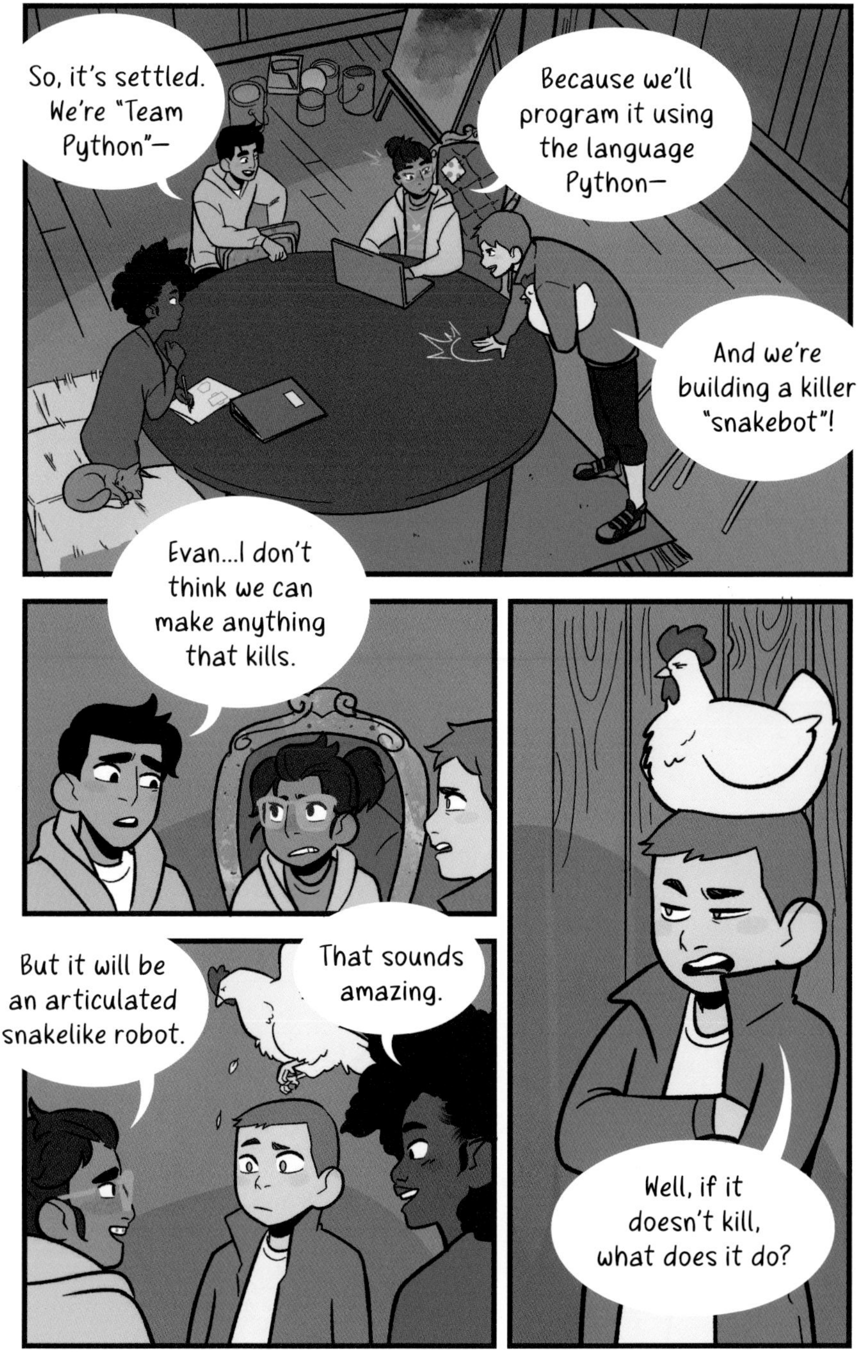
So, it's settled. We're "Team Python"—
Because we'll program it using the language Python—
And we're building a killer "snakebot"!
Evan...I don't think we can make anything that kills.
But it will be an articulated snakelike robot.
That sounds amazing.
Well, if it doesn't kill, what does it do?

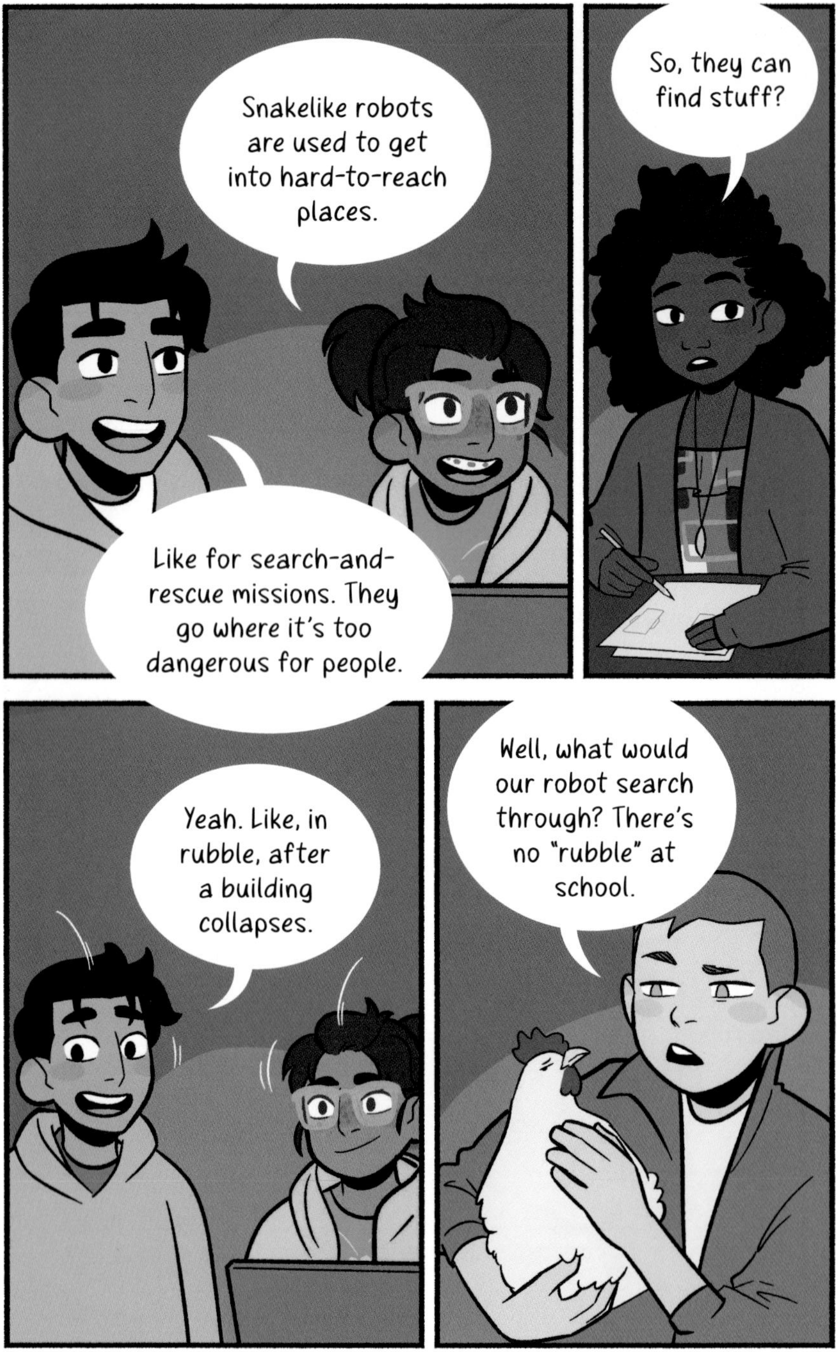

Snakelike robots are used to get into hard-to-reach places.
Like for search-and-rescue missions. They go where it's too dangerous for people.
So, they can find stuff?
Yeah. Like, in rubble, after a building collapses.
Well, what would our robot search through? There's no "rubble" at school.

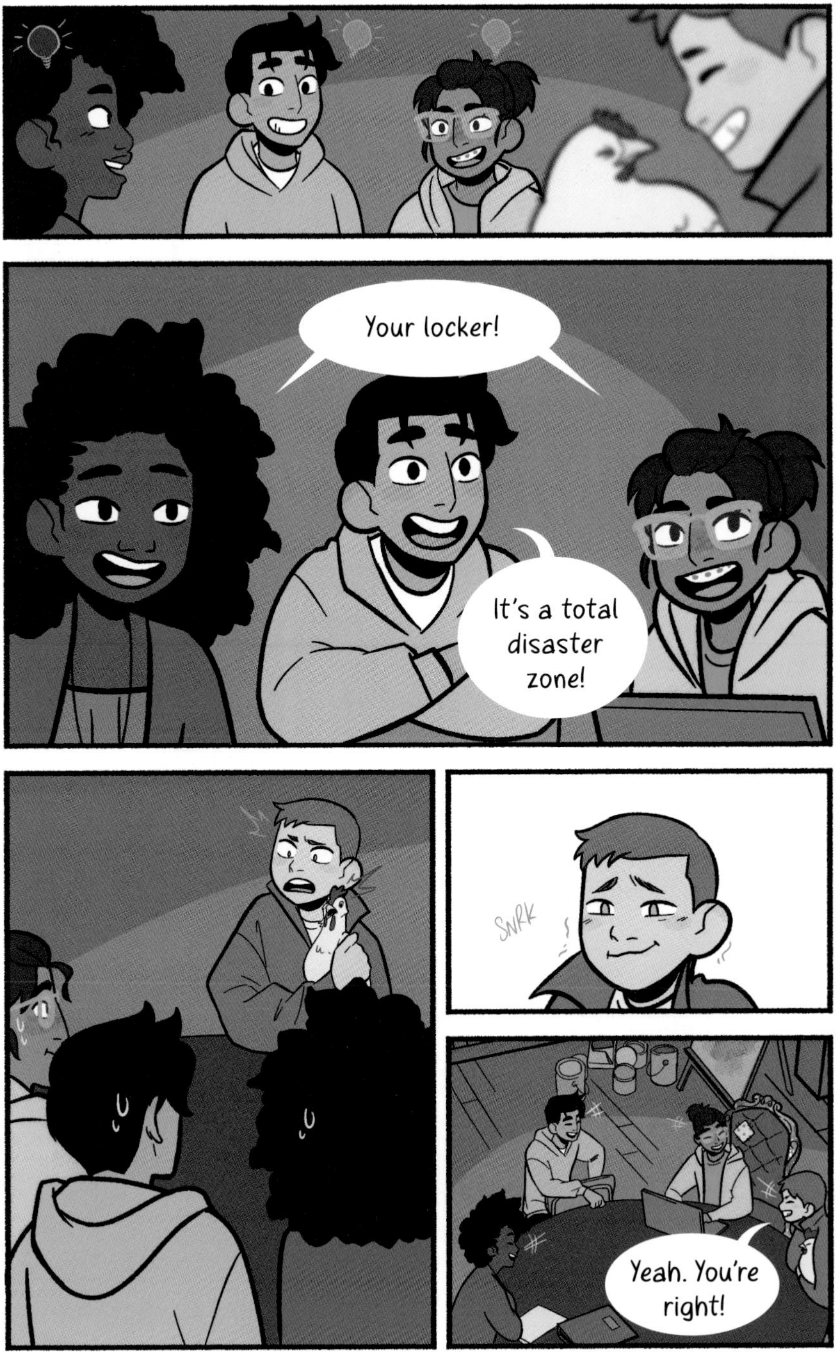
Your locker!
It's a total disaster zone!
SNRK
Yeah. You're right!

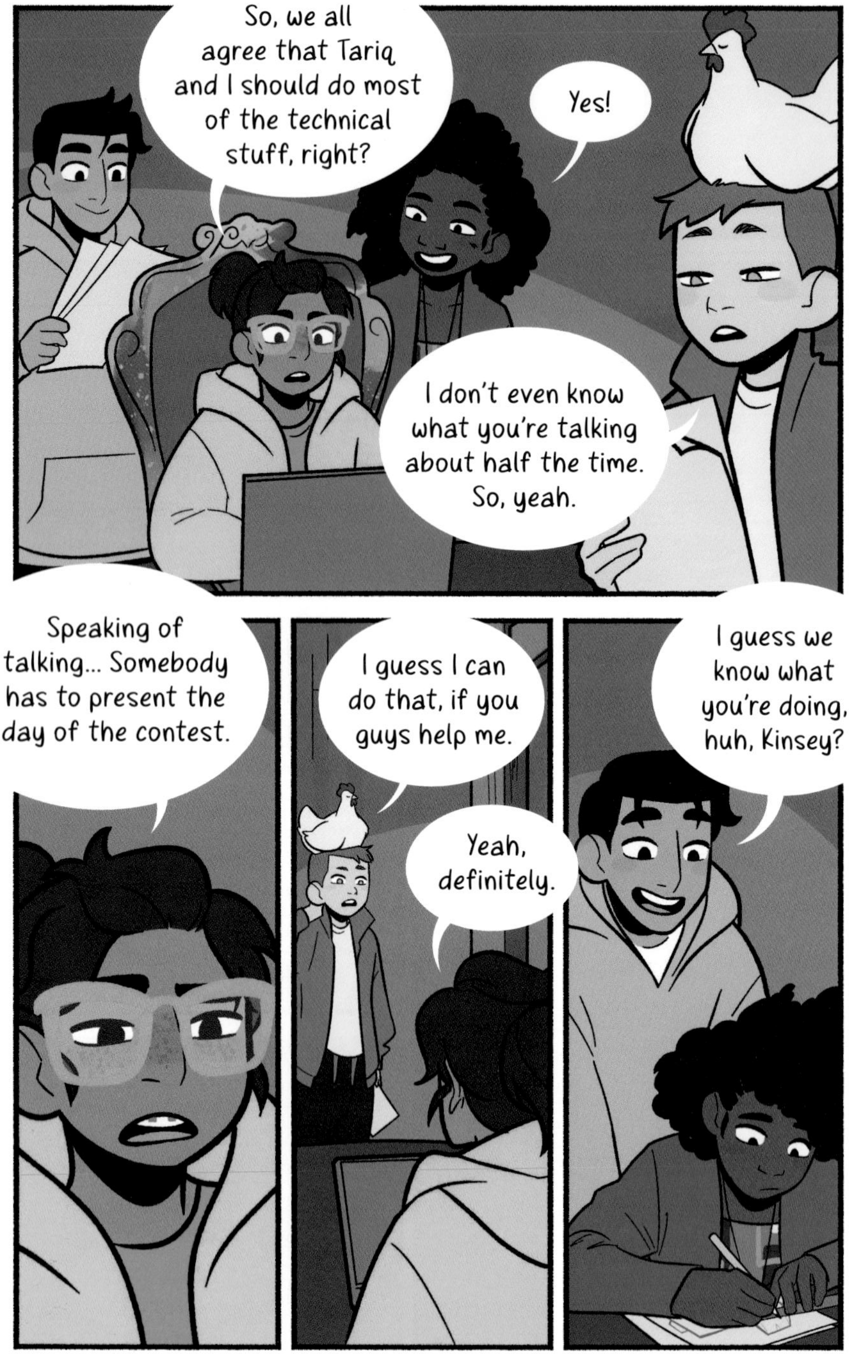
So, we all agree that Tariq and I should do most of the technical stuff, right?
Yes!
I don't even know what you're talking about half the time. So, yeah.
Speaking of talking... Somebody has to present the day of the contest.
I guess I can do that, if you guys help me.
Yeah, definitely.
I guess we know what you're doing, huh, Kinsey?

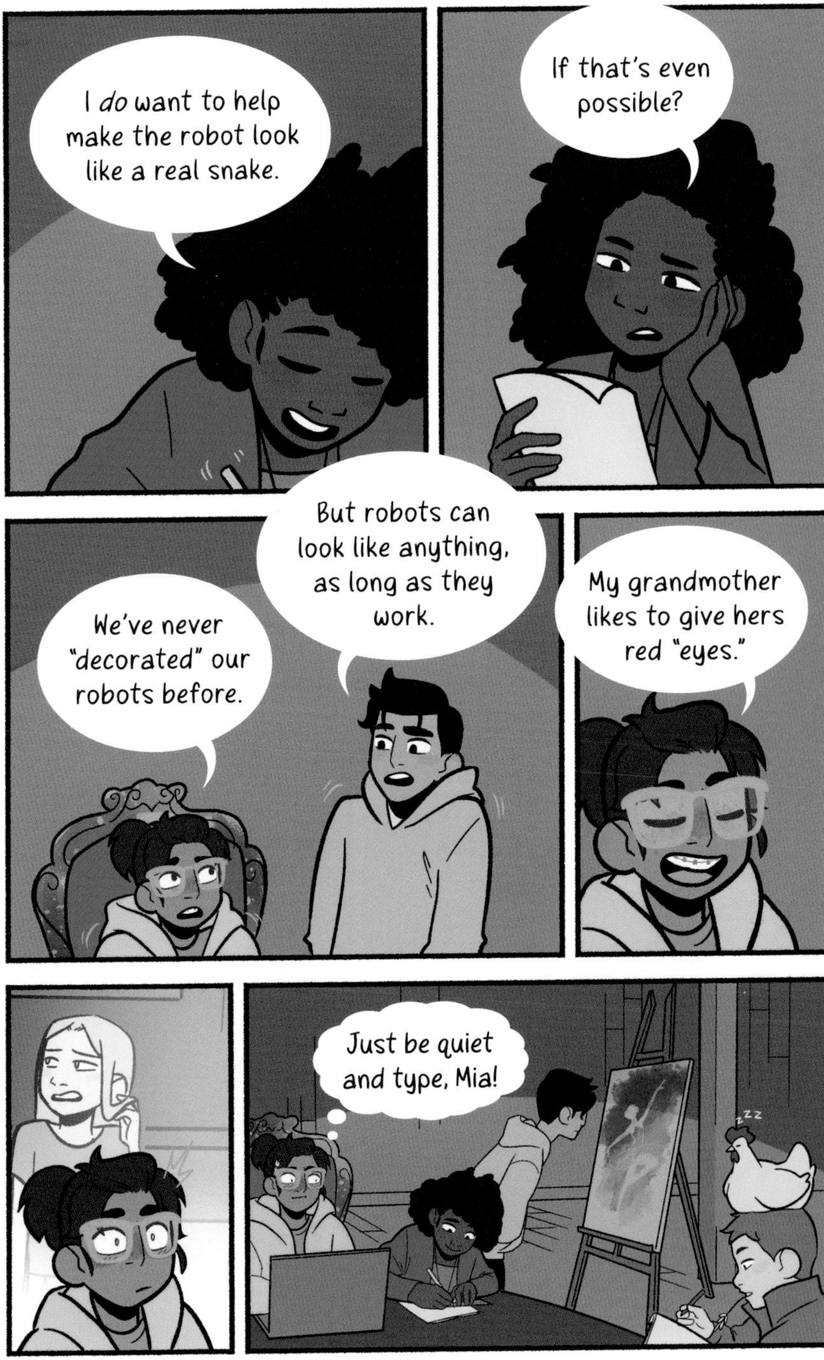
I *do* want to help make the robot look like a real snake.
If that's even possible?
We've never "decorated" our robots before.
But robots can look like anything, as long as they work.
My grandmother likes to give hers red "eyes."
Just be quiet and type, Mia!
ZZZ

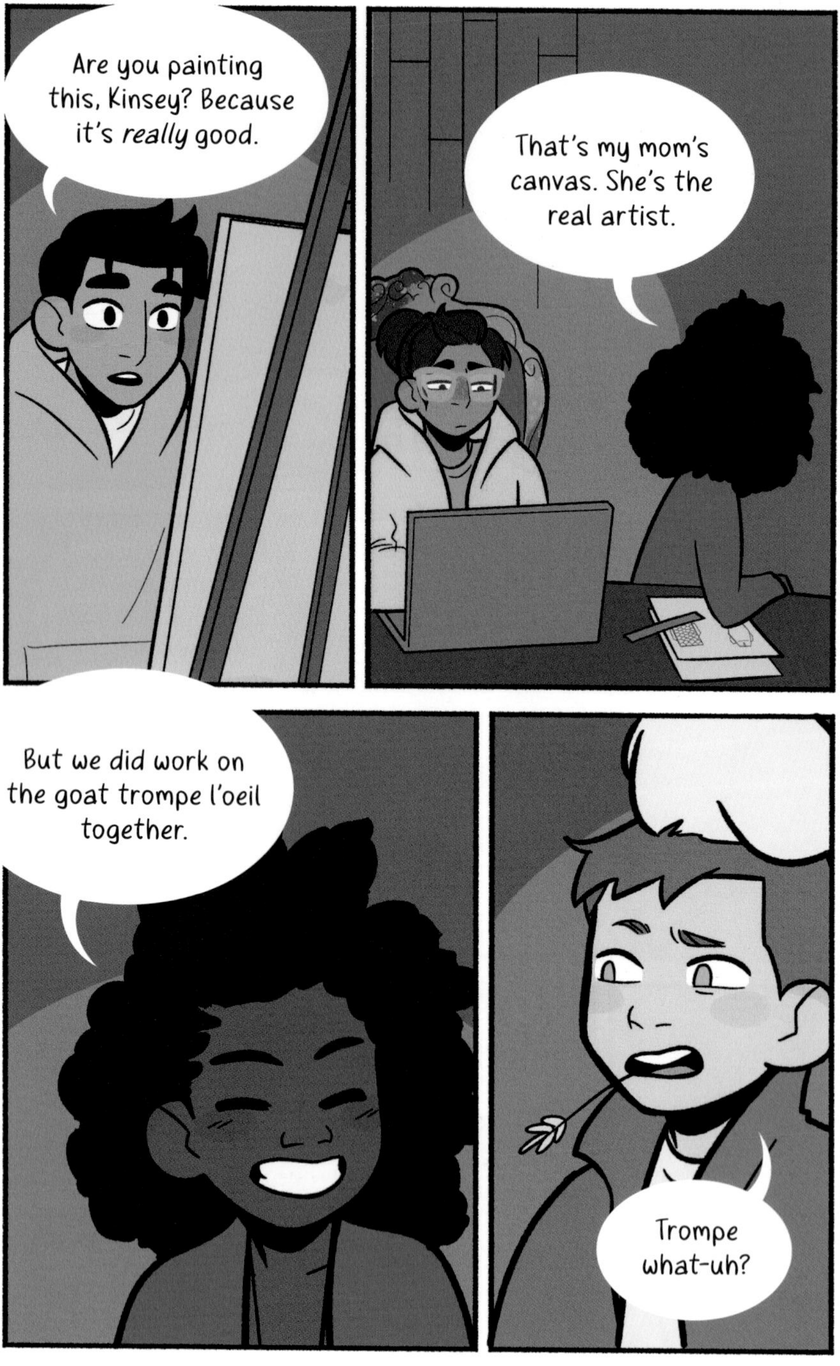
Are you painting this, Kinsey? Because it's *really* good.
That's my mom's canvas. She's the real artist.
But we did work on the goat trompe l'oeil together.
Trompe what-uh?

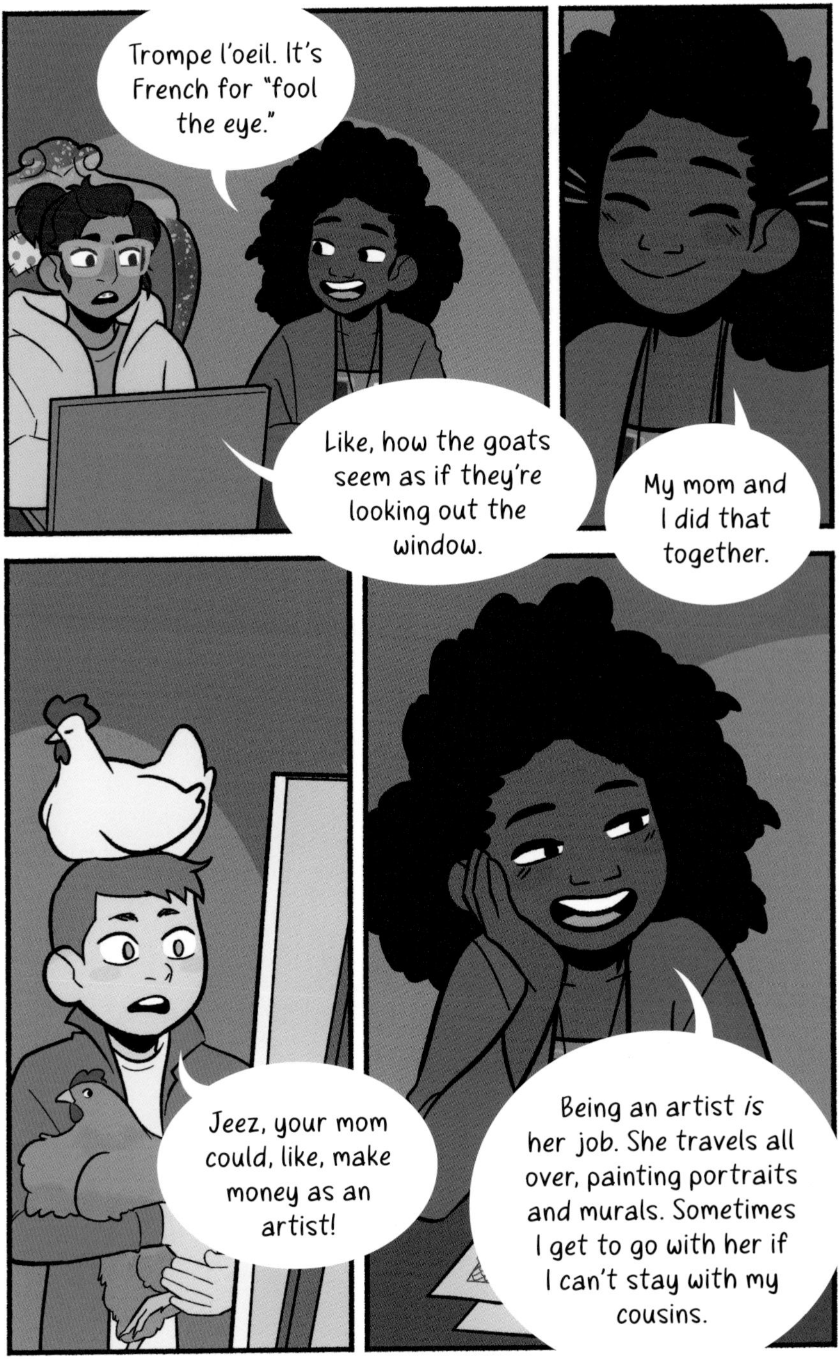
Trompe l'oeil. It's French for "fool the eye."
Like, how the goats seem as if they're looking out the window.
My mom and I did that together.
Jeez, your mom could, like, make money as an artist!
Being an artist *is* her job. She travels all over, painting portraits and murals. Sometimes I get to go with her if I can't stay with my cousins.

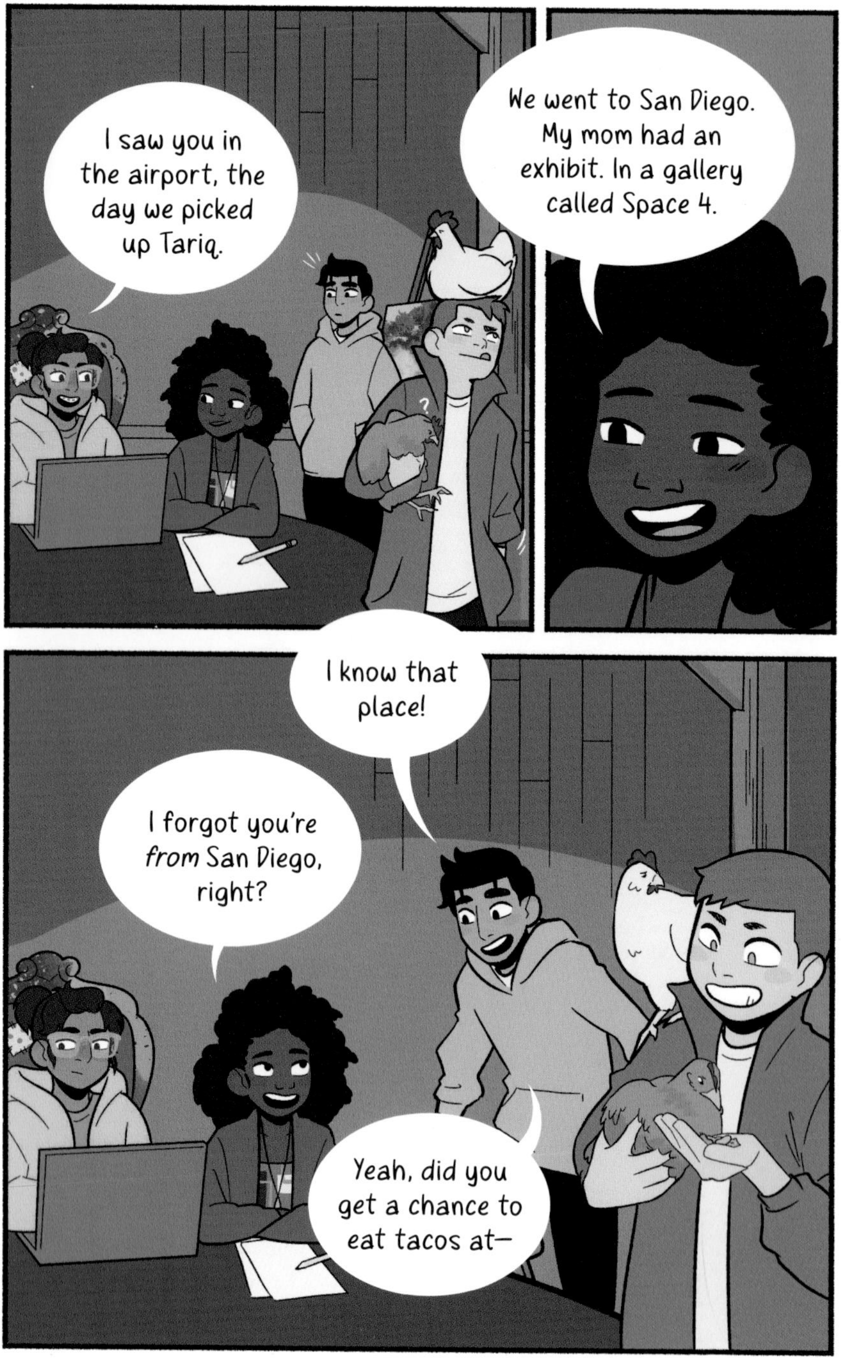
I saw you in the airport, the day we picked up Tariq.
We went to San Diego. My mom had an exhibit. In a gallery called Space 4.
I know that place!
I forgot you're *from* San Diego, right?
Yeah, did you get a chance to eat tacos at—

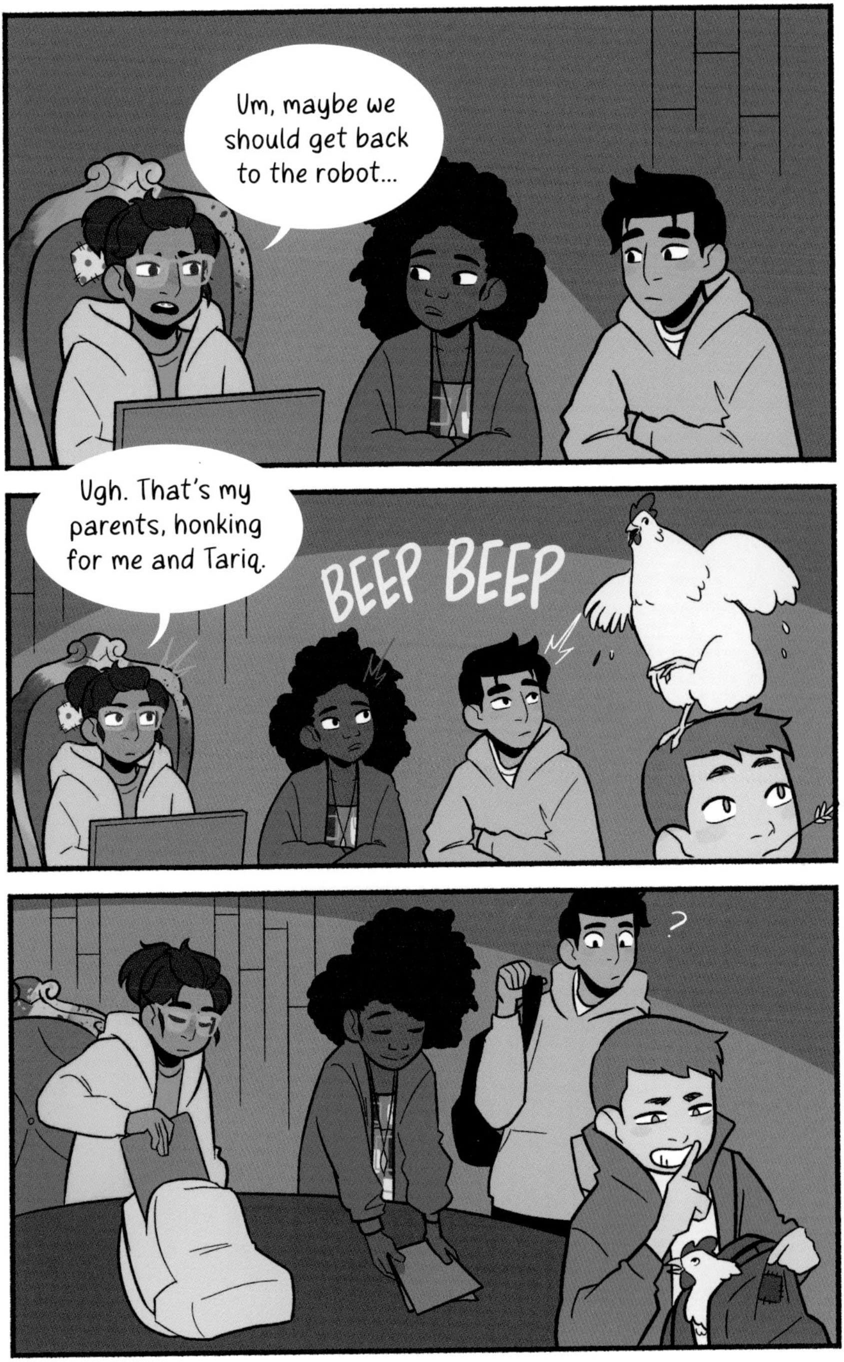
Um, maybe we should get back to the robot...
Ugh. That's my parents, honking for me and Tariq.
BEEP BEEP
?

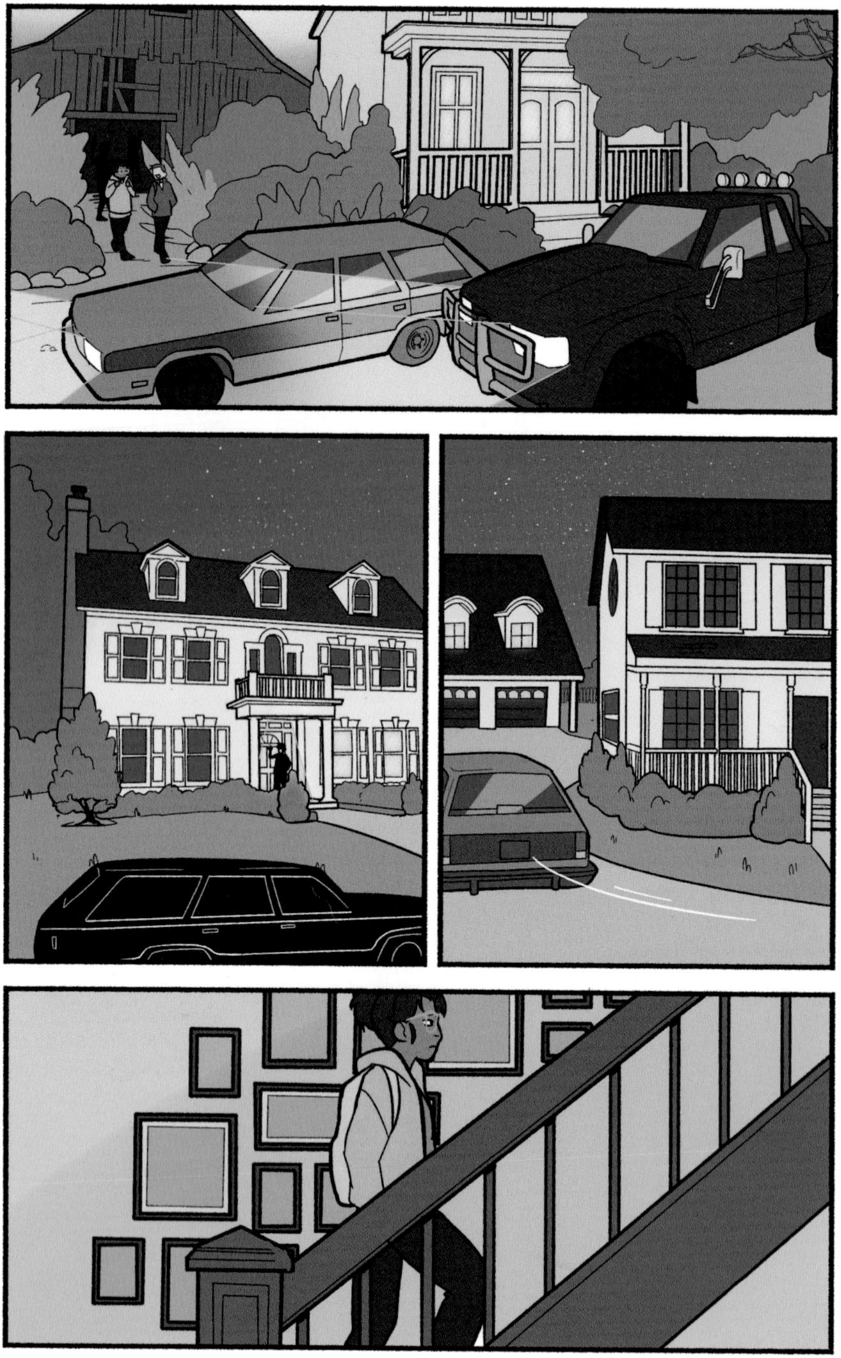

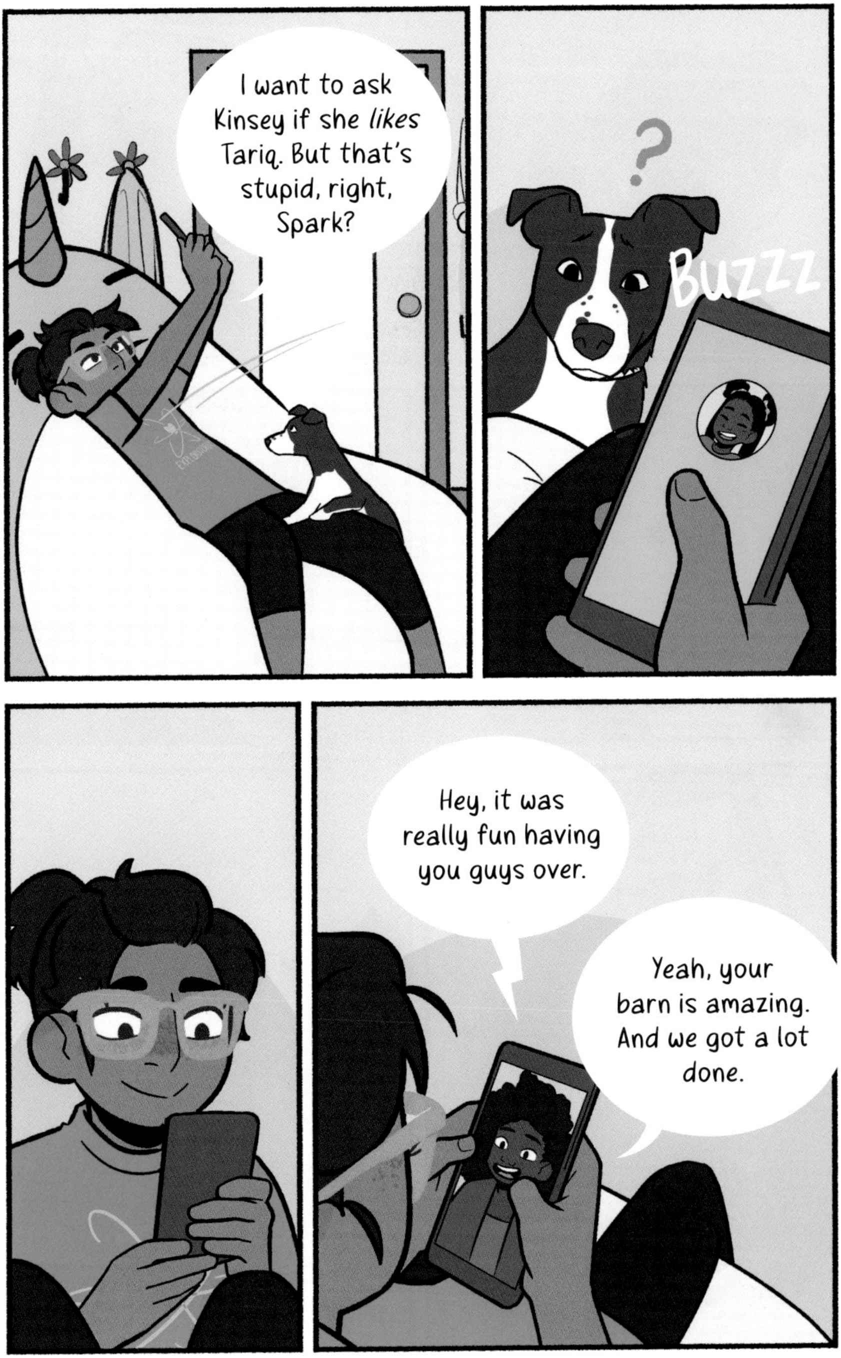
I want to ask Kinsey if she *likes* Tariq. But that's stupid, right, Spark?
?
BUZZZ
Hey, it was really fun having you guys over.
Yeah, your barn is amazing. And we got a lot done.

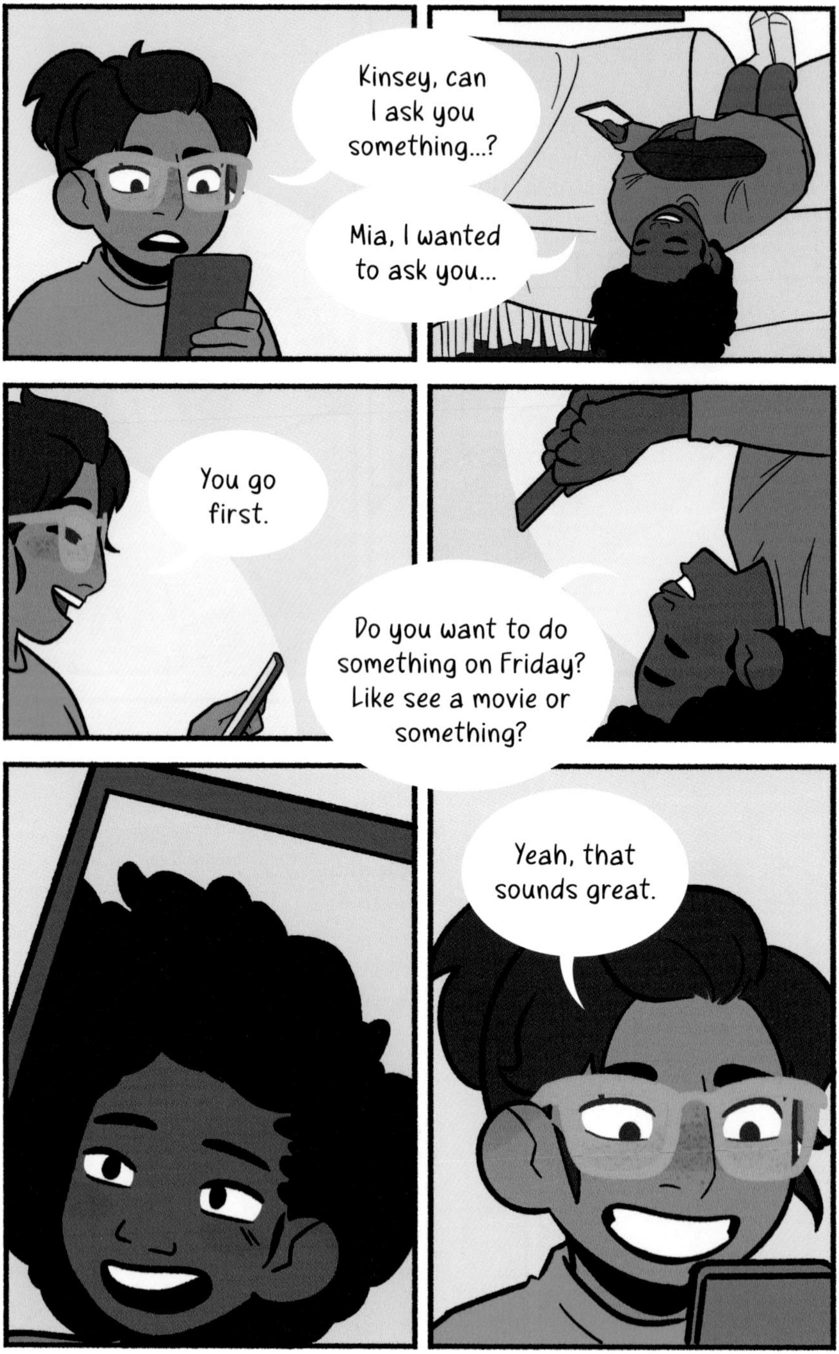
Kinsey, can I ask you something...?
Mia, I wanted to ask you...
You go first.
Do you want to do something on Friday? Like see a movie or something?
Yeah, that sounds great.

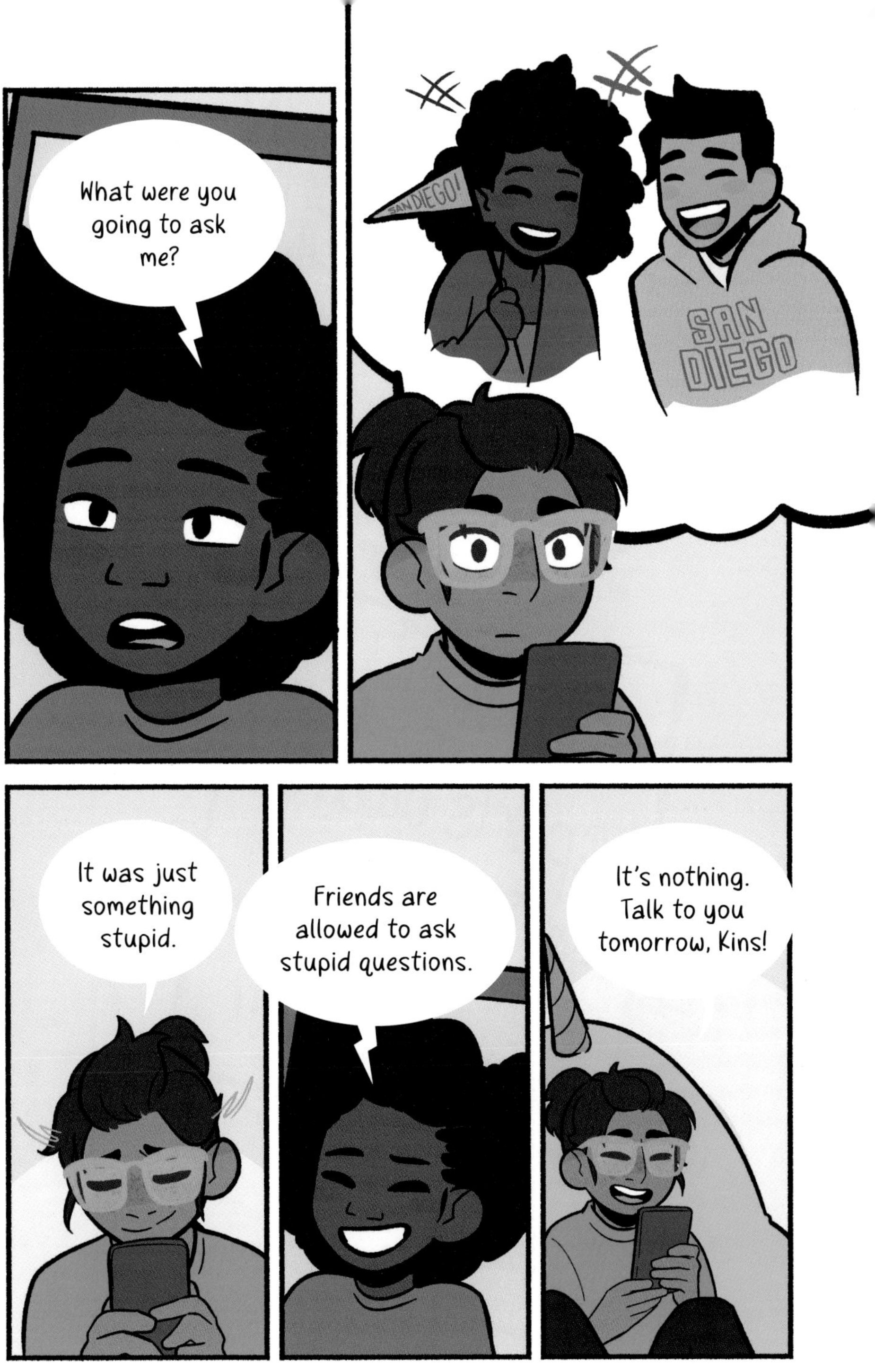
What were you going to ask me?
SAN DIEGO!
SAN DIEGO
It was just something stupid.
Friends are allowed to ask stupid questions.
It's nothing. Talk to you tomorrow, Kins!

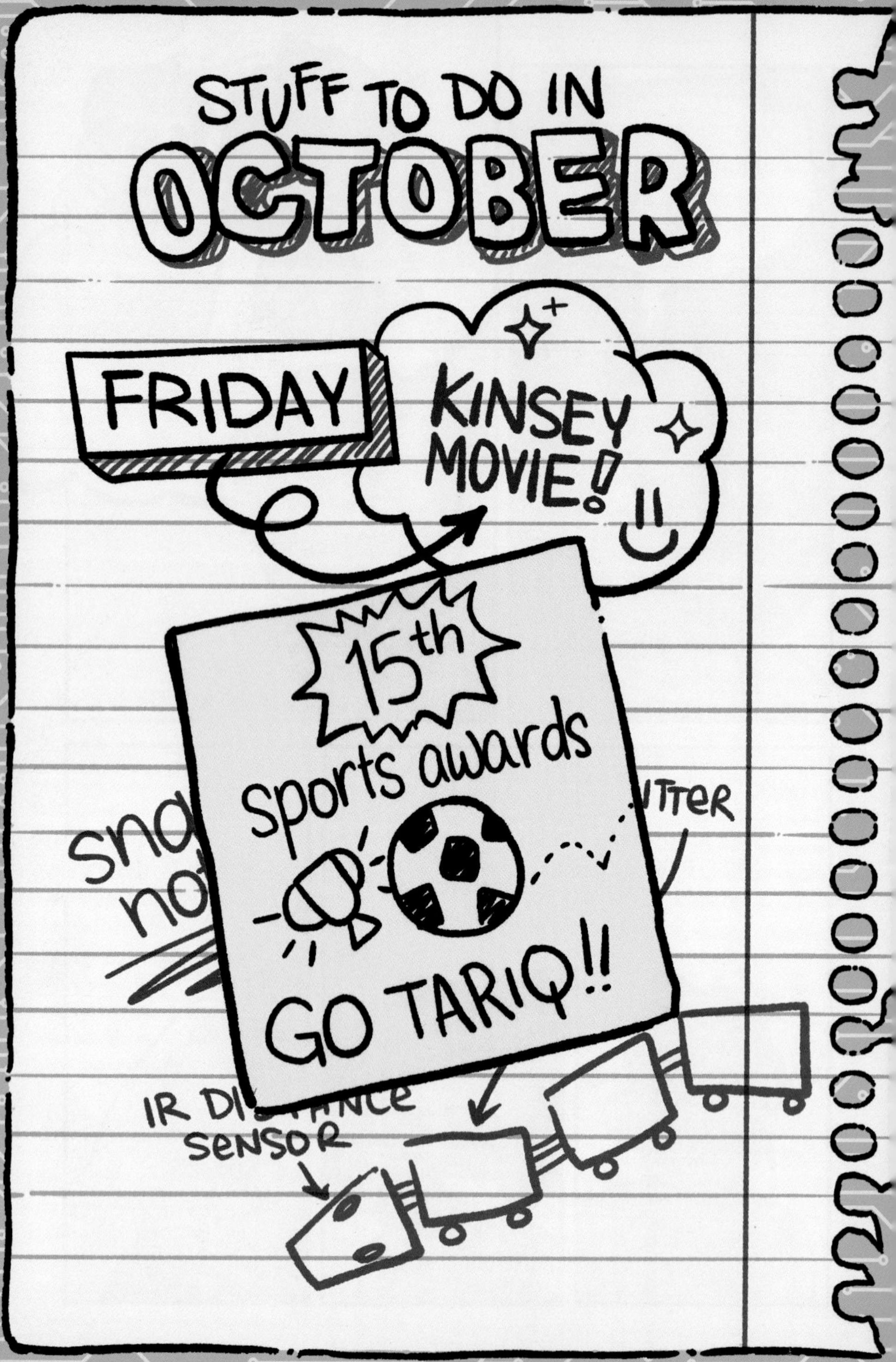

STUFF TO DO IN
OCTOBER
FRIDAY
KINSEY MOVIE!
15th
sports awards
GO TARIQ!!
IR DISTANCE SENSOR

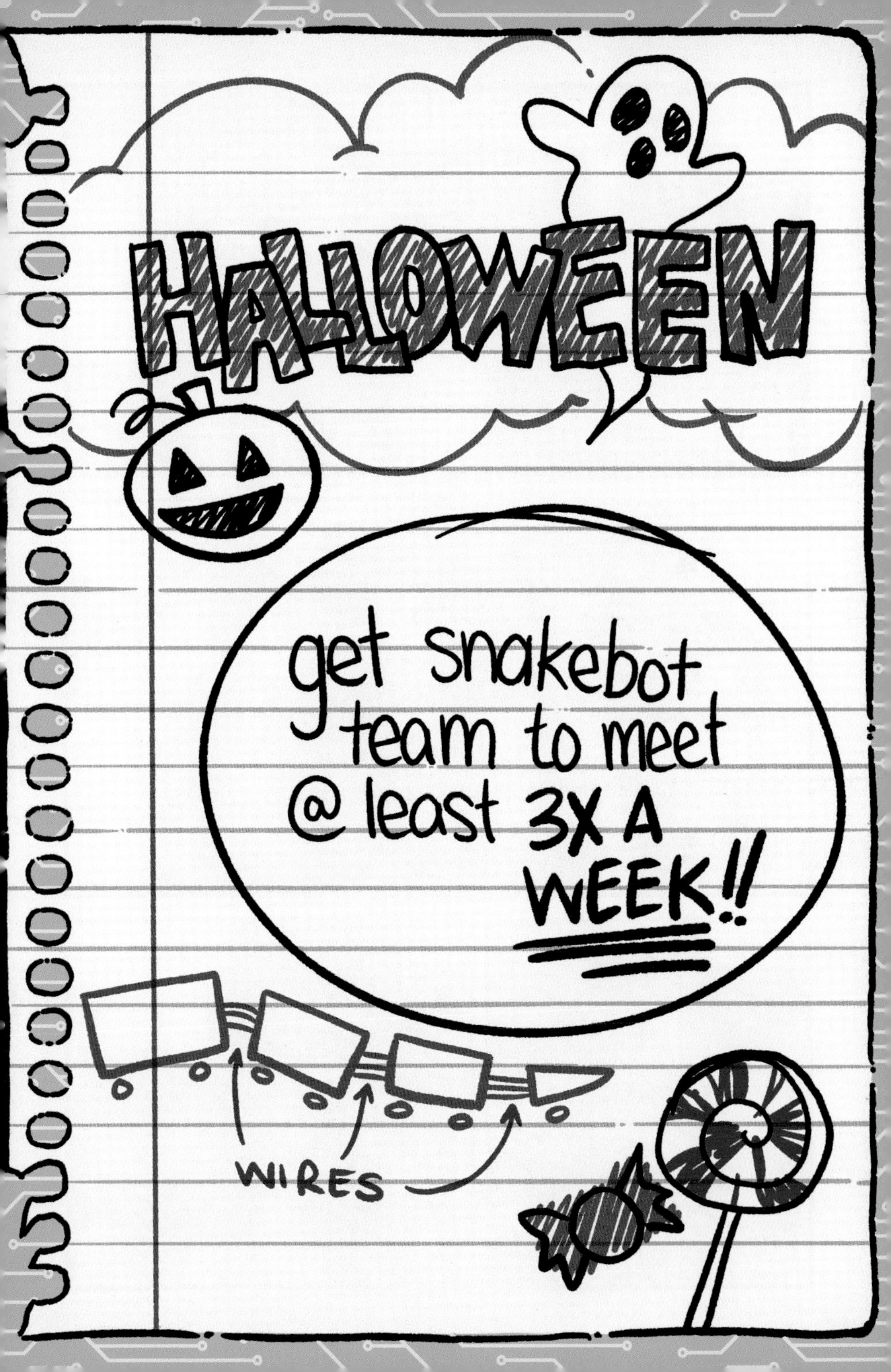

HALLOWEEN
get snakebot team to meet @ least 3X A WEEK!!
WIRES

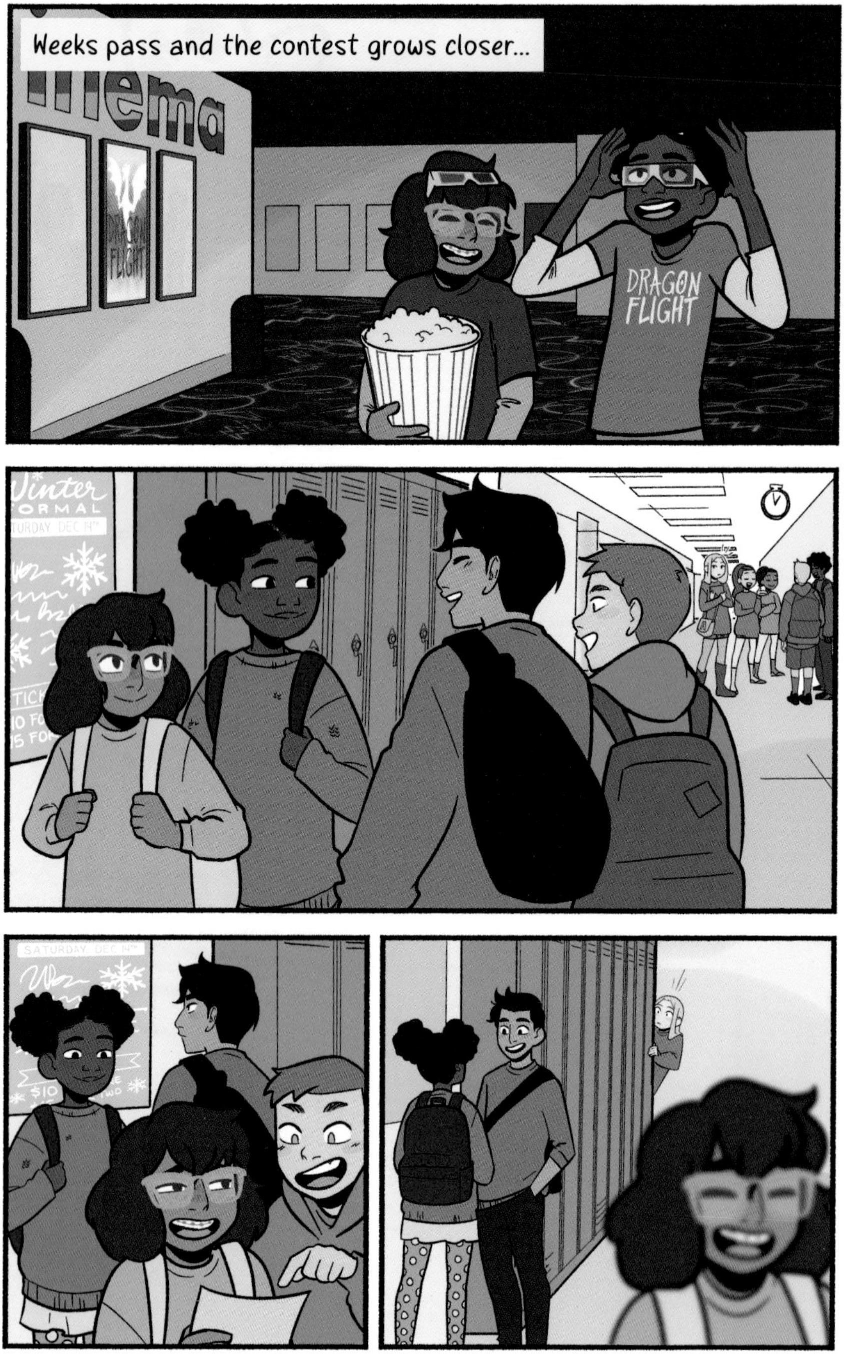
Weeks pass and the contest grows closer...
DRAGON FLIGHT
SATURDAY DEC 14TH

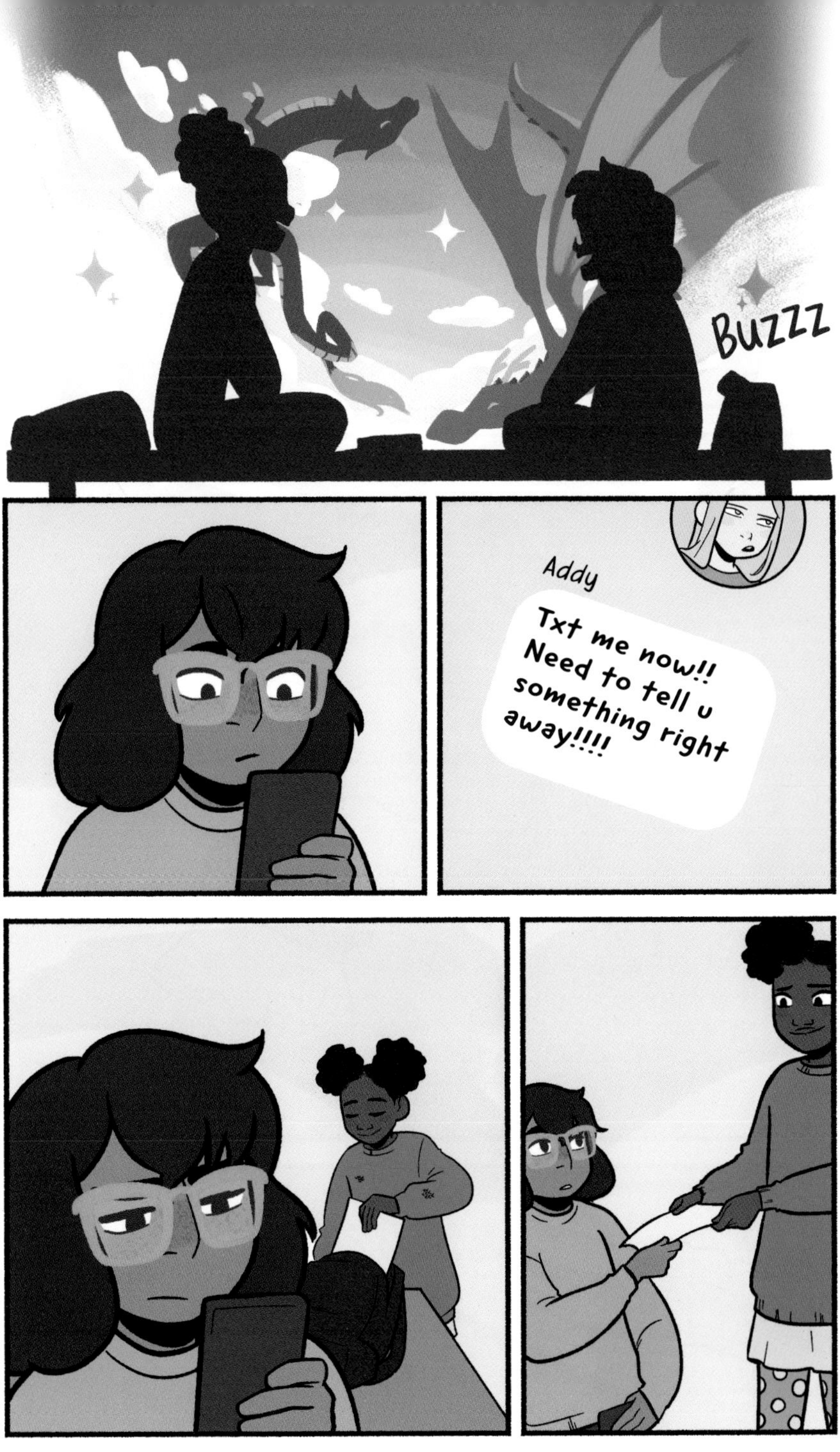
Buzzz
Addy
Txt me now!! Need to tell u something right away!!!!

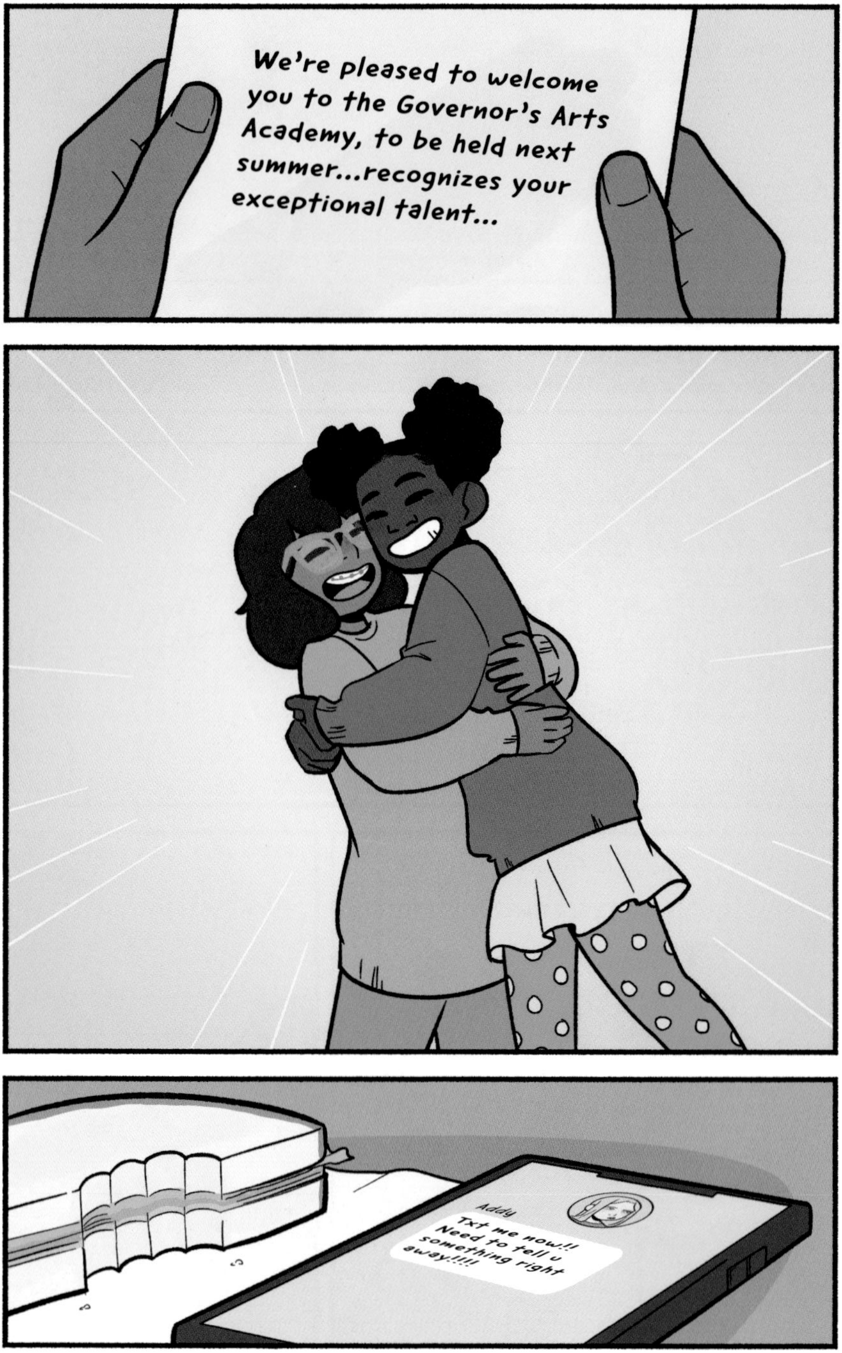
We're pleased to welcome you to the Governor's Arts Academy, to be held next summer...recognizes your exceptional talent...
Addy
Txt me now!! Need to tell u something right away!!!!

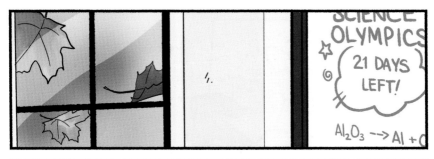

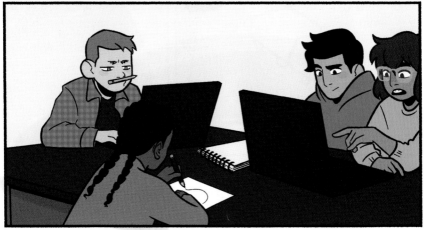

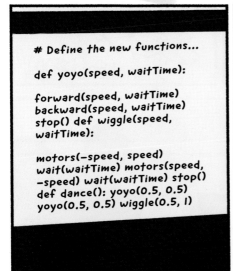

OLYMPICS
21 DAYS LEFT!
Al2O3 --> Al +
# Define the new functions...
def yoyo(speed, waitTime):
forward(speed, waitTime)
backward(speed, waitTime)
stop() def wiggle(speed,
waitTime):
motors(-speed, speed)
wait(waitTime) motors(speed,
-speed) wait(waitTime) stop()
def dance(): yoyo(0.5, 0.5)
yoyo(0.5, 0.5) wiggle(0.5, 1)

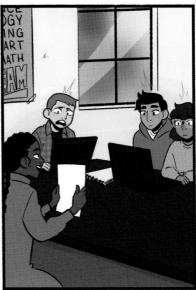

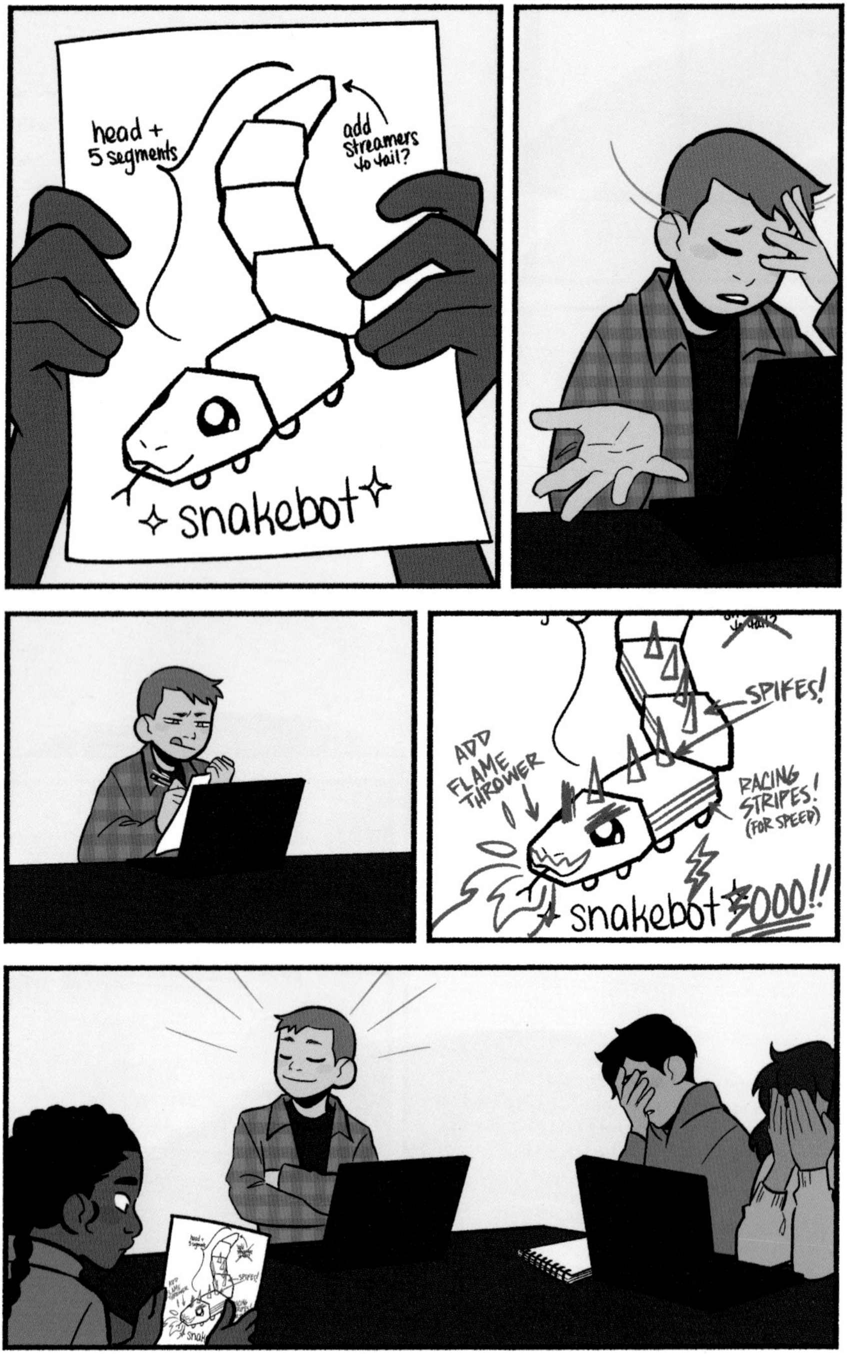
head +
5 segments
add
streamers
to tail?
snakebot
SPIKES!
ADD
FLAME
THROWER
RACING
STRIPES!
(FOR SPEED)
snakebot 3000!!

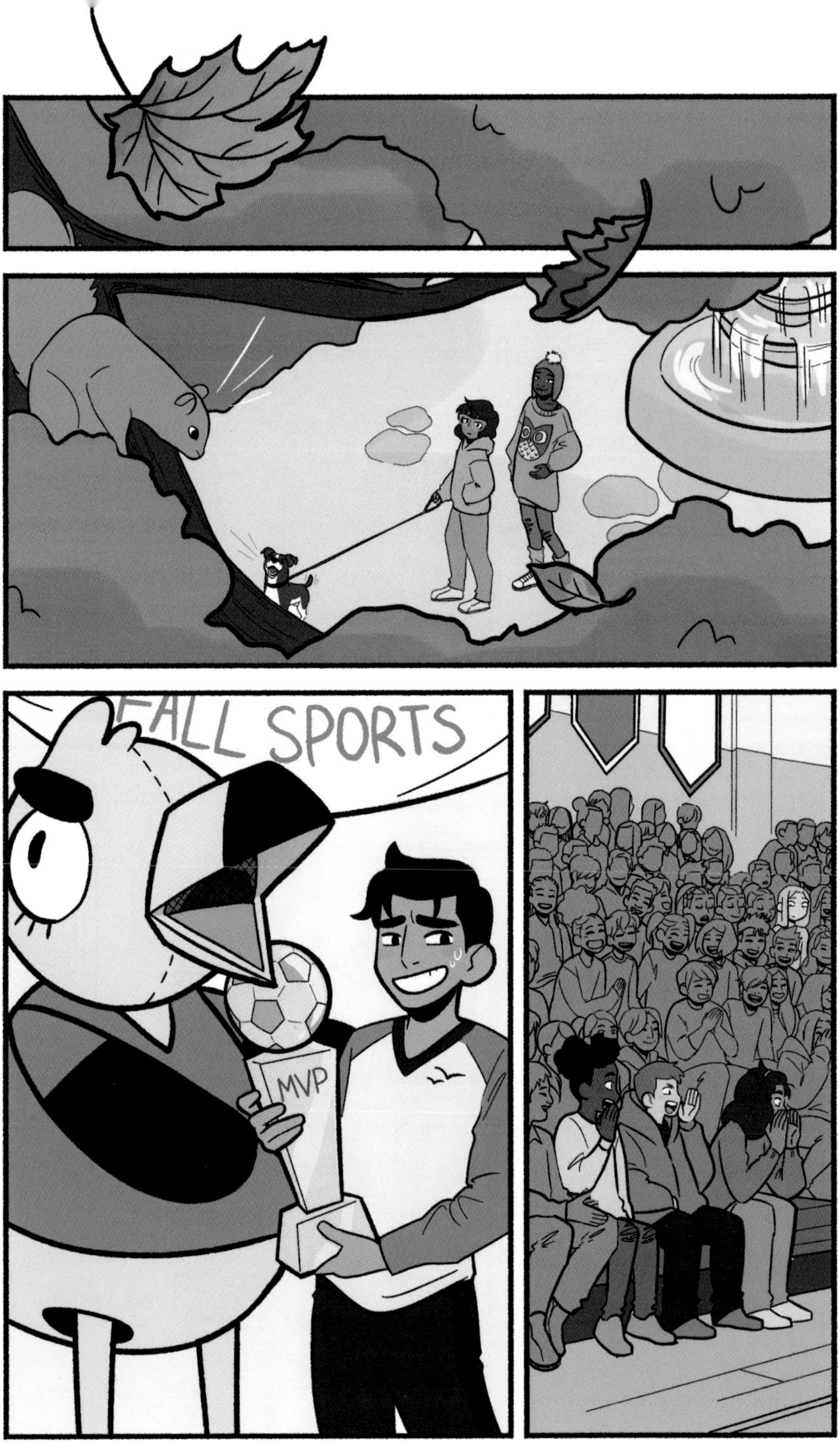
FALL SPORTS
MVP

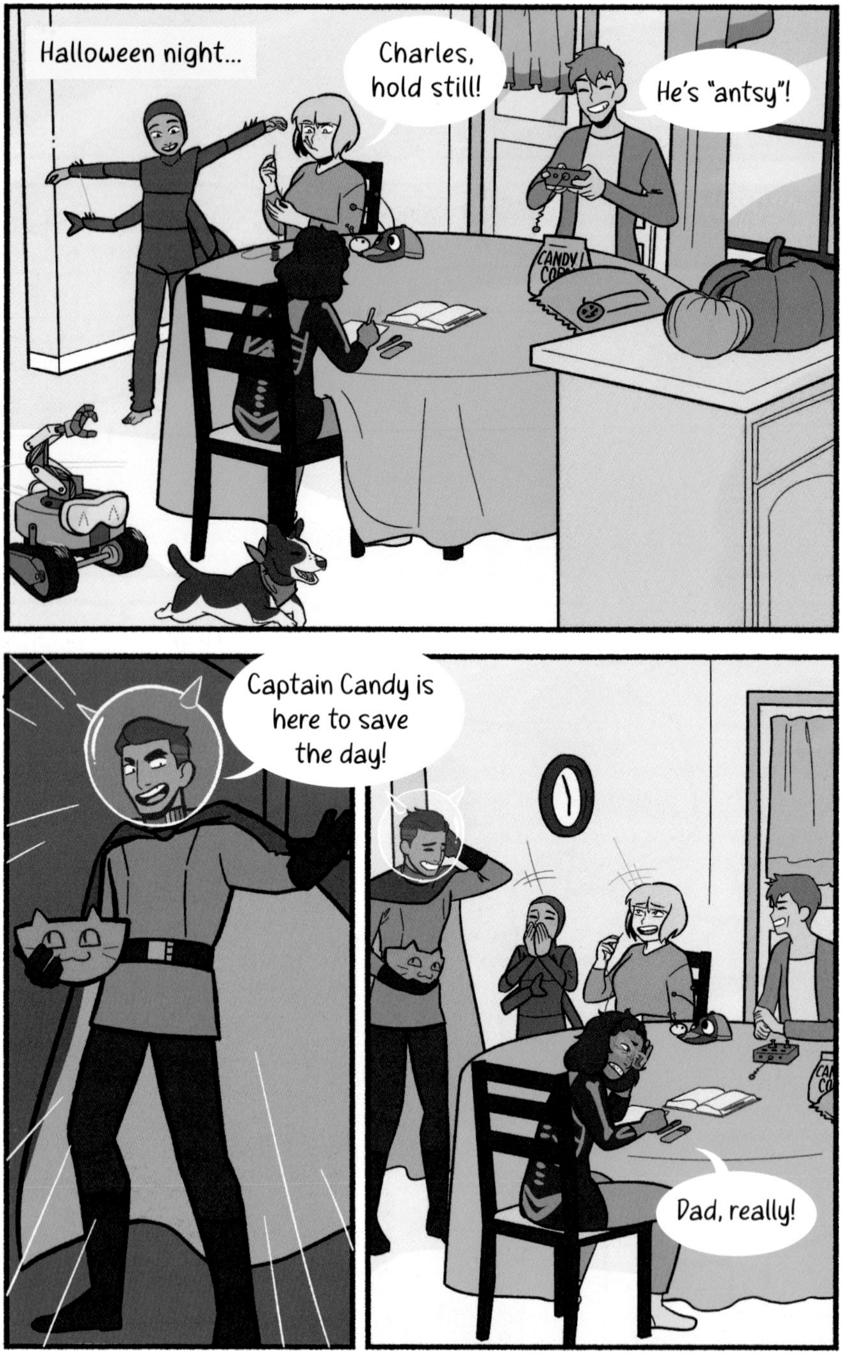
Halloween night...
Charles, hold still!
He's "antsy"!
Captain Candy is here to save the day!
Dad, really!

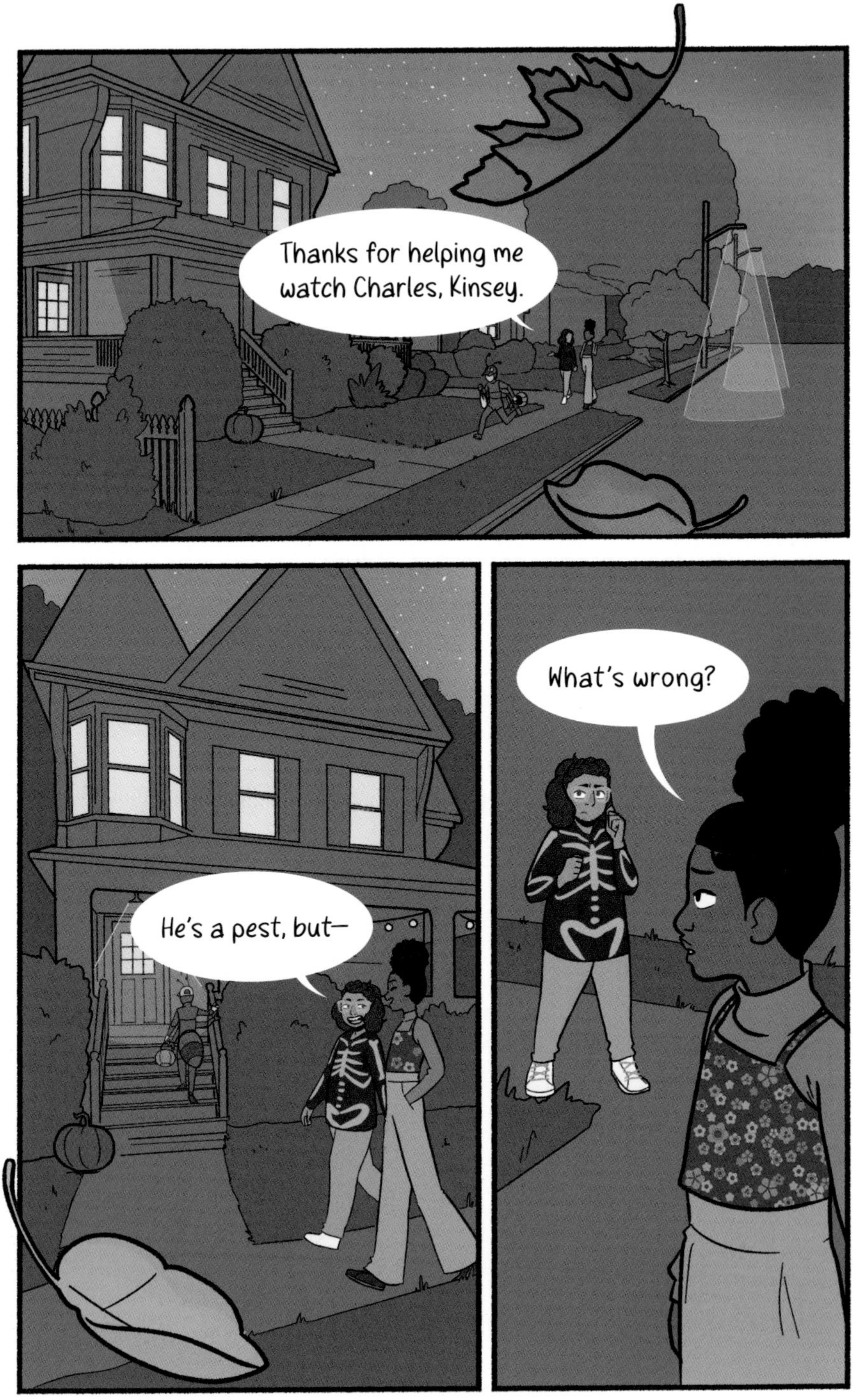
Thanks for helping me watch Charles, Kinsey.
He's a pest, but—
What's wrong?

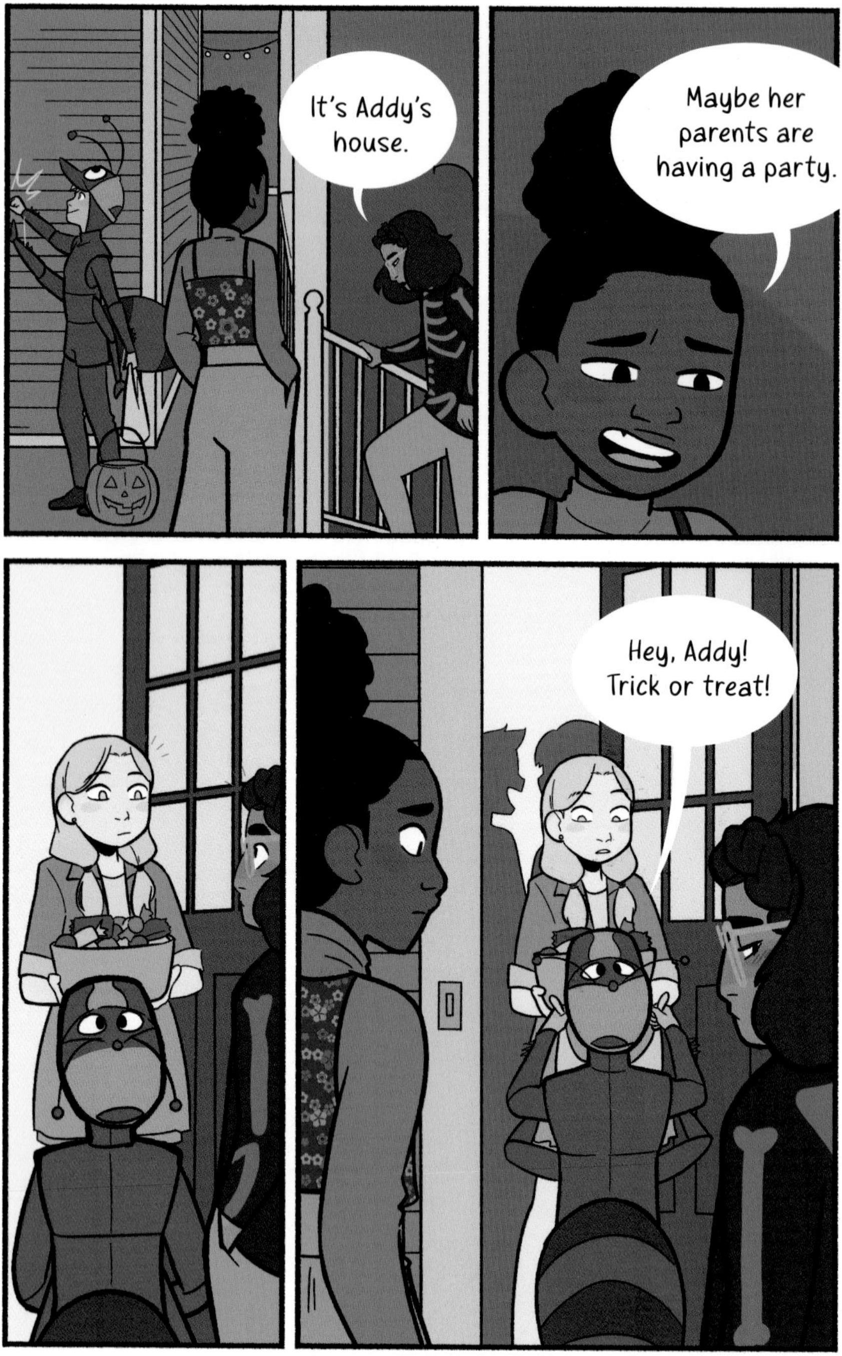
It's Addy's house.
Maybe her parents are having a party.
Hey, Addy! Trick or treat!

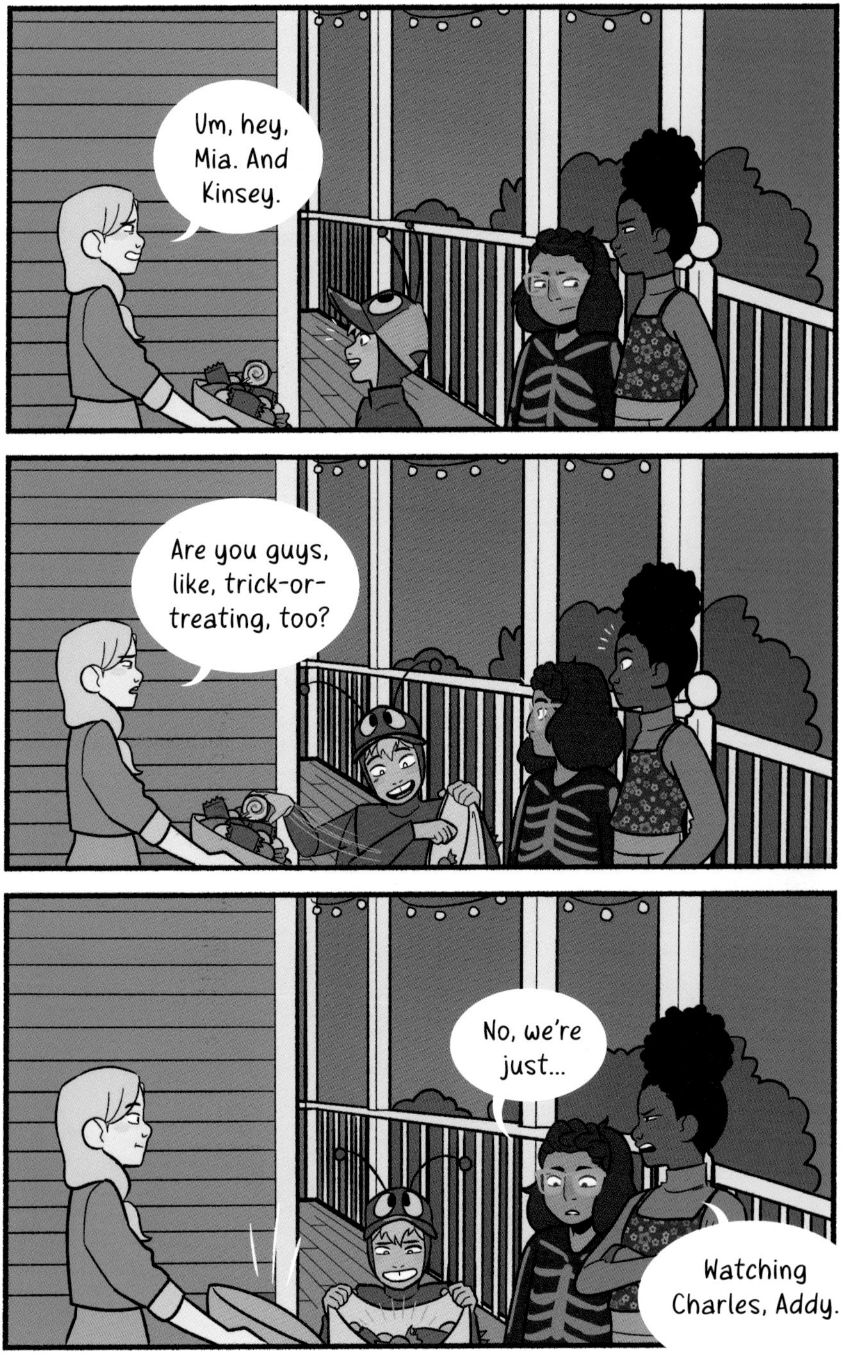
Um, hey, Mia. And Kinsey.
Are you guys, like, trick-or-treating, too?
No, we're just...
Watching Charles, Addy.

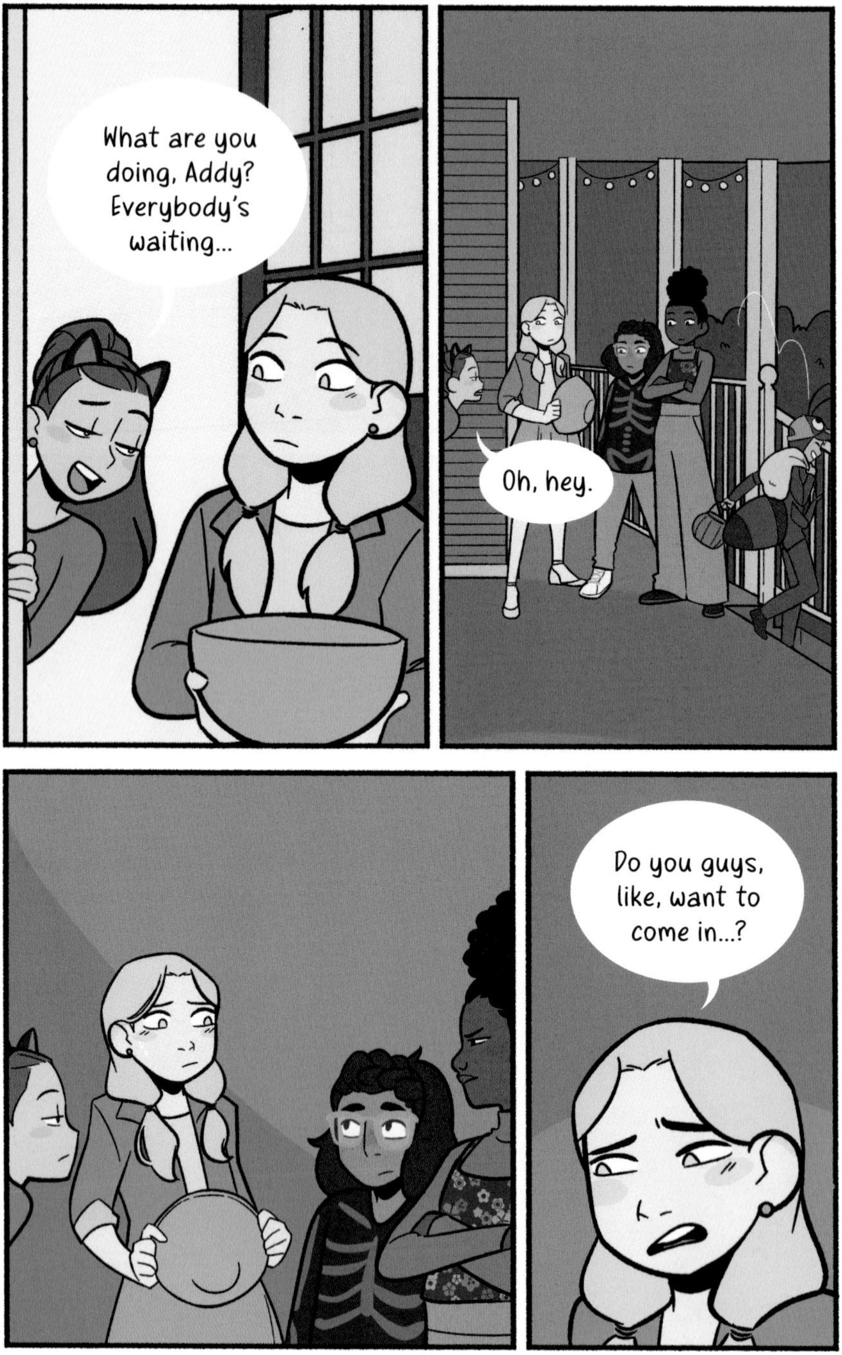
What are you doing, Addy? Everybody's waiting...
Oh, hey.
Do you guys, like, want to come in...?

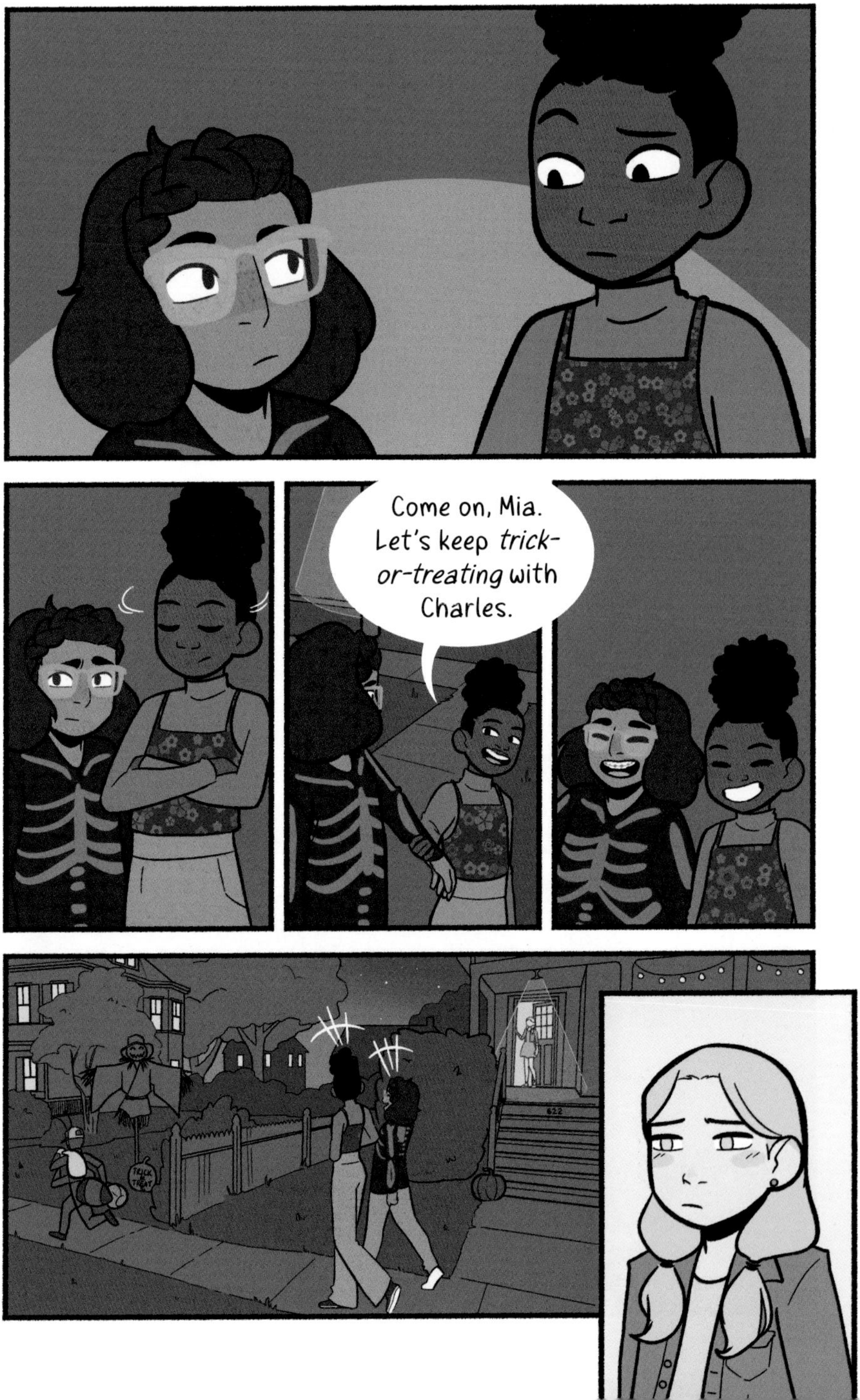
Come on, Mia. Let's keep *trick-or-treating* with Charles.
TRICK OR TREAT
622

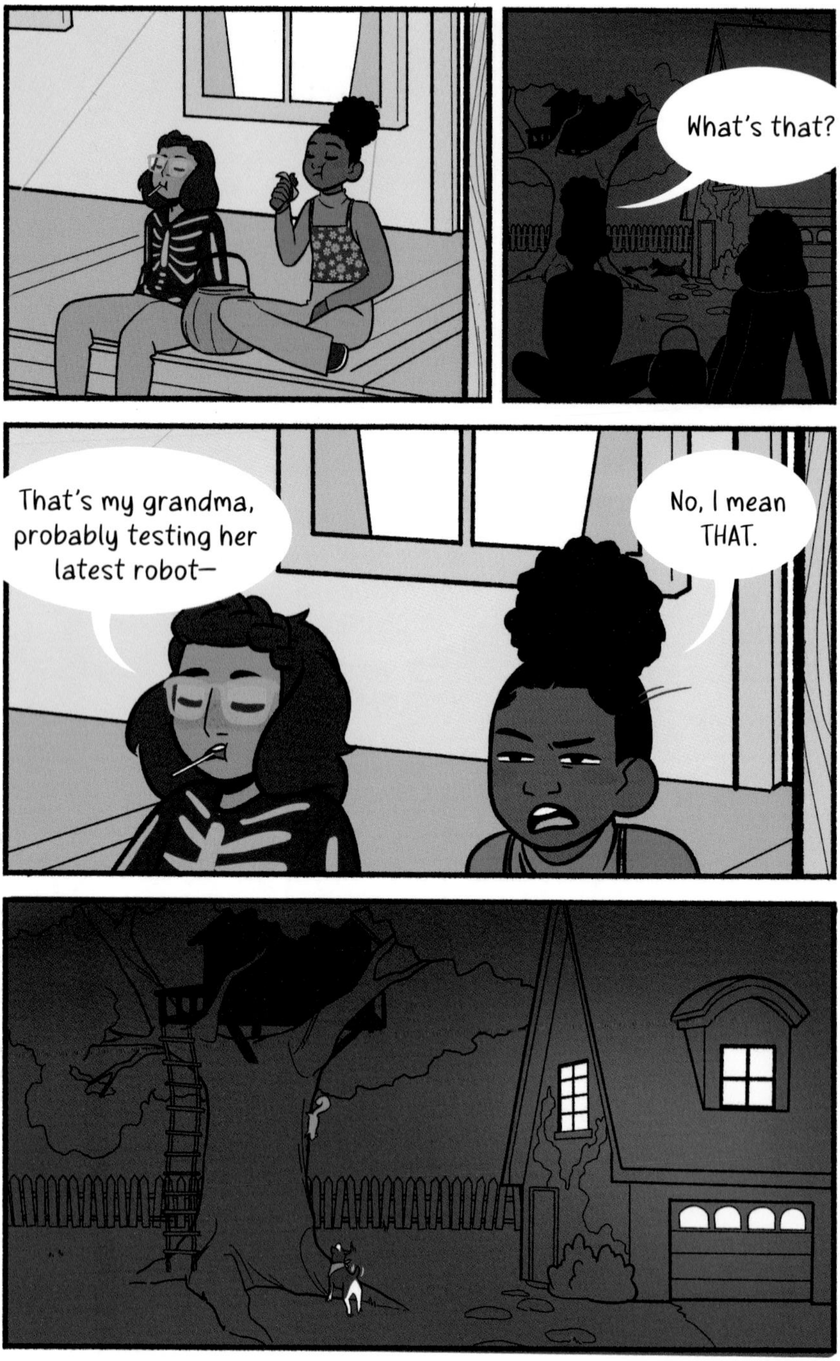
What's that?
That's my grandma, probably testing her latest robot—
No, I mean THAT.

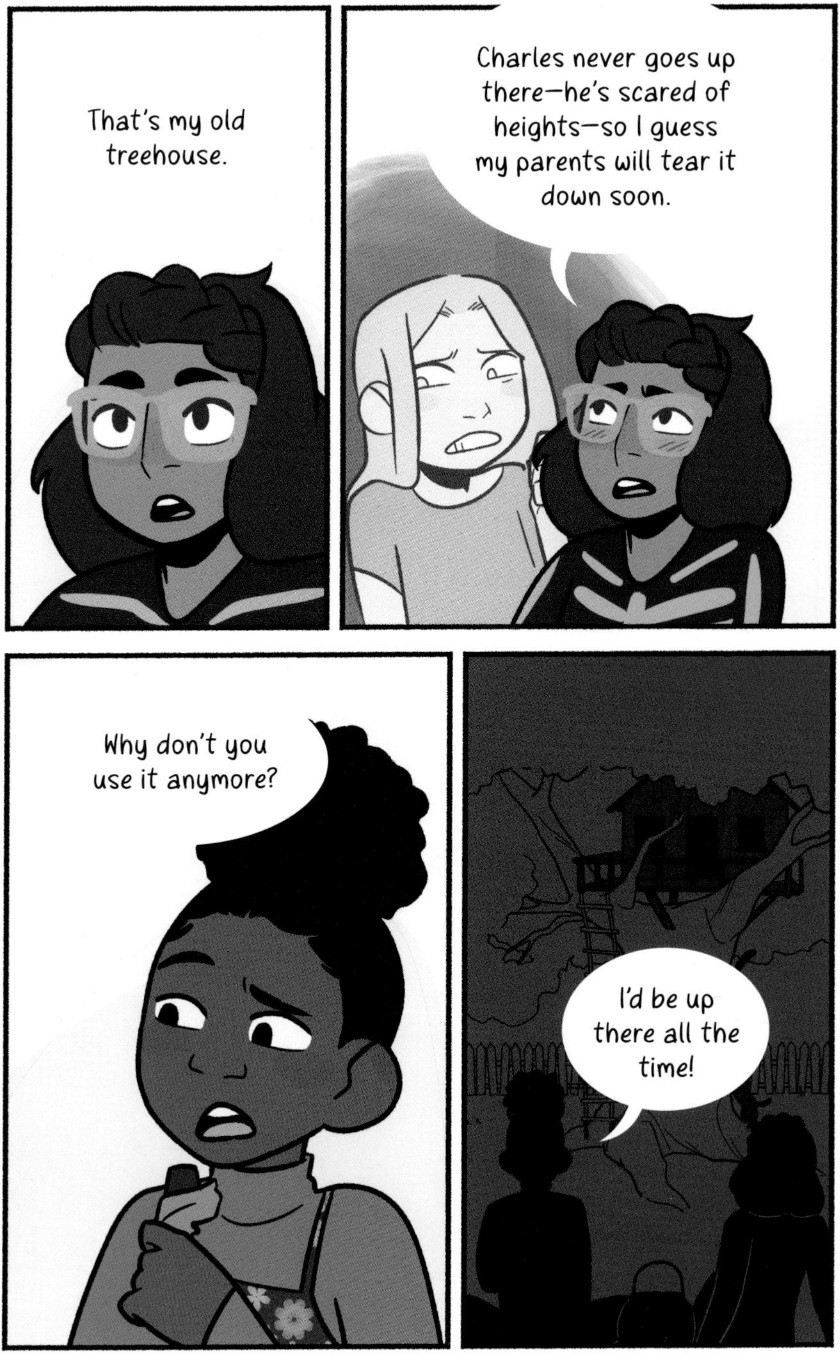

That's my old treehouse.
Charles never goes up there—he's scared of heights—so I guess my parents will tear it down soon.
Why don't you use it anymore?
I'd be up there all the time!

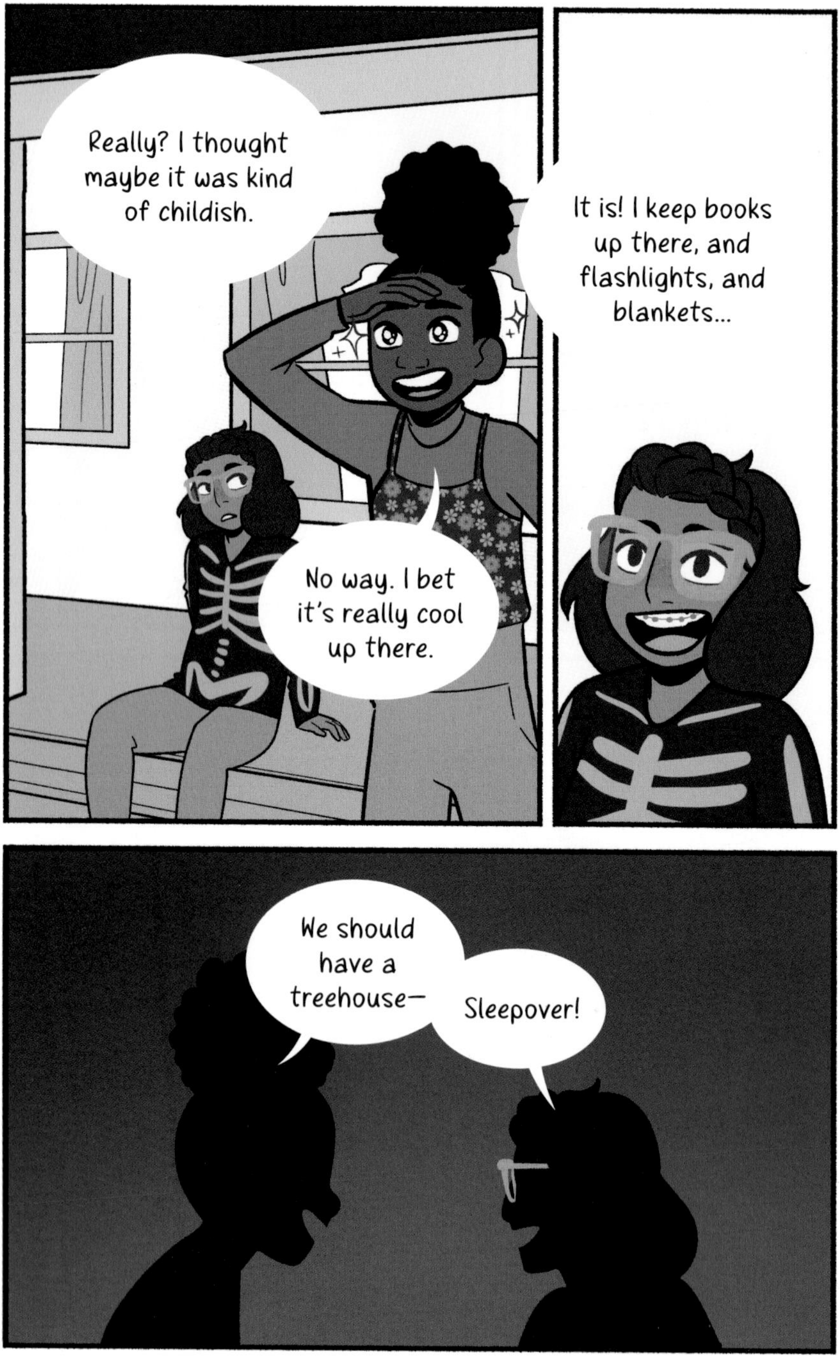
Really? I thought maybe it was kind of childish.
No way. I bet it's really cool up there.
It is! I keep books up there, and flashlights, and blankets...
We should have a treehouse—
Sleepover!

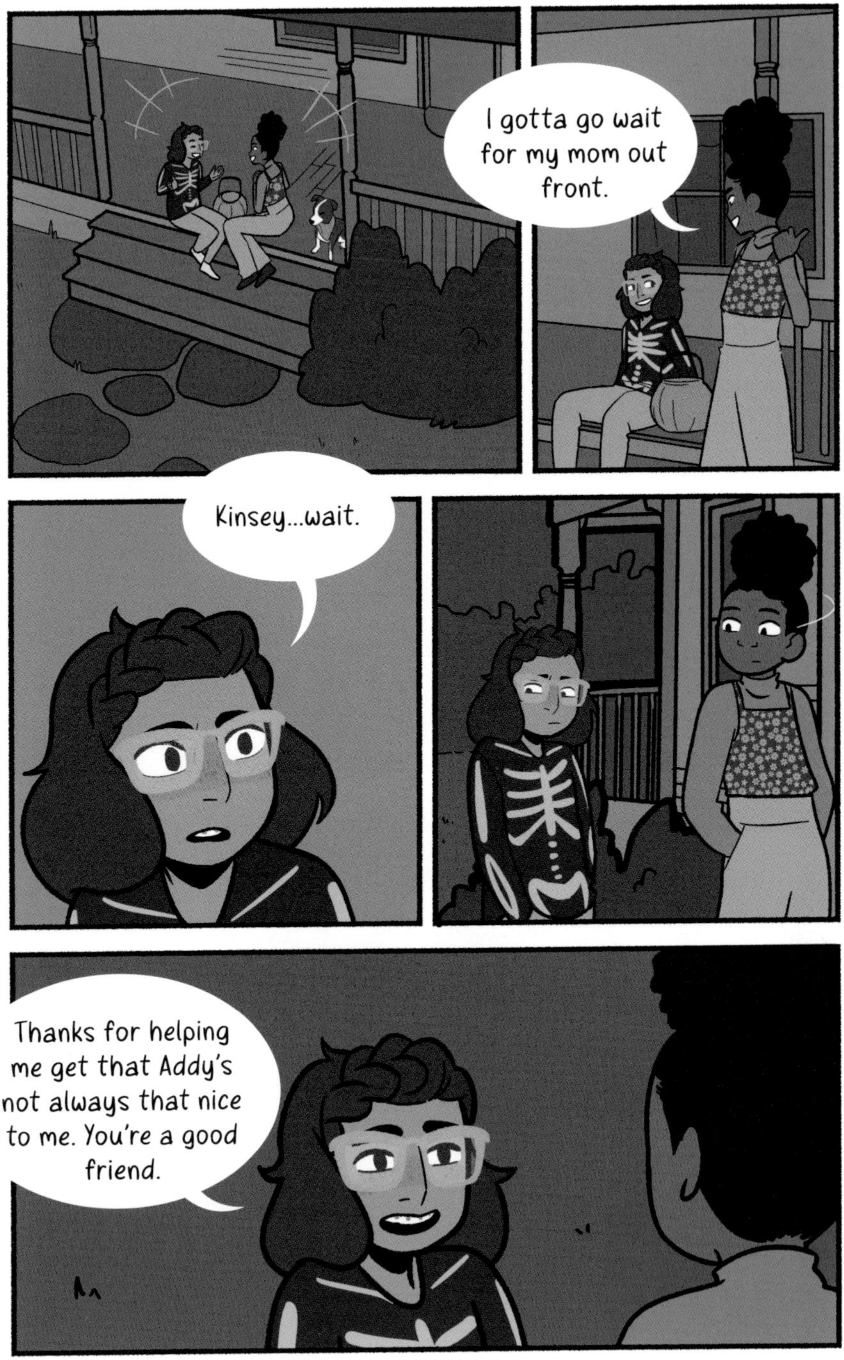
I gotta go wait for my mom out front.
Kinsey...wait.
Thanks for helping me get that Addy's not always that nice to me. You're a good friend.

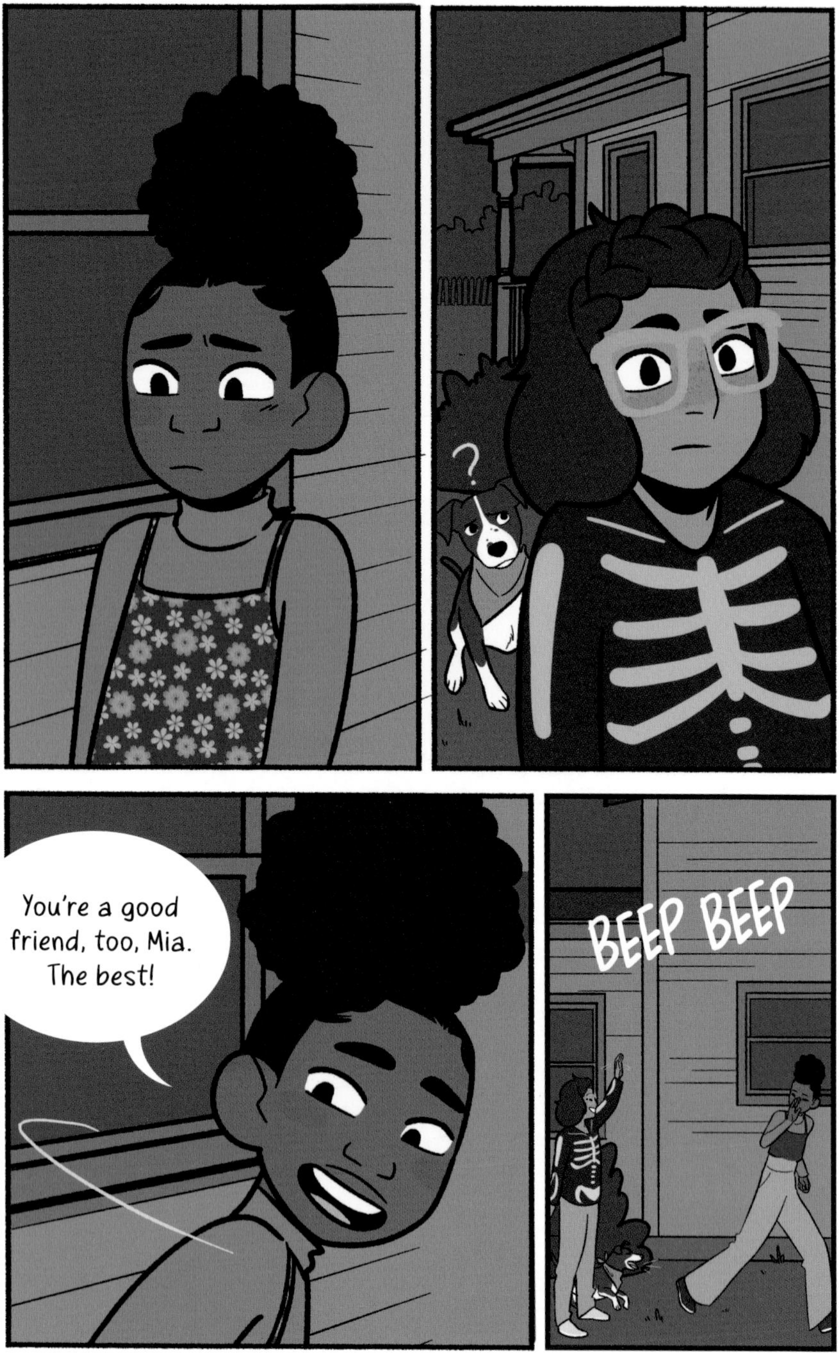
You're a good friend, too, Mia. The best!
BEEP BEEP

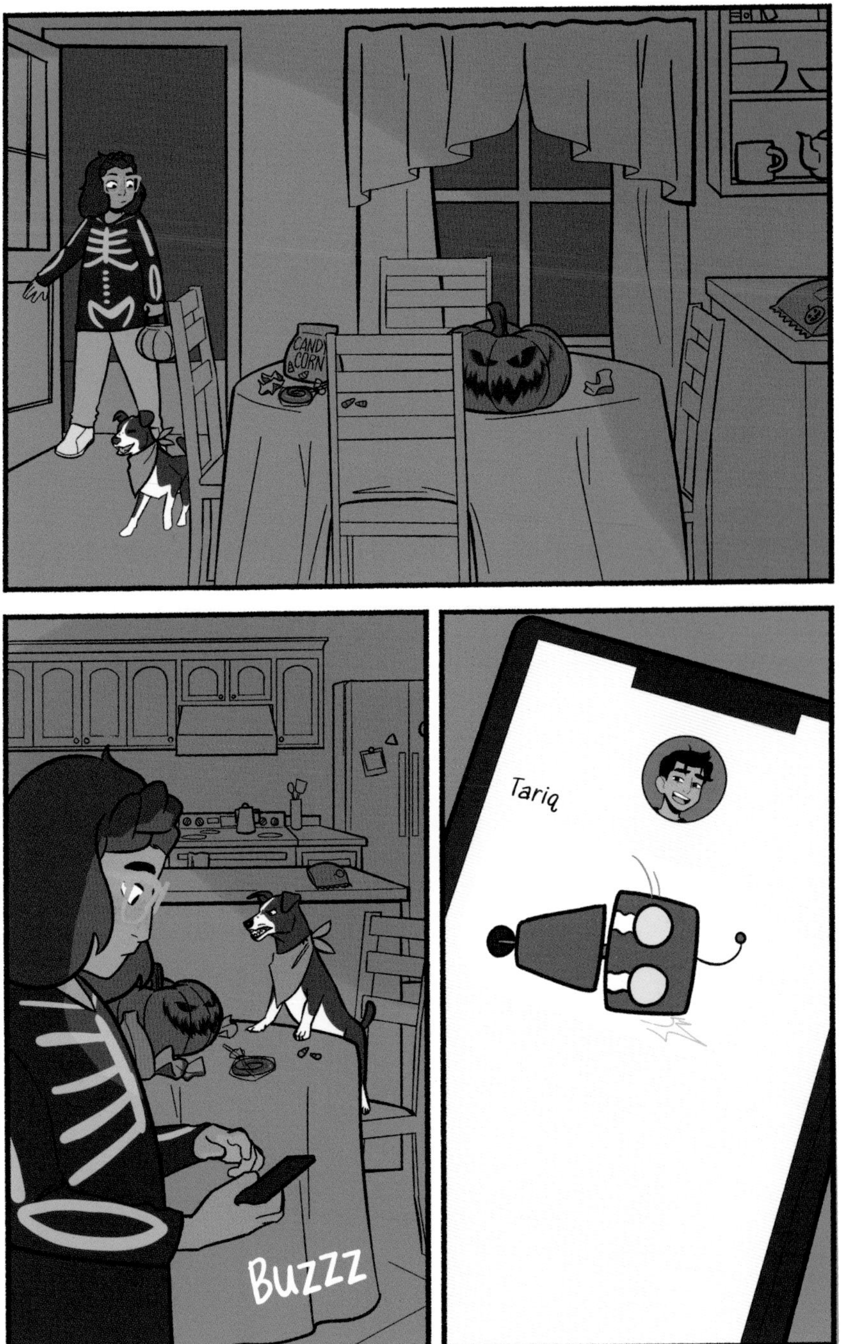

CANDY CORN
Tariq
BUZZZ

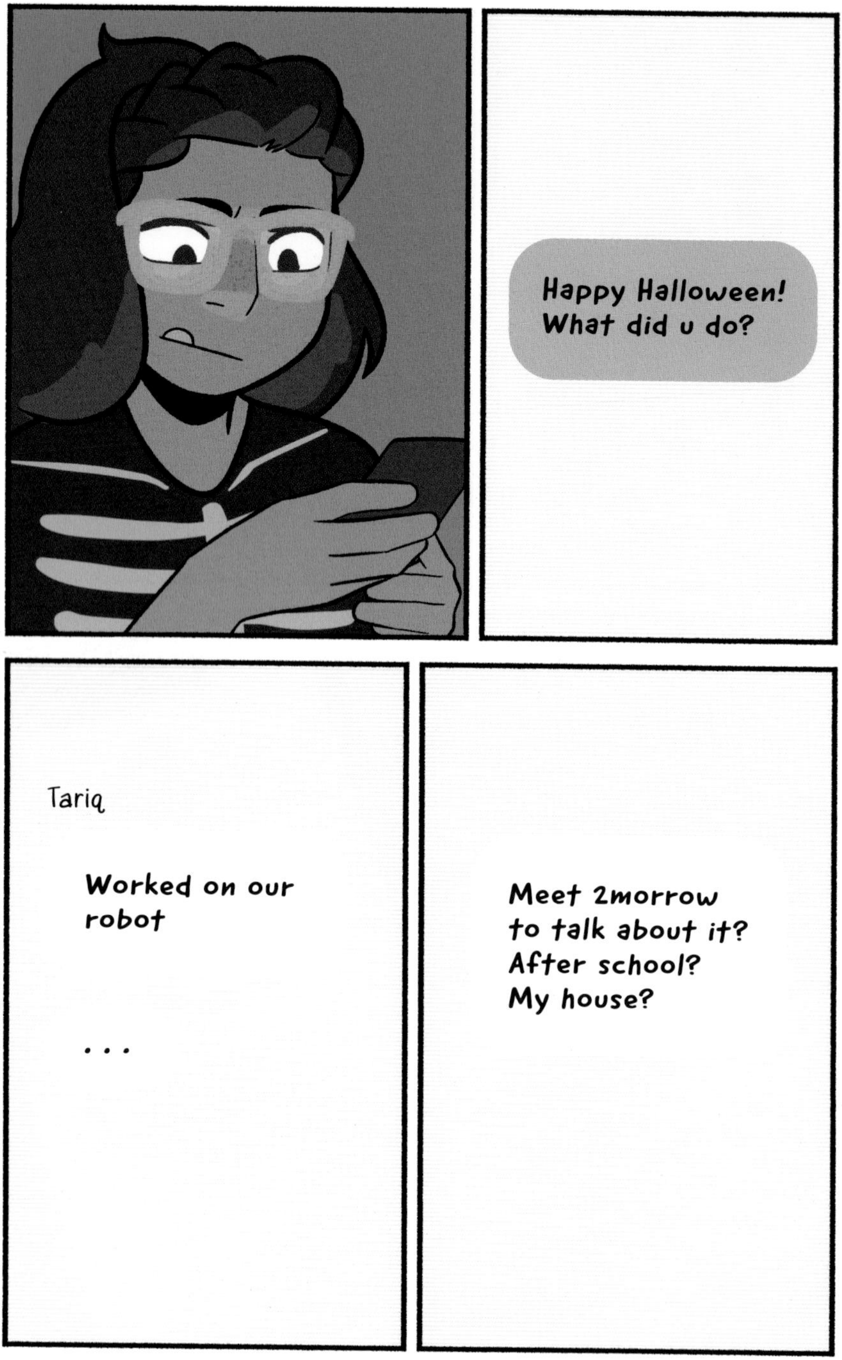
Happy Halloween!
What did u do?
Tariq
Worked on our robot
. . .
Meet 2morrow to talk about it? After school? My house?

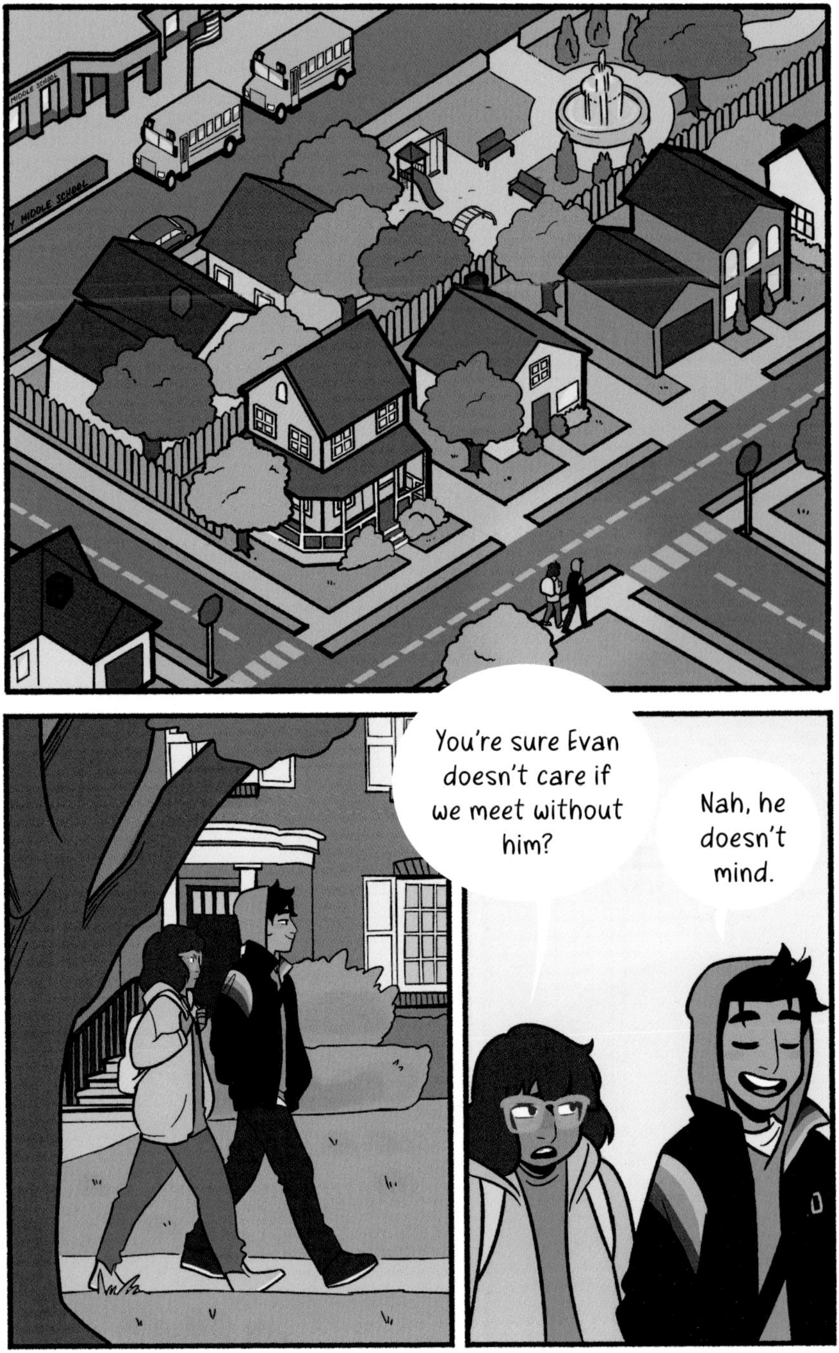
MIDDLE SCHOOL
MIDDLE SCHOOL
You're sure Evan doesn't care if we meet without him?
Nah, he doesn't mind.

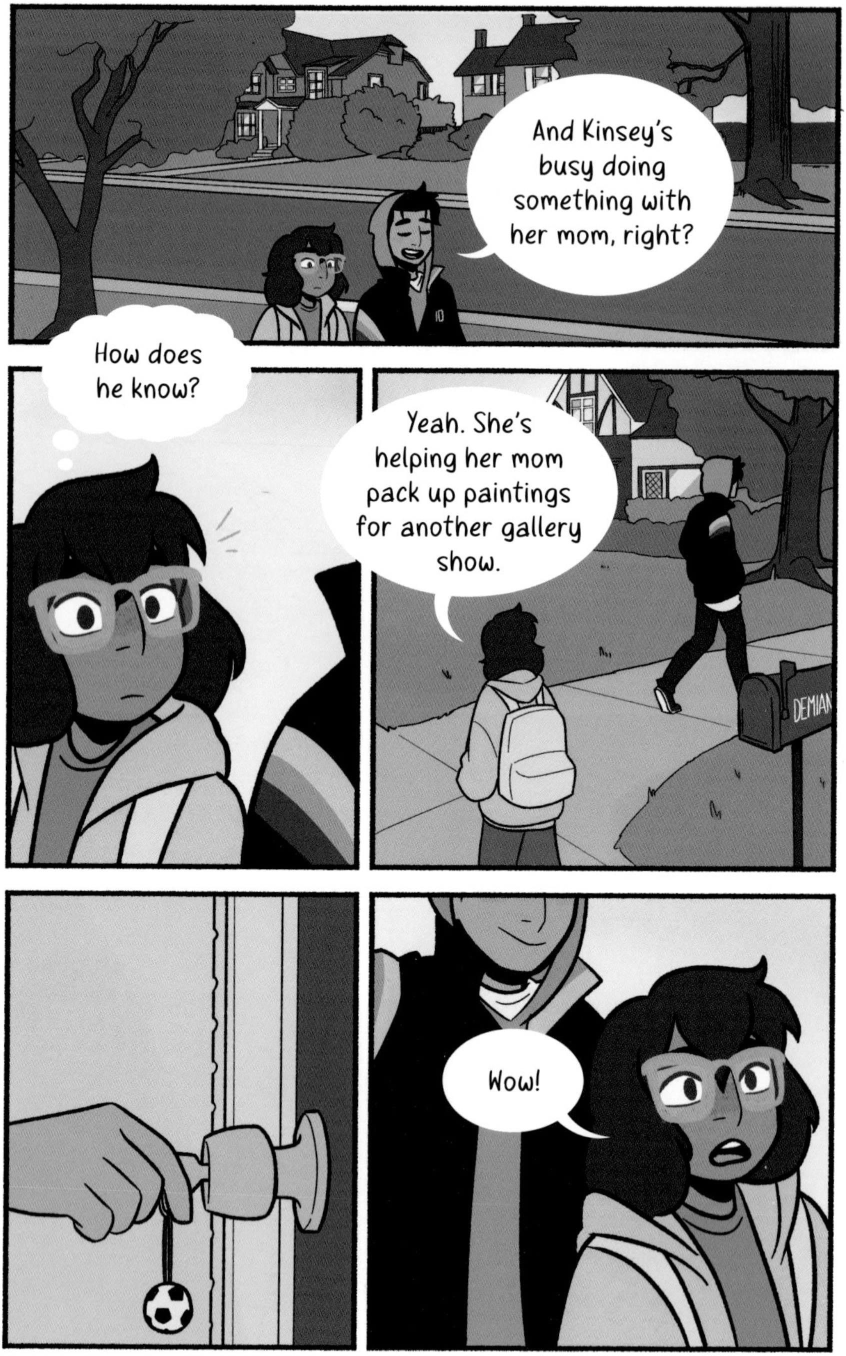
And Kinsey's busy doing something with her mom, right?
How does he know?
Yeah. She's helping her mom pack up paintings for another gallery show.
DEMIAN
Wow!

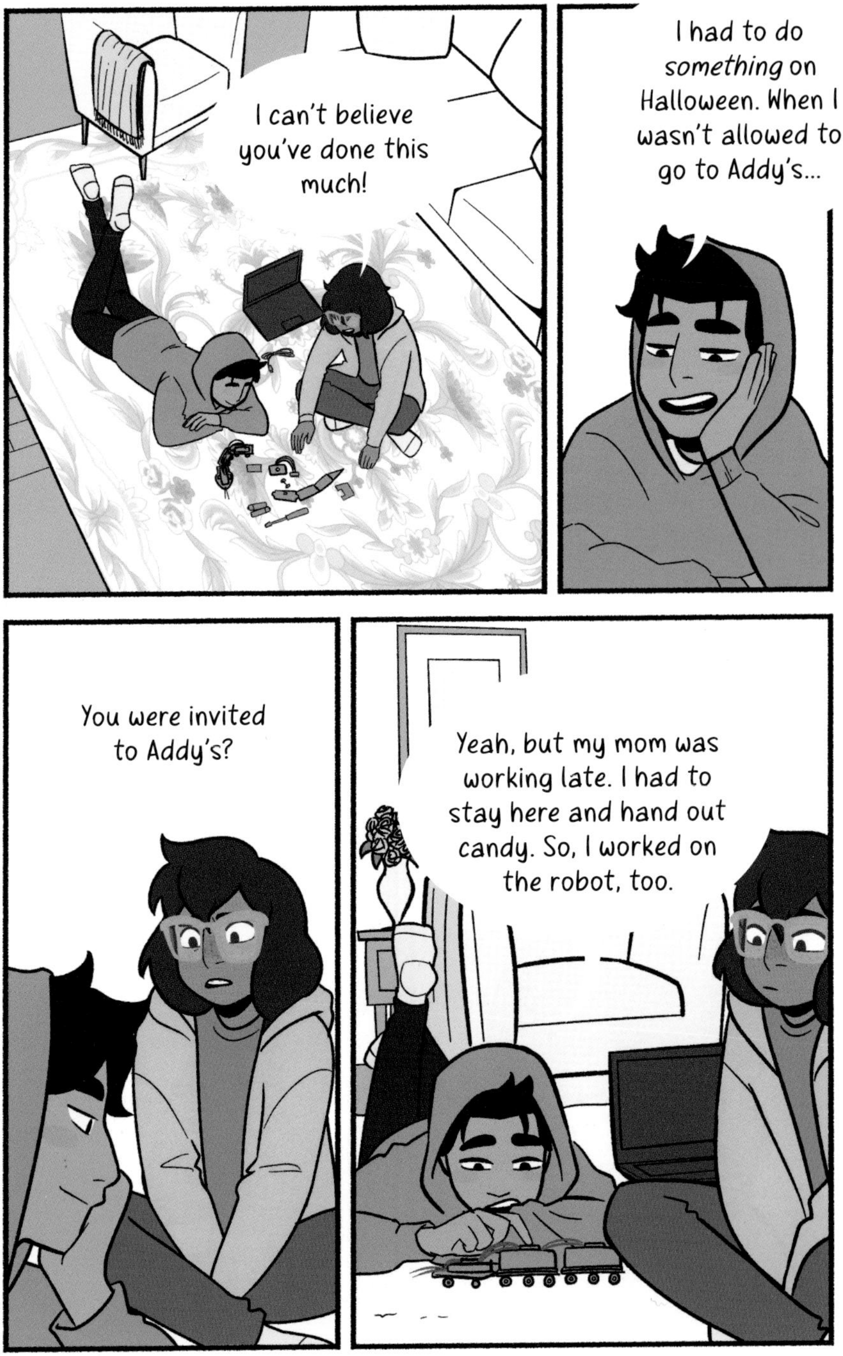
I can't believe you've done this much!
I had to do *something* on Halloween. When I wasn't allowed to go to Addy's...
You were invited to Addy's?
Yeah, but my mom was working late. I had to stay here and hand out candy. So, I worked on the robot, too.

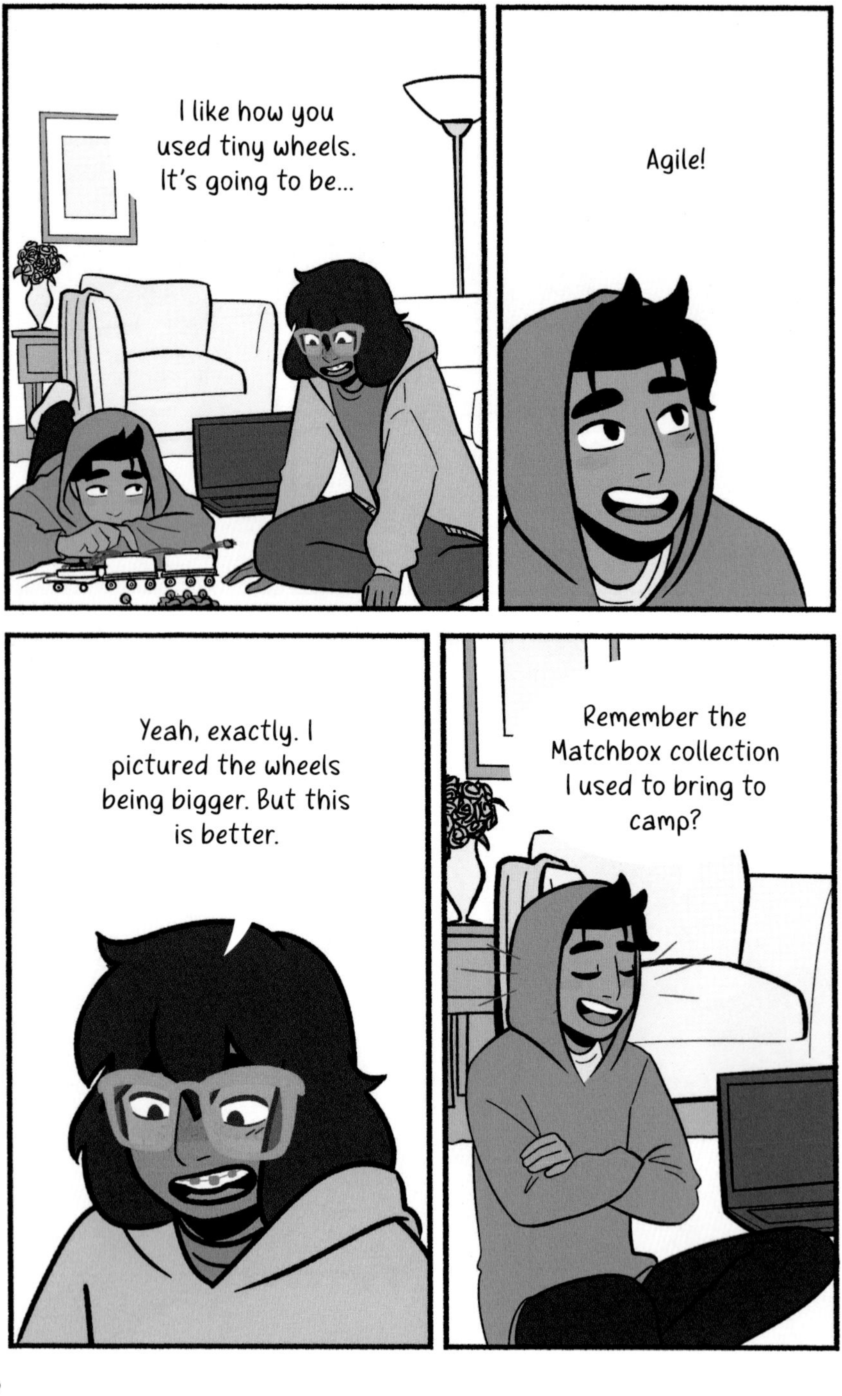
I like how you used tiny wheels. It's going to be...
Agile!
Yeah, exactly. I pictured the wheels being bigger. But this is better.
Remember the Matchbox collection I used to bring to camp?

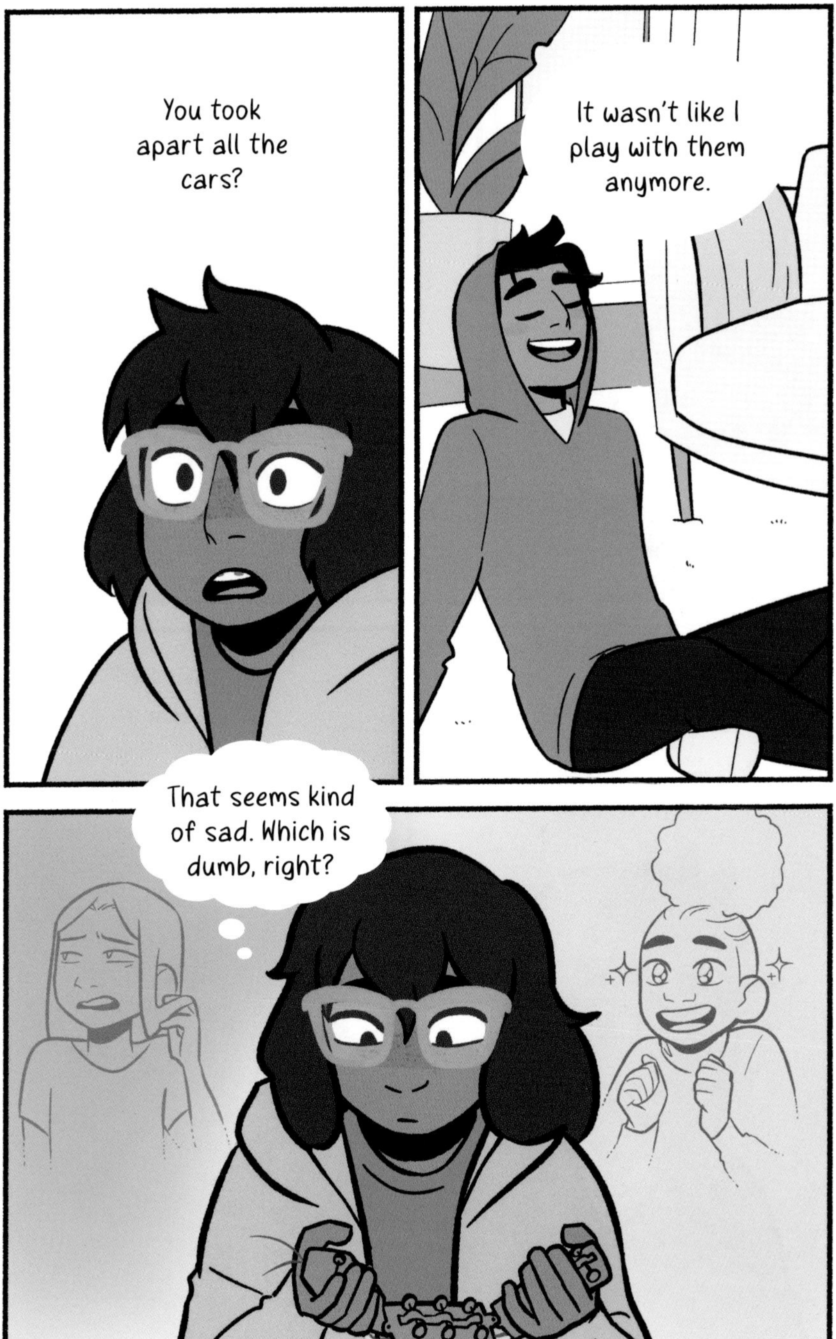
You took apart all the cars?
It wasn't like I play with them anymore.
That seems kind of sad. Which is dumb, right?

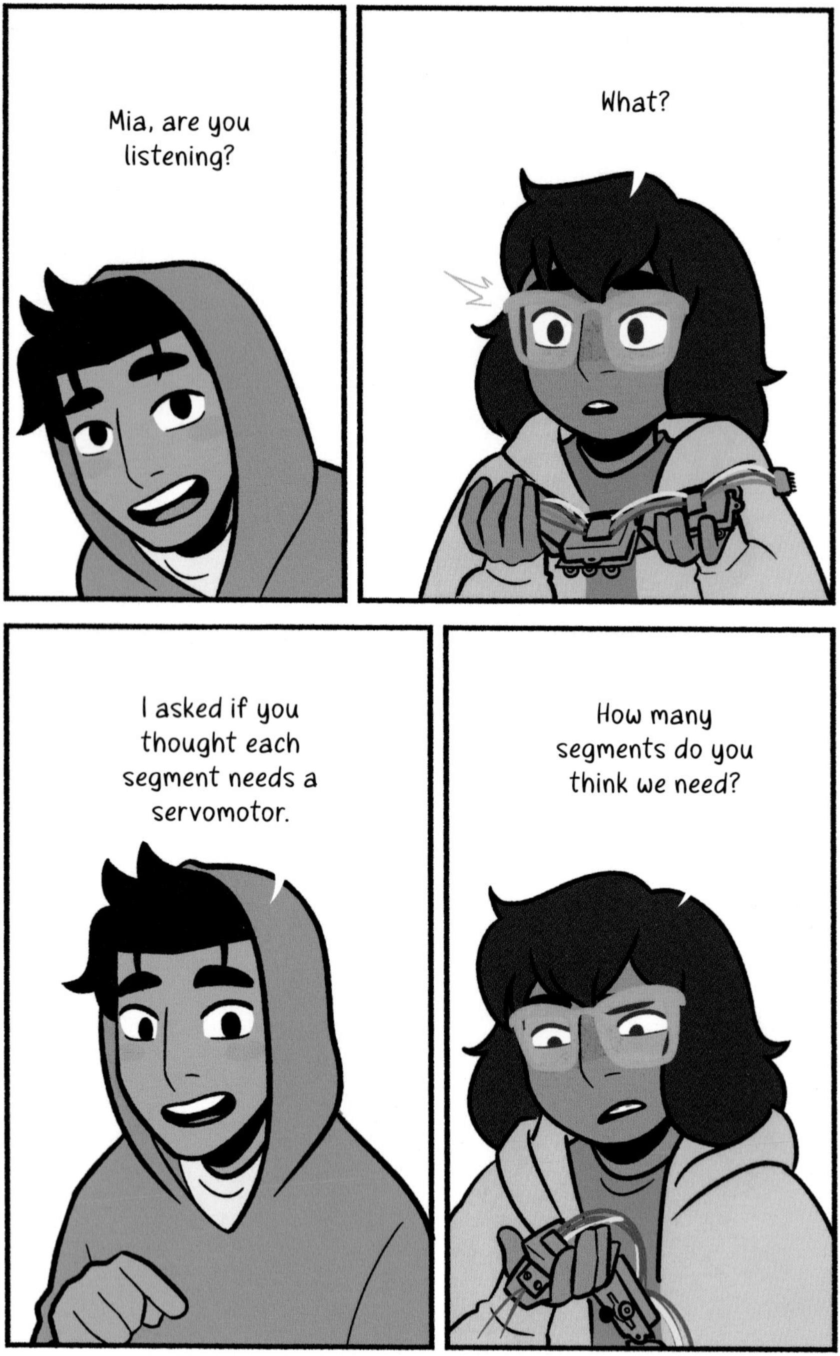
Mia, are you listening?
What?
I asked if you thought each segment needs a servomotor.
How many segments do you think we need?

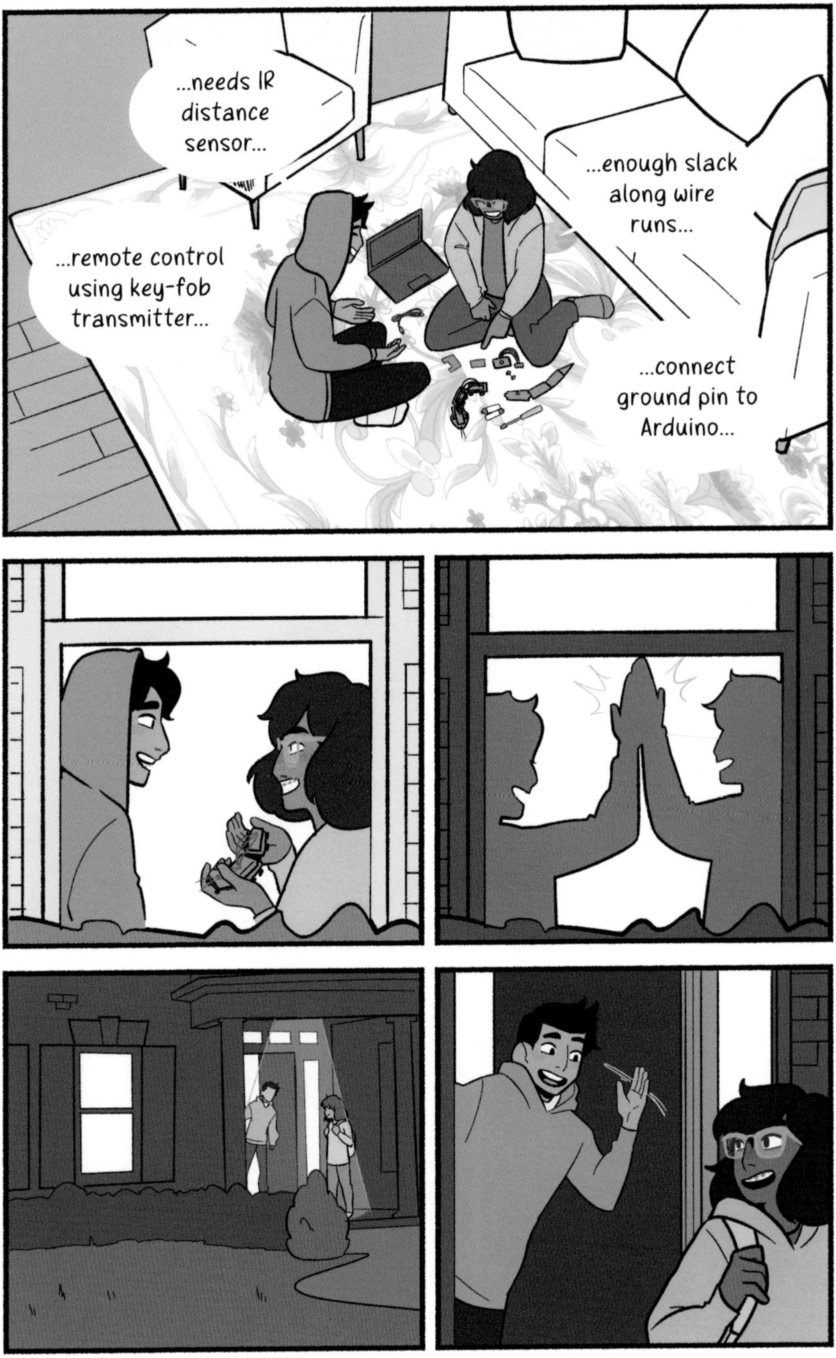
...needs IR distance sensor...
...remote control using key-fob transmitter...
...enough slack along wire runs...
...connect ground pin to Arduino...

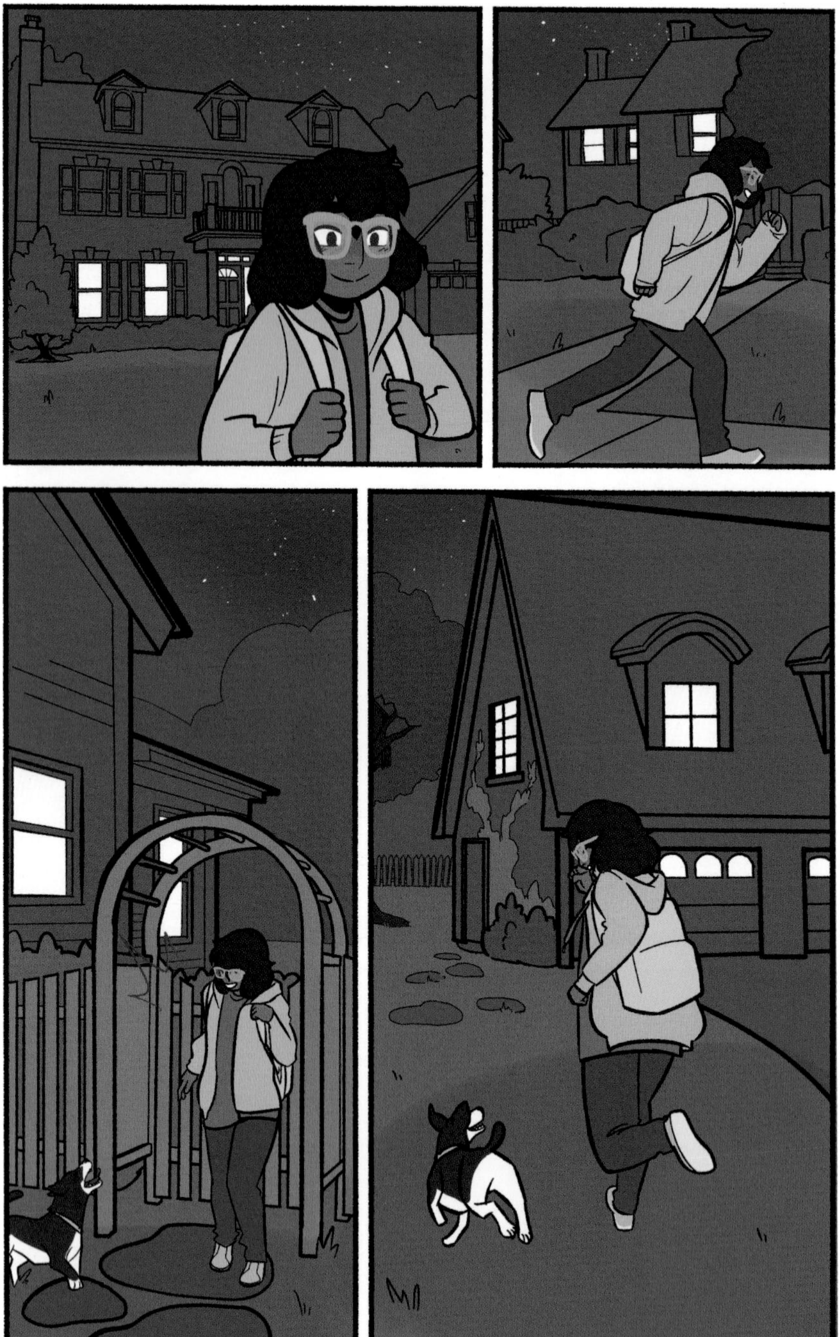

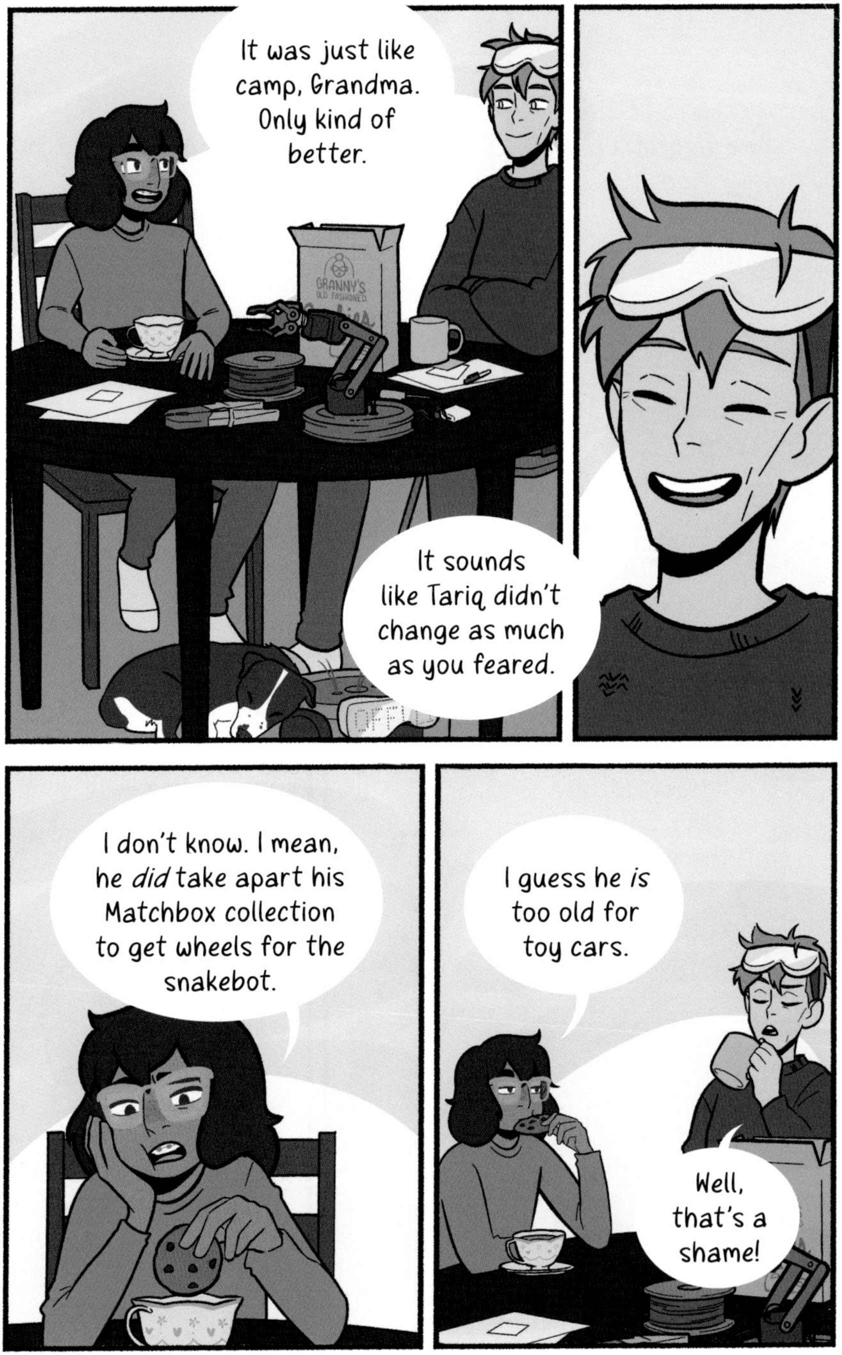
It was just like camp, Grandma. Only kind of better.
GRANNY'S OLD FASHIONED
It sounds like Tariq didn't change as much as you feared.
I don't know. I mean, he *did* take apart his Matchbox collection to get wheels for the snakebot.
I guess he *is* too old for toy cars.
Well, that's a shame!

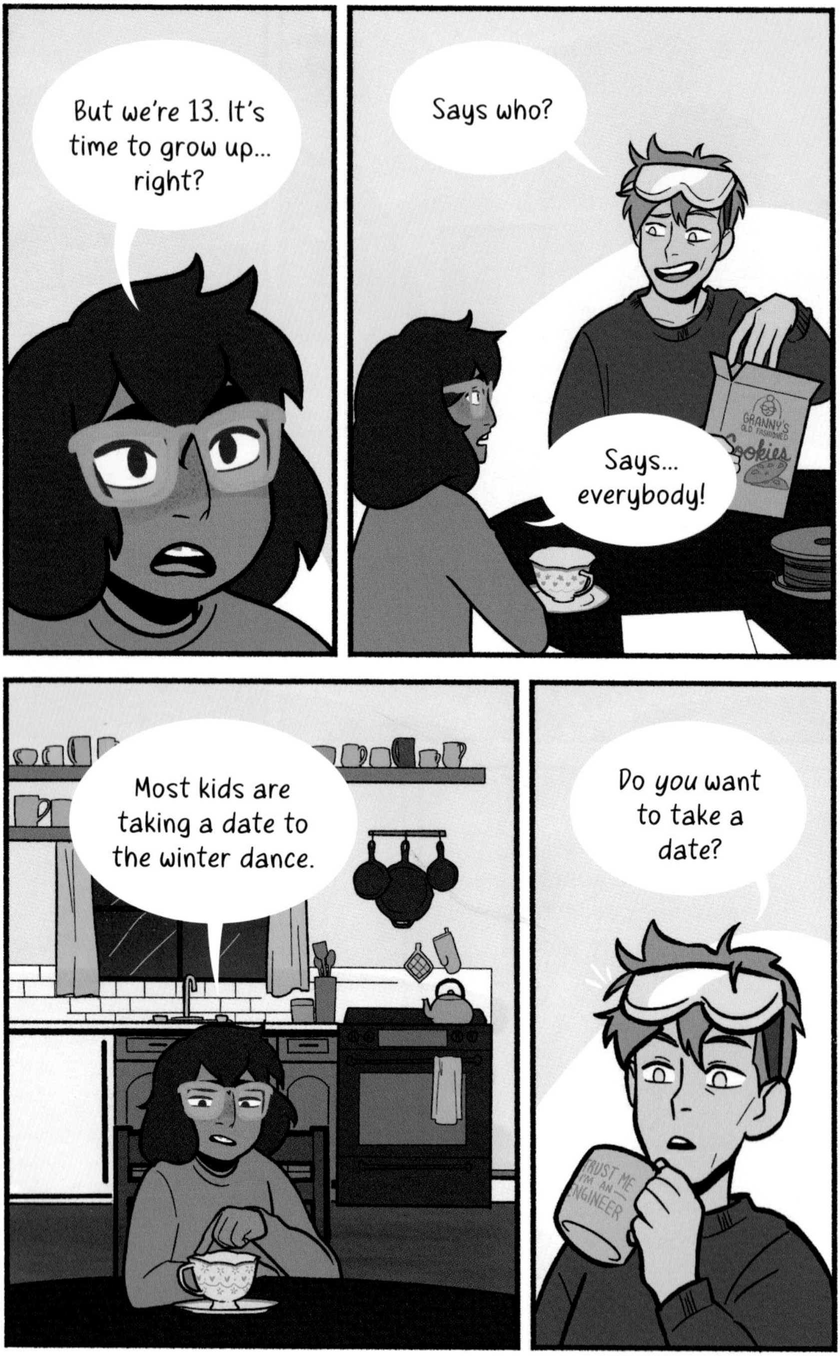
But we're 13. It's time to grow up... right?
Says who?
GRANNY'S OLD FASHIONED Cookies
Says... everybody!
Most kids are taking a date to the winter dance.
Do *you* want to take a date?
TRUST ME I'M AN ENGINEER

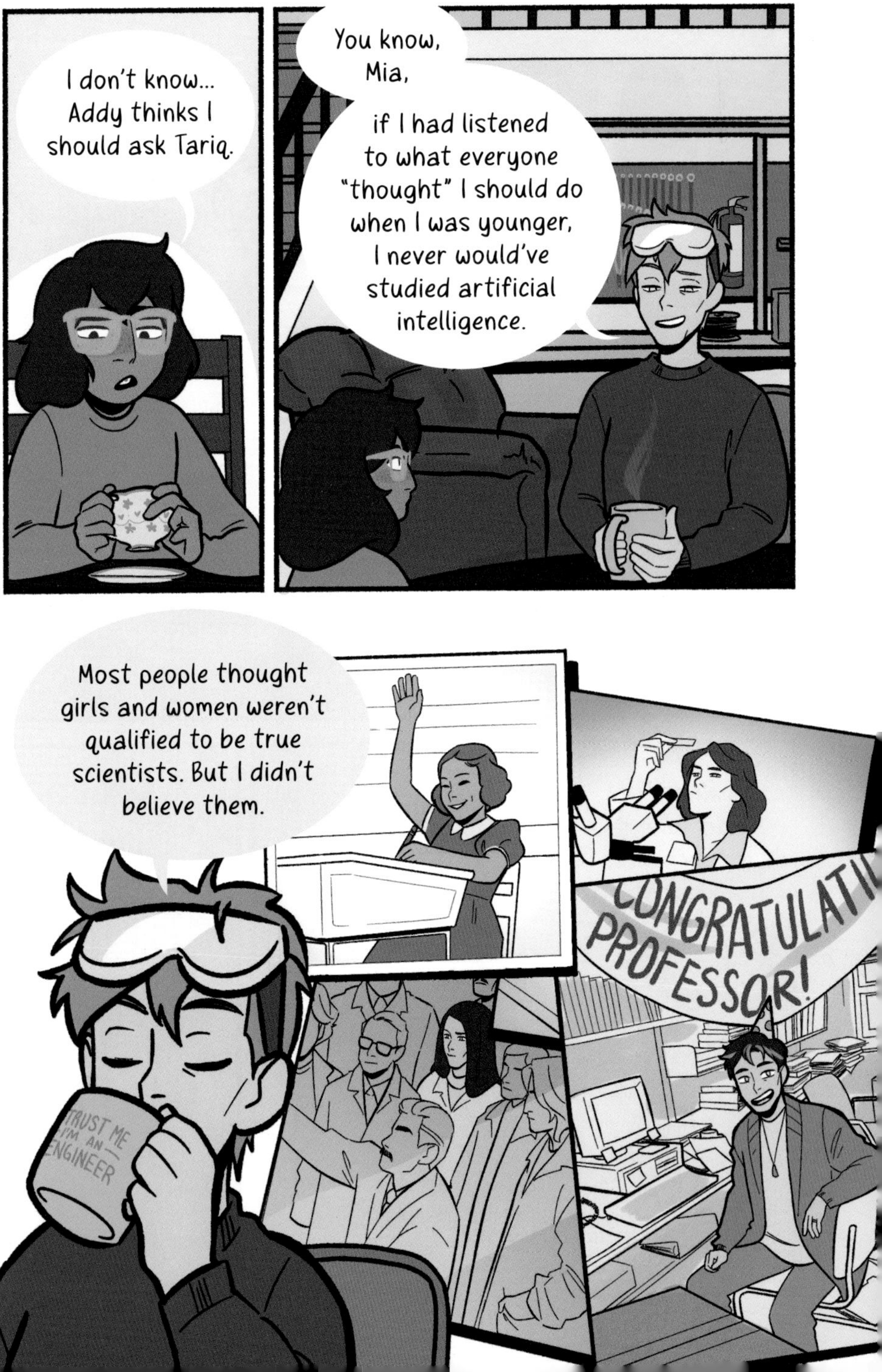
I don't know... Addy thinks I should ask Tariq.
You know, Mia,
if I had listened to what everyone "thought" I should do when I was younger, I never would've studied artificial intelligence.
Most people thought girls and women weren't qualified to be true scientists. But I didn't believe them.
CONGRATULATI
PROFESSOR!
TRUST ME I'M AN ENGINEER

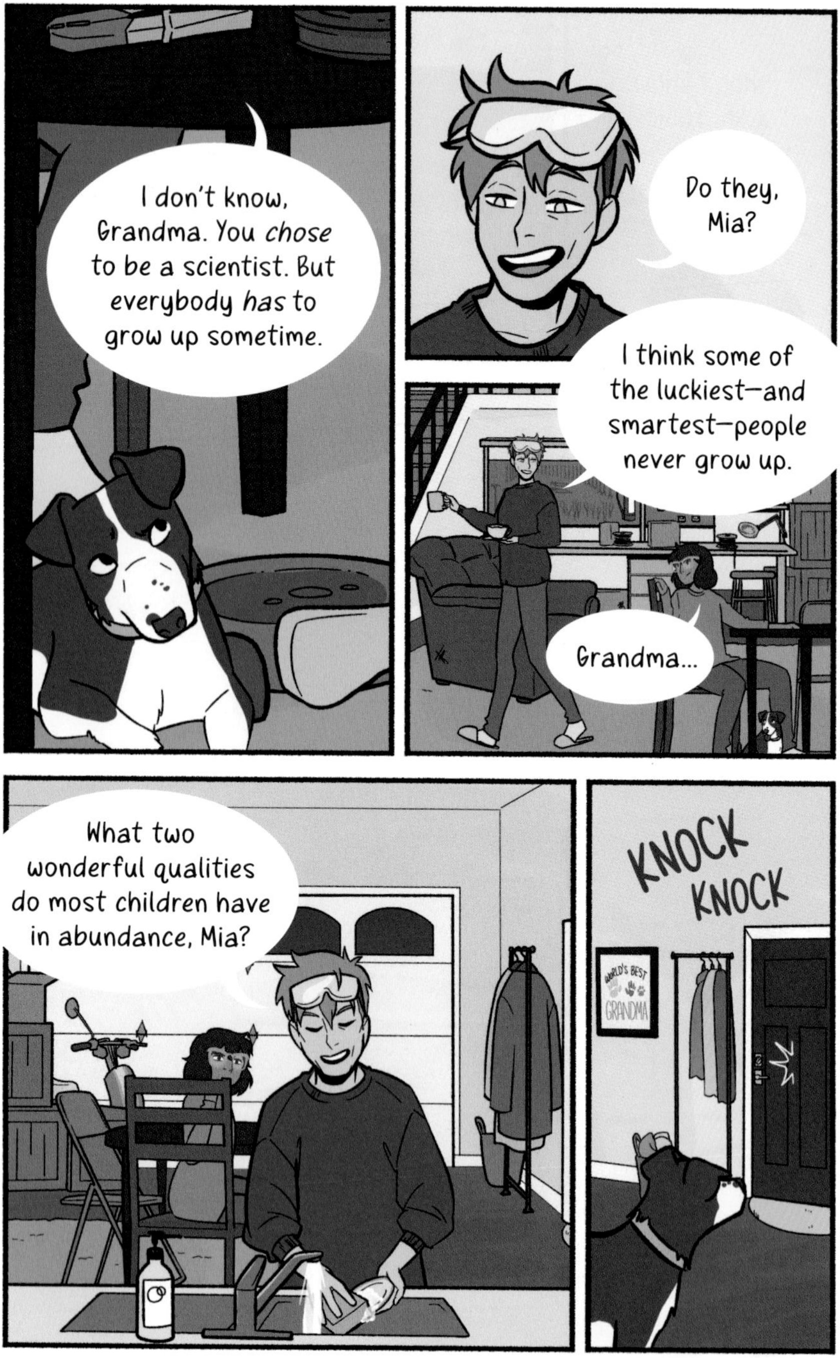
I don't know, Grandma. You *chose* to be a scientist. But everybody *has* to grow up sometime.
Do they, Mia?
I think some of the luckiest—and smartest—people never grow up.
Grandma...
What two wonderful qualities do most children have in abundance, Mia?
KNOCK KNOCK
WORLD'S BEST GRANDMA

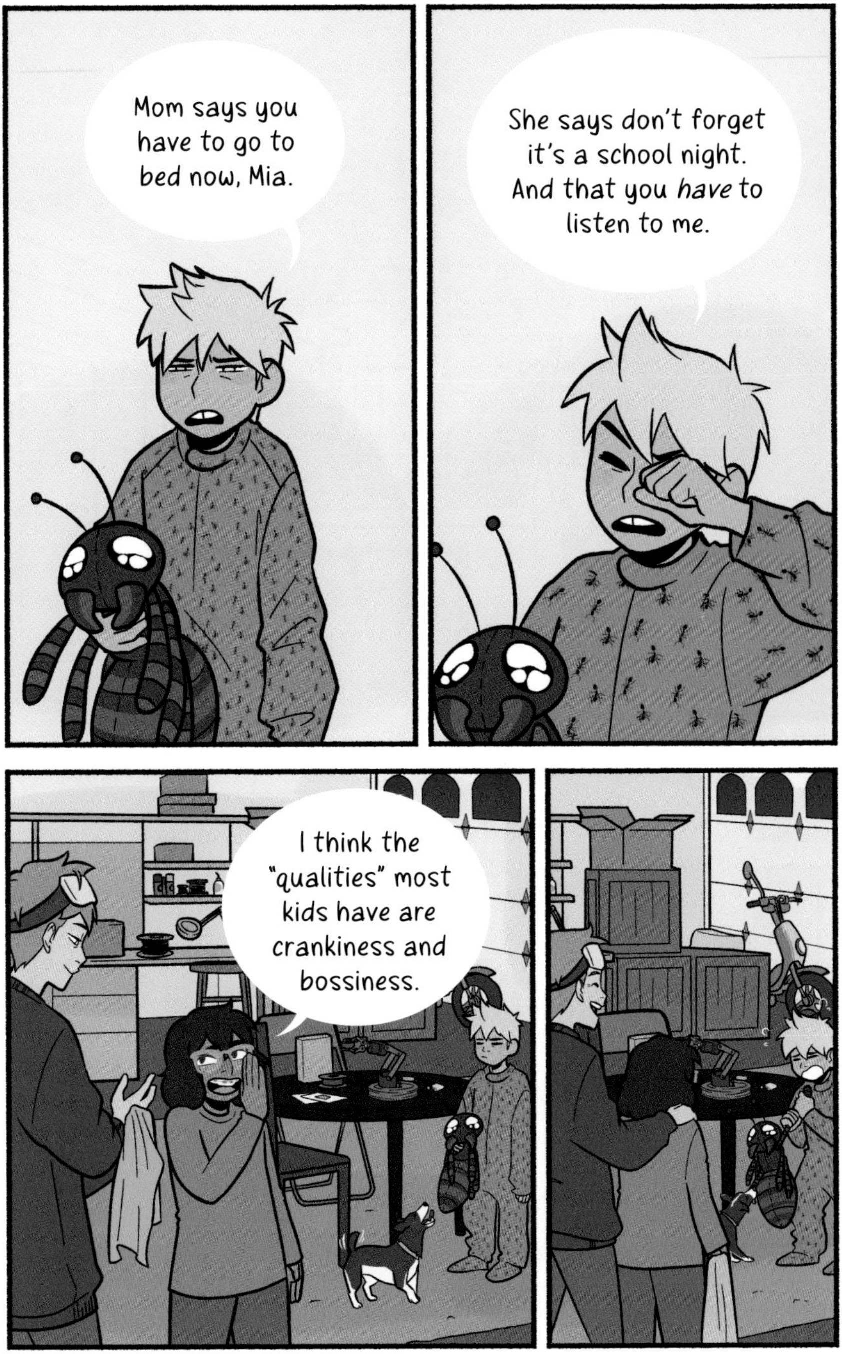
Mom says you have to go to bed now, Mia.
She says don't forget it's a school night. And that you *have* to listen to me.
I think the "qualities" most kids have are crankiness and bossiness.

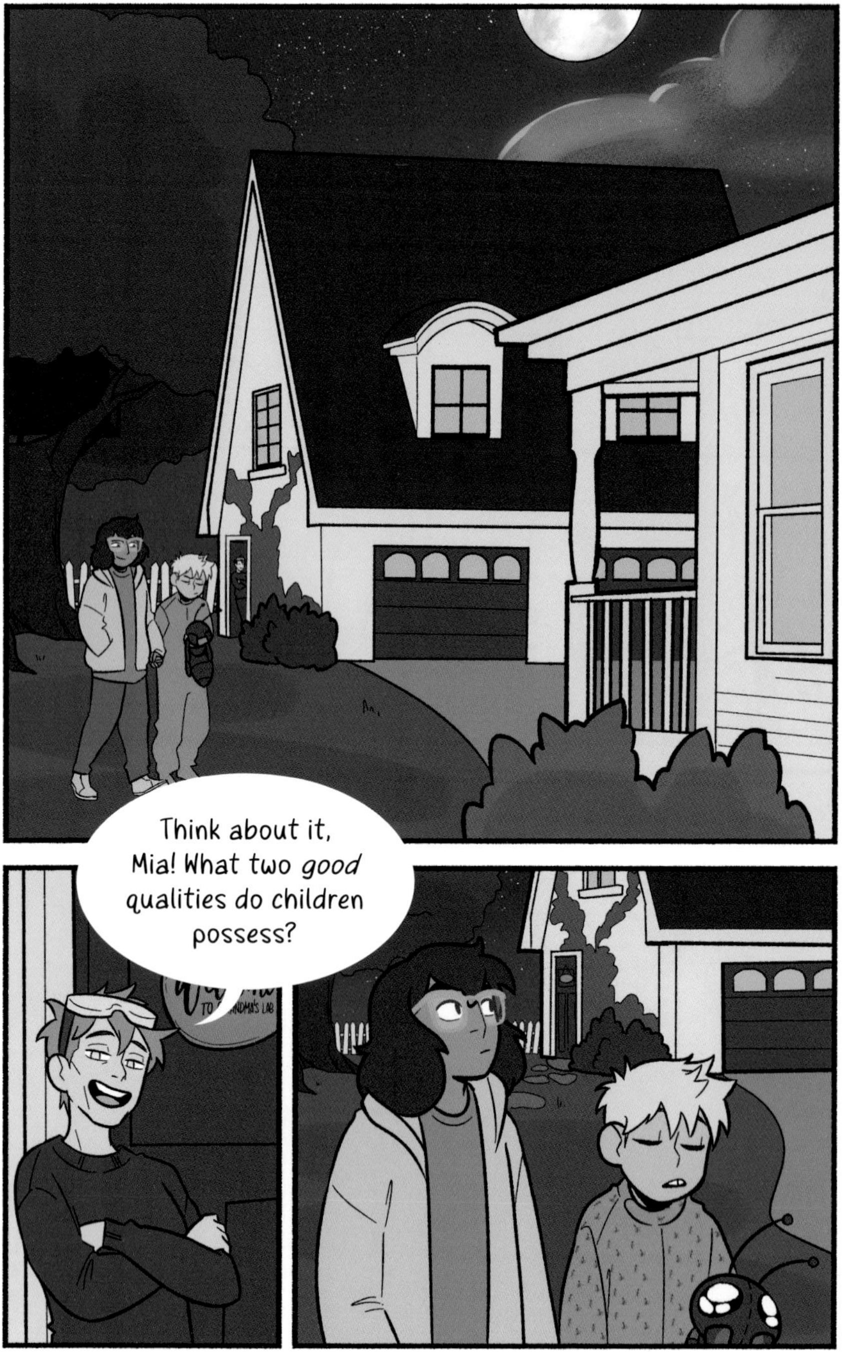
Think about it, Mia! What two *good* qualities do children possess?
TO GRANDMA'S LAB

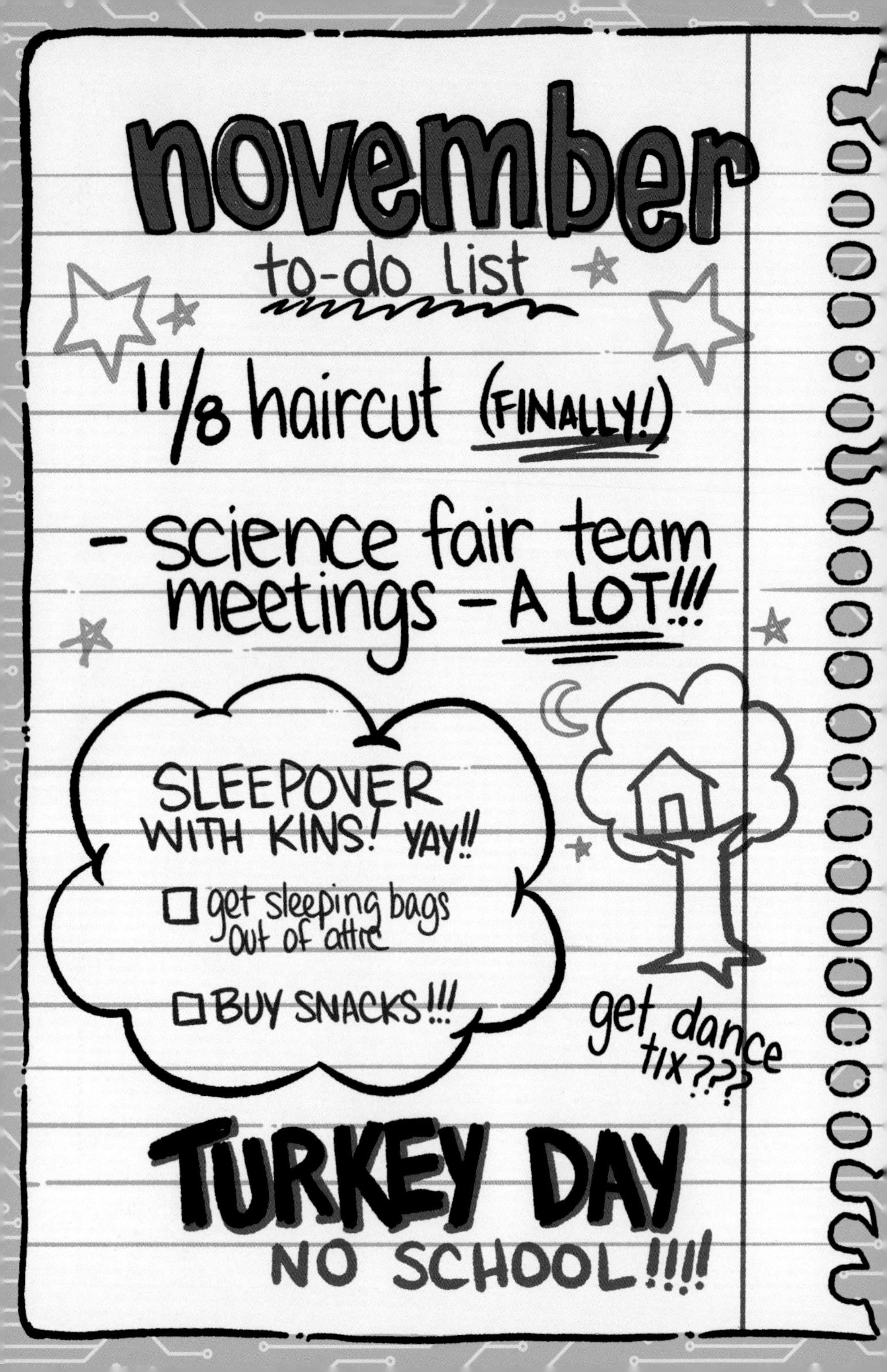
november
to-do list
11/8 haircut (FINALLY!)
- science fair team meetings - A LOT!!!
SLEEPOVER WITH KINS! YAY!!
get sleeping bags out of attic
BUY SNACKS!!!
get dance tix???
TURKEY DAY
NO SCHOOL!!!!

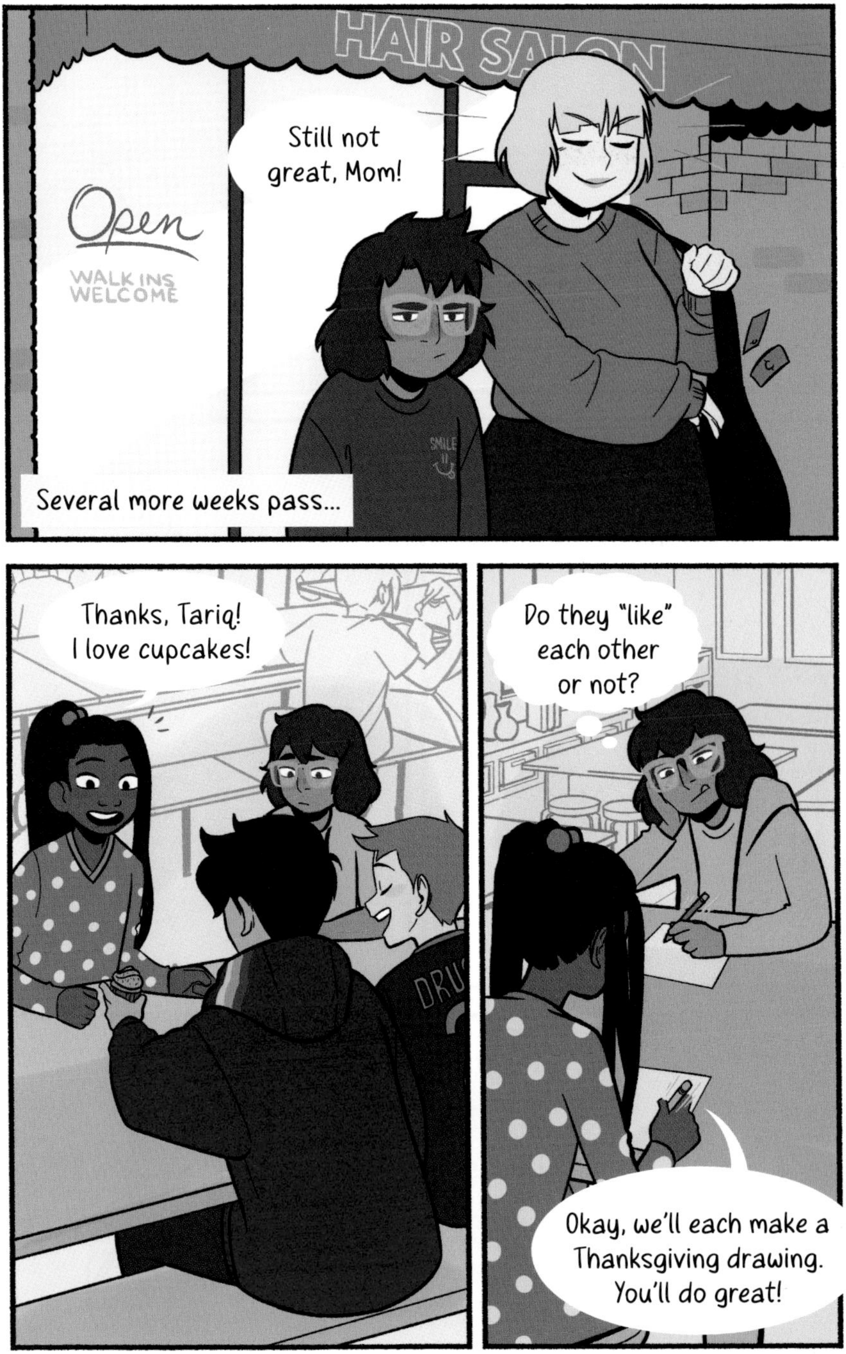
HAIR SALON
Open
WALK INS WELCOME
Still not great, Mom!
SMILE
Several more weeks pass...
Thanks, Tariq! I love cupcakes!
DRUS
Do they "like" each other or not?
Okay, we'll each make a Thanksgiving drawing. You'll do great!

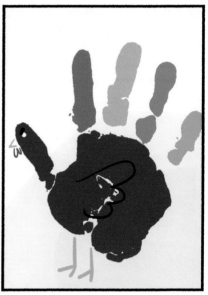

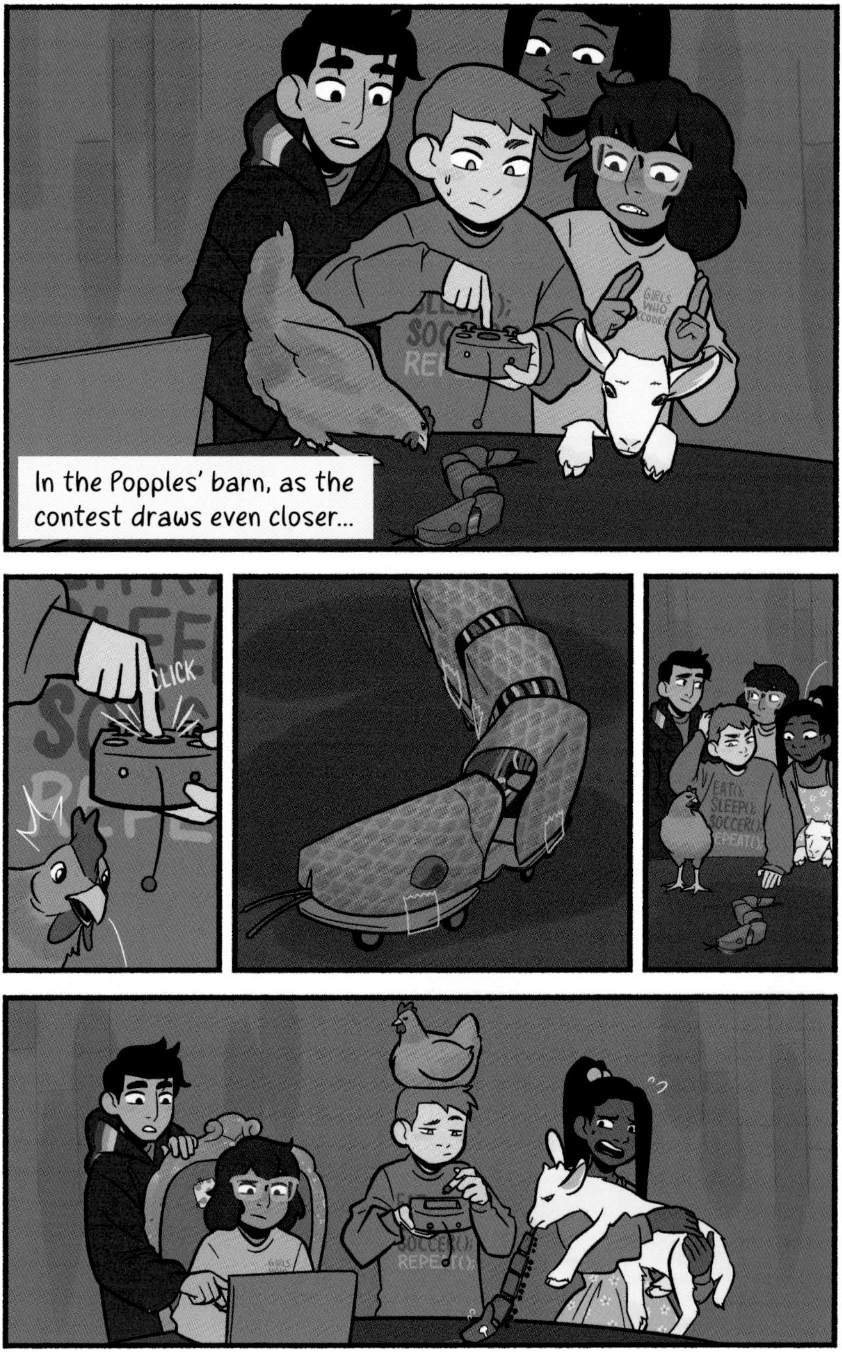

In the Popples' barn, as the contest draws even closer...
GIRLS WHO CODE()
CLICK
EAT();
SLEEP();
SOCCER();
REPEAT();

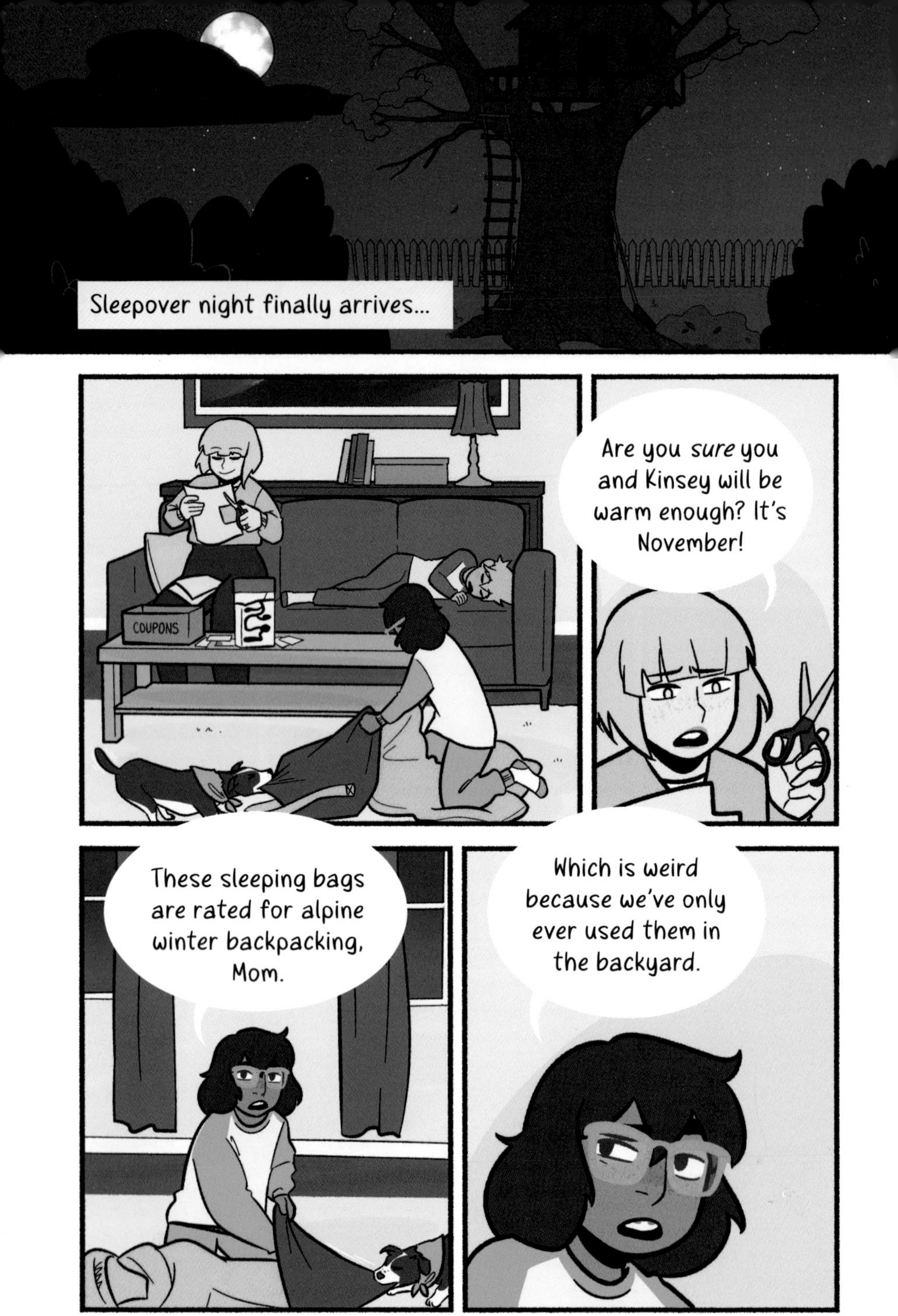
Sleepover night finally arrives...
COUPONS
Are you *sure* you and Kinsey will be warm enough? It's November!
These sleeping bags are rated for alpine winter backpacking, Mom.
Which is weird because we've only ever used them in the backyard.

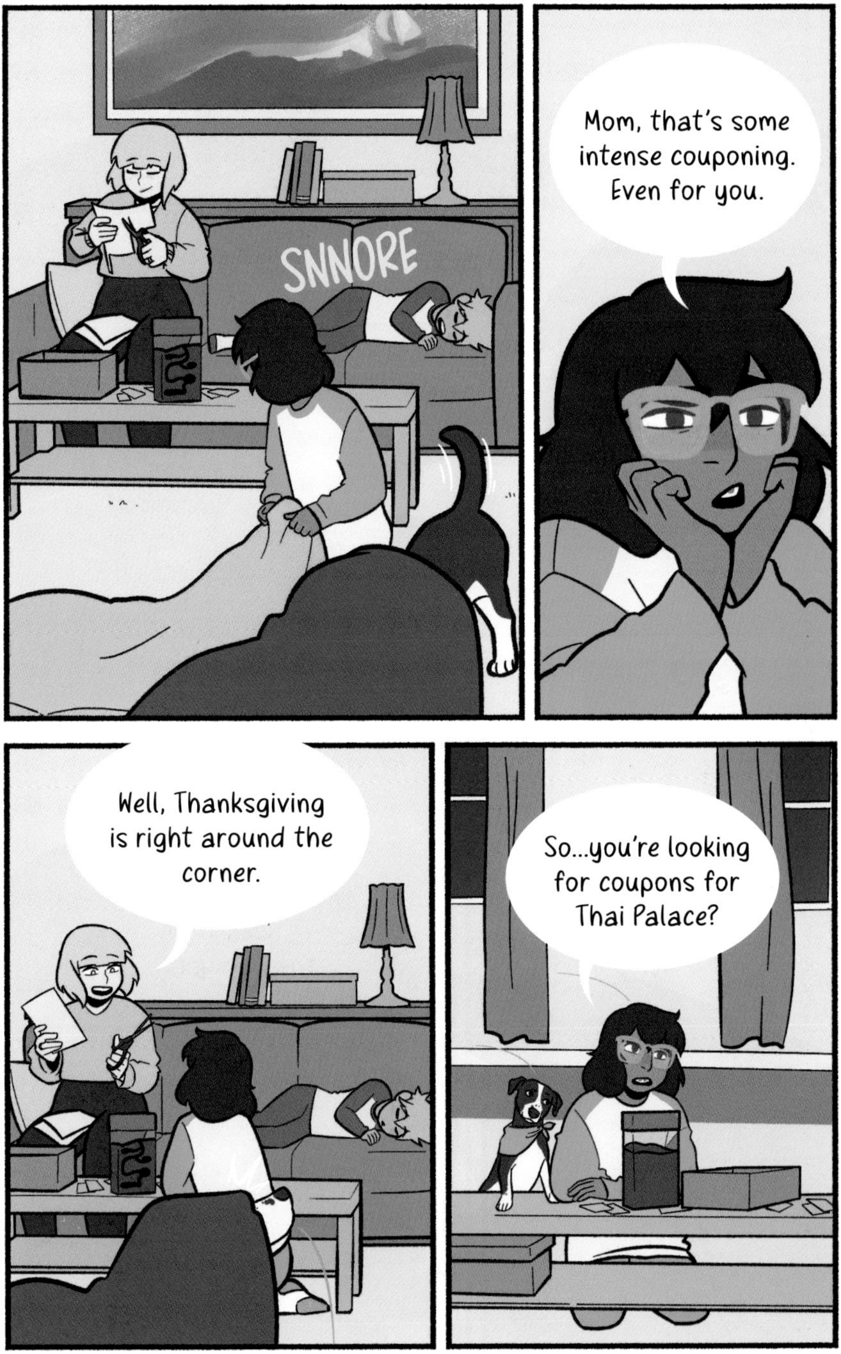
SNNORE
Mom, that's some intense couponing. Even for you.
Well, Thanksgiving is right around the corner.
So...you're looking for coupons for Thai Palace?

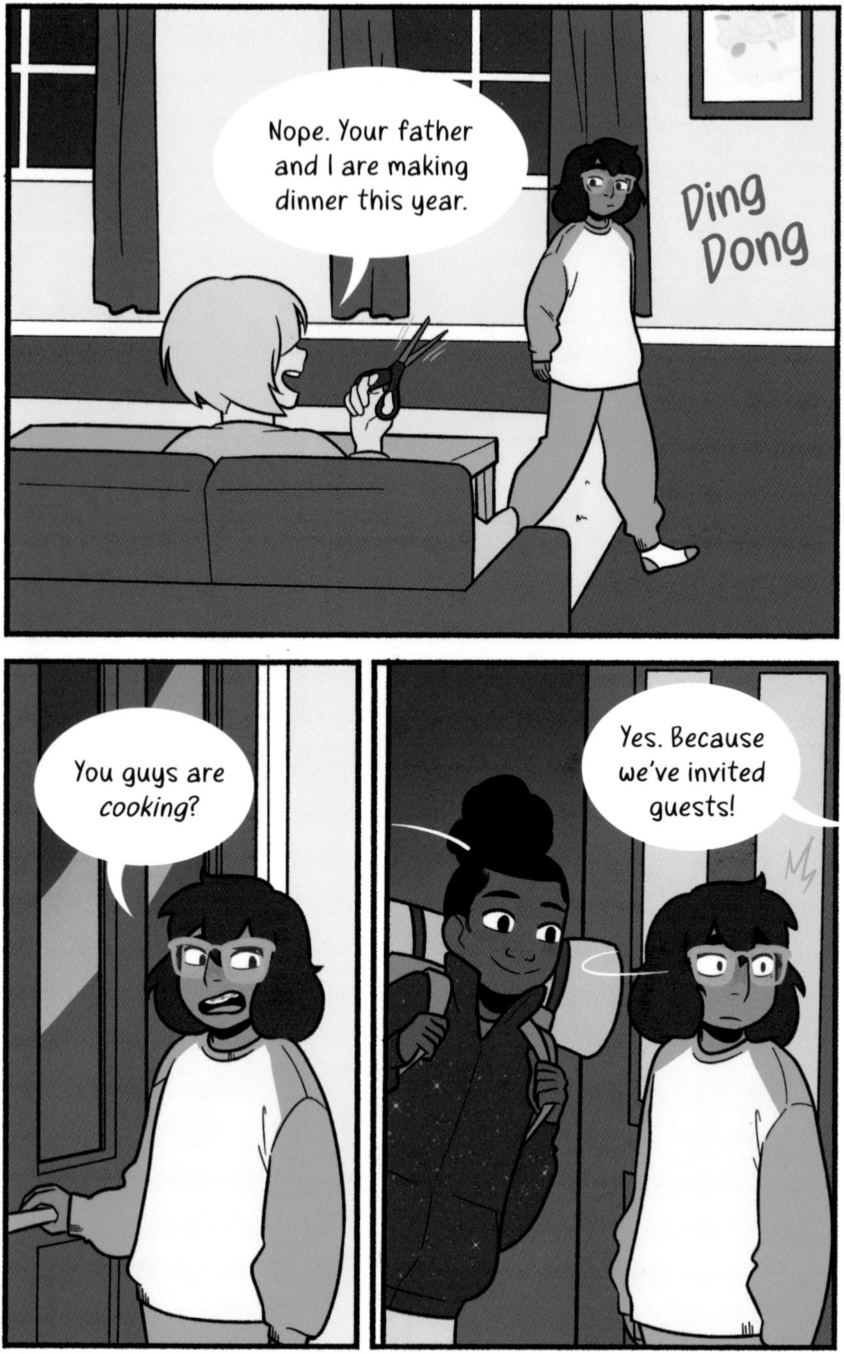
Nope. Your father and I are making dinner this year.
Ding Dong
You guys are *cooking*?
Yes. Because we've invited guests!

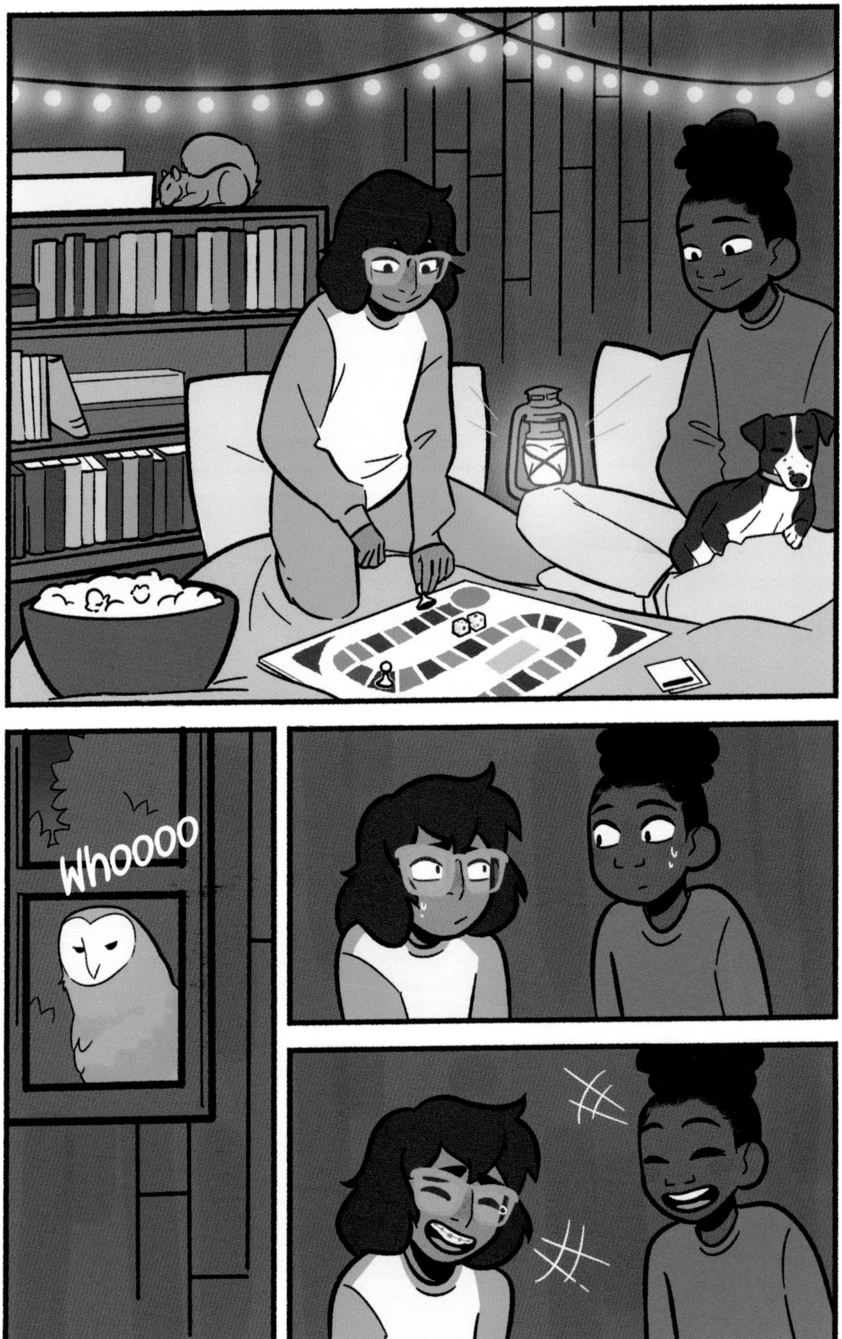
Whoooo

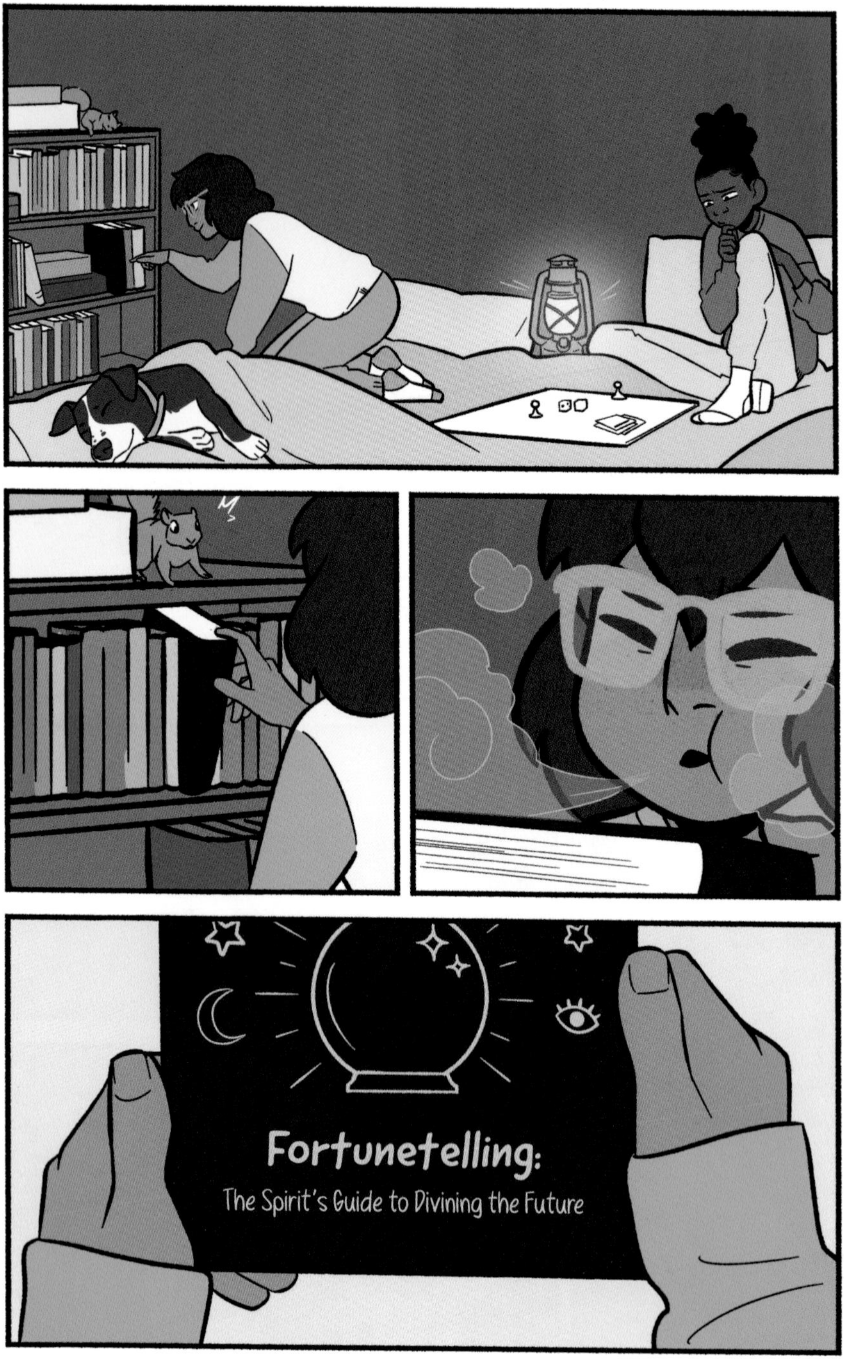
Fortunetelling:
The Spirit's Guide to Divining the Future

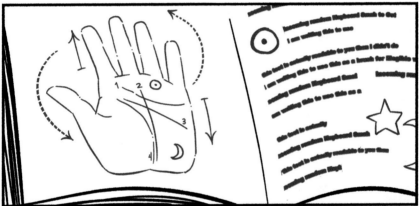

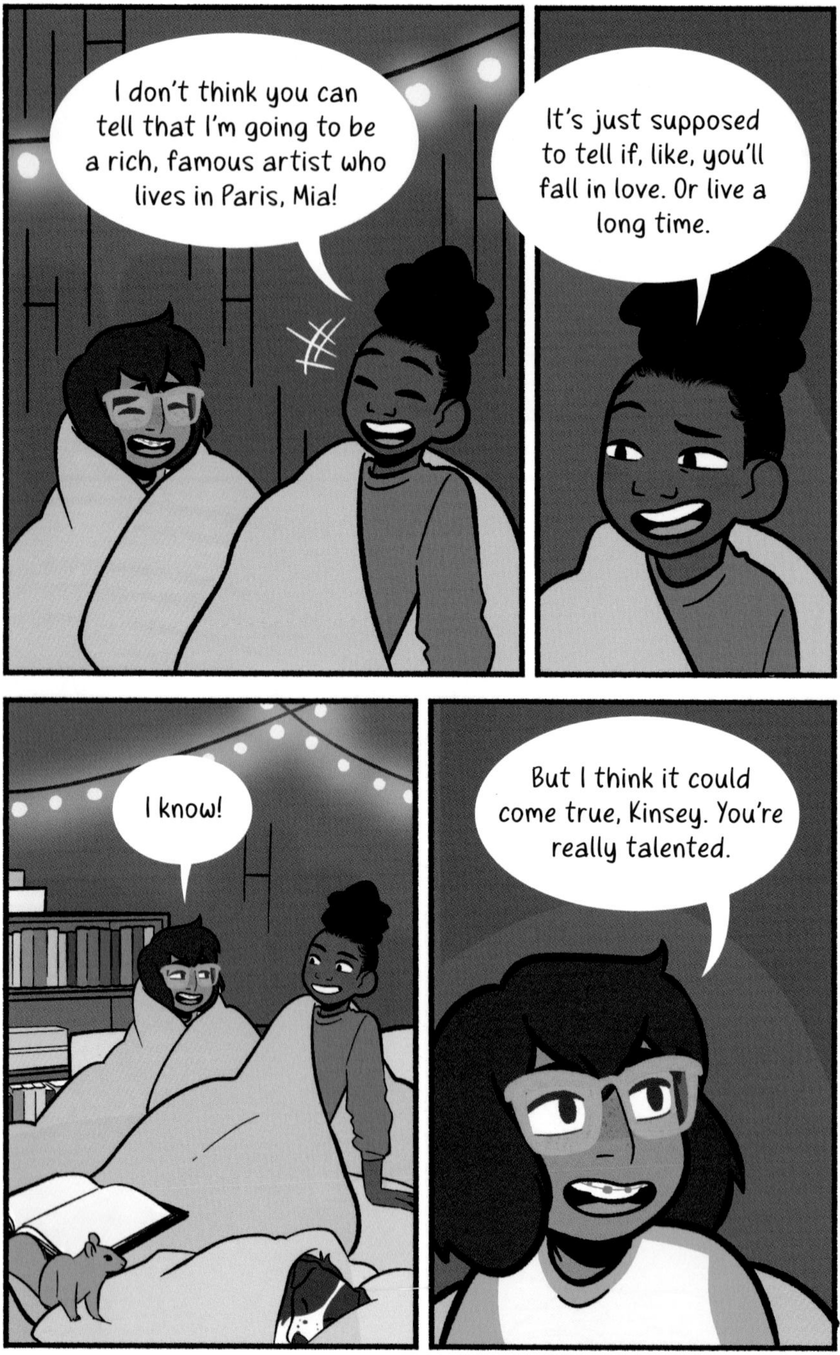
I don't think you can tell that I'm going to be a rich, famous artist who lives in Paris, Mia!
It's just supposed to tell if, like, you'll fall in love. Or live a long time.
I know!
But I think it could come true, Kinsey. You're really talented.

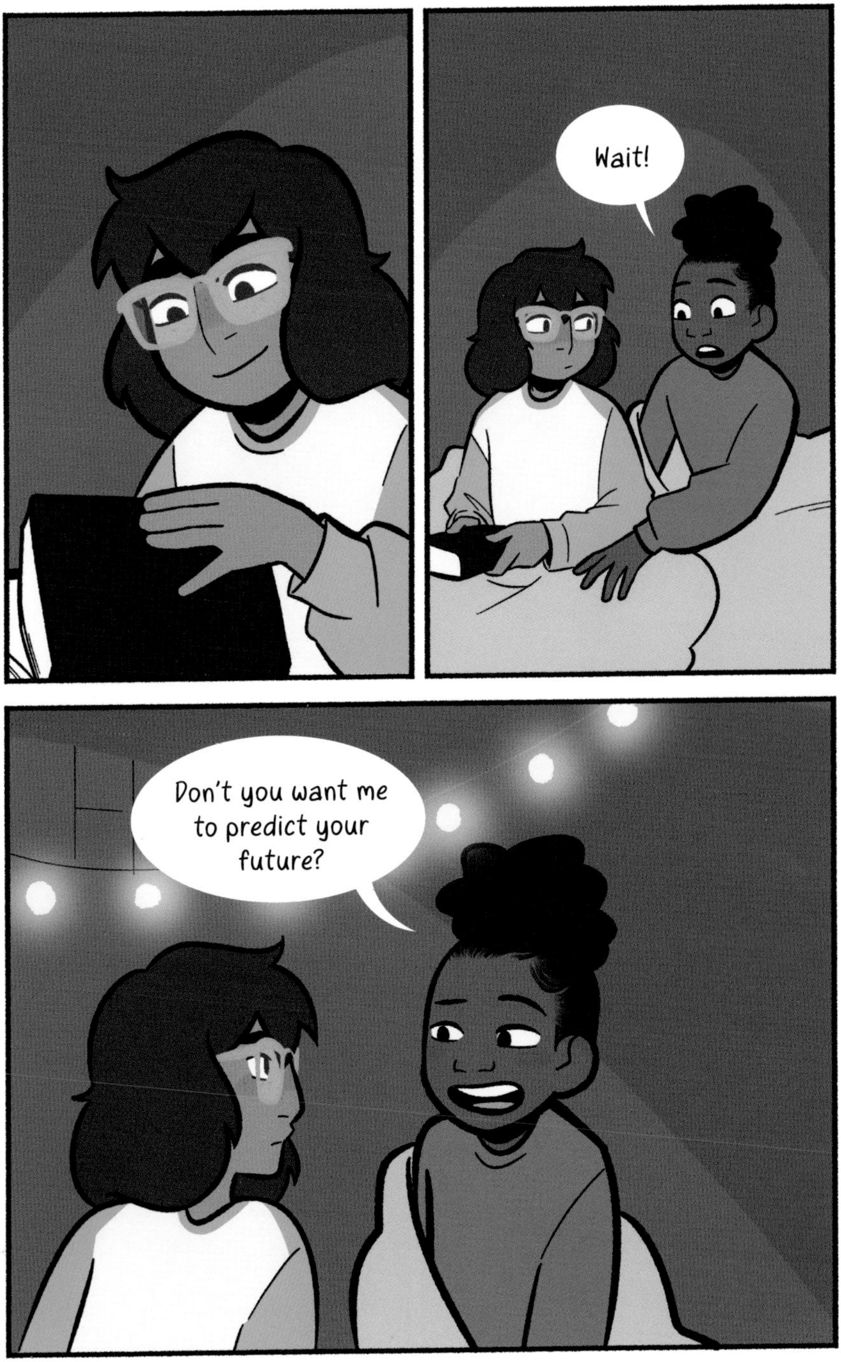
Wait!
Don't you want me to predict your future?

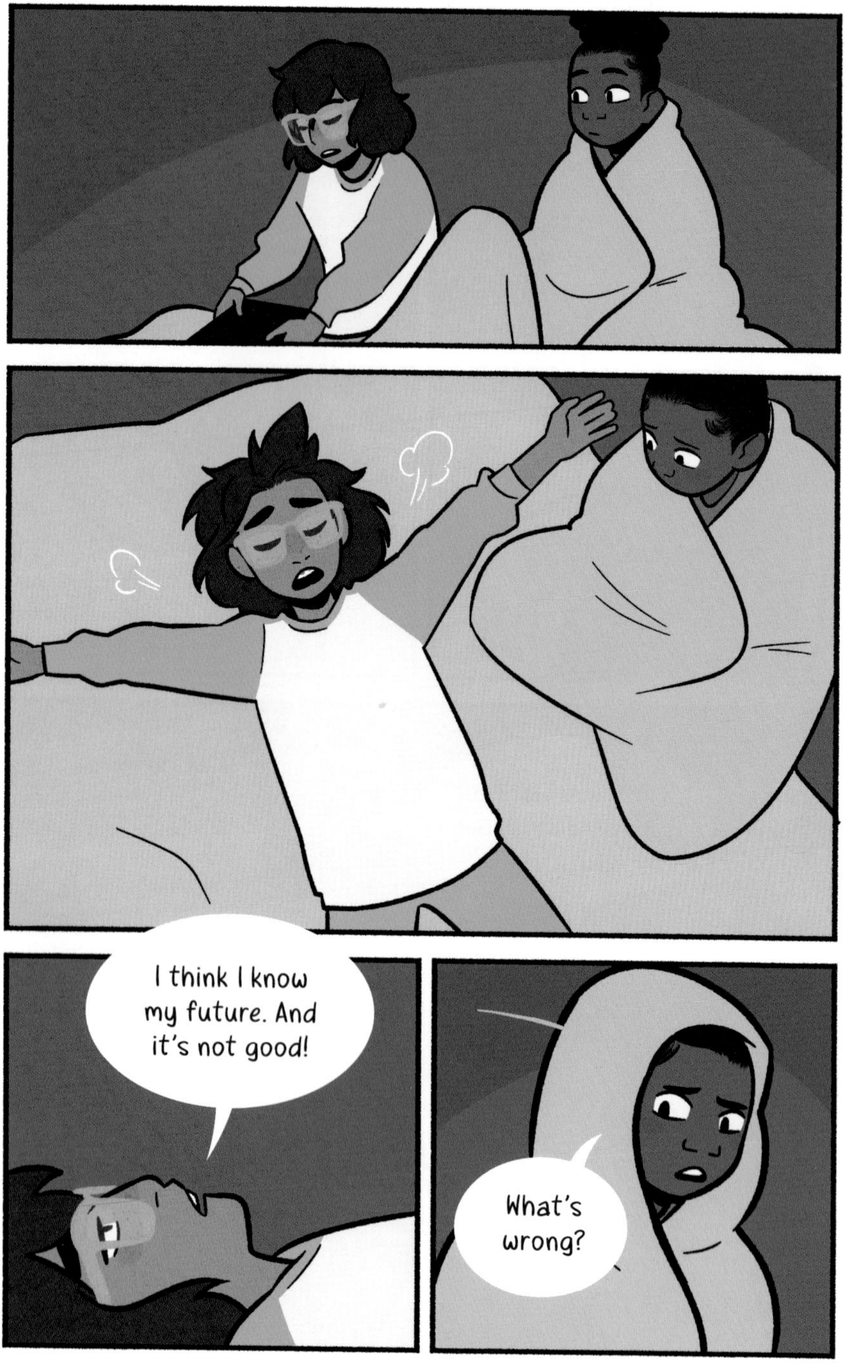
I think I know my future. And it's not good!
What's wrong?

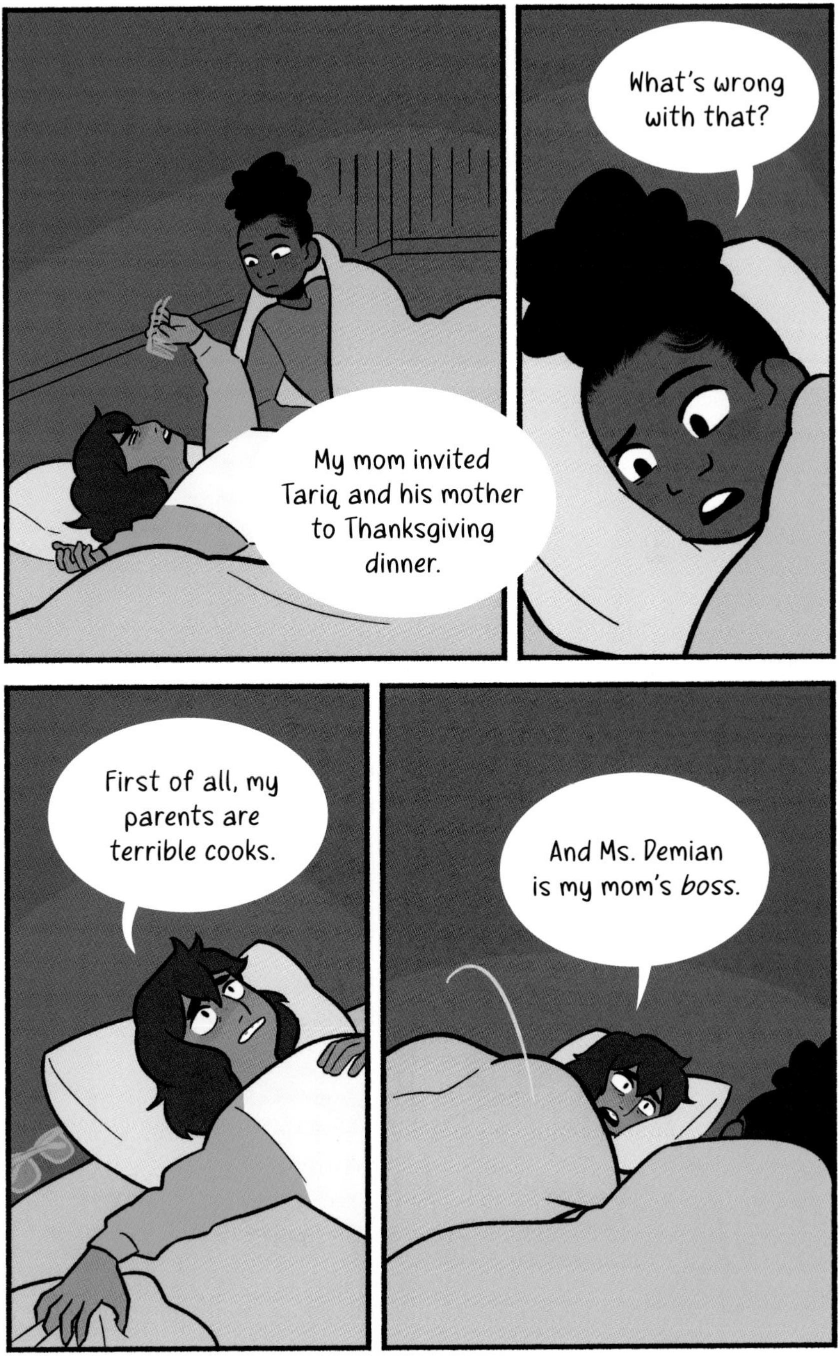
My mom invited Tariq and his mother to Thanksgiving dinner.
What's wrong with that?
First of all, my parents are terrible cooks.
And Ms. Demian is my mom's *boss*.

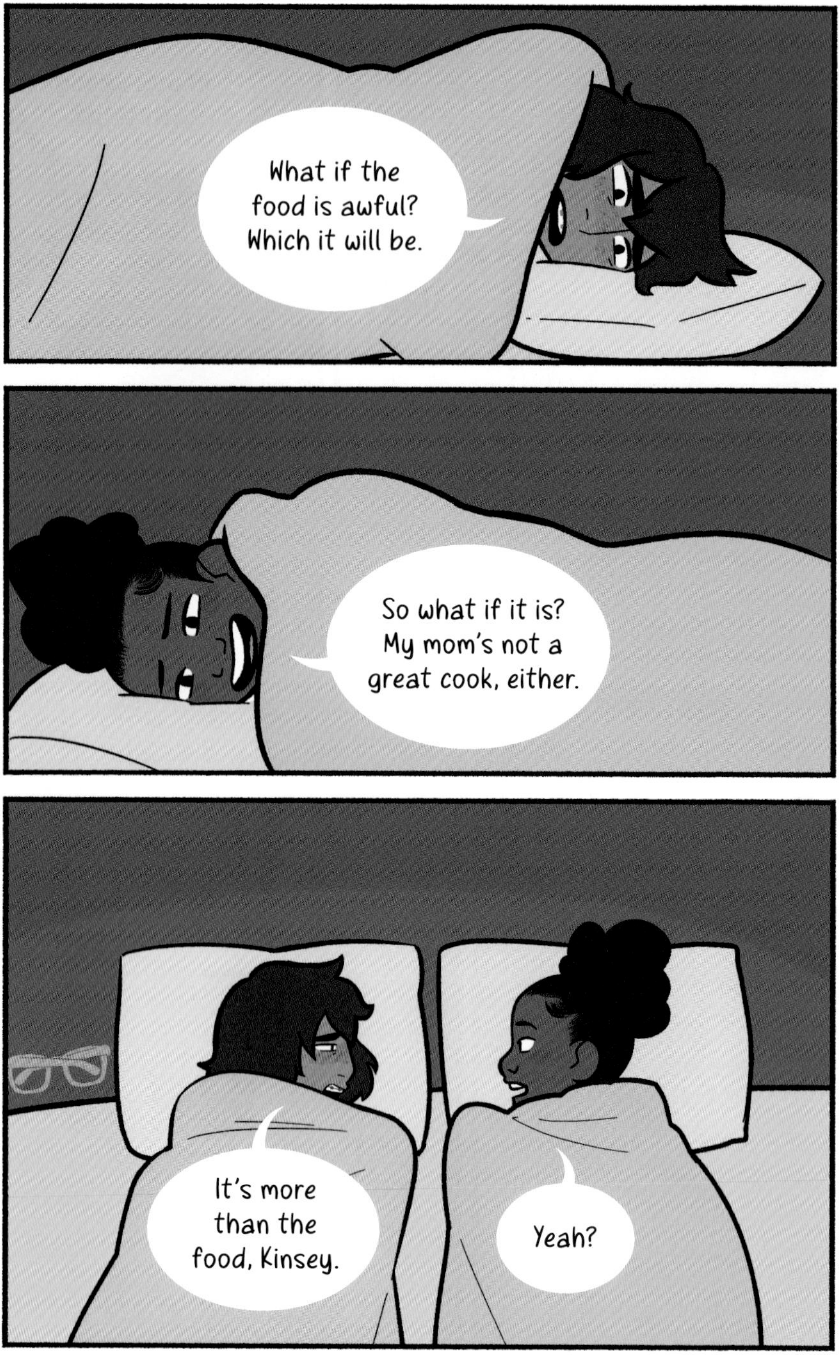
What if the food is awful? Which it will be.
So what if it is? My mom's not a great cook, either.
It's more than the food, Kinsey.
Yeah?

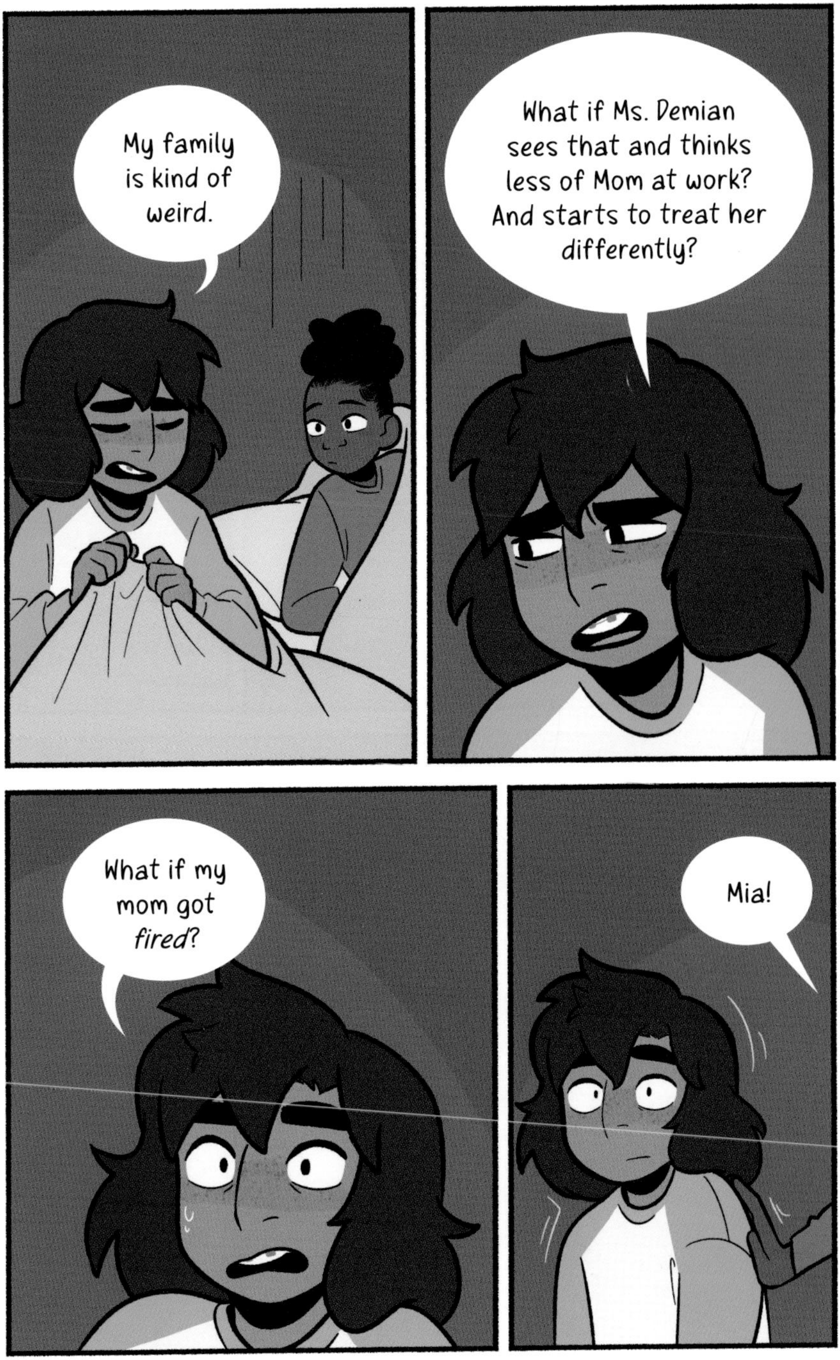
My family is kind of weird.
What if Ms. Demian sees that and thinks less of Mom at work? And starts to treat her differently?
What if my mom got *fired*?
Mia!

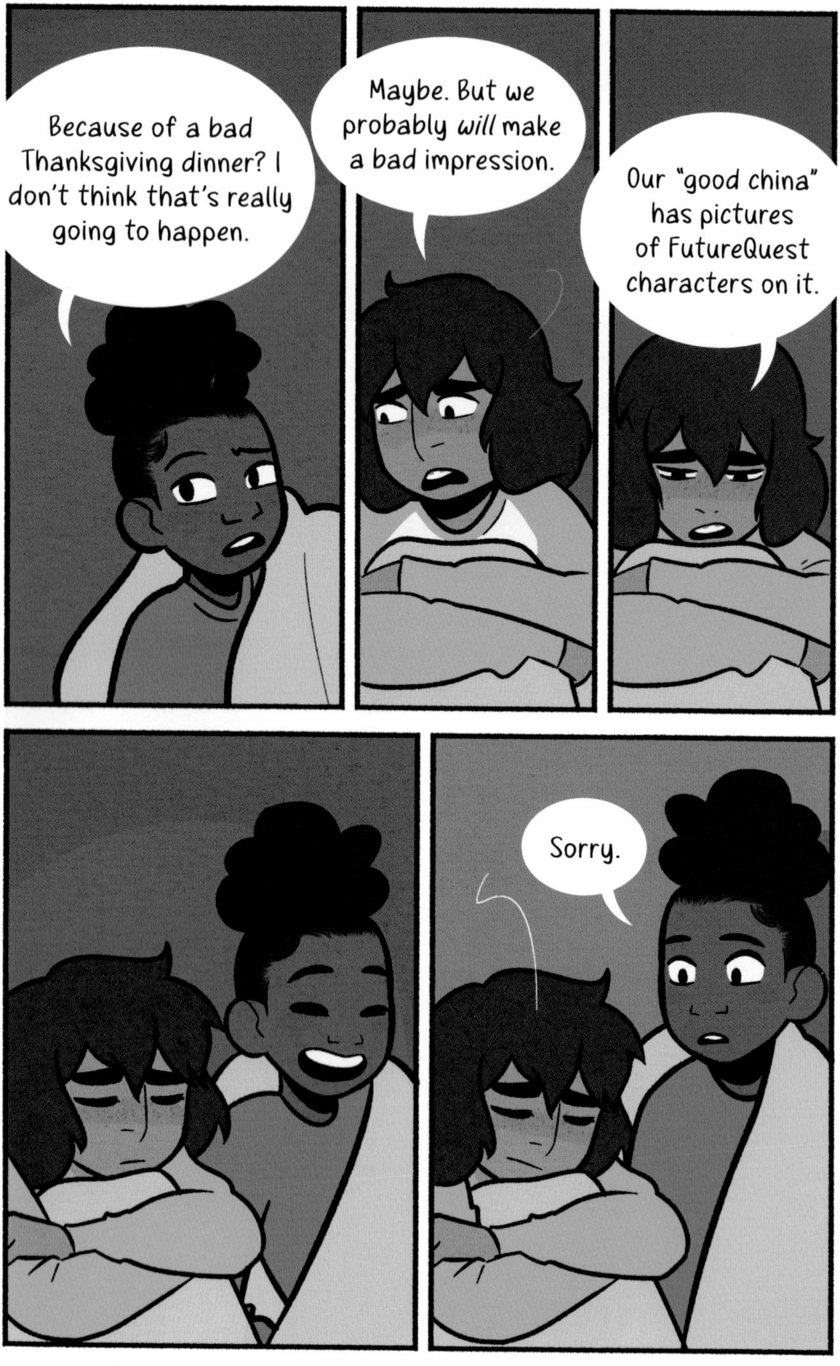
Because of a bad Thanksgiving dinner? I don't think that's really going to happen.
Maybe. But we probably *will* make a bad impression.
Our "good china" has pictures of FutureQuest characters on it.
Sorry.

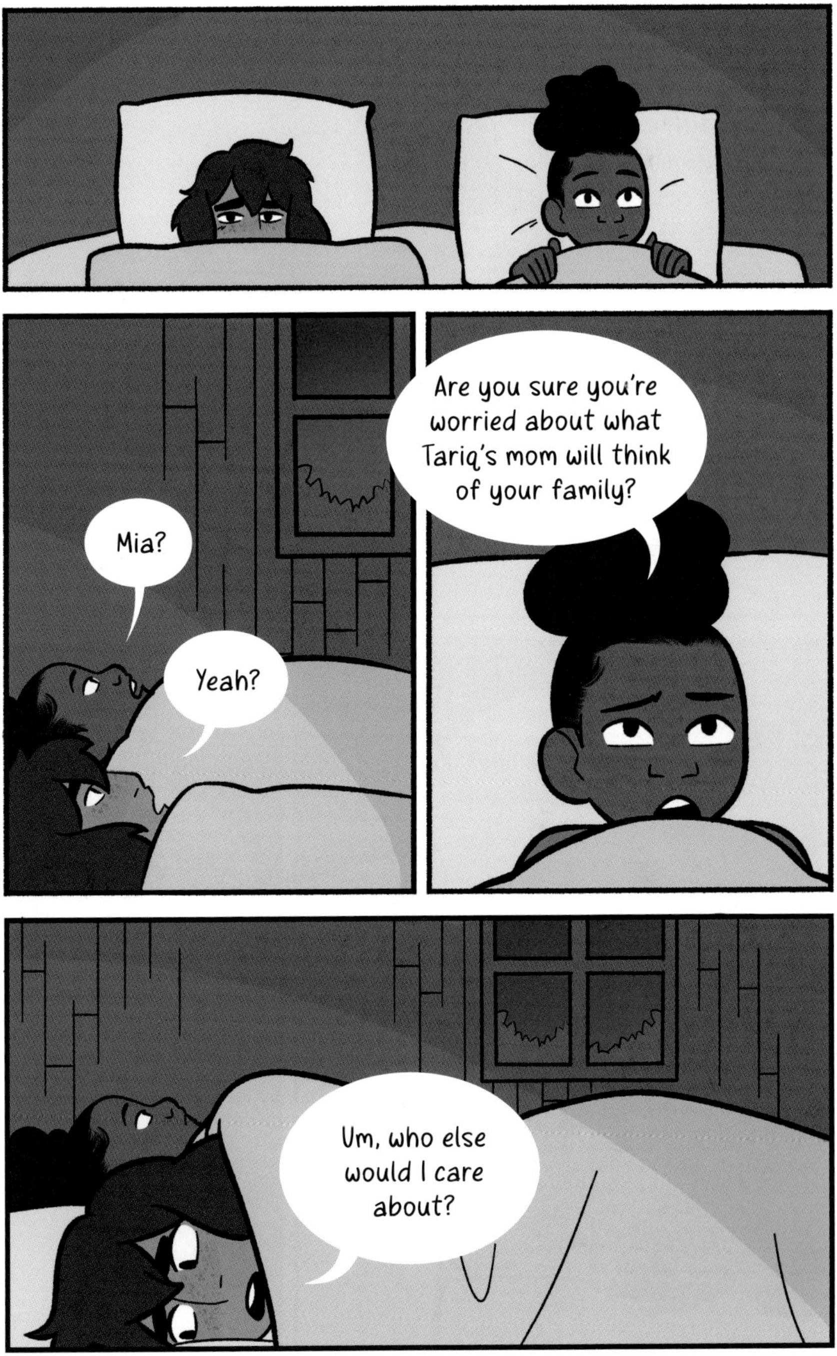
Are you sure you're worried about what Tariq's mom will think of your family?
Mia?
Yeah?
Um, who else would I care about?

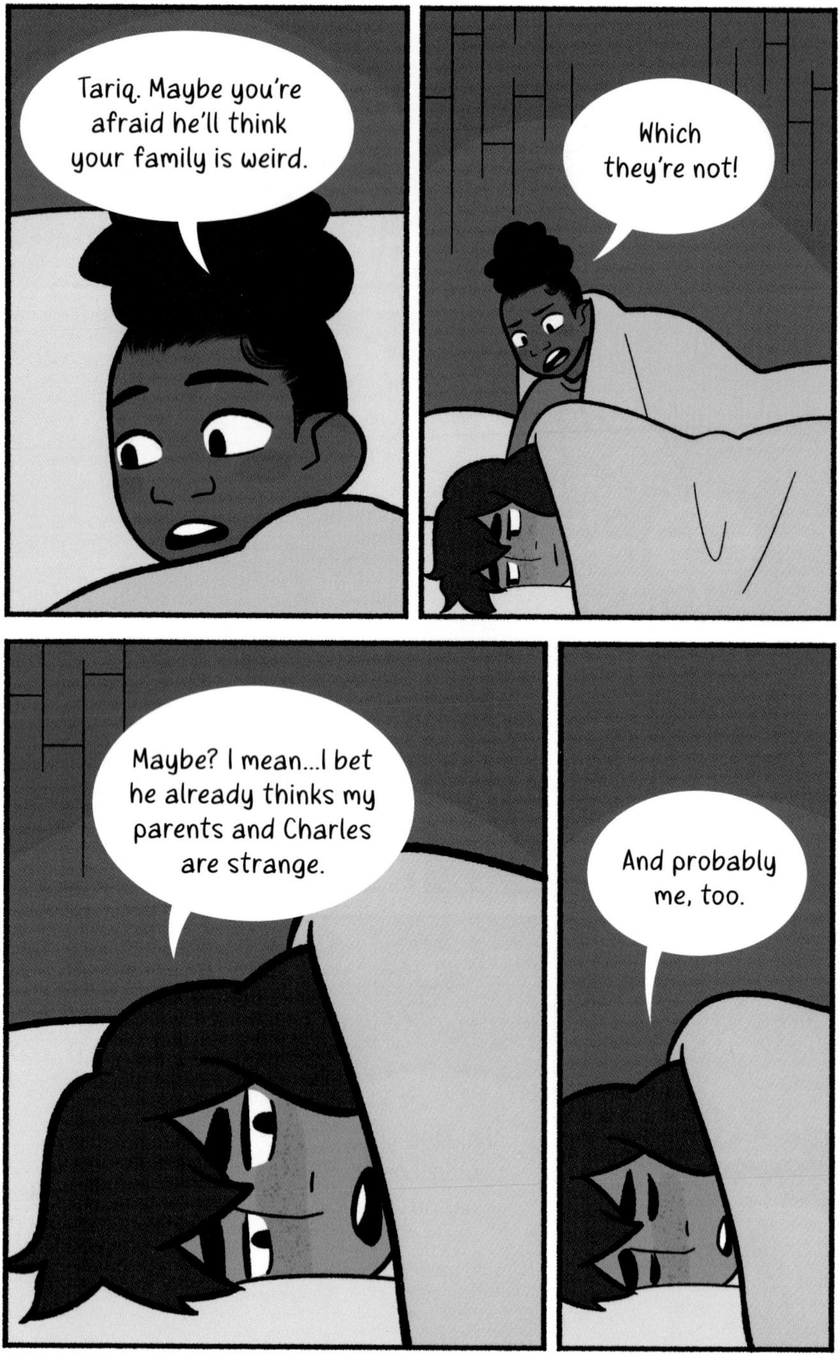
Tariq. Maybe you're afraid he'll think your family is weird.
Which they're not!
Maybe? I mean...I bet he already thinks my parents and Charles are strange.
And probably me, too.

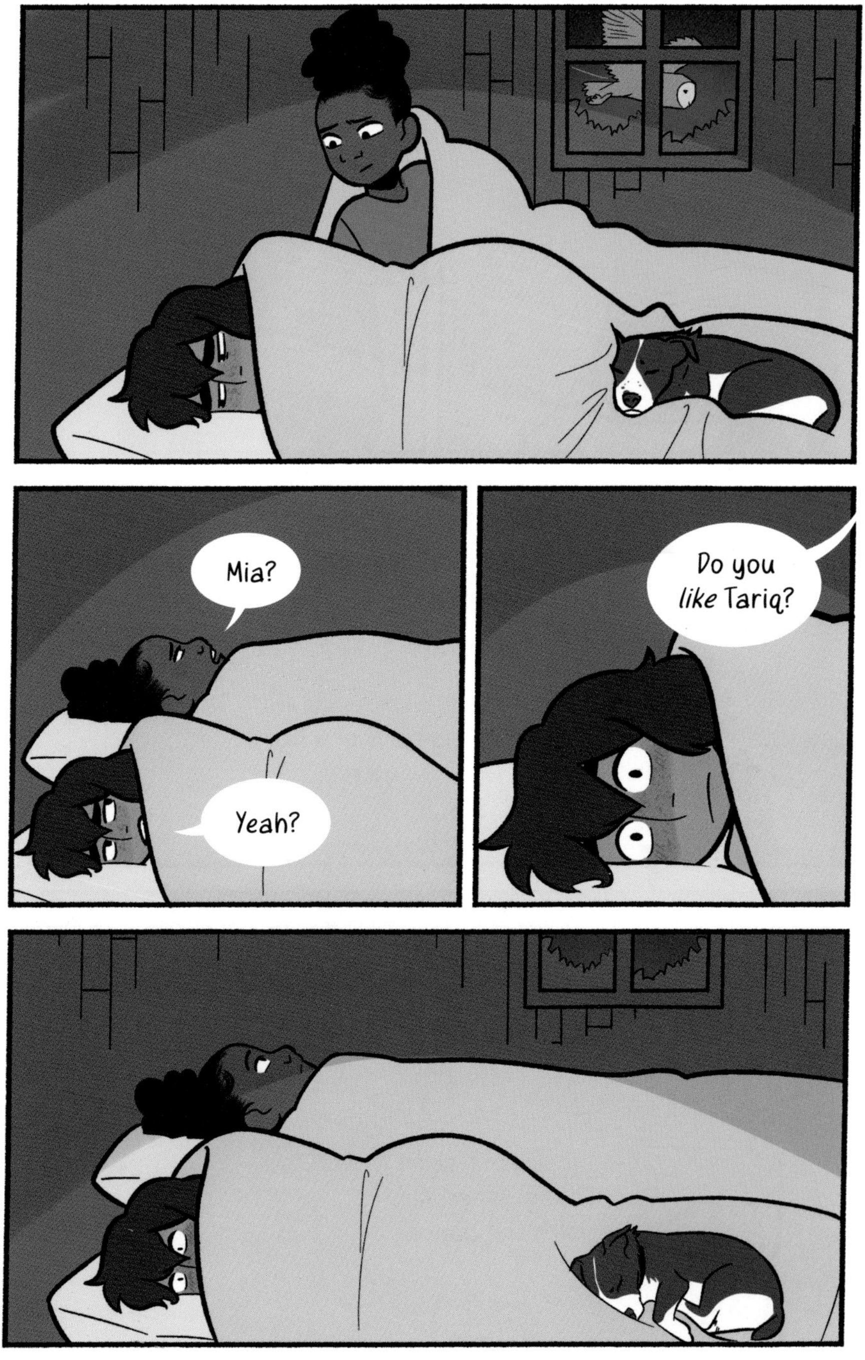
Mia?
Yeah?
Do you like Tariq?

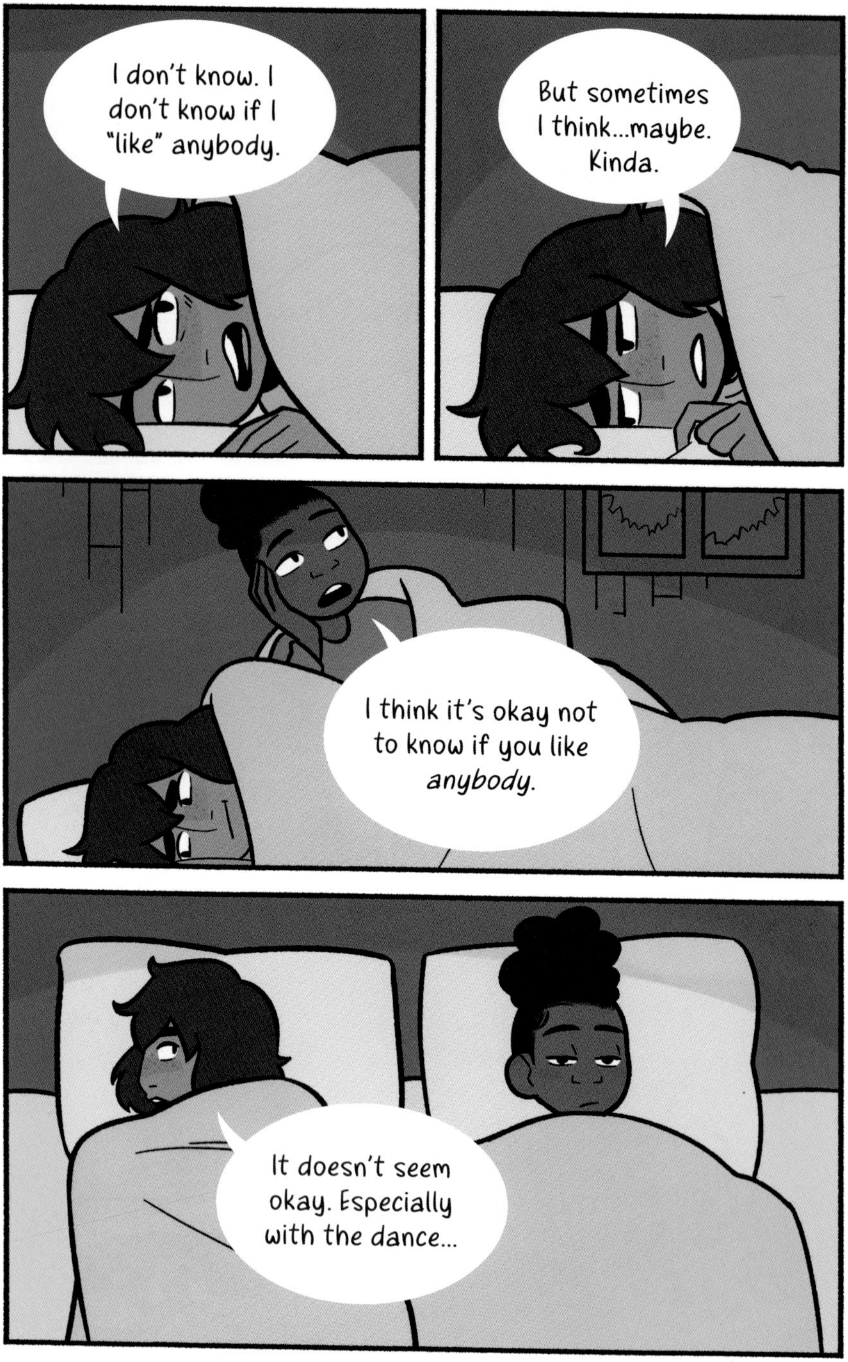
I don't know. I don't know if I "like" anybody.
But sometimes I think...maybe. Kinda.
I think it's okay not to know if you like *anybody*.
It doesn't seem okay. Especially with the dance...

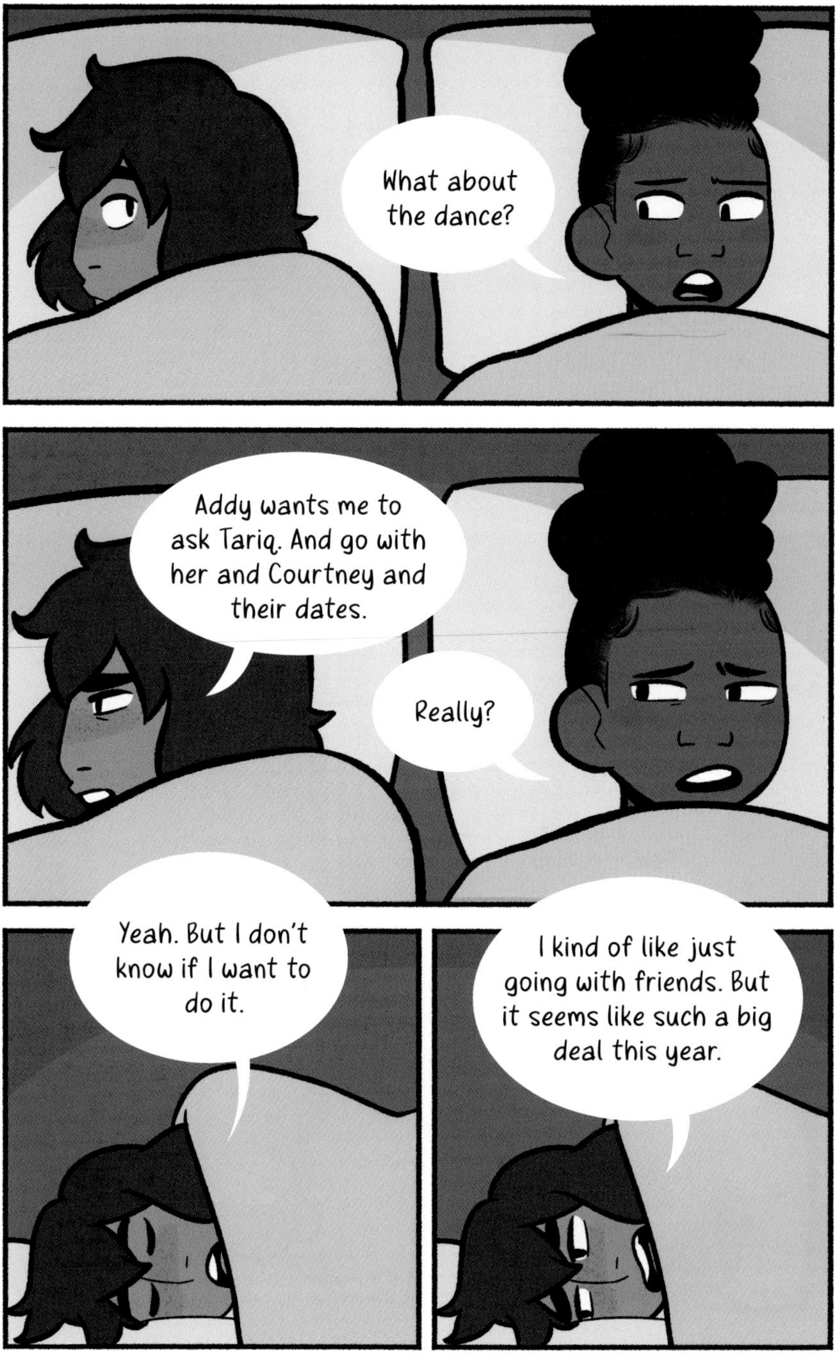
What about the dance?
Addy wants me to ask Tariq. And go with her and Courtney and their dates.
Really?
Yeah. But I don't know if I want to do it.
I kind of like just going with friends. But it seems like such a big deal this year.

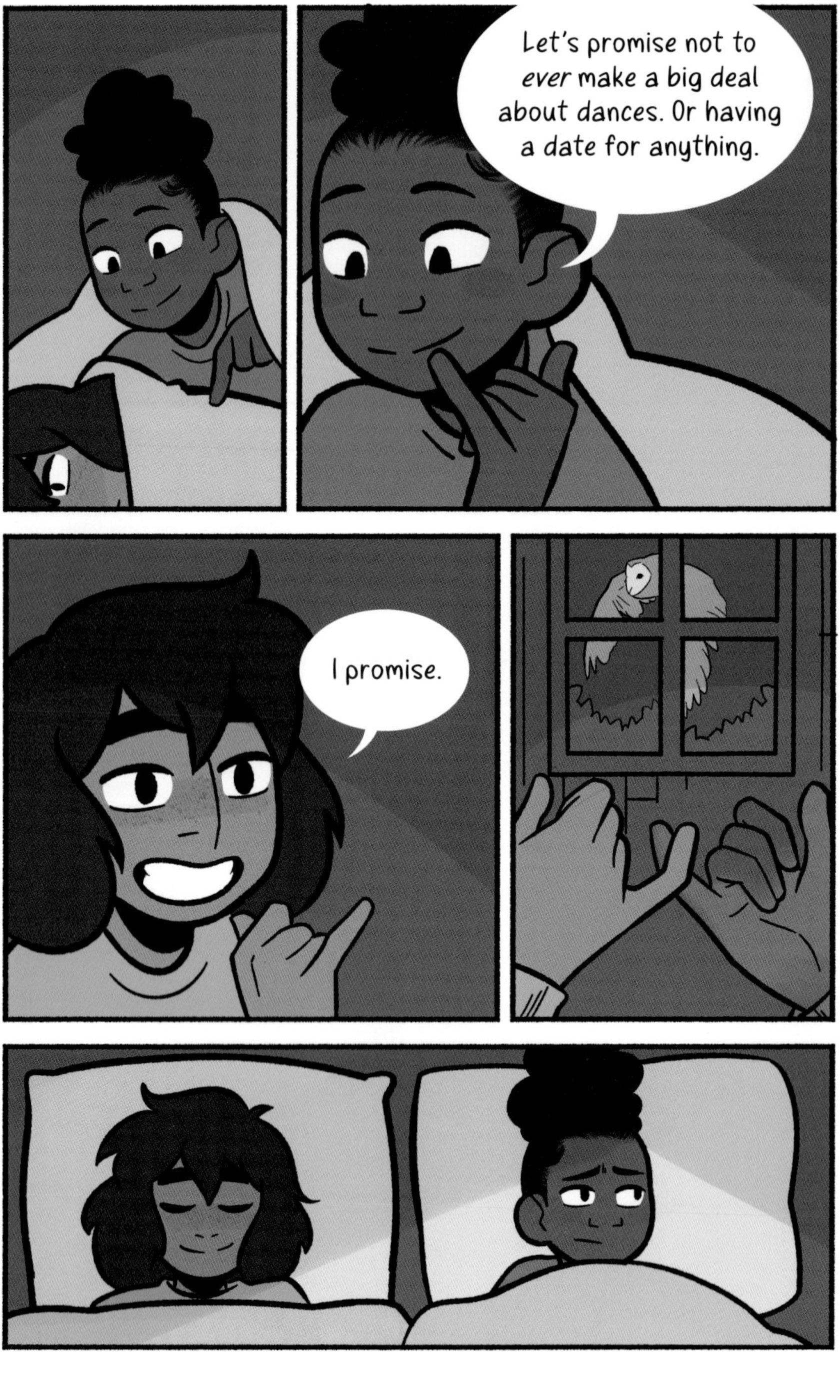
Let's promise not to *ever* make a big deal about dances. Or having a date for anything.
I promise.

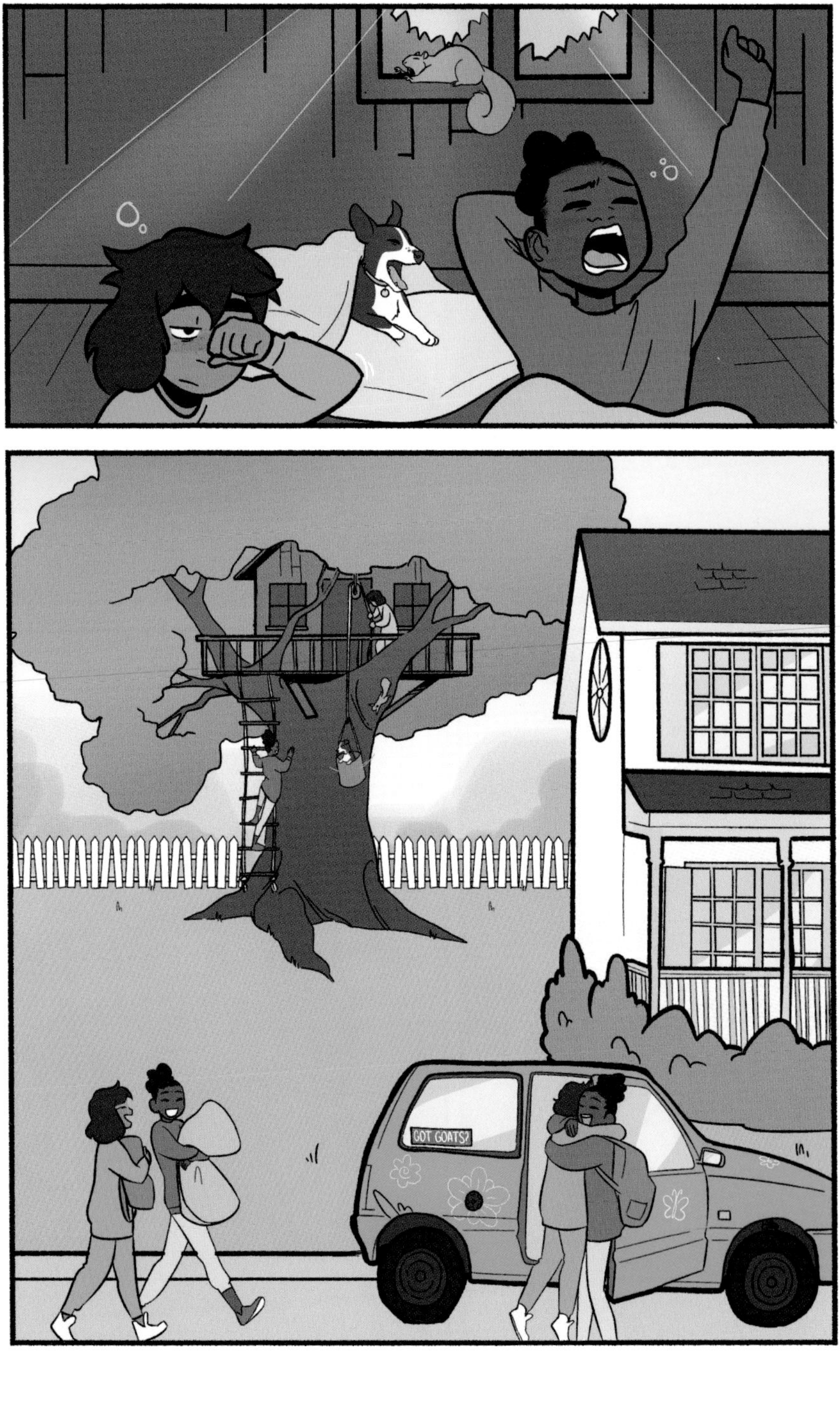
GOT GOATS?

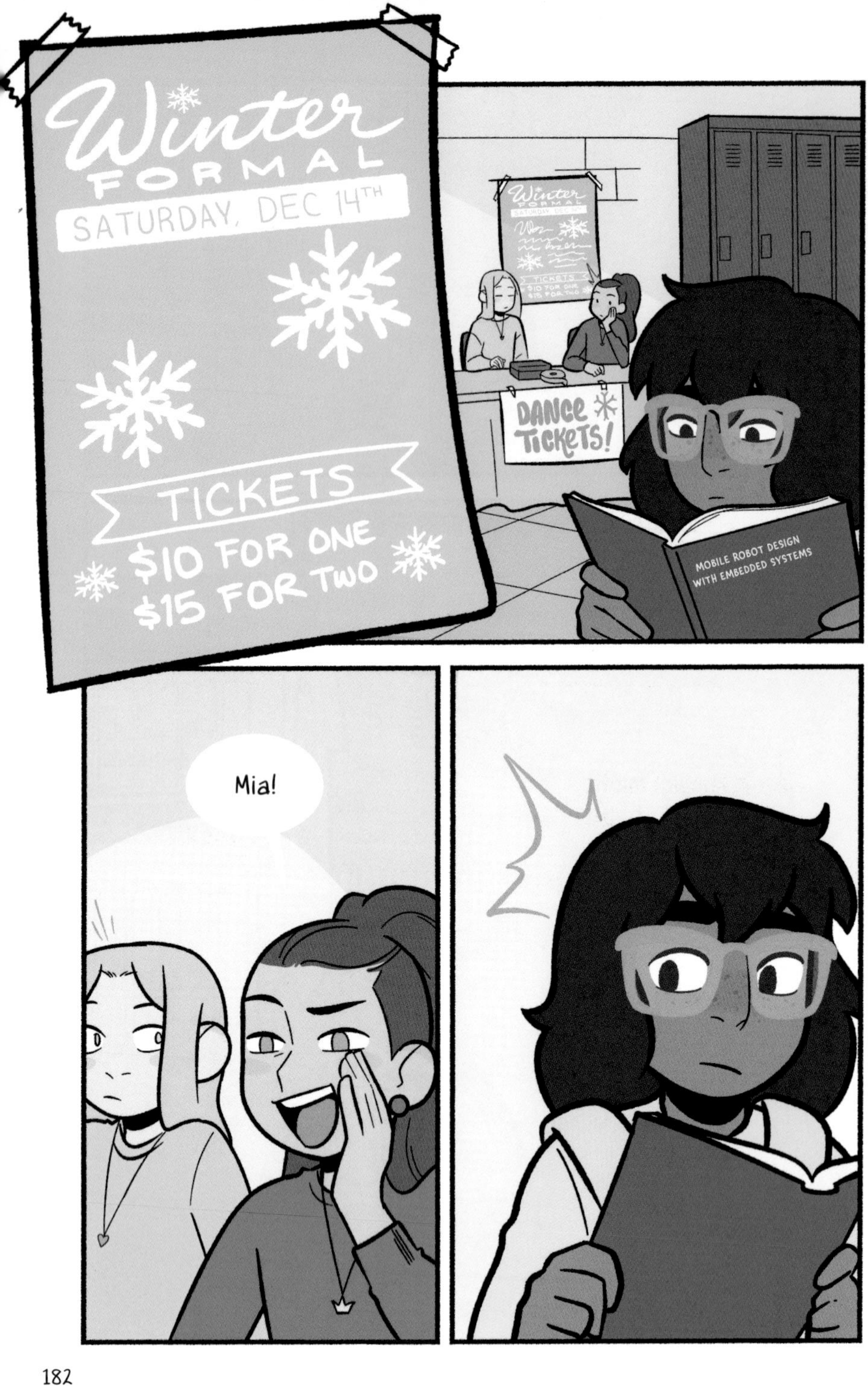
Winter
FORMAL
SATURDAY, DEC 14TH
TICKETS
$10 FOR ONE
$15 FOR TWO
DANCE TICKETS!
MOBILE ROBOT DESIGN
WITH EMBEDDED SYSTEMS
Mia!

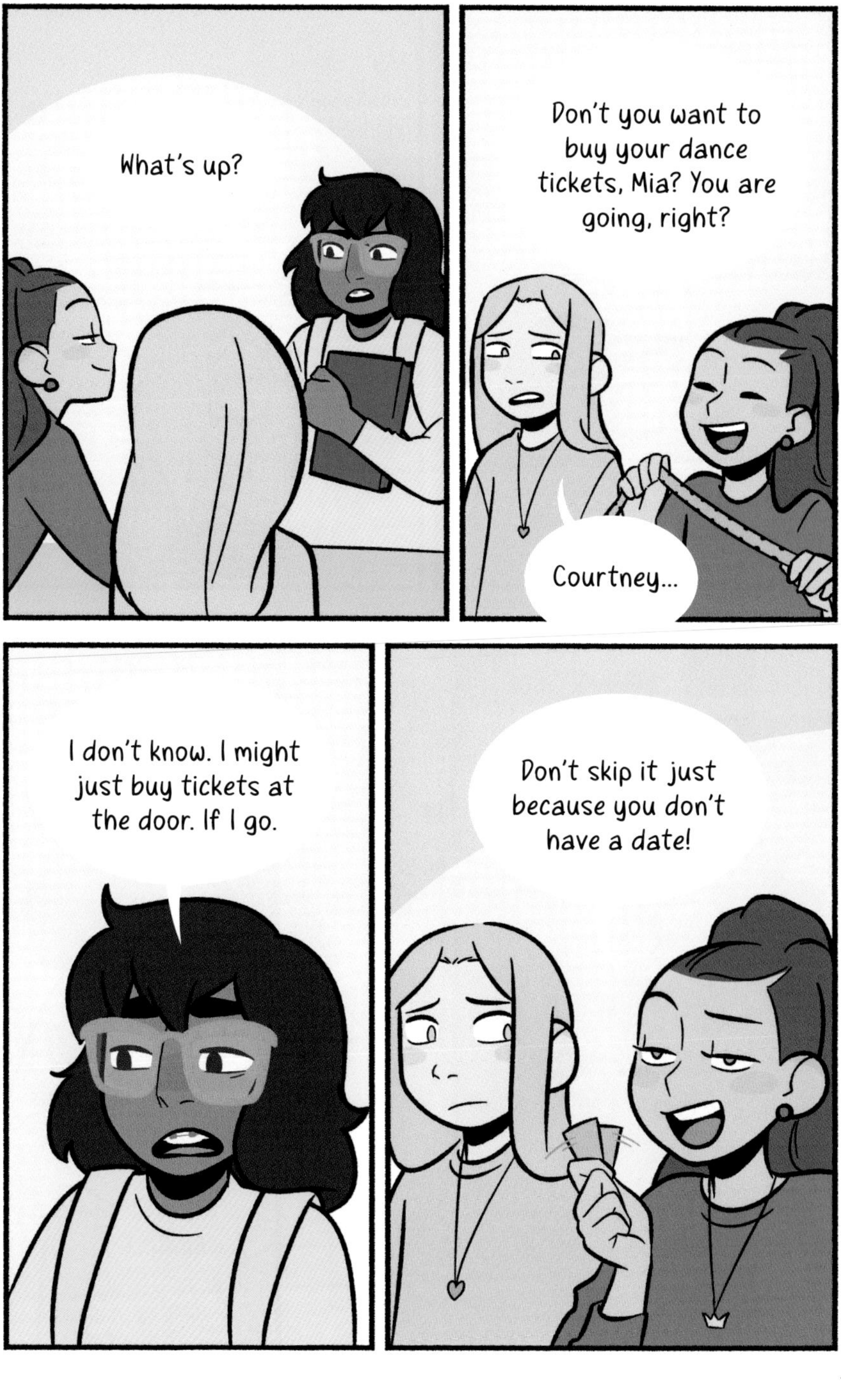
What's up?
Don't you want to buy your dance tickets, Mia? You are going, right?
Courtney...
I don't know. I might just buy tickets at the door. If I go.
Don't skip it just because you don't have a date!

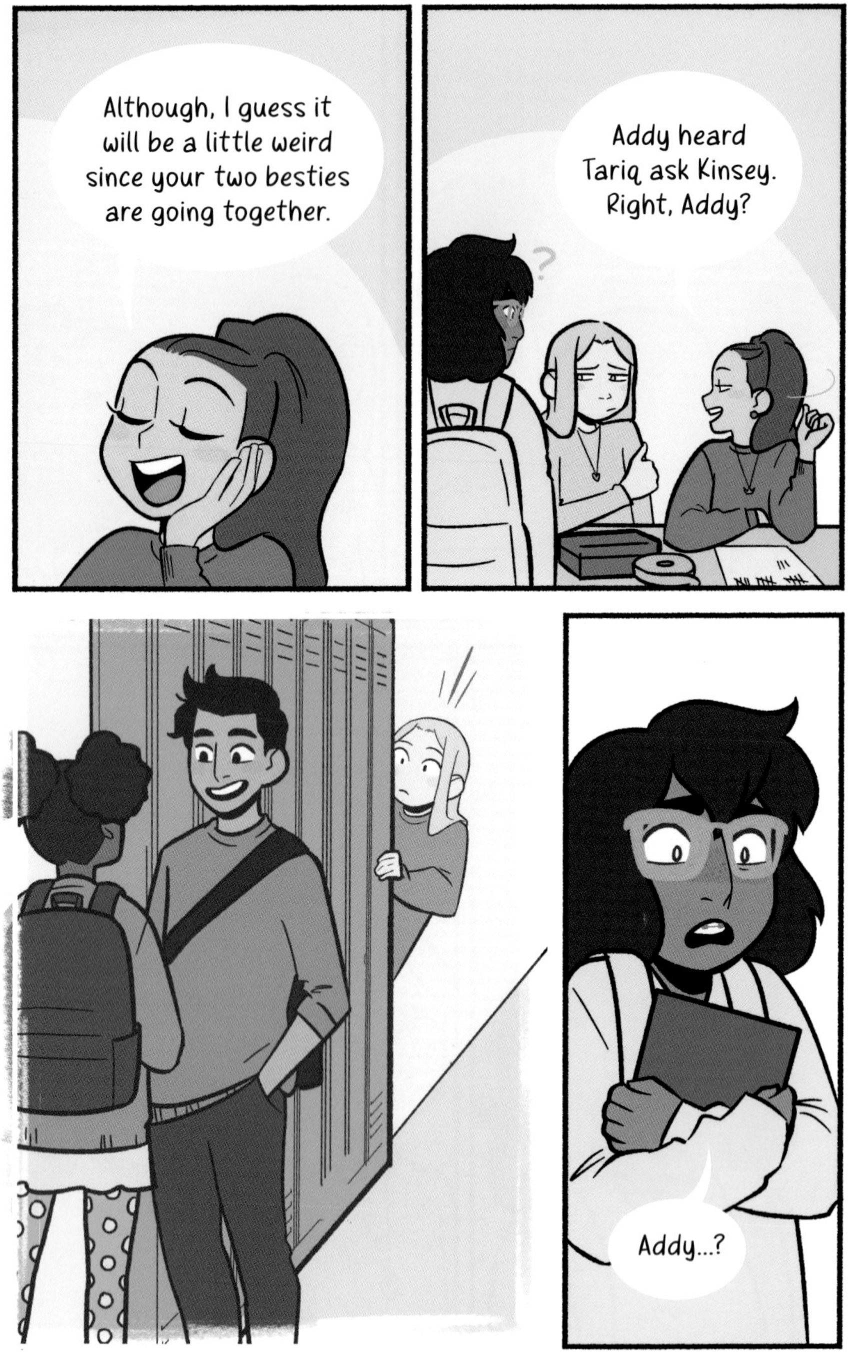
Although, I guess it will be a little weird since your two besties are going together.
Addy heard Tariq ask Kinsey. Right, Addy?
?
Addy...?

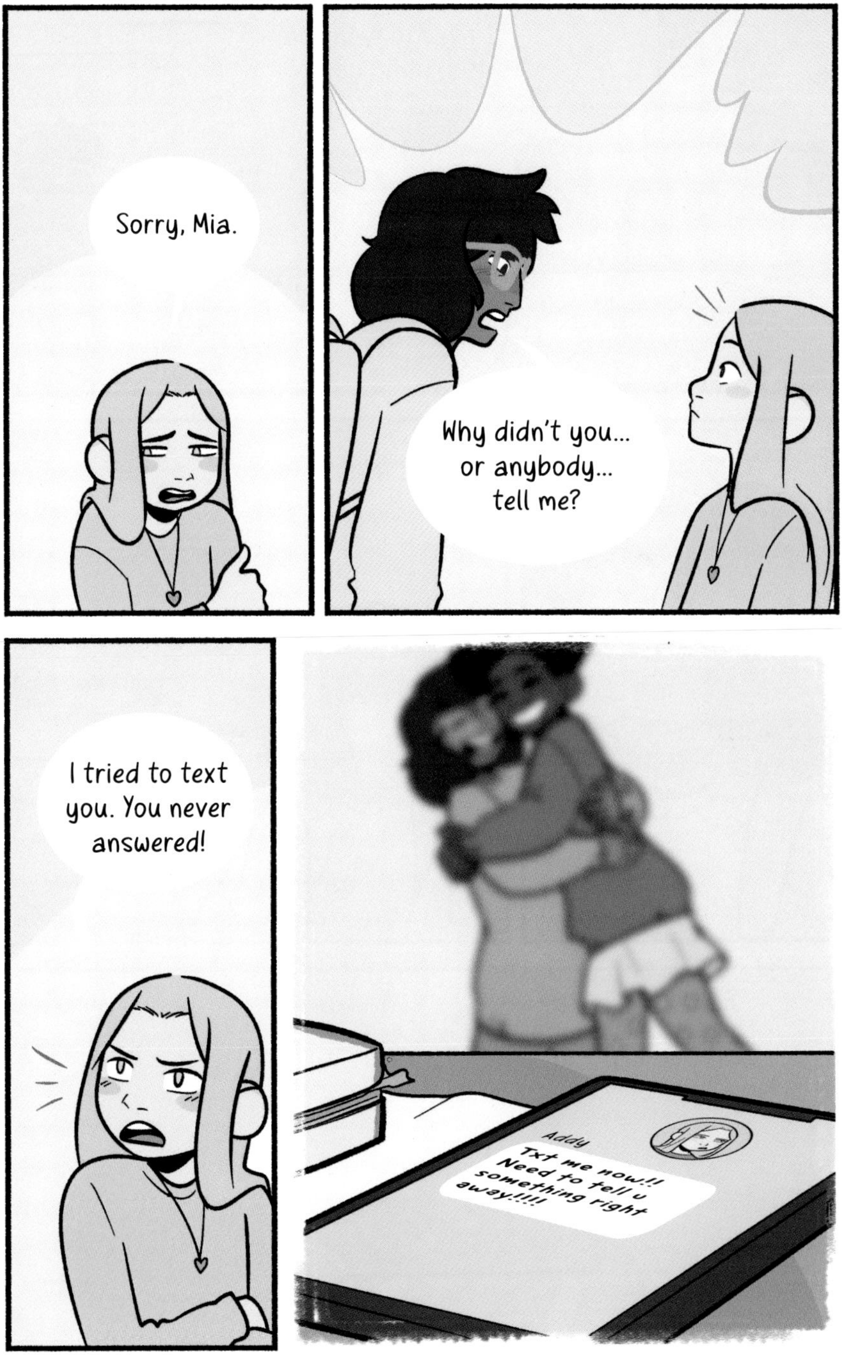
Sorry, Mia.
Why didn't you... or anybody... tell me?
I tried to text you. You never answered!
Addy
Txt me now!! Need to tell u something right away!!!!

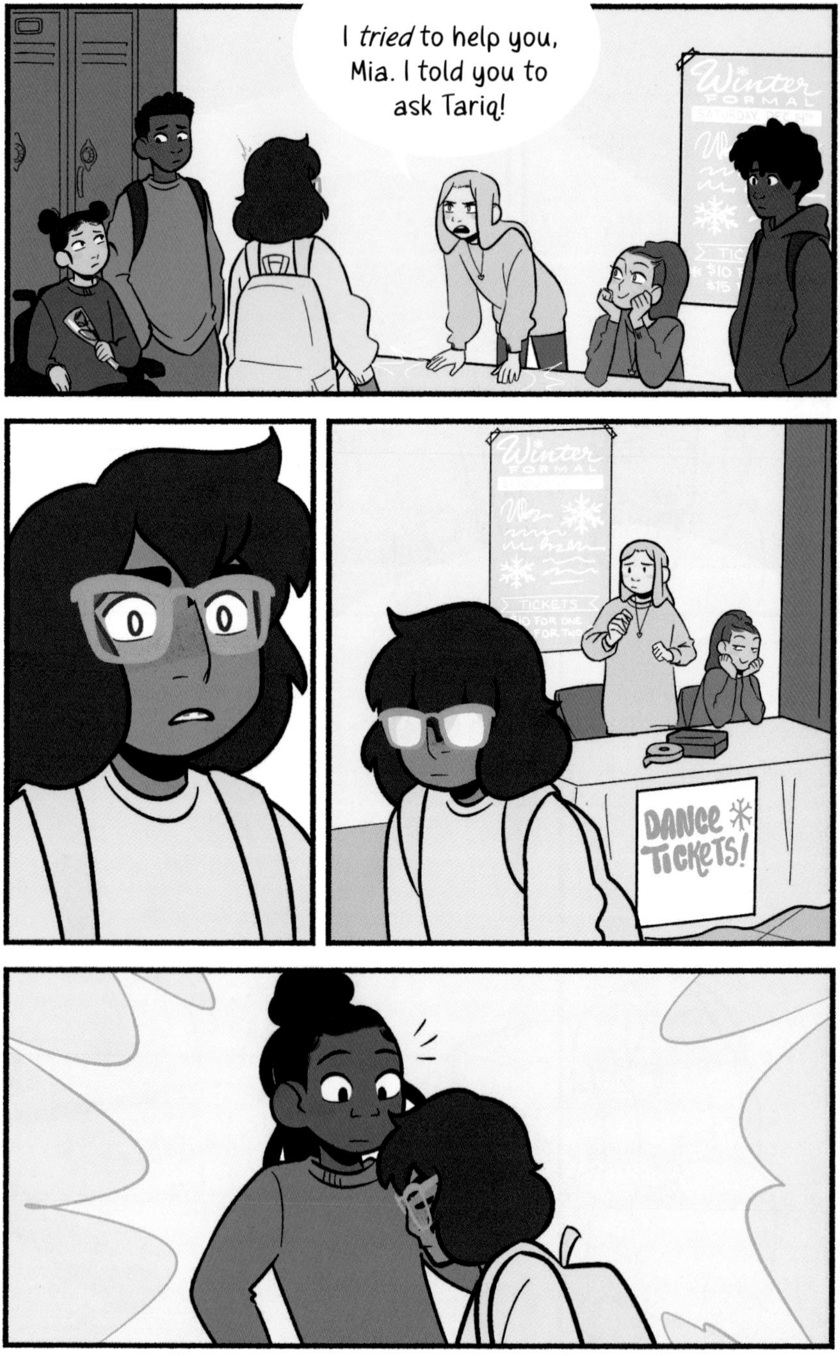
I *tried* to help you, Mia. I told you to ask Tariq!
Winter FORMAL
TICKETS
DANCE TICKETS!

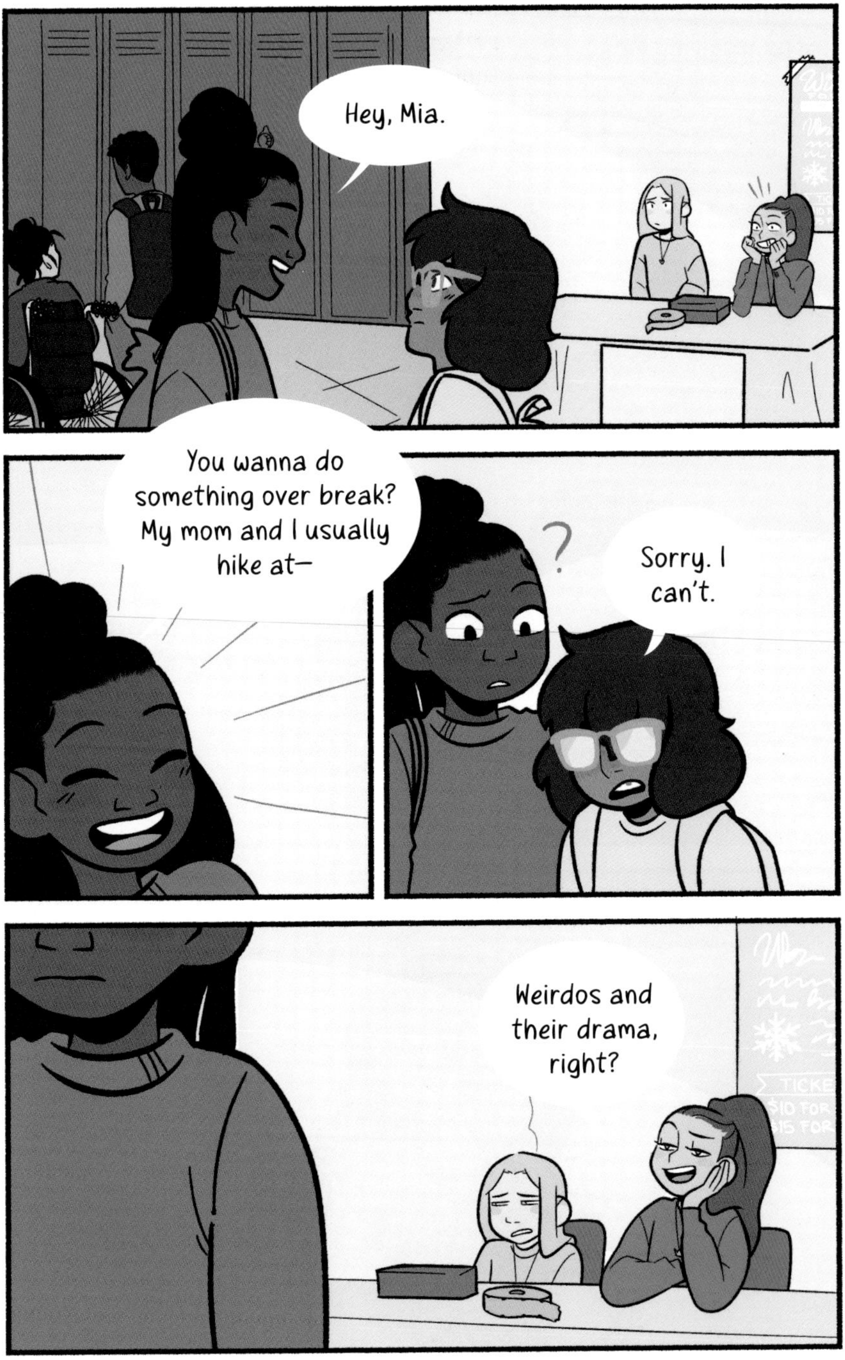
Hey, Mia.
You wanna do something over break? My mom and I usually hike at—
Sorry. I can't.
Weirdos and their drama, right?

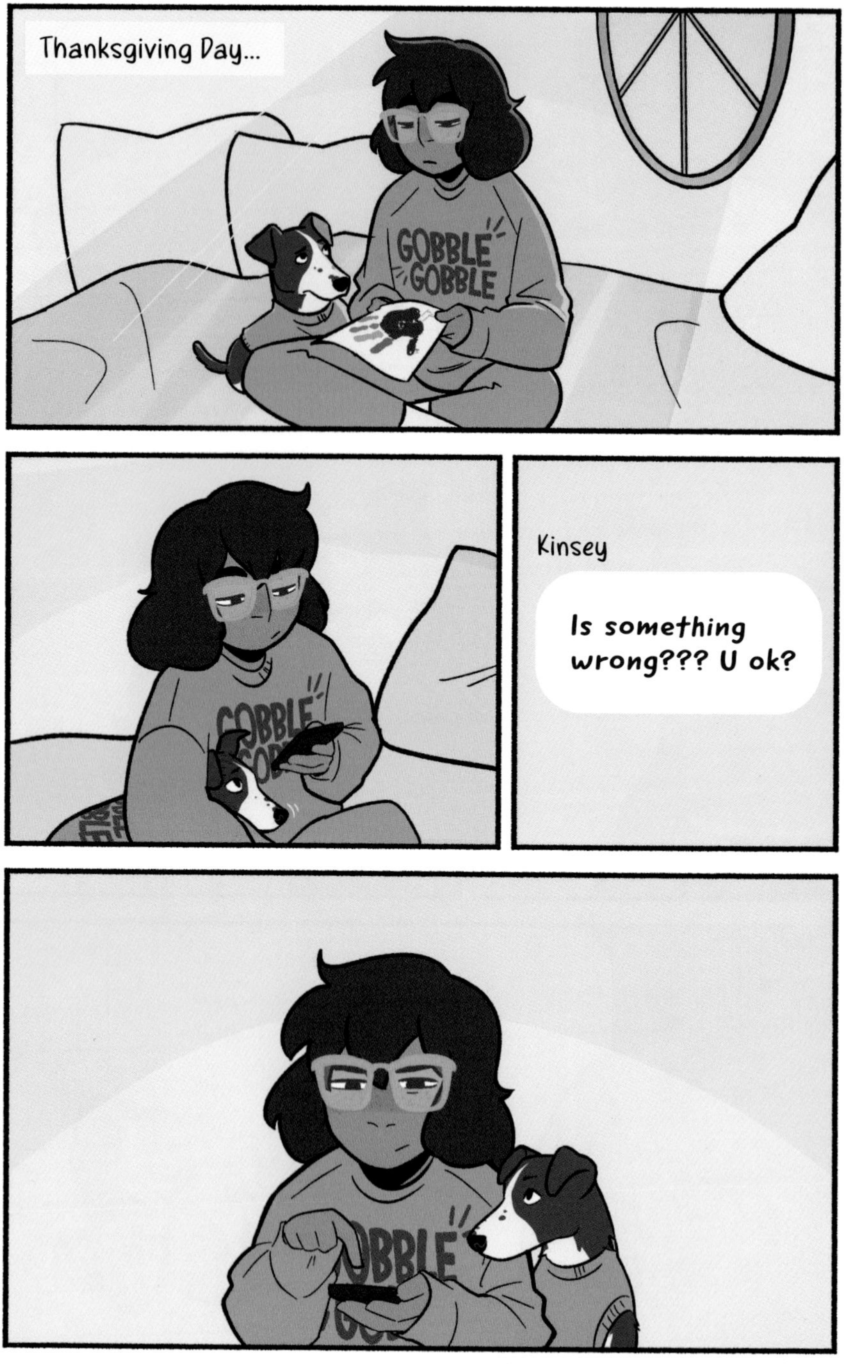
Thanksgiving Day...
GOBBLE GOBBLE
Kinsey
Is something wrong??? U ok?

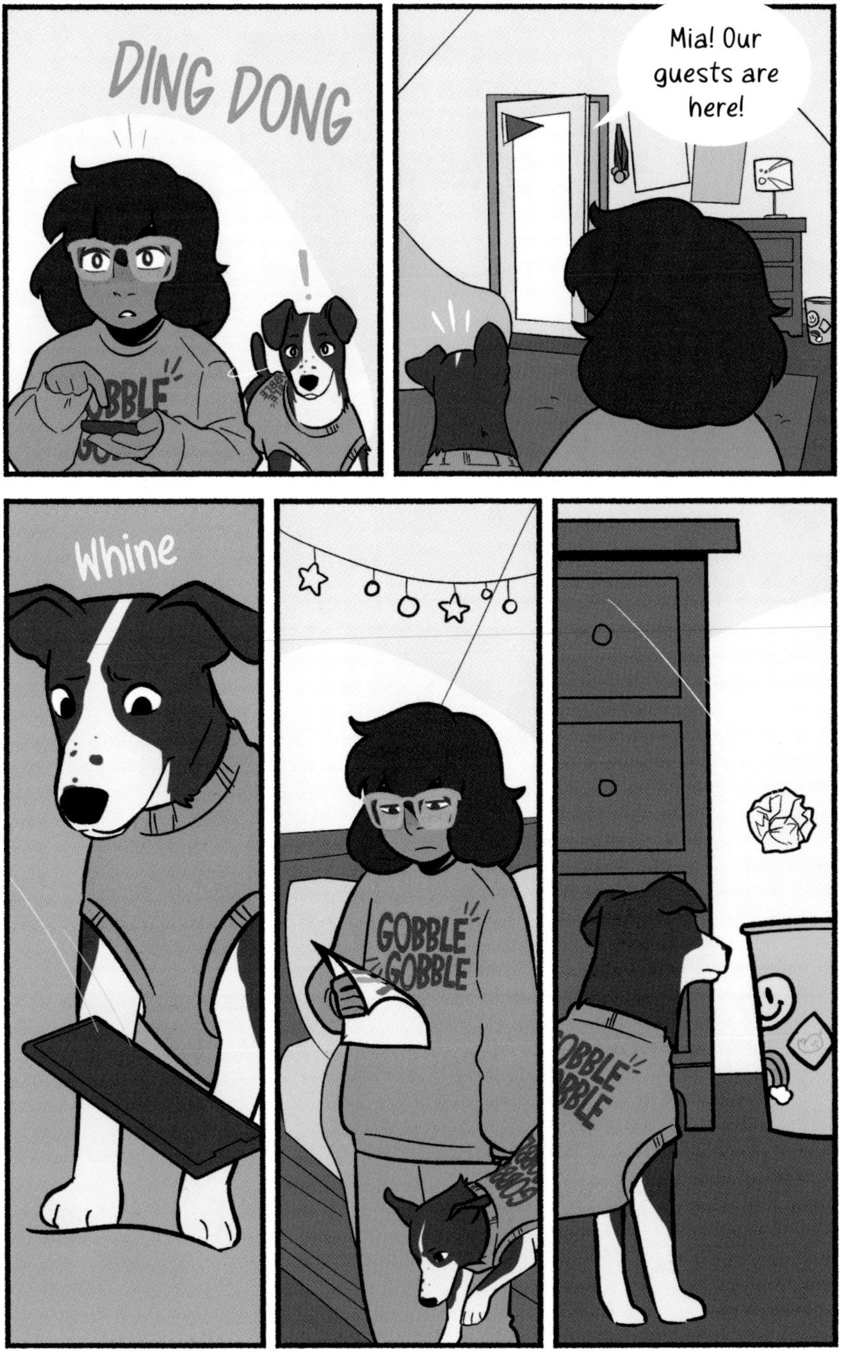
DING DONG
Mia! Our guests are here!
Whine
GOBBLE GOBBLE

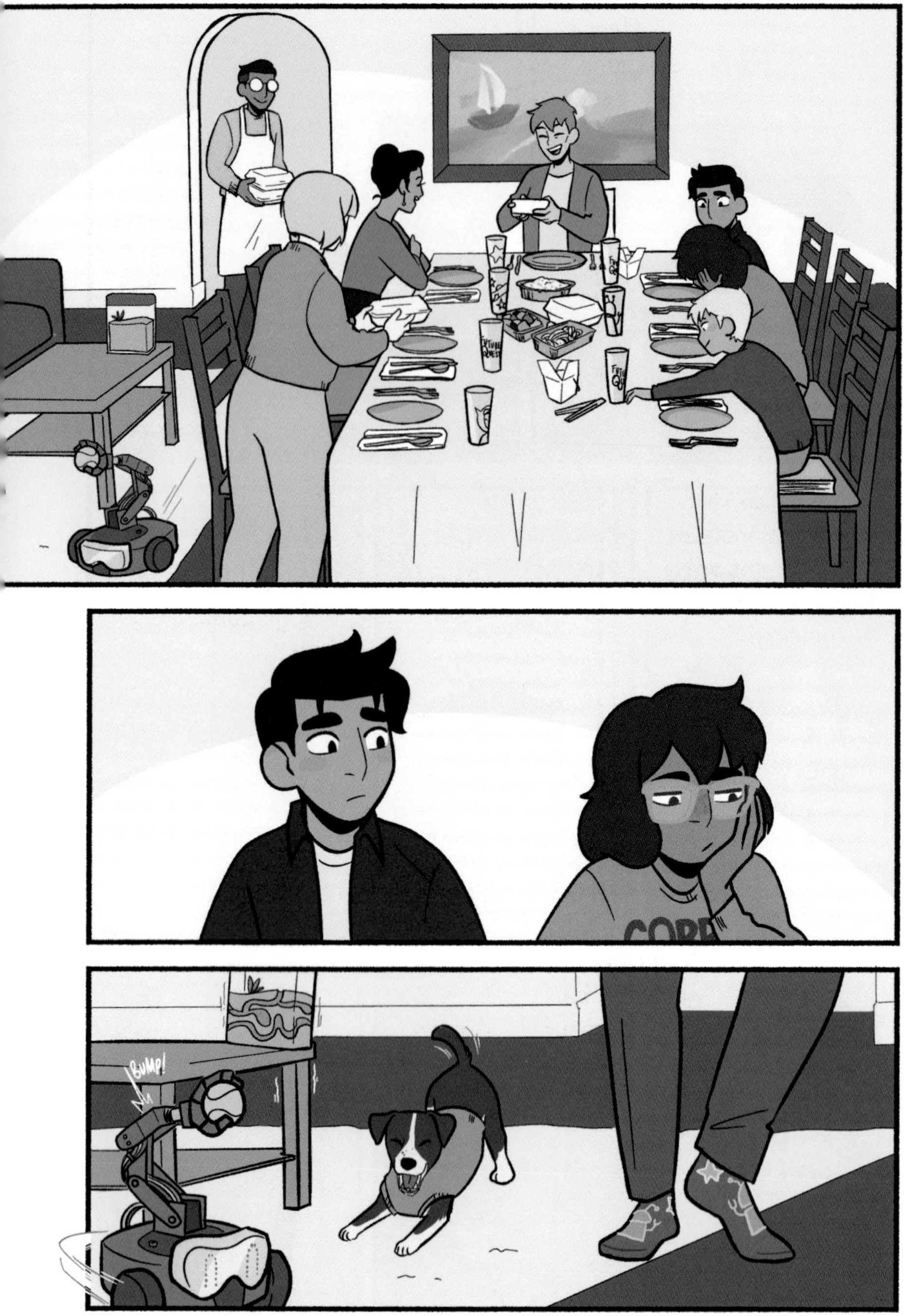
FUTURE QUEST
BUMP!

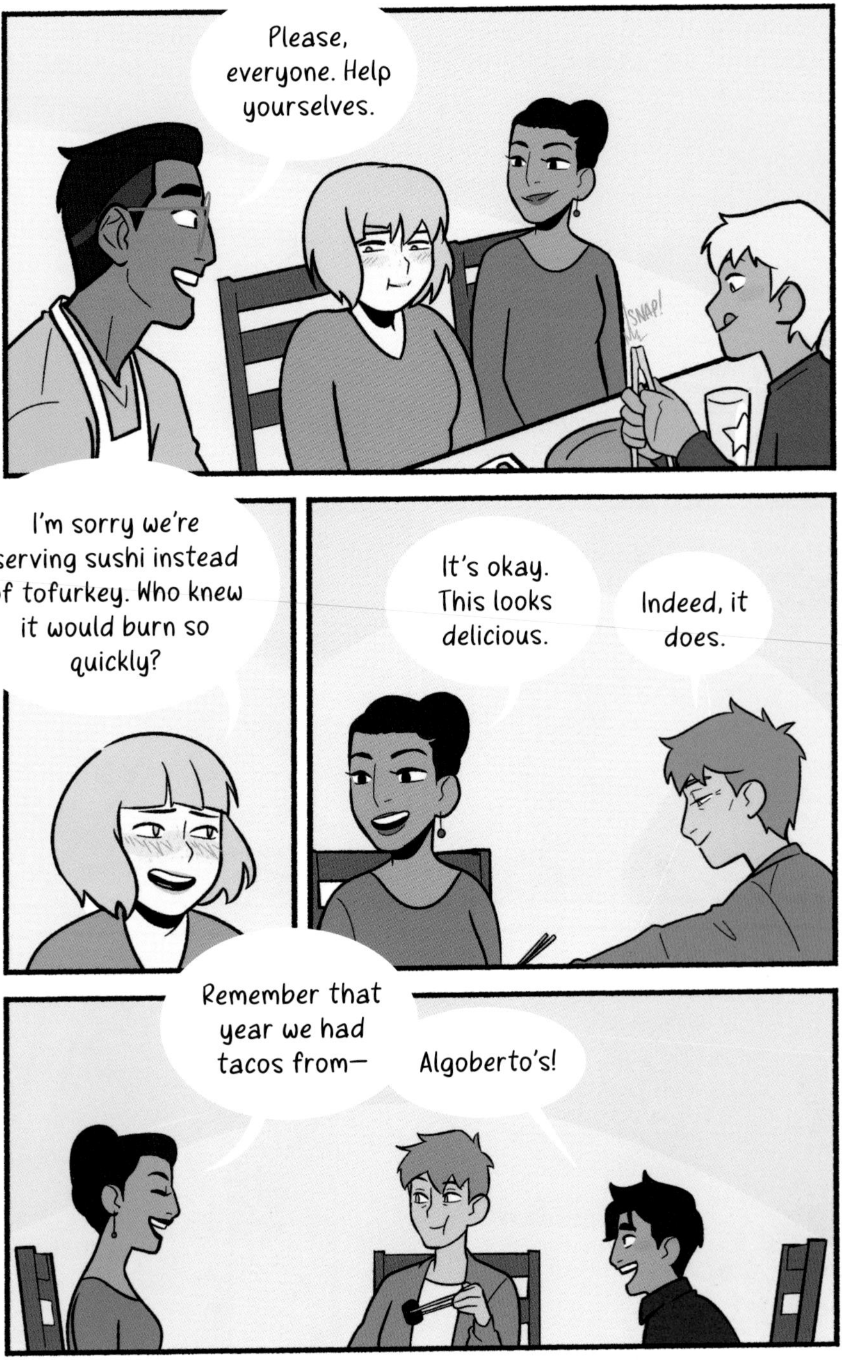
Please, everyone. Help yourselves.
SNAP!
I'm sorry we're serving sushi instead of tofurkey. Who knew it would burn so quickly?
It's okay. This looks delicious.
Indeed, it does.
Remember that year we had tacos from—
Algoberto's!

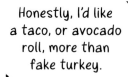

Honestly, I'd like a taco, or avocado roll, more than fake turkey.

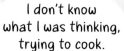

I don't know what I was thinking, trying to cook.

You have other talents—no doubt inherited from your legendary mother!

You're too kind.

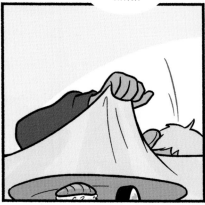

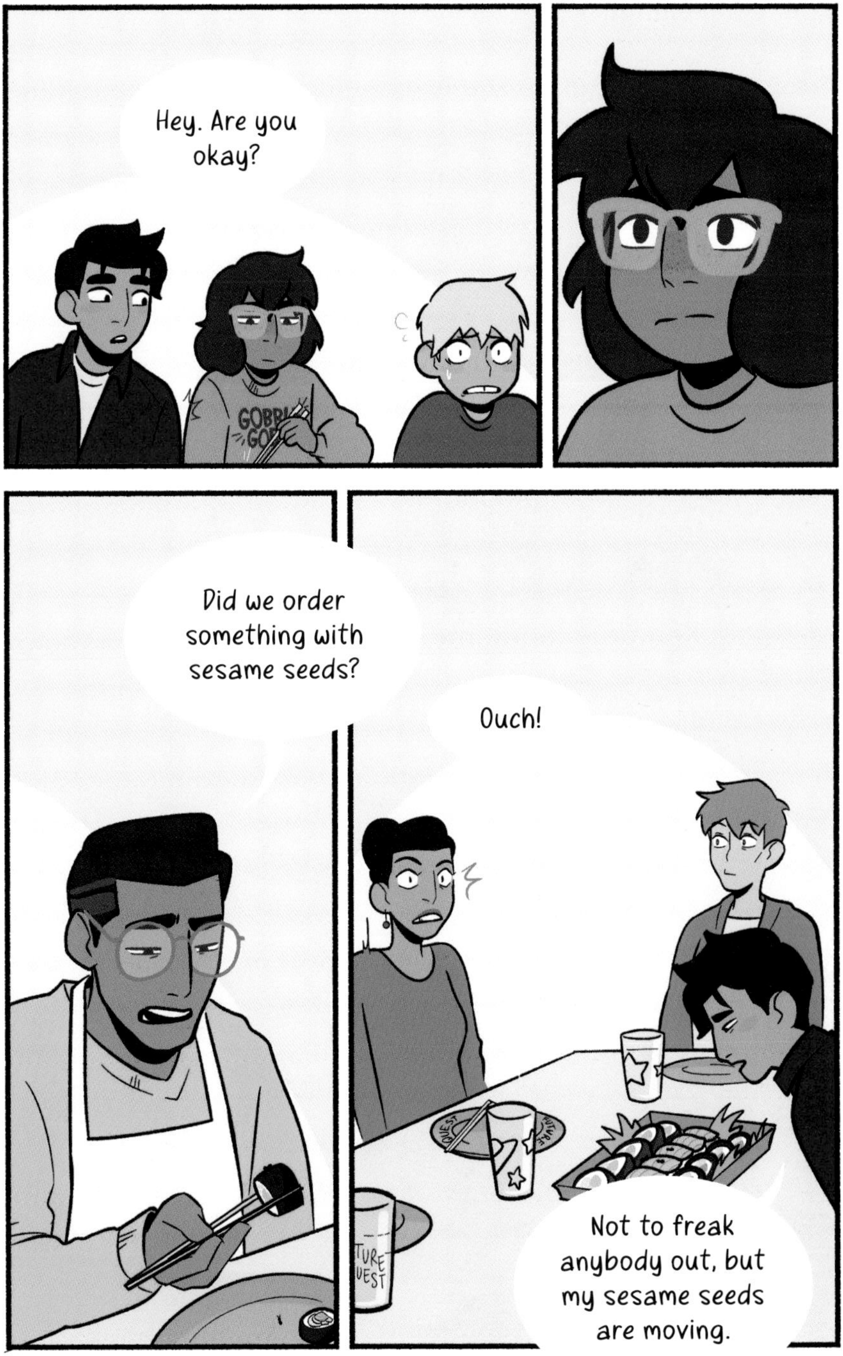
Hey. Are you okay?
GOBBLE GOB
Did we order something with sesame seeds?
Ouch!
Not to freak anybody out, but my sesame seeds are moving.

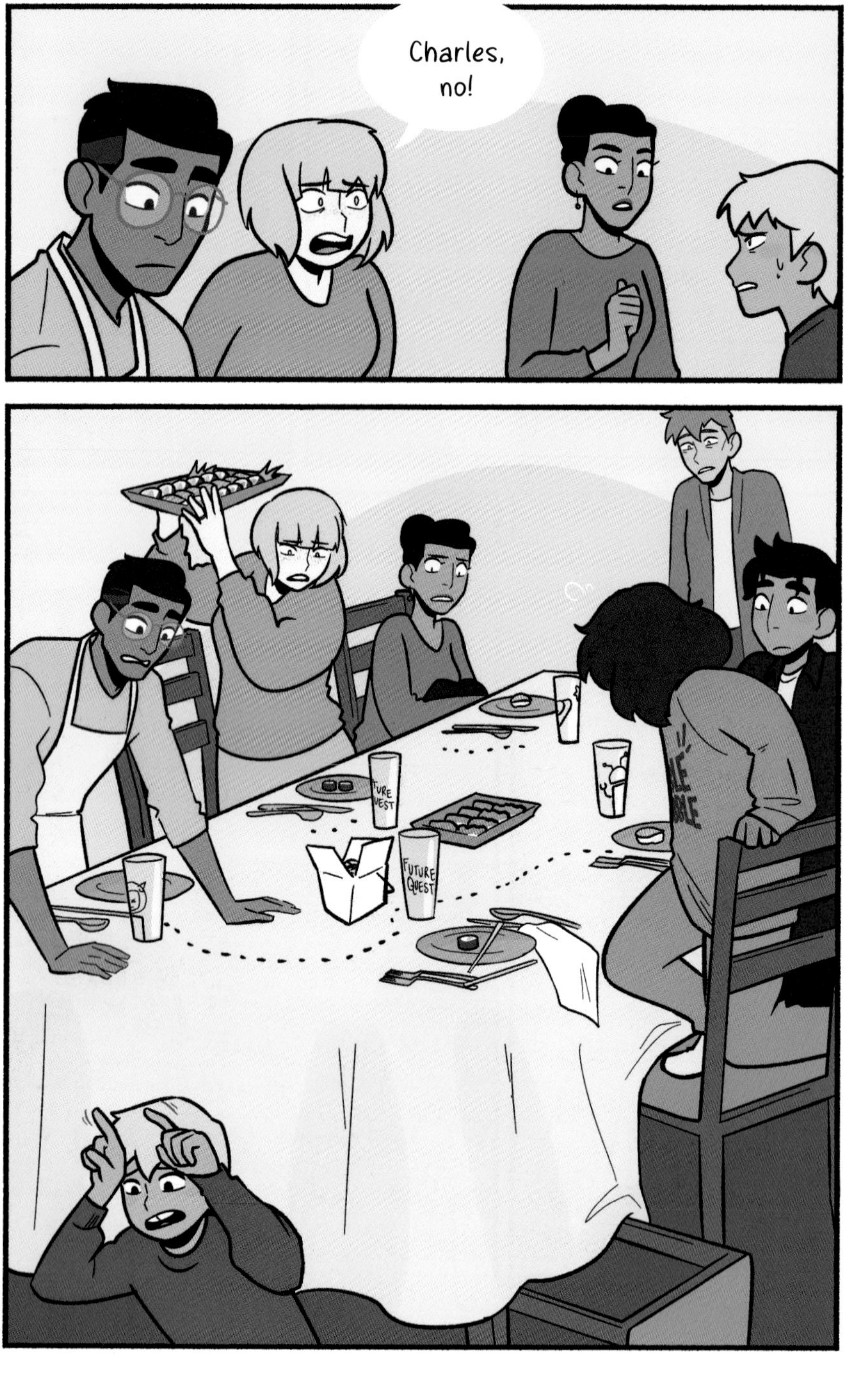
Charles,
no!
FUTURE QUEST
FUTURE QUEST

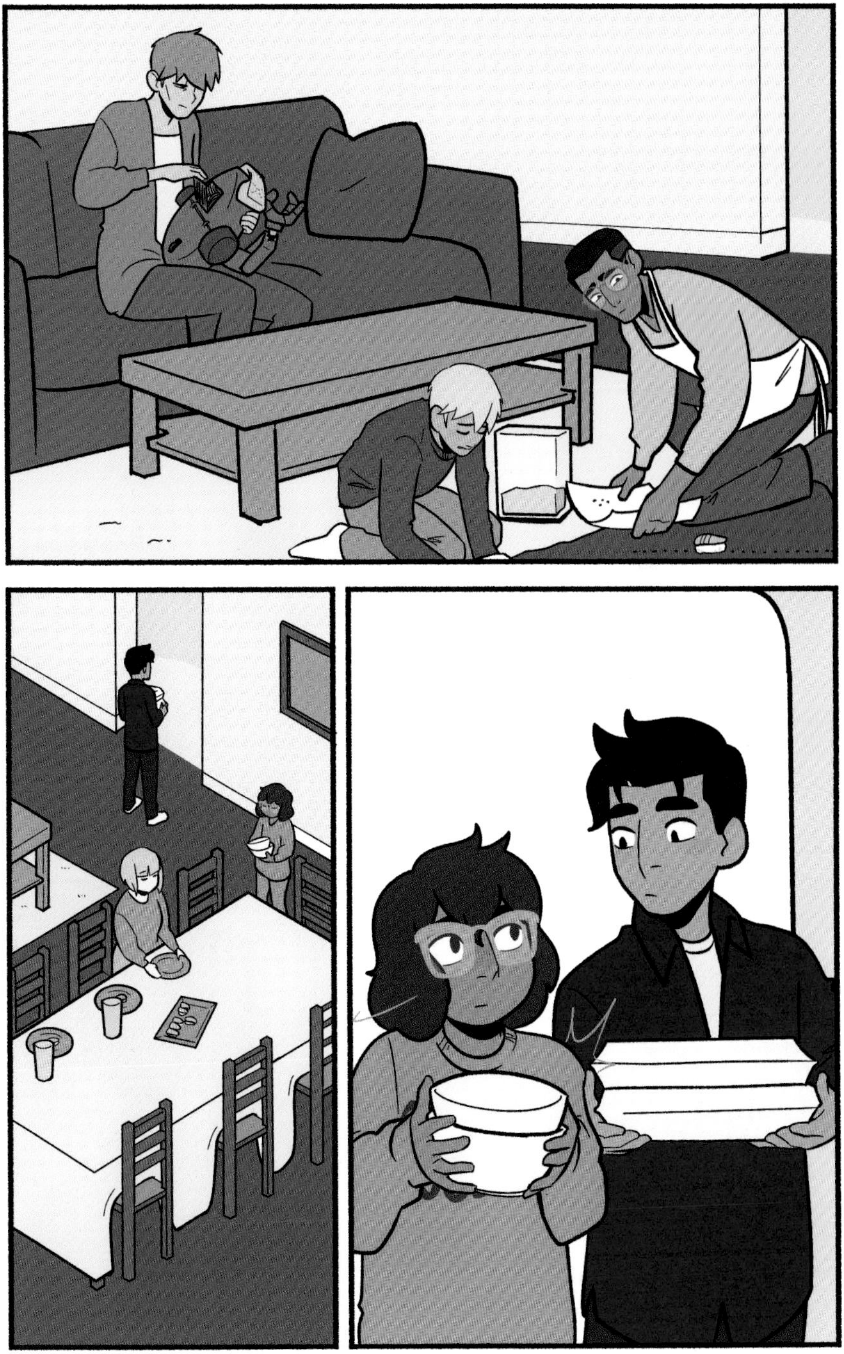

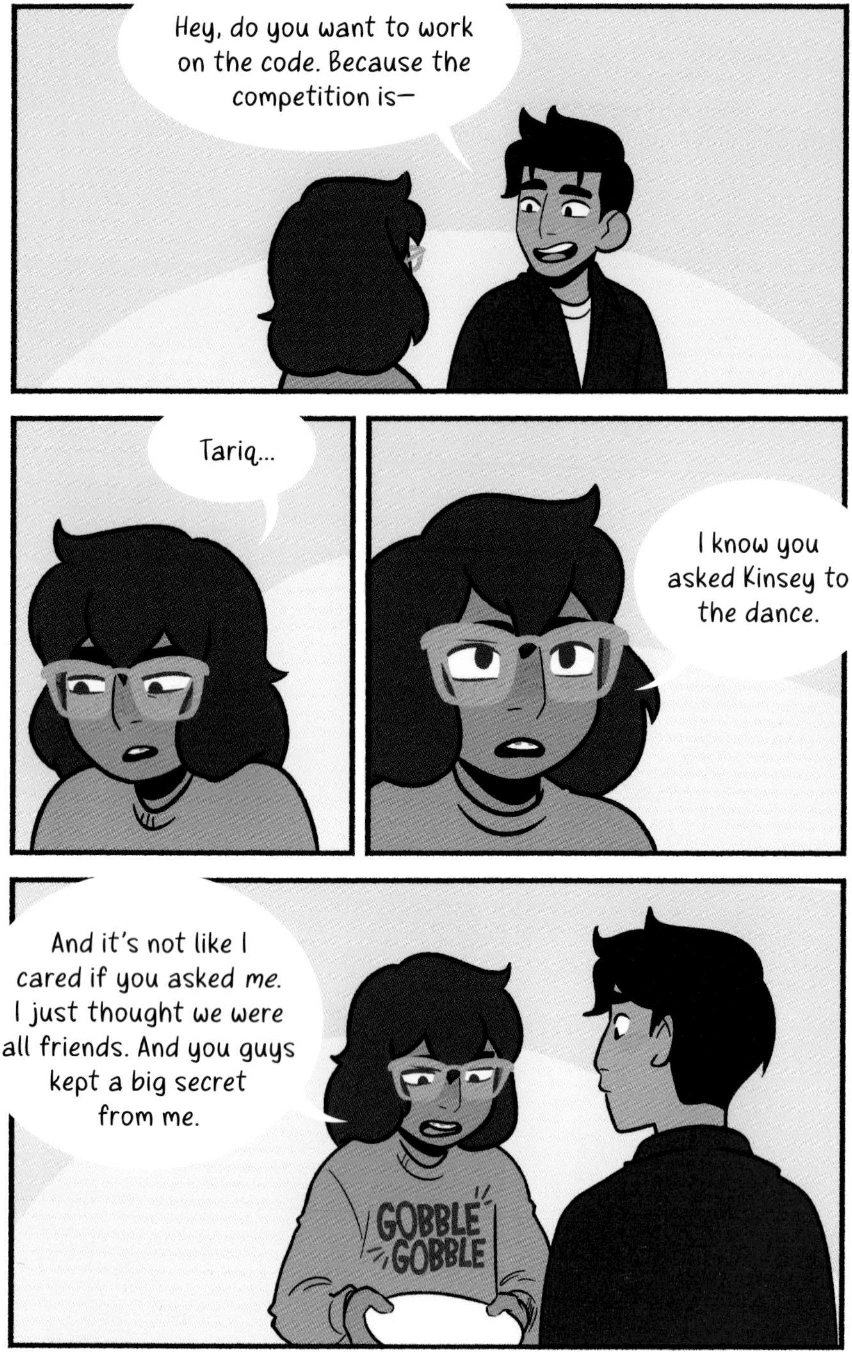
Hey, do you want to work on the code. Because the competition is—
Tariq...
I know you asked Kinsey to the dance.
And it's not like I cared if you asked *me*. I just thought we were all friends. And you guys kept a big secret from me.
GOBBLE GOBBLE

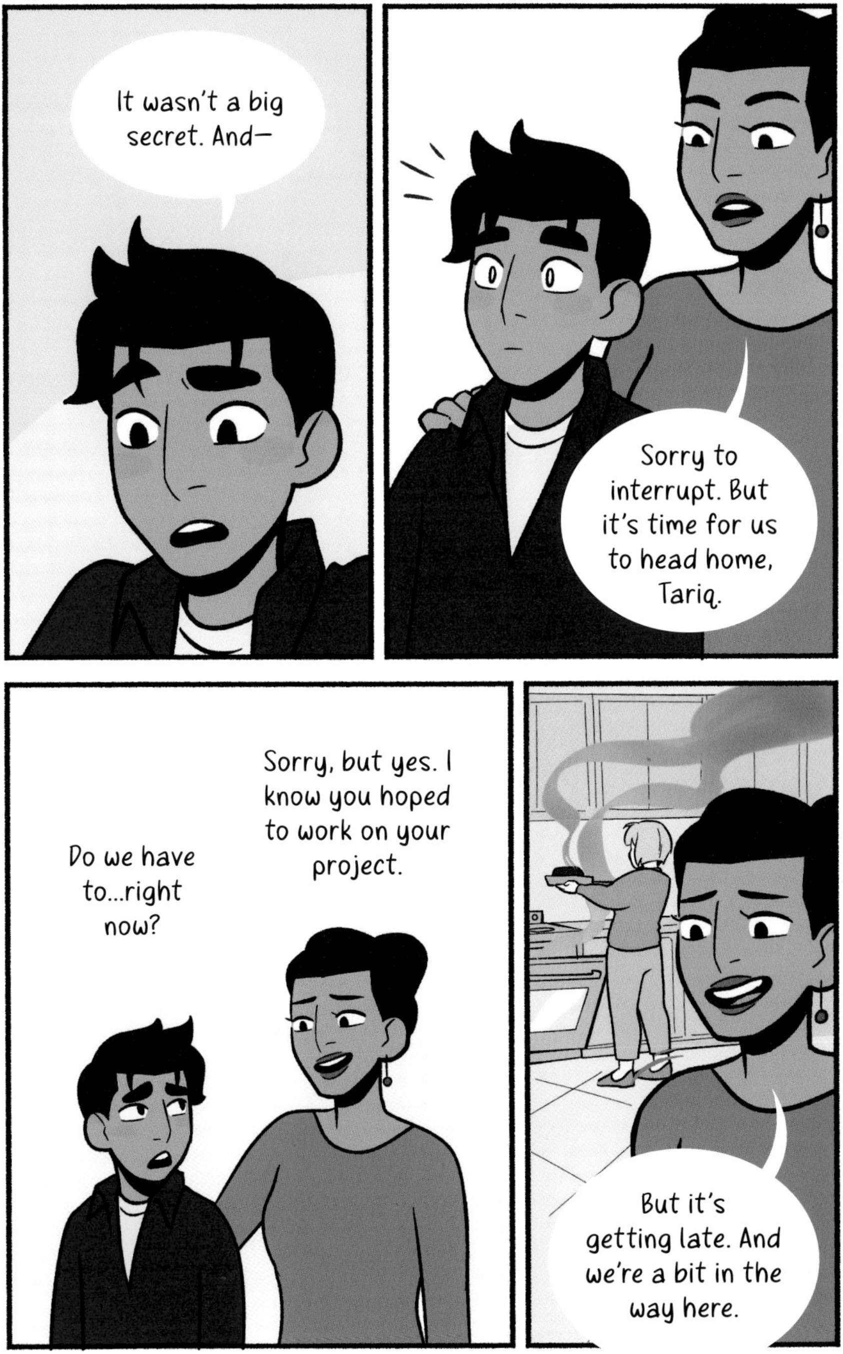
It wasn't a big secret. And—
Sorry to interrupt. But it's time for us to head home, Tariq.
Do we have to...right now?
Sorry, but yes. I know you hoped to work on your project.
But it's getting late. And we're a bit in the way here.

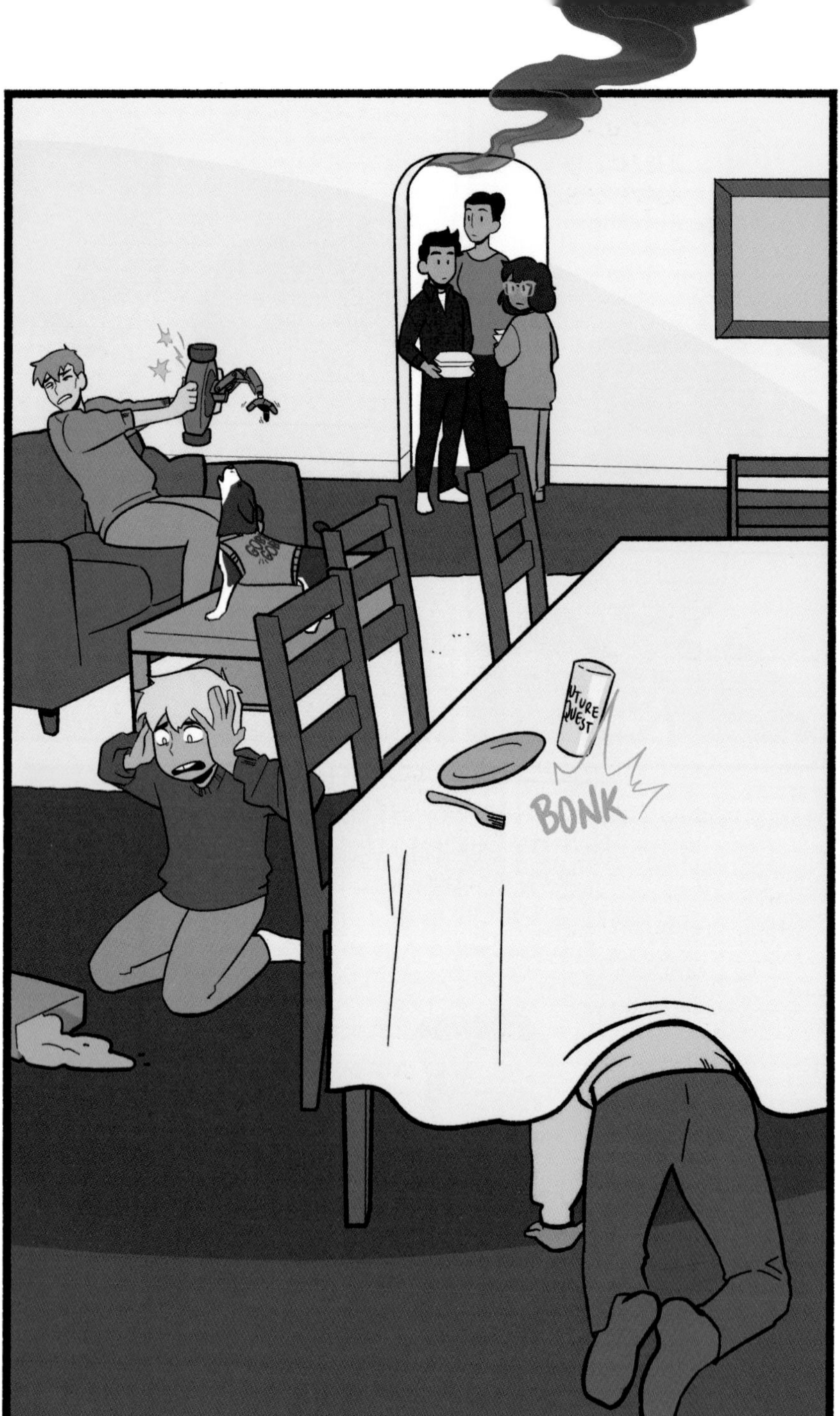
...
..
UTURE
QUEST
BONK

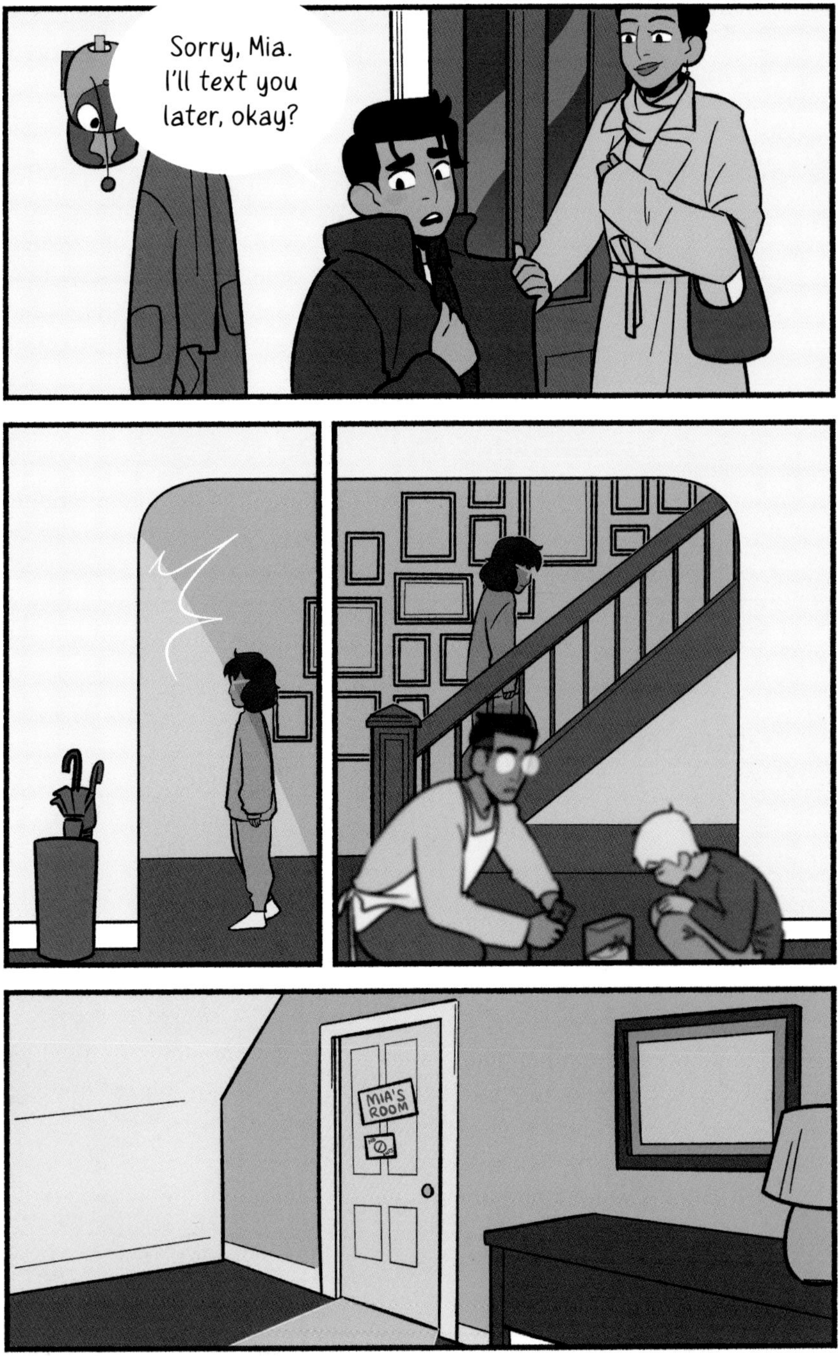
Sorry, Mia. I'll text you later, okay?
MIA'S ROOM

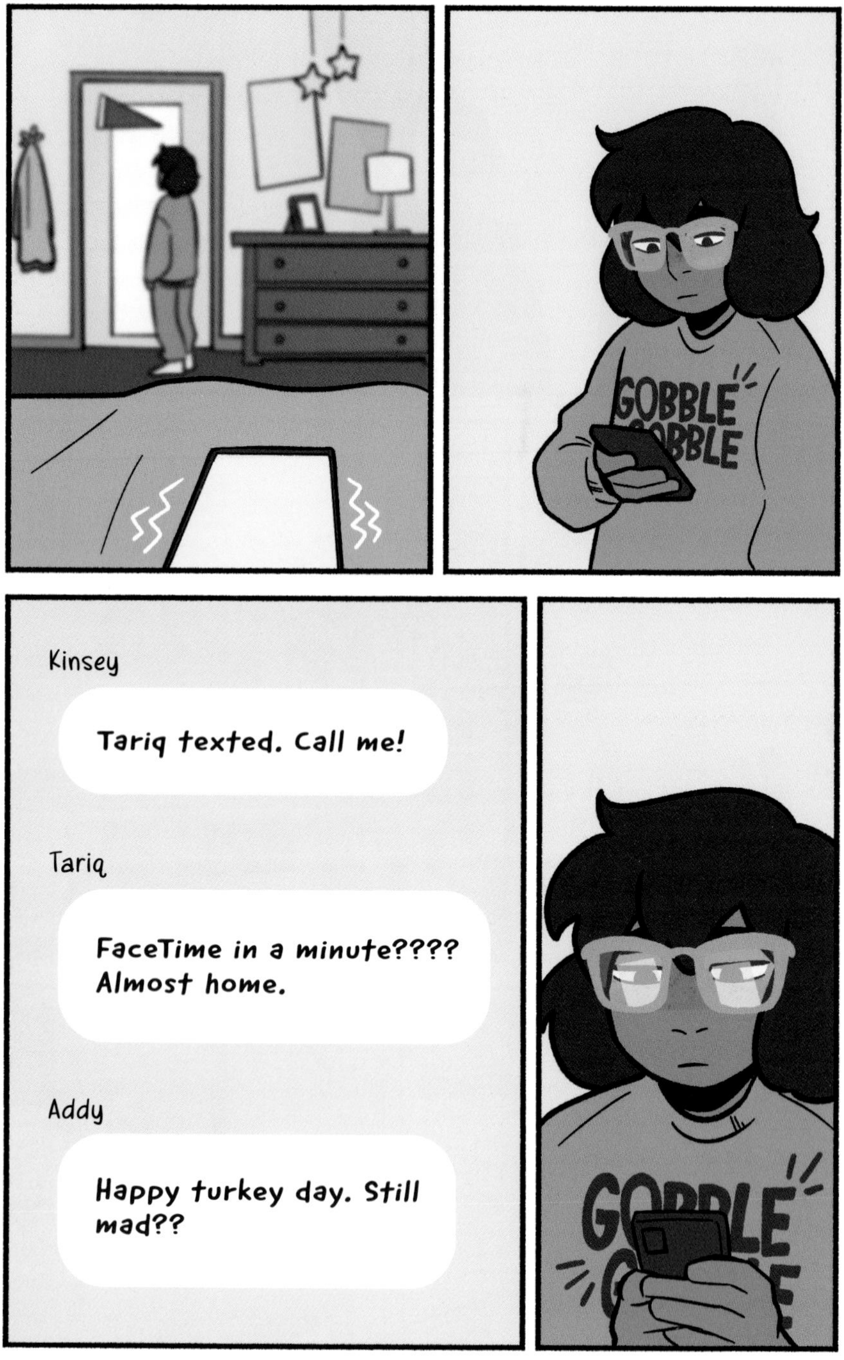
GOBBLE GOBBLE
Kinsey
Tariq texted. Call me!
Tariq
FaceTime in a minute????
Almost home.
Addy
Happy turkey day. Still
mad??

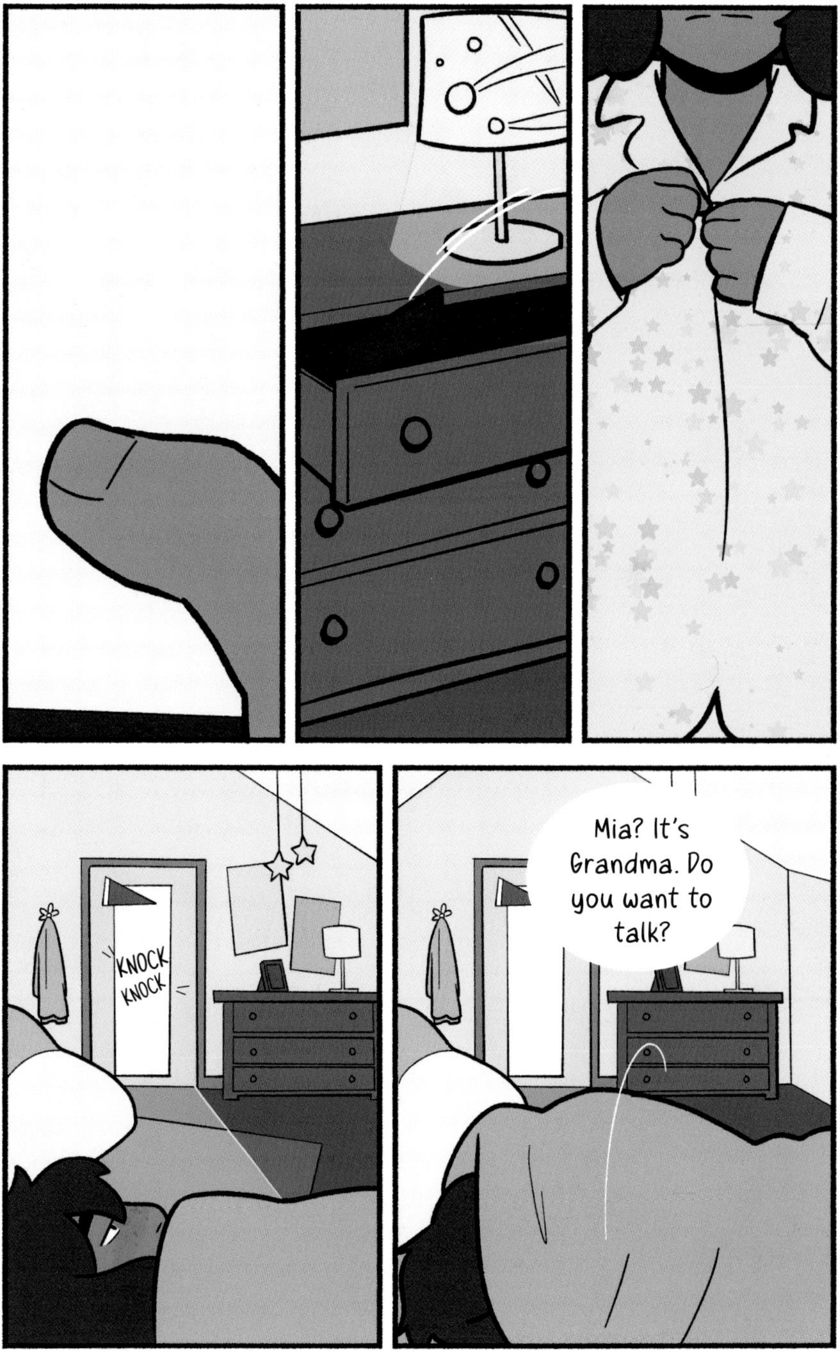
KNOCK KNOCK
Mia? It's Grandma. Do you want to talk?

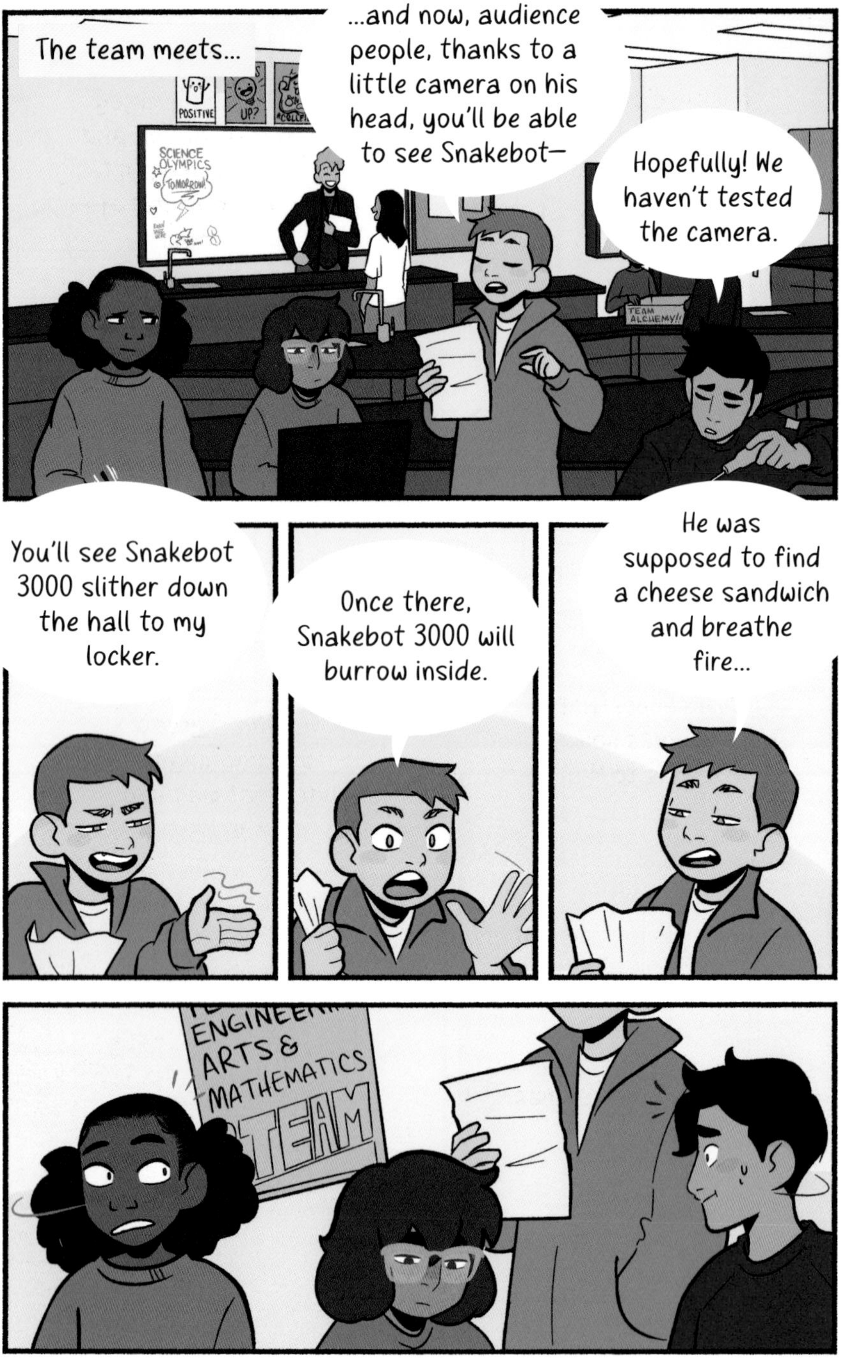
The team meets...
POSITIVE
UP?
SCIENCE OLYMPICS
TOMORROW!
...and now, audience people, thanks to a little camera on his head, you'll be able to see Snakebot—
Hopefully! We haven't tested the camera.
TEAM ALCHEMY!!
You'll see Snakebot 3000 slither down the hall to my locker.
Once there, Snakebot 3000 will burrow inside.
He was supposed to find a cheese sandwich and breathe fire...
ARTS &
MATHEMATICS
TEAM

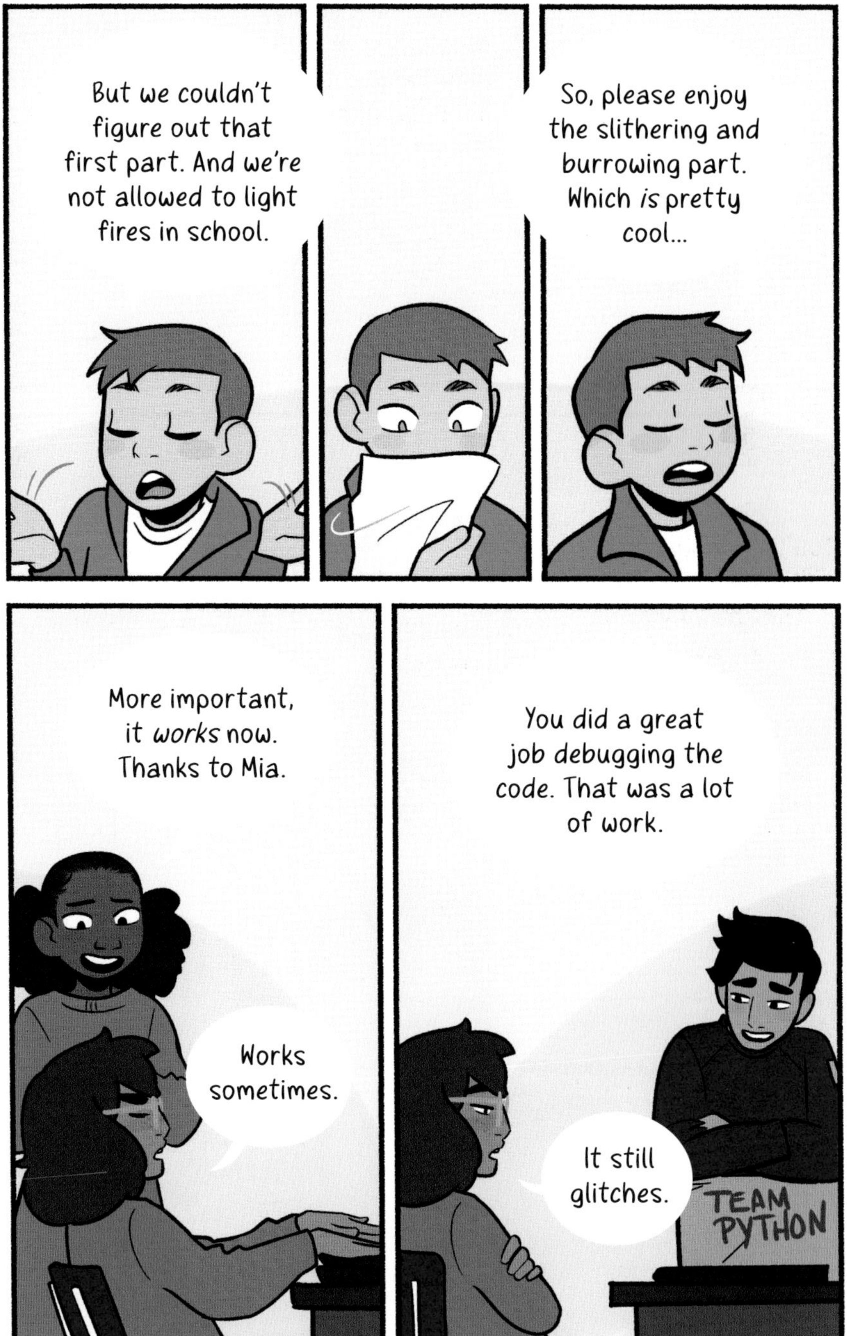
But we couldn't figure out that first part. And we're not allowed to light fires in school.
So, please enjoy the slithering and burrowing part. Which *is* pretty cool...
More important, it *works* now. Thanks to Mia.
Works sometimes.
You did a great job debugging the code. That was a lot of work.
It still glitches.
TEAM PYTHON

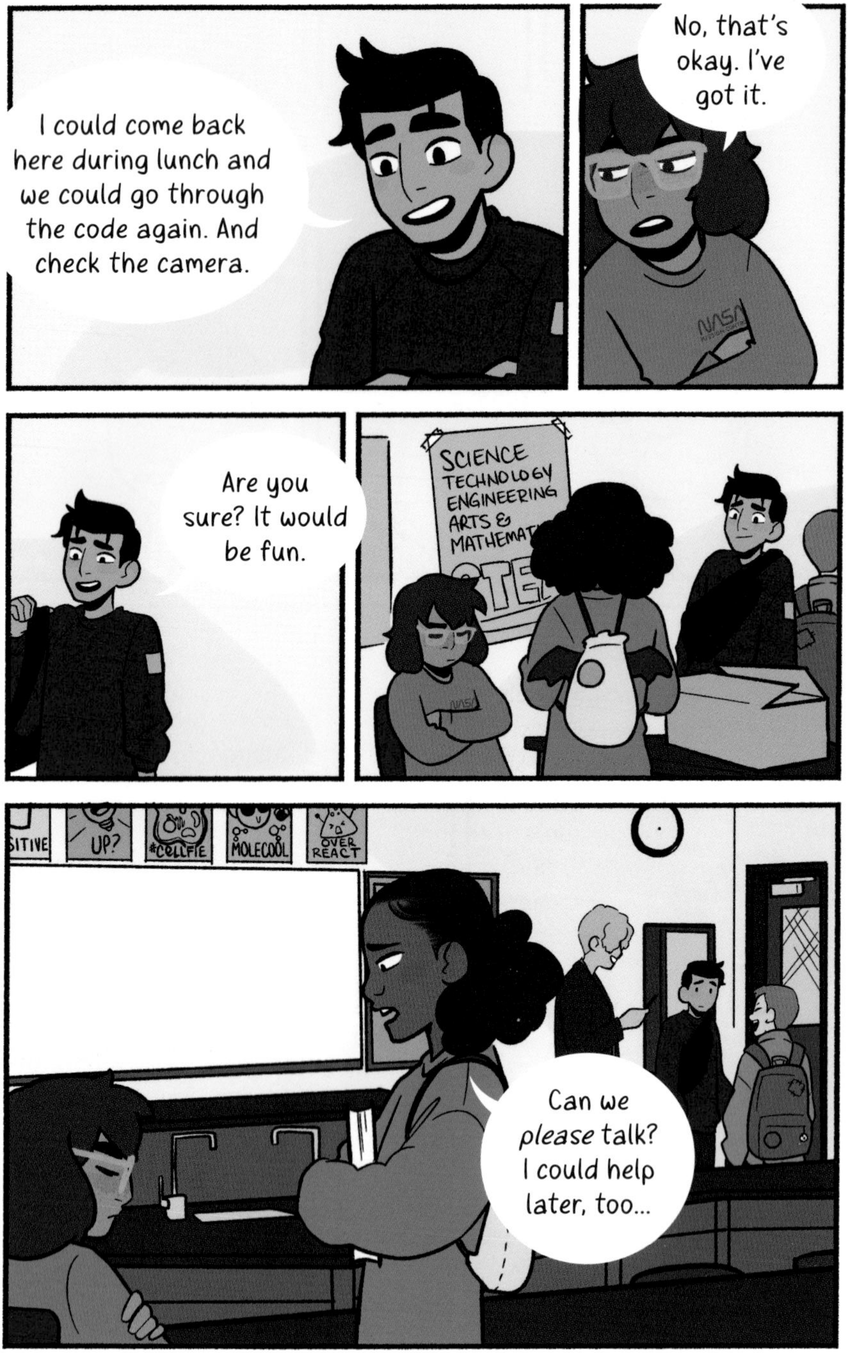
I could come back here during lunch and we could go through the code again. And check the camera.
No, that's okay. I've got it.
Are you sure? It would be fun.
SCIENCE
TECHNOLOGY
ENGINEERING
ARTS &
SITIVE
UP?
#CELLFIE
MOLECOOL
OVER REACT
Can we *please* talk? I could help later, too...

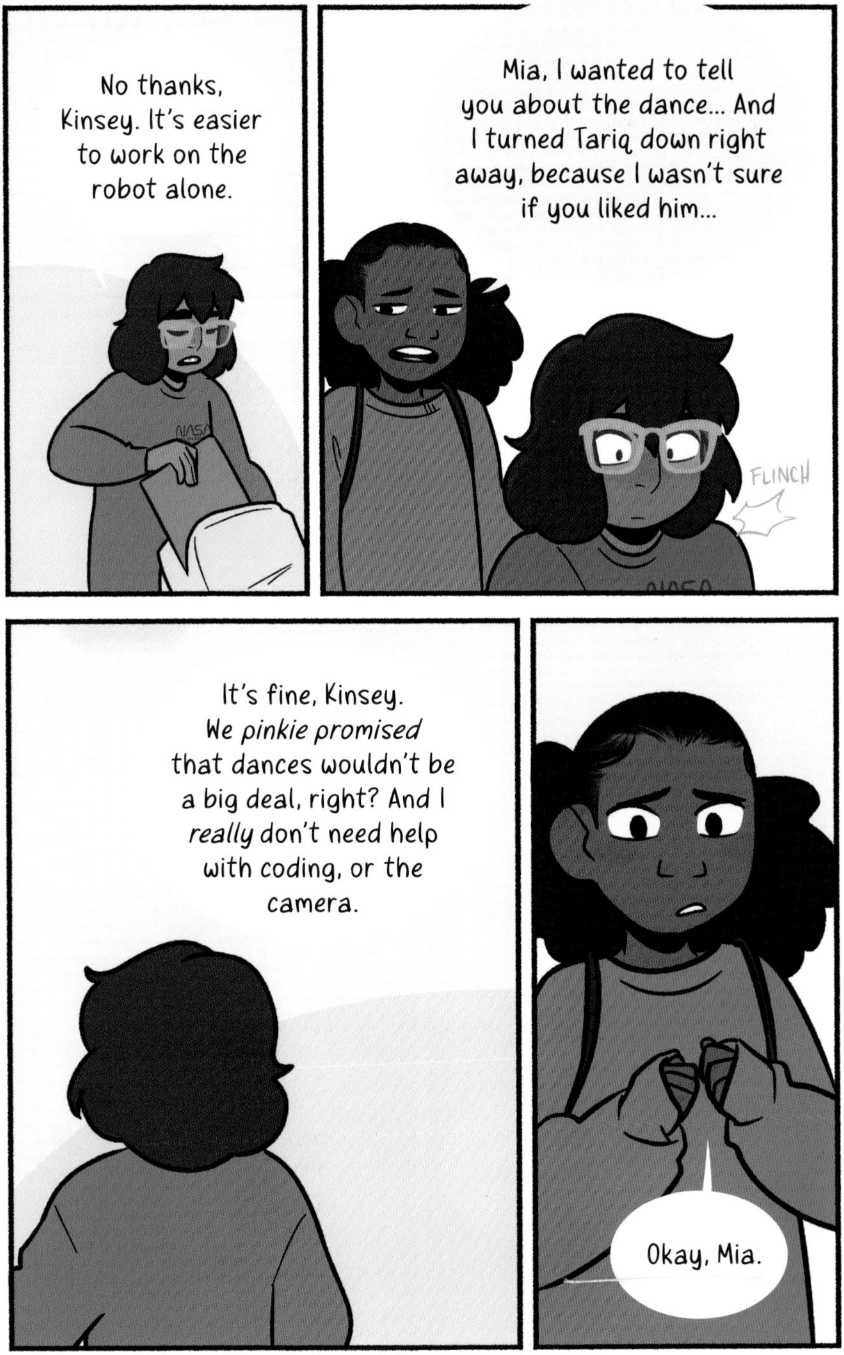
No thanks, Kinsey. It's *easier* to work on the robot alone.
Mia, I wanted to tell you about the dance... And I turned Tariq down right away, because I wasn't sure if you liked him...
FLINCH
It's fine, Kinsey. We *pinkie promised* that dances wouldn't be a big deal, right? And I *really* don't need help with coding, or the camera.
Okay, Mia.

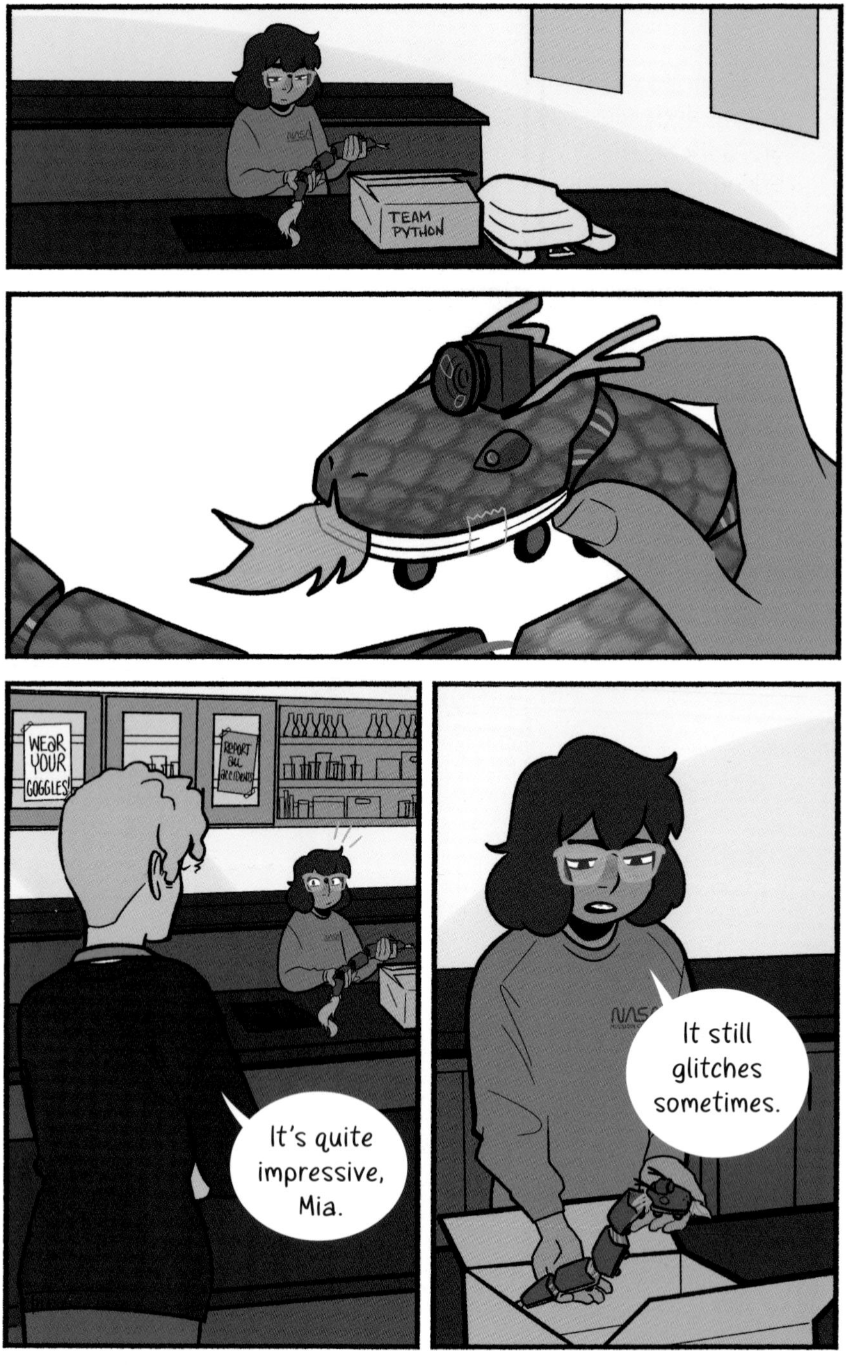
TEAM PYTHON
WEAR YOUR GOGGLES!
REPORT ALL ACCIDENTS
It's quite impressive, Mia.
It still glitches sometimes.

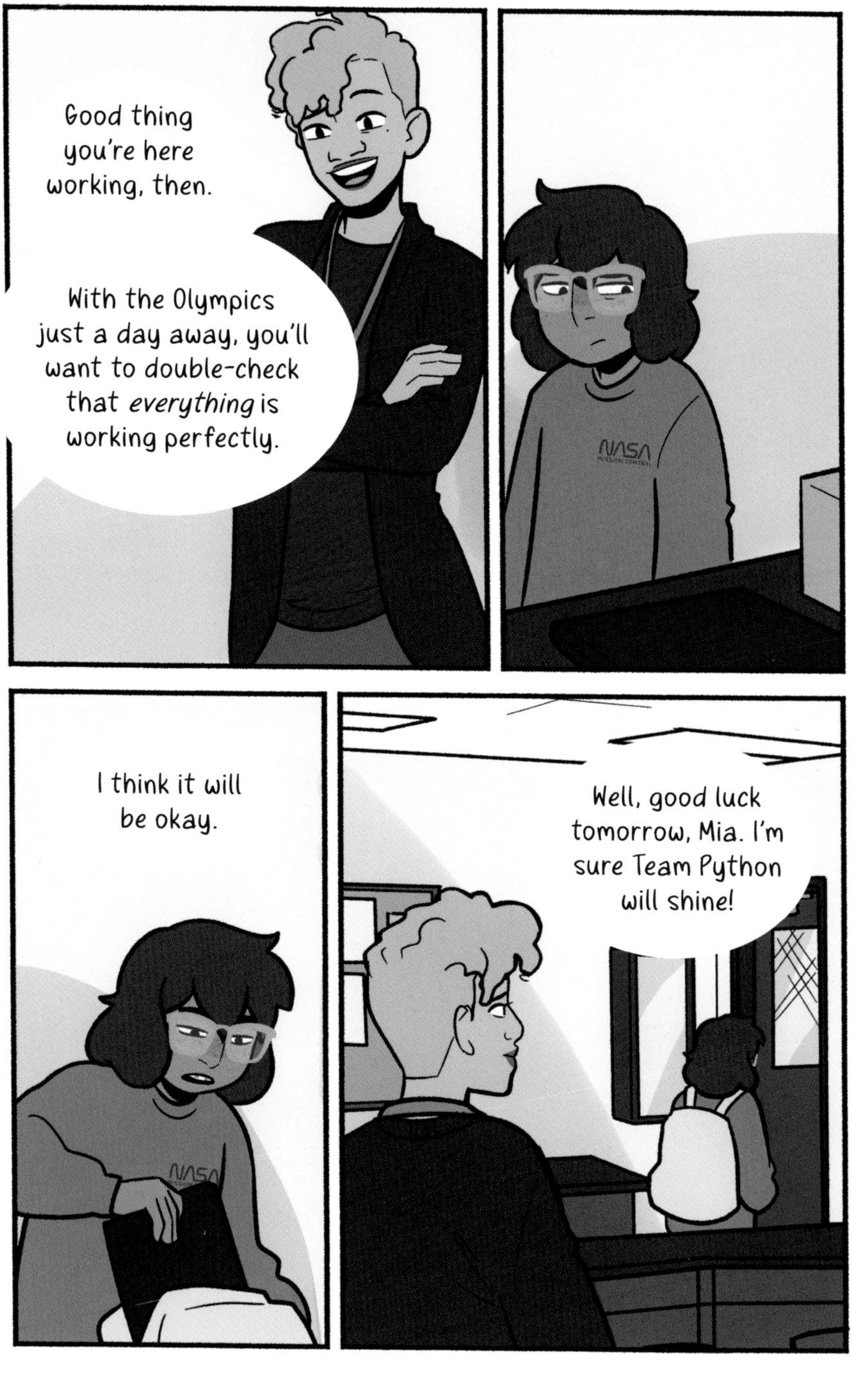
Good thing you're here working, then.
With the Olympics just a day away, you'll want to double-check that *everything* is working perfectly.
NASA
I think it will be okay.
NASA
Well, good luck tomorrow, Mia. I'm sure Team Python will shine!

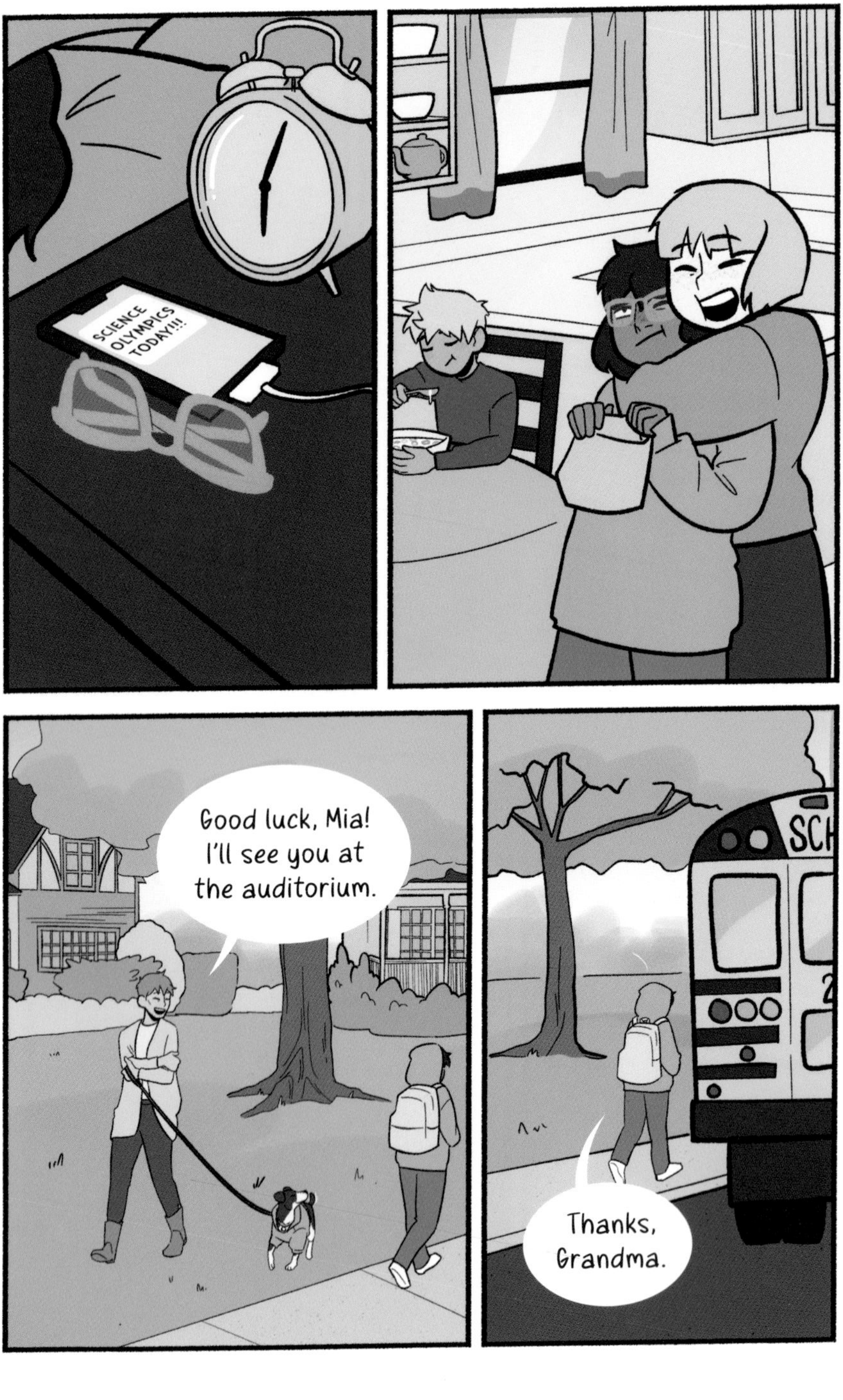
SCIENCE OLYMPICS TODAY!!!
Good luck, Mia! I'll see you at the auditorium.
SCH
Thanks, Grandma.

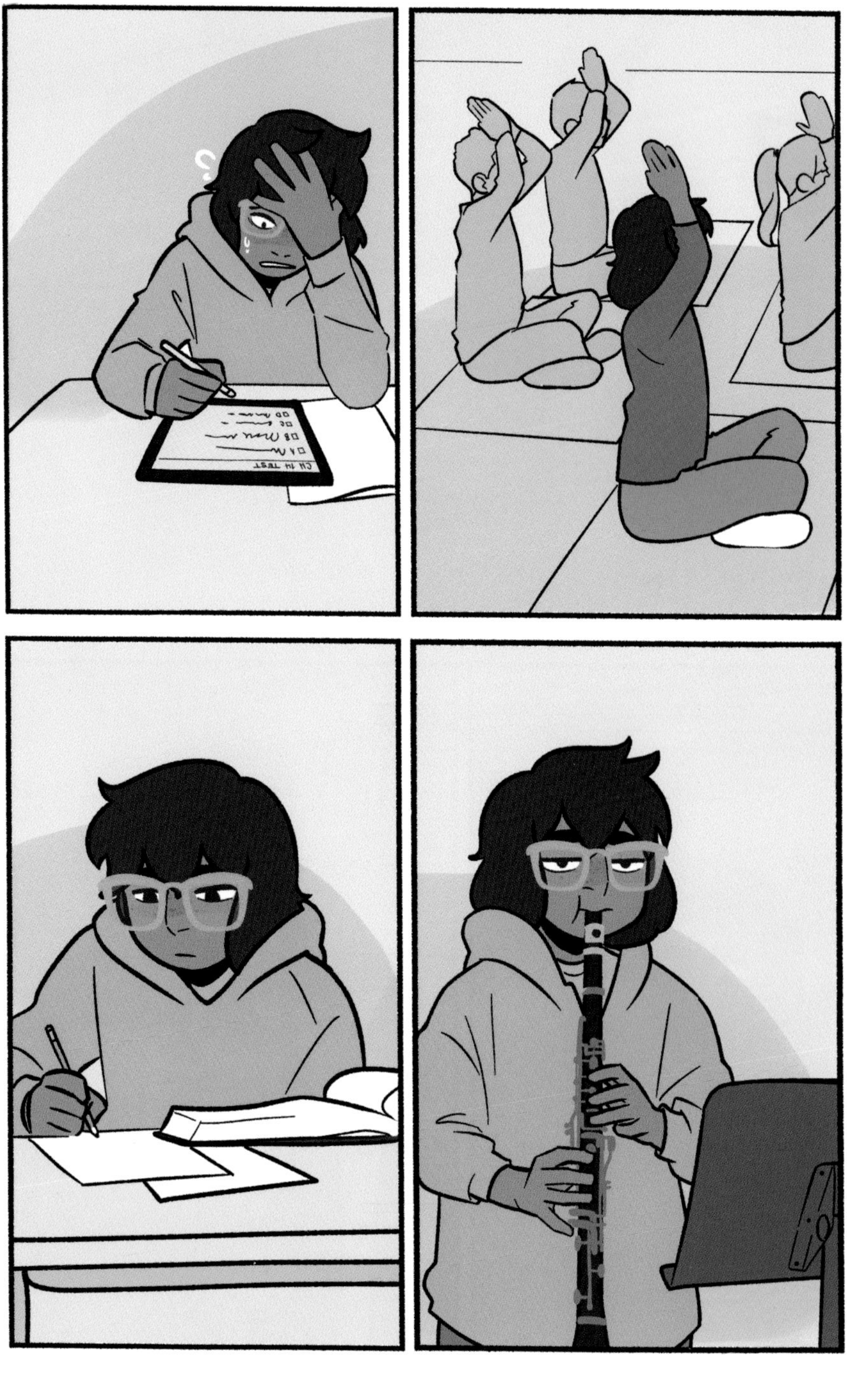
CH 14 TEST

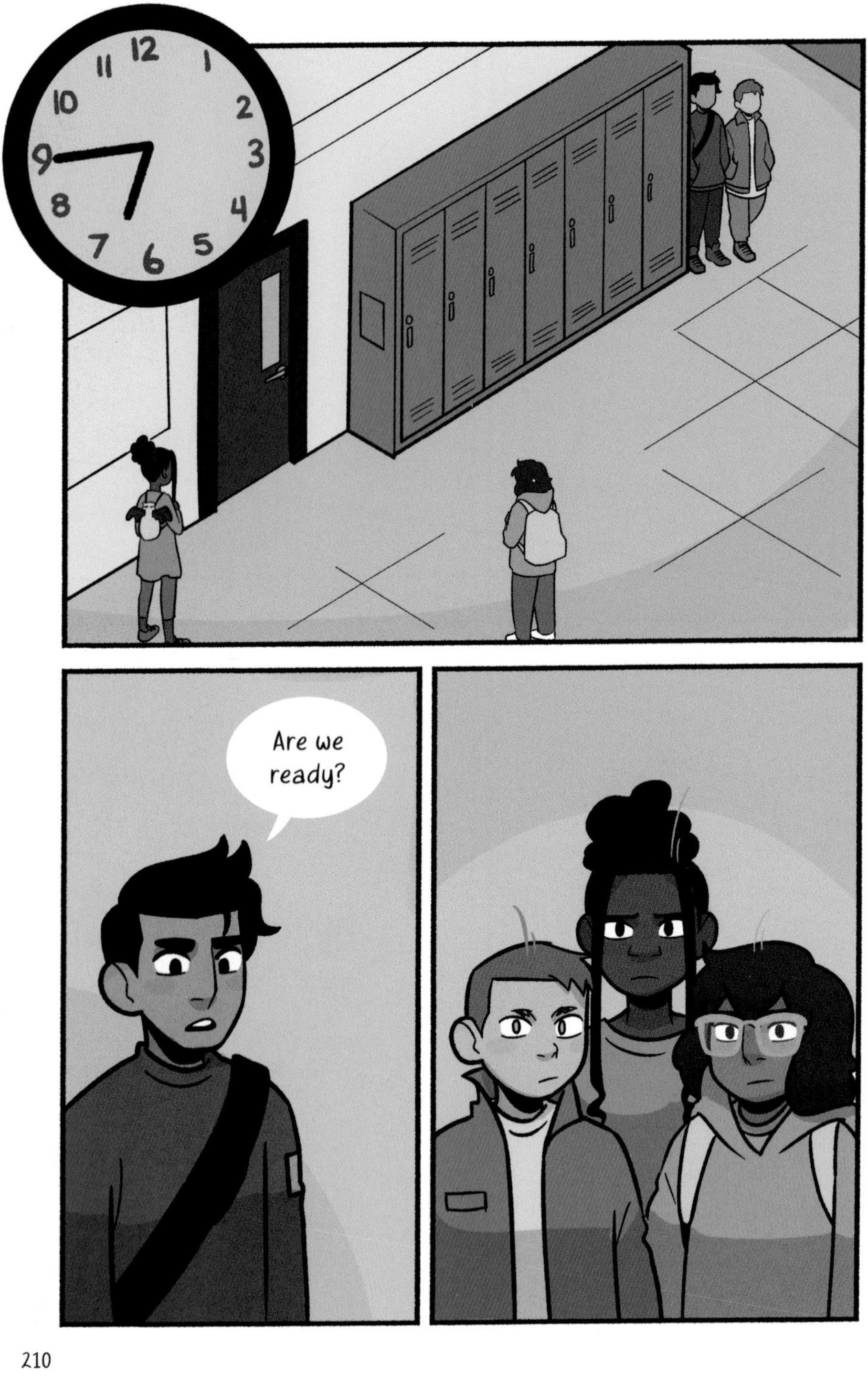
Are we ready?

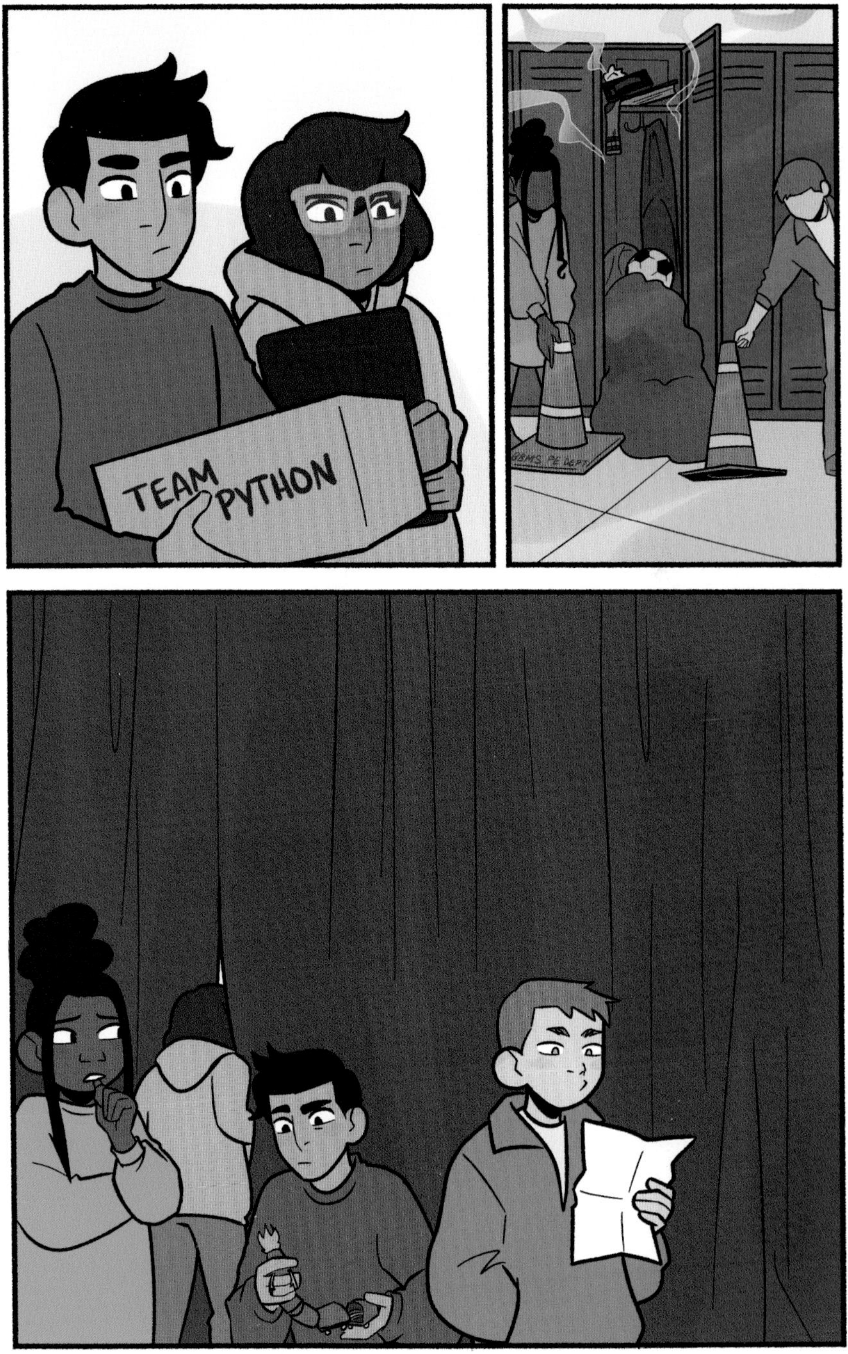
TEAM PYTHON

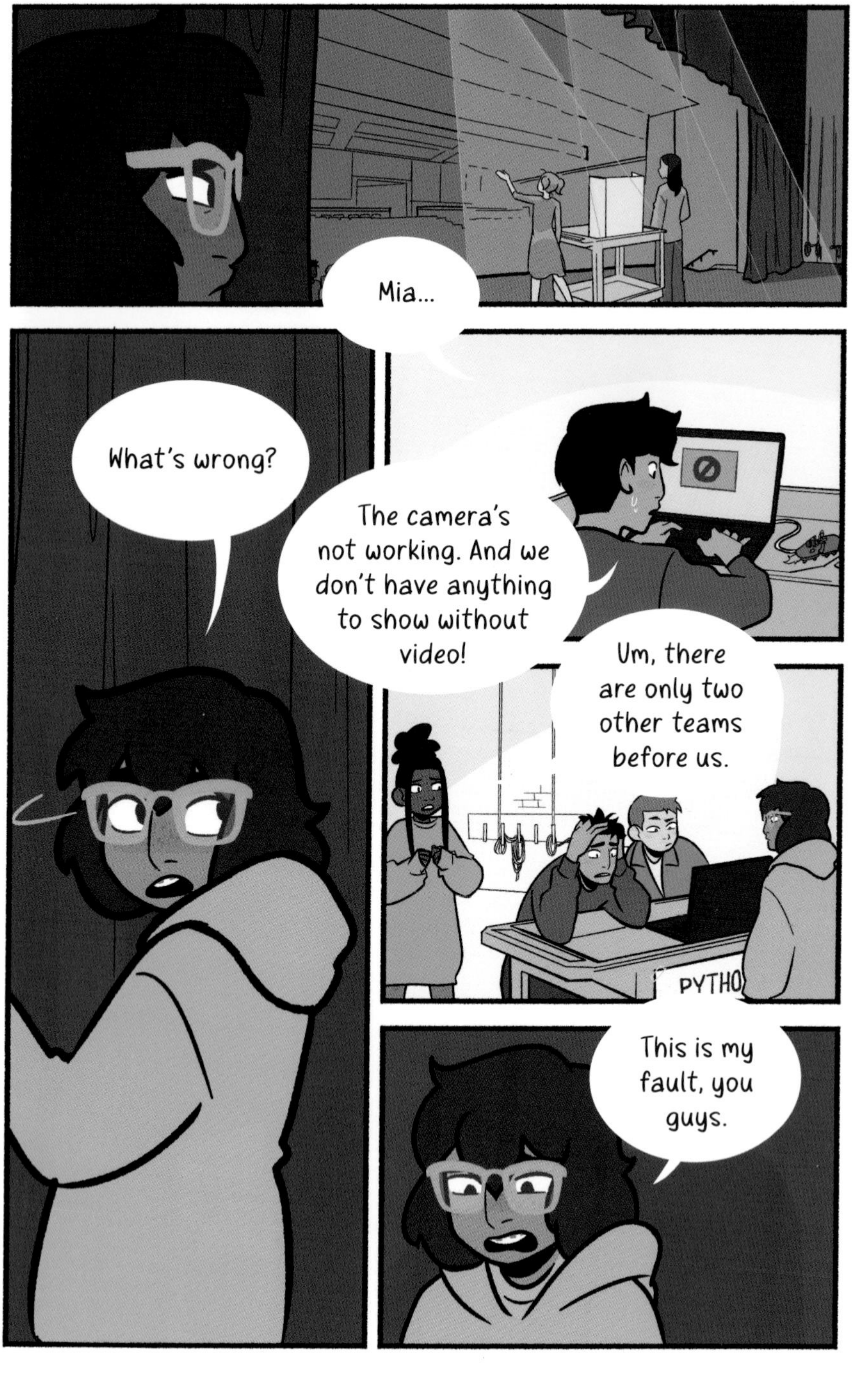
Mia...
What's wrong?
The camera's not working. And we don't have anything to show without video!
Um, there are only two other teams before us.
PYTHO
This is my fault, you guys.

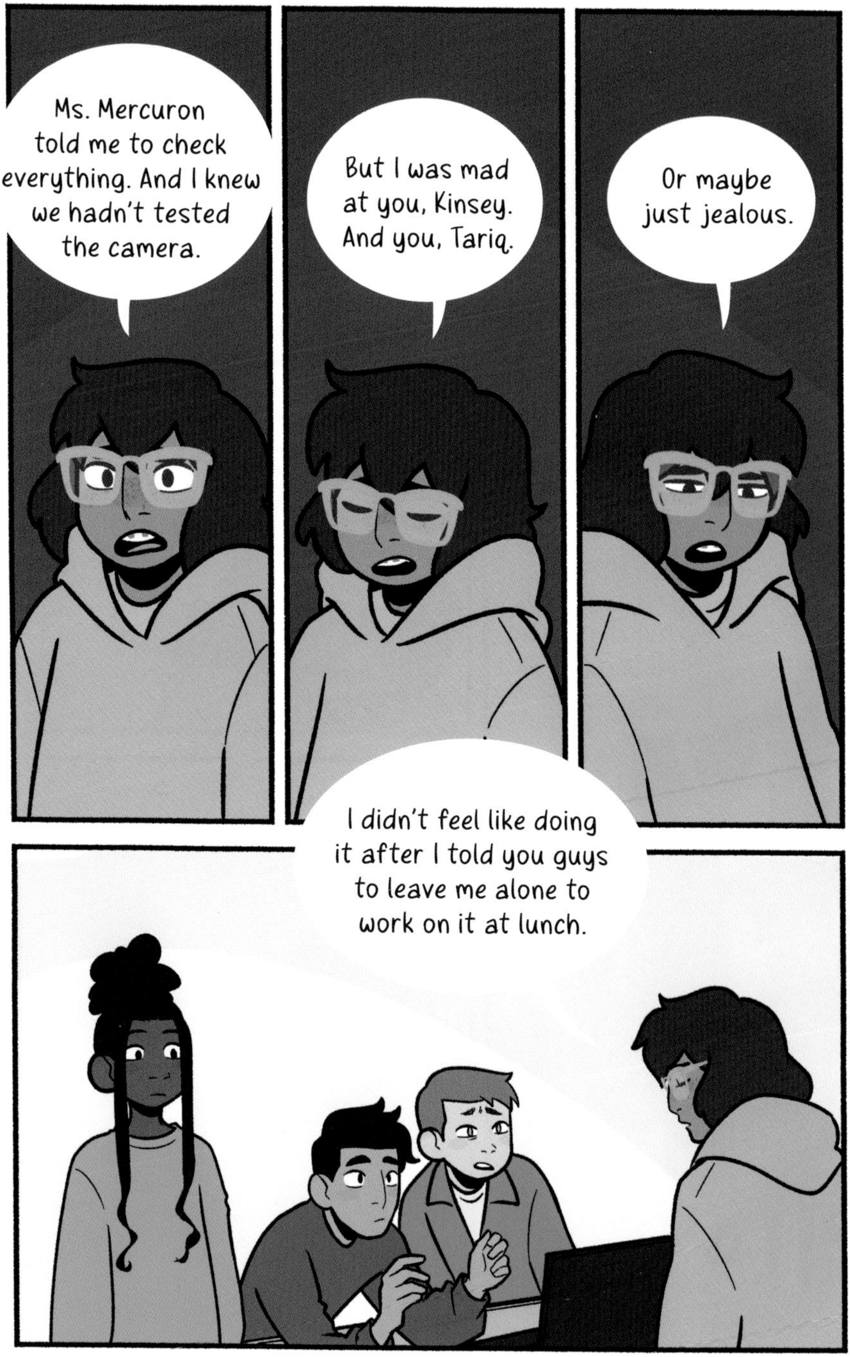
Ms. Mercuron told me to check everything. And I knew we hadn't tested the camera.
But I was mad at you, Kinsey. And you, Tariq.
Or maybe just jealous.
I didn't feel like doing it after I told you guys to leave me alone to work on it at lunch.

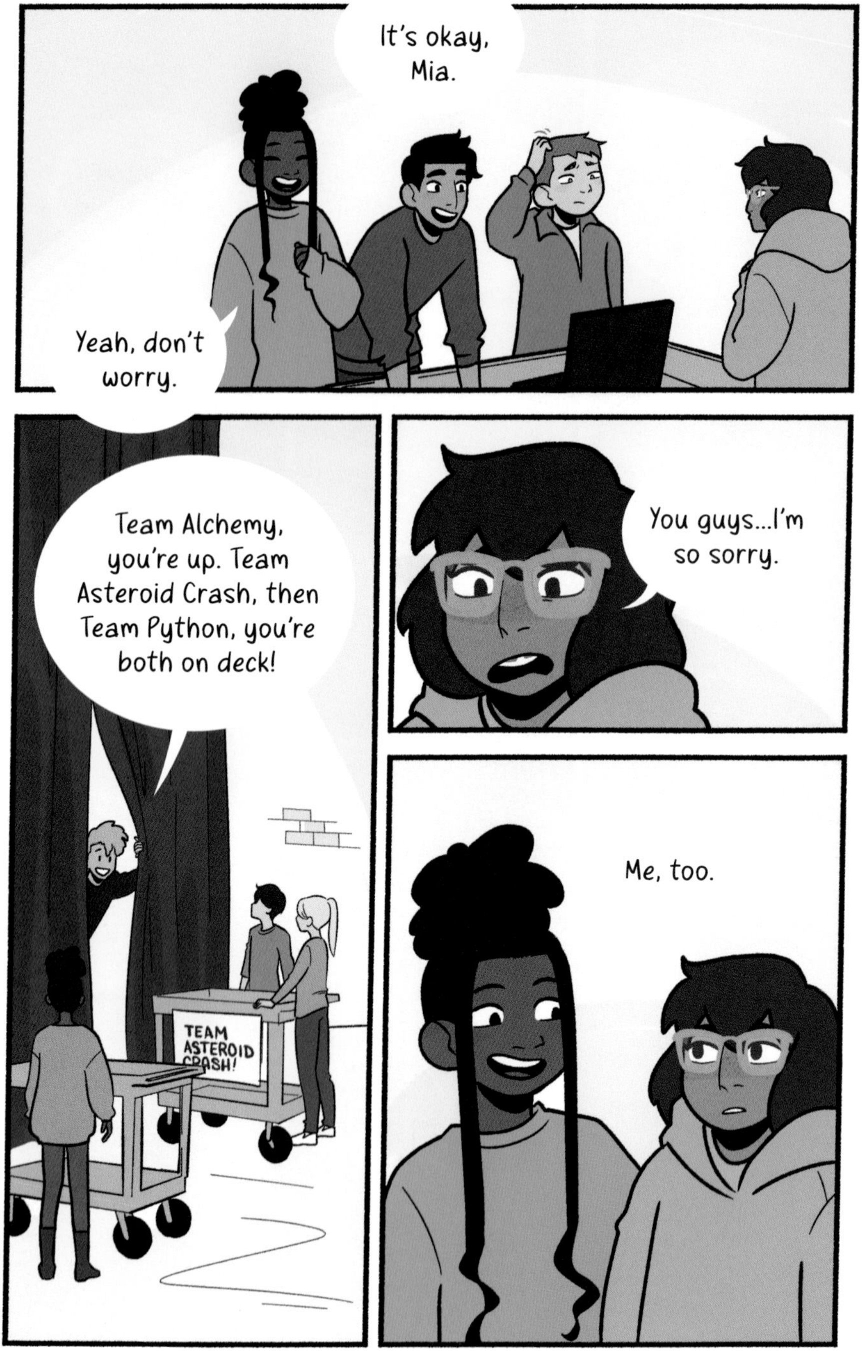
It's okay, Mia.
Yeah, don't worry.
Team Alchemy, you're up. Team Asteroid Crash, then Team Python, you're both on deck!
TEAM ASTEROID CRASH!
You guys...I'm so sorry.
Me, too.

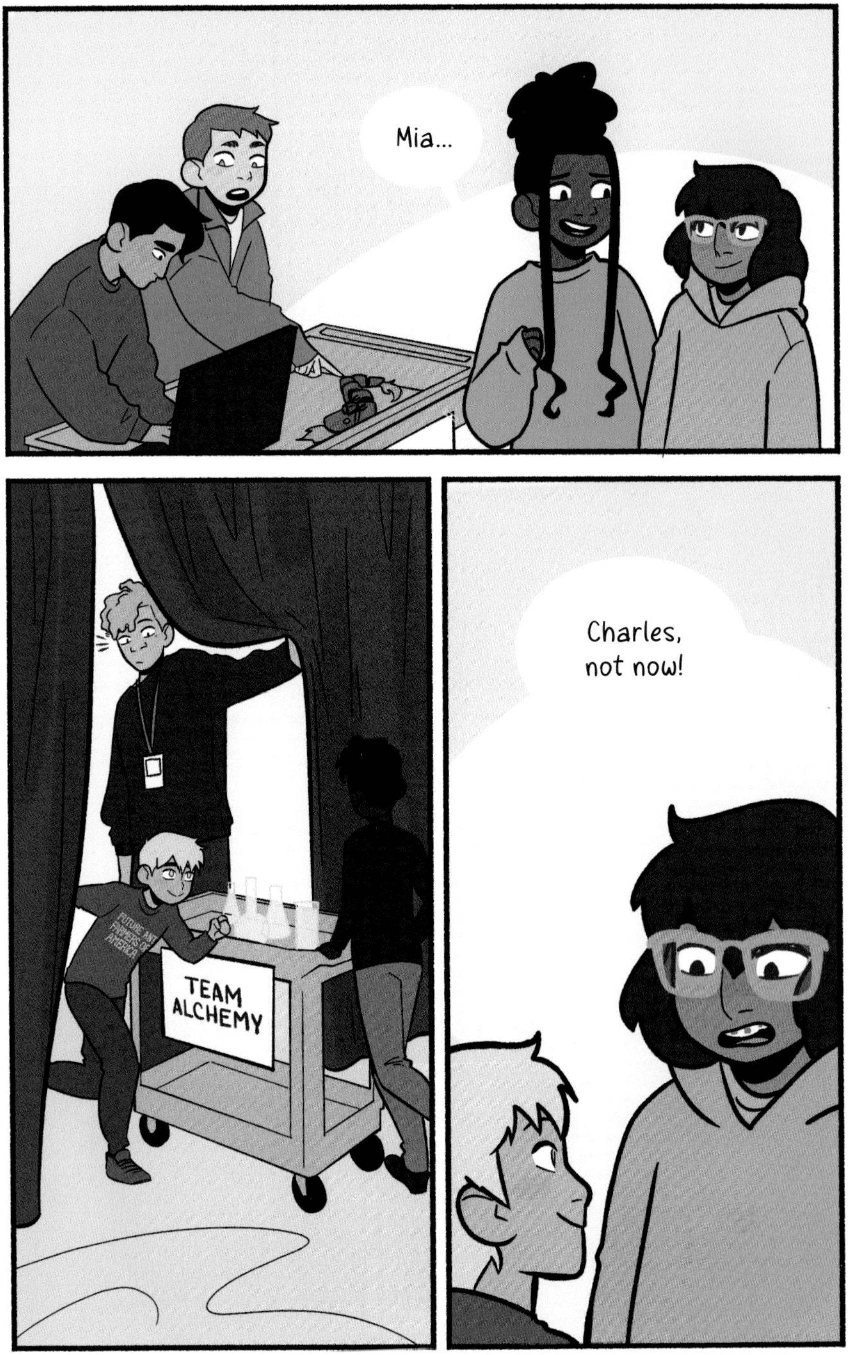
Mia...
FUTURE ANT FARMERS OF AMERICA
TEAM ALCHEMY
Charles, not now!

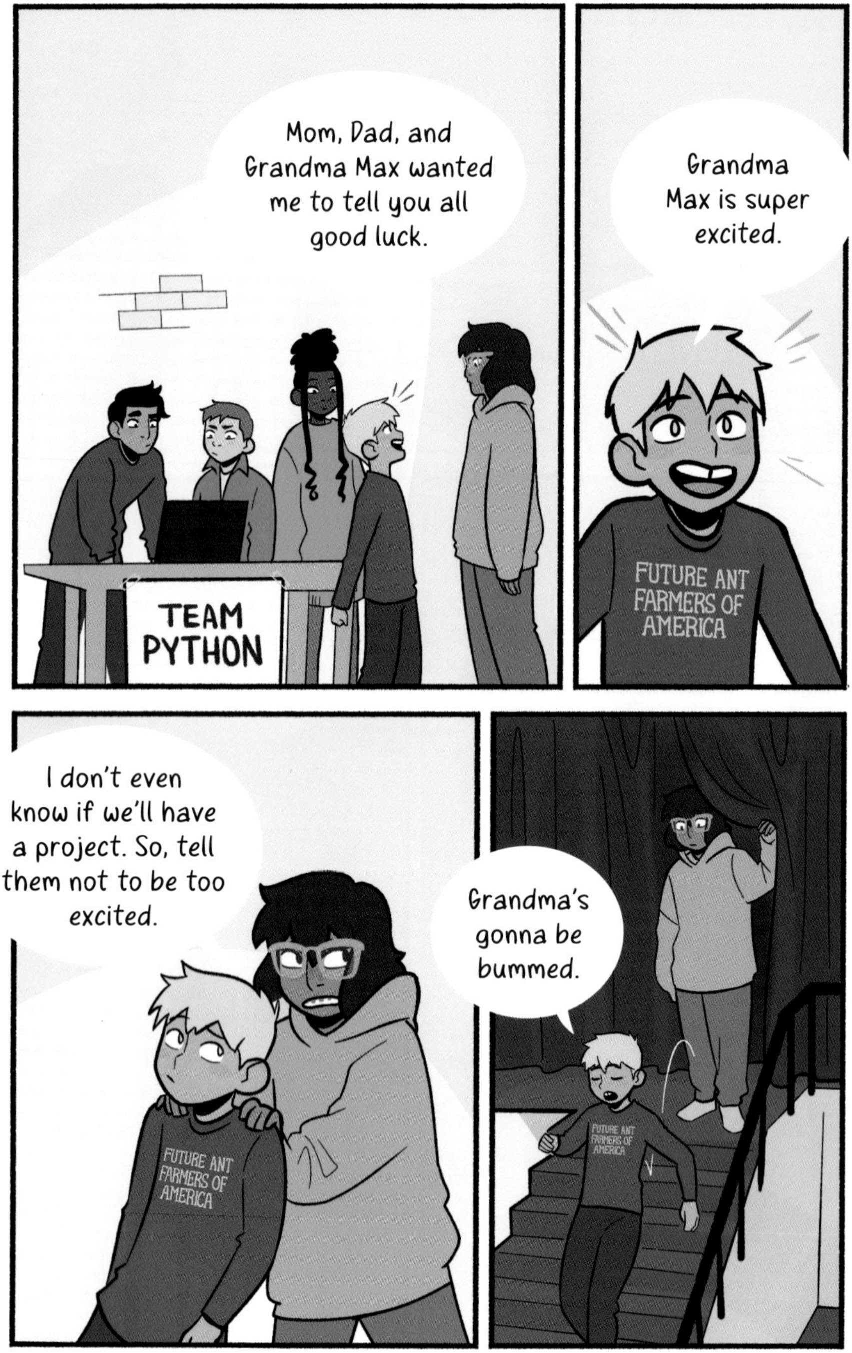
Mom, Dad, and Grandma Max wanted me to tell you all good luck.
TEAM PYTHON
Grandma Max is super excited.
FUTURE ANT FARMERS OF AMERICA
I don't even know if we'll have a project. So, tell them not to be too excited.
FUTURE ANT FARMERS OF AMERICA
Grandma's gonna be bummed.
FUTURE ANT FARMERS OF AMERICA

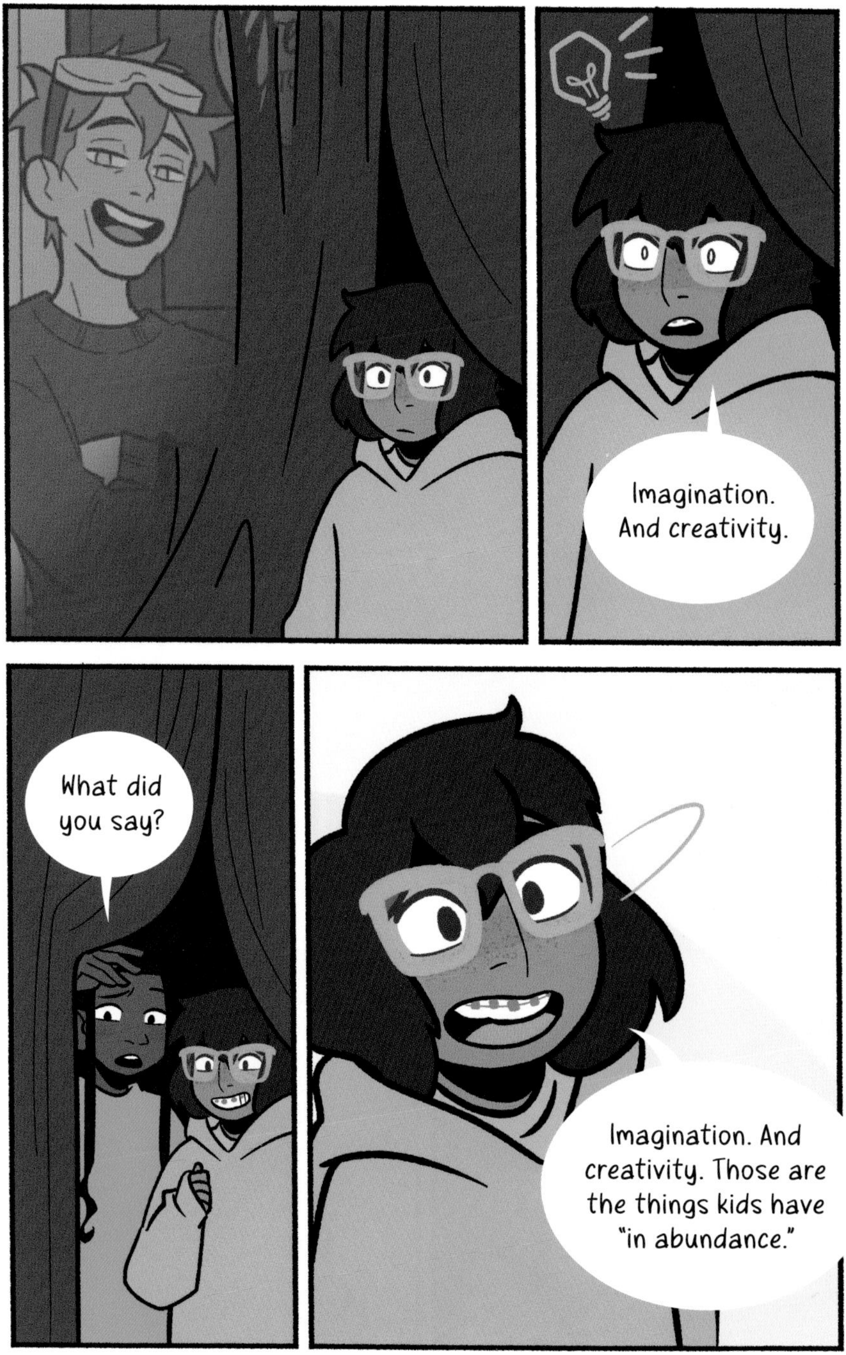
Imagination.
And creativity.
What did you say?
Imagination. And creativity. Those are the things kids have "in abundance."

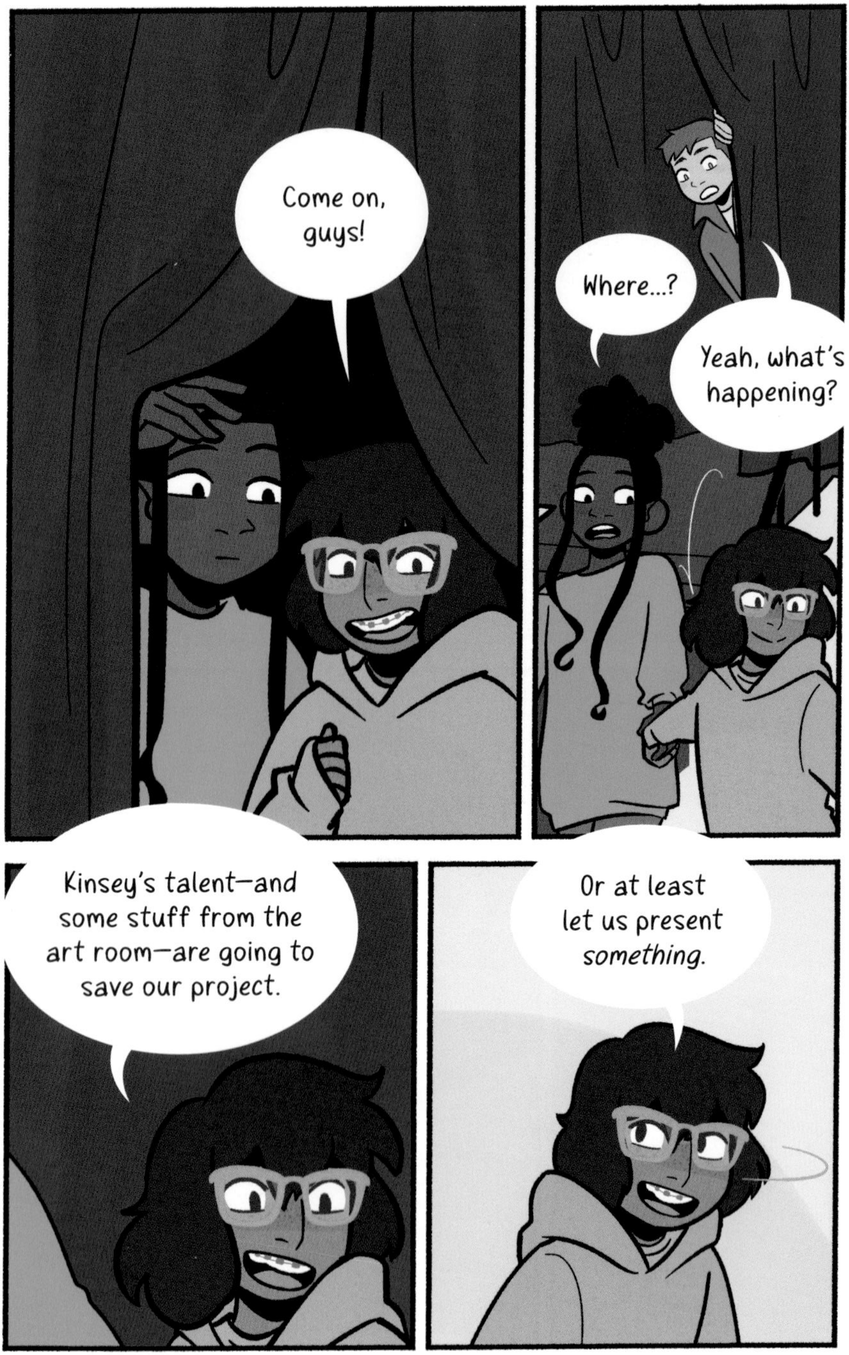
Come on, guys!
Where...?
Yeah, what's happening?
Kinsey's talent—and some stuff from the art room—are going to save our project.
Or at least let us present *something.*

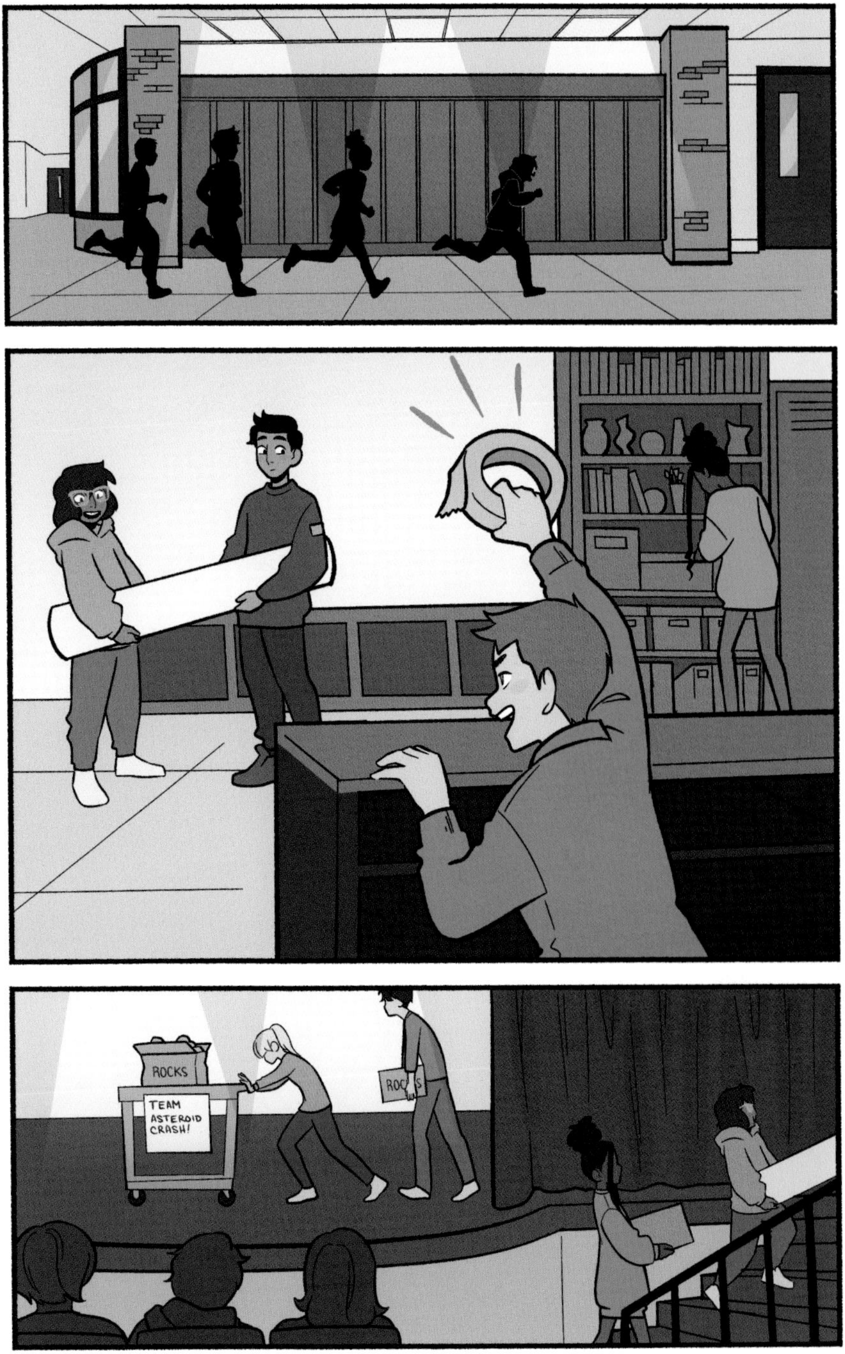
ROCKS
TEAM ASTEROID CRASH!
ROCKS

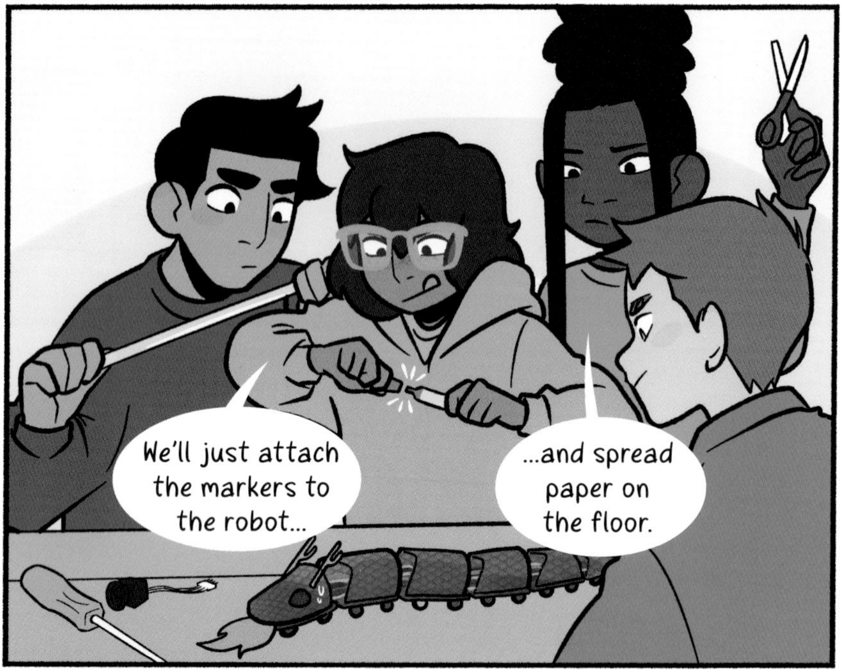
We'll just attach the markers to the robot...
...and spread paper on the floor.

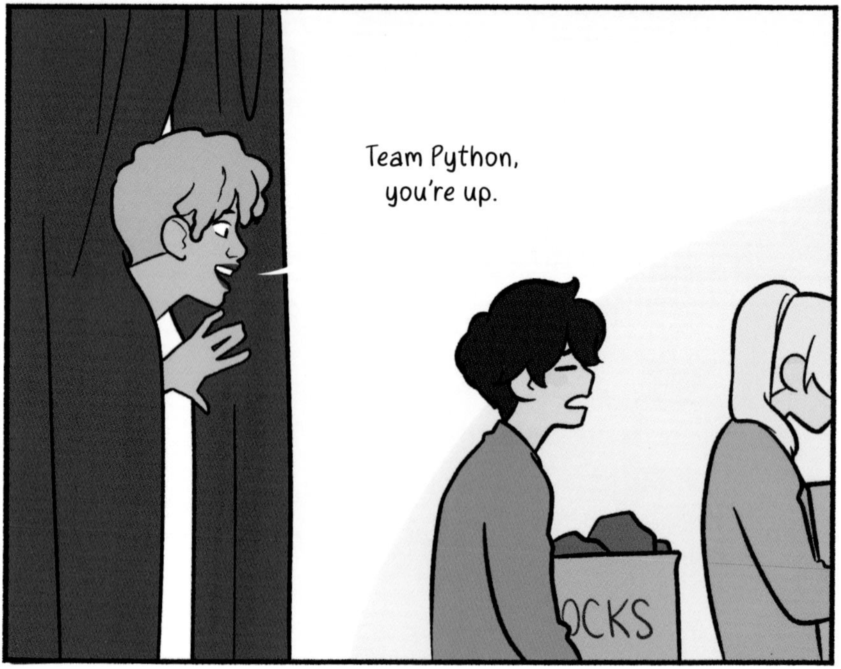
Team Python, you're up.
OCKS

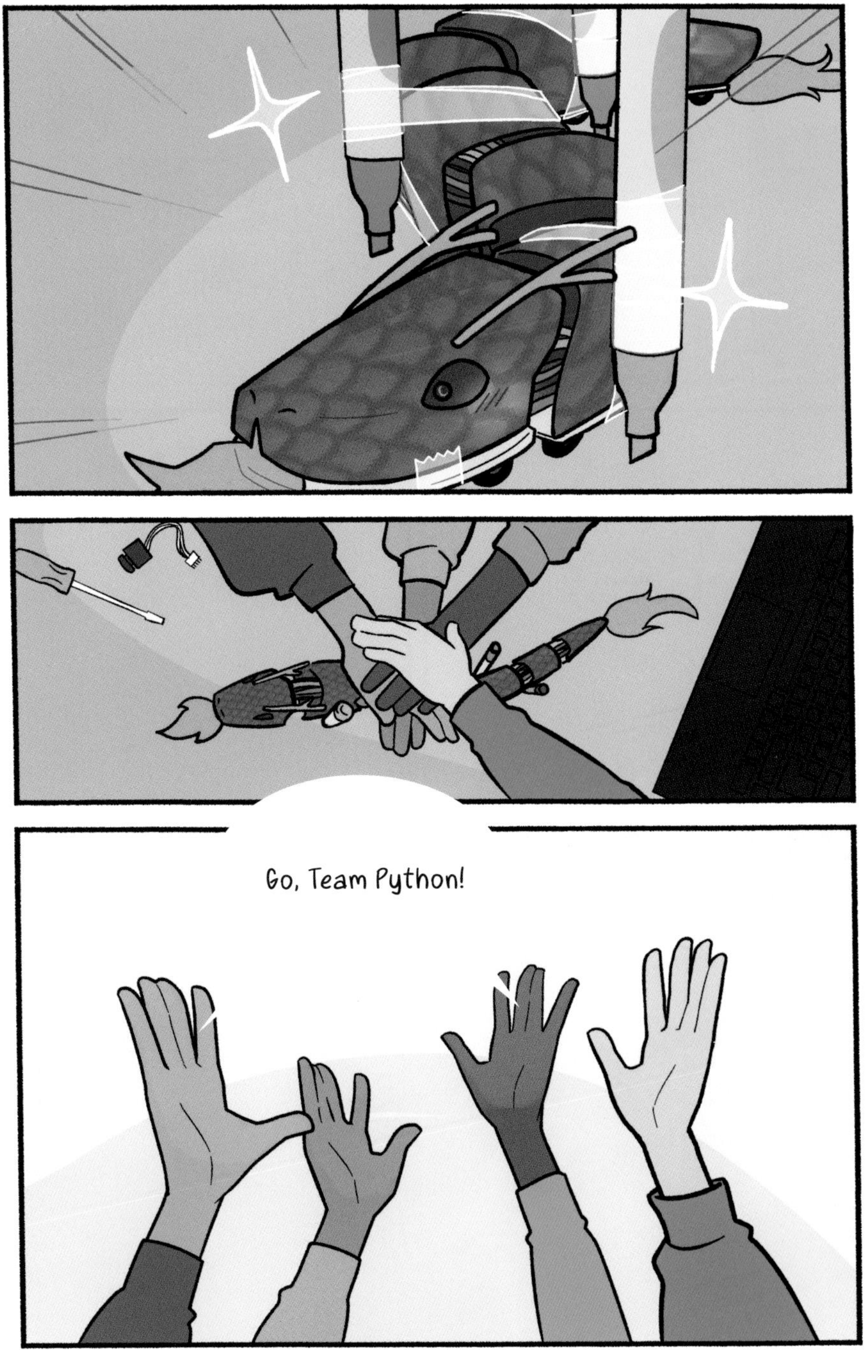
Go, Team Python!

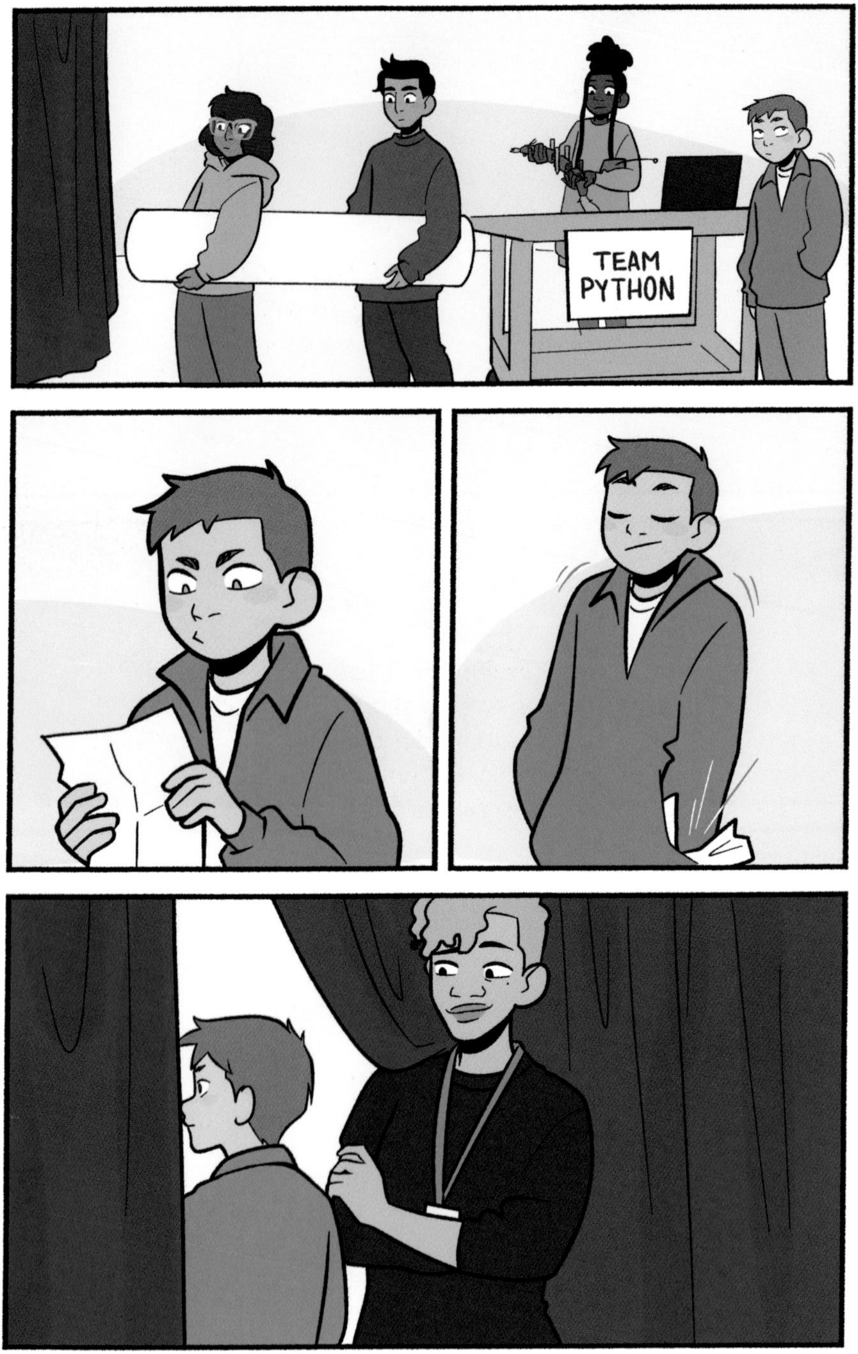
TEAM
PYTHON

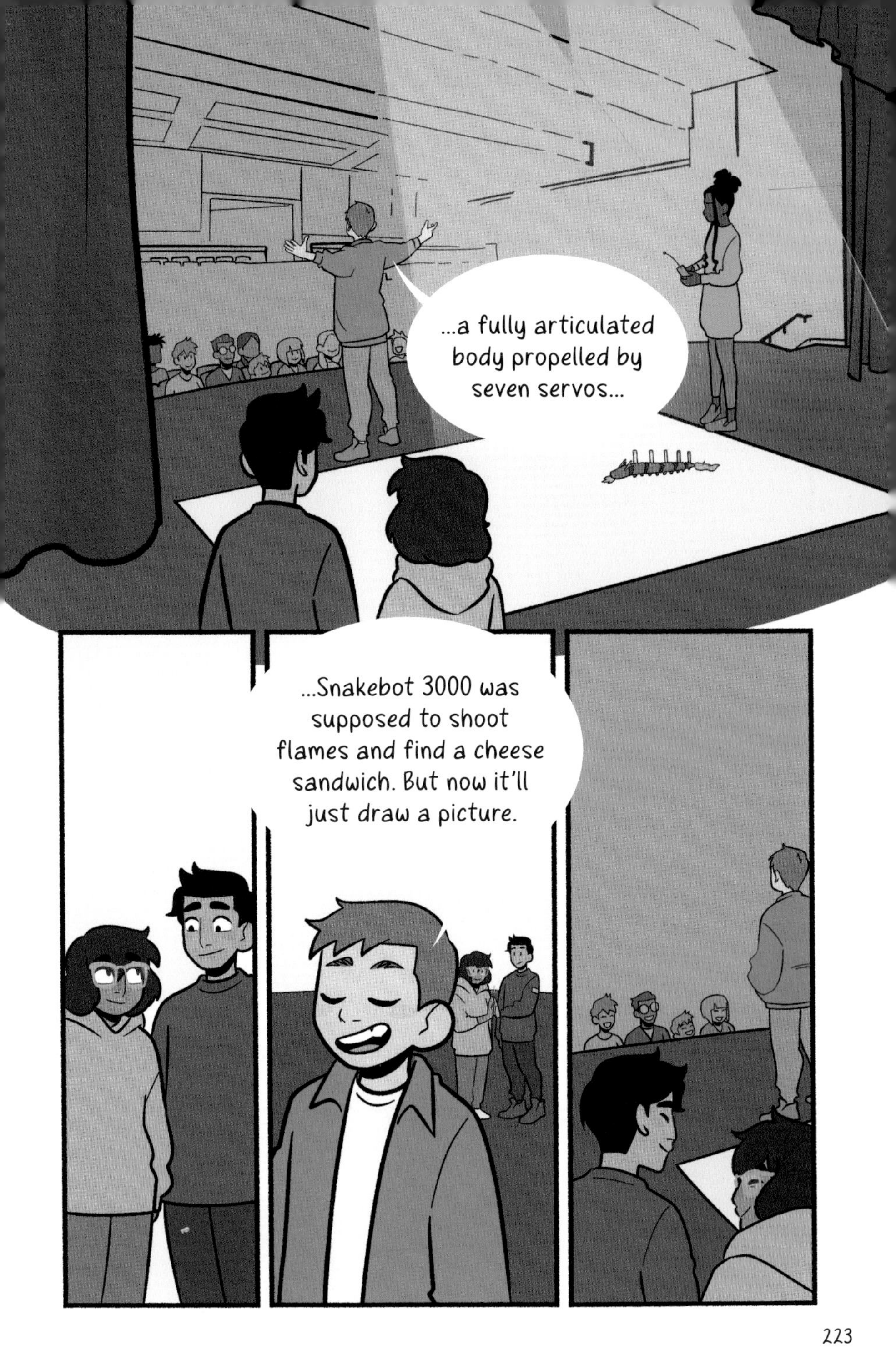
...a fully articulated body propelled by seven servos...
...Snakebot 3000 was supposed to shoot flames and find a cheese sandwich. But now it'll just draw a picture.

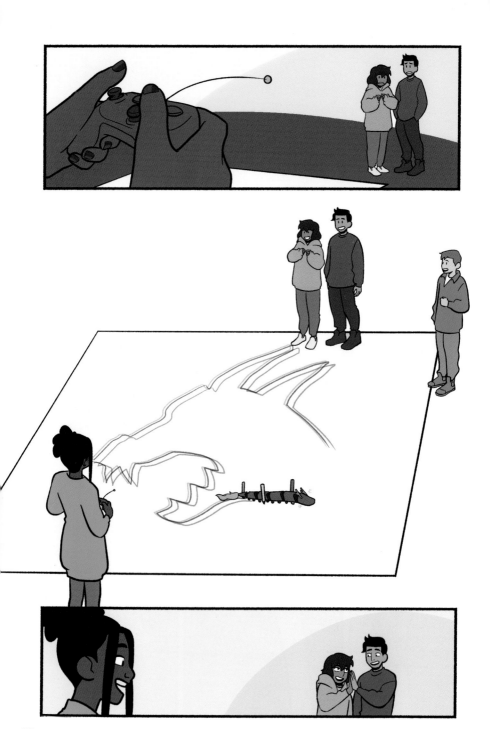

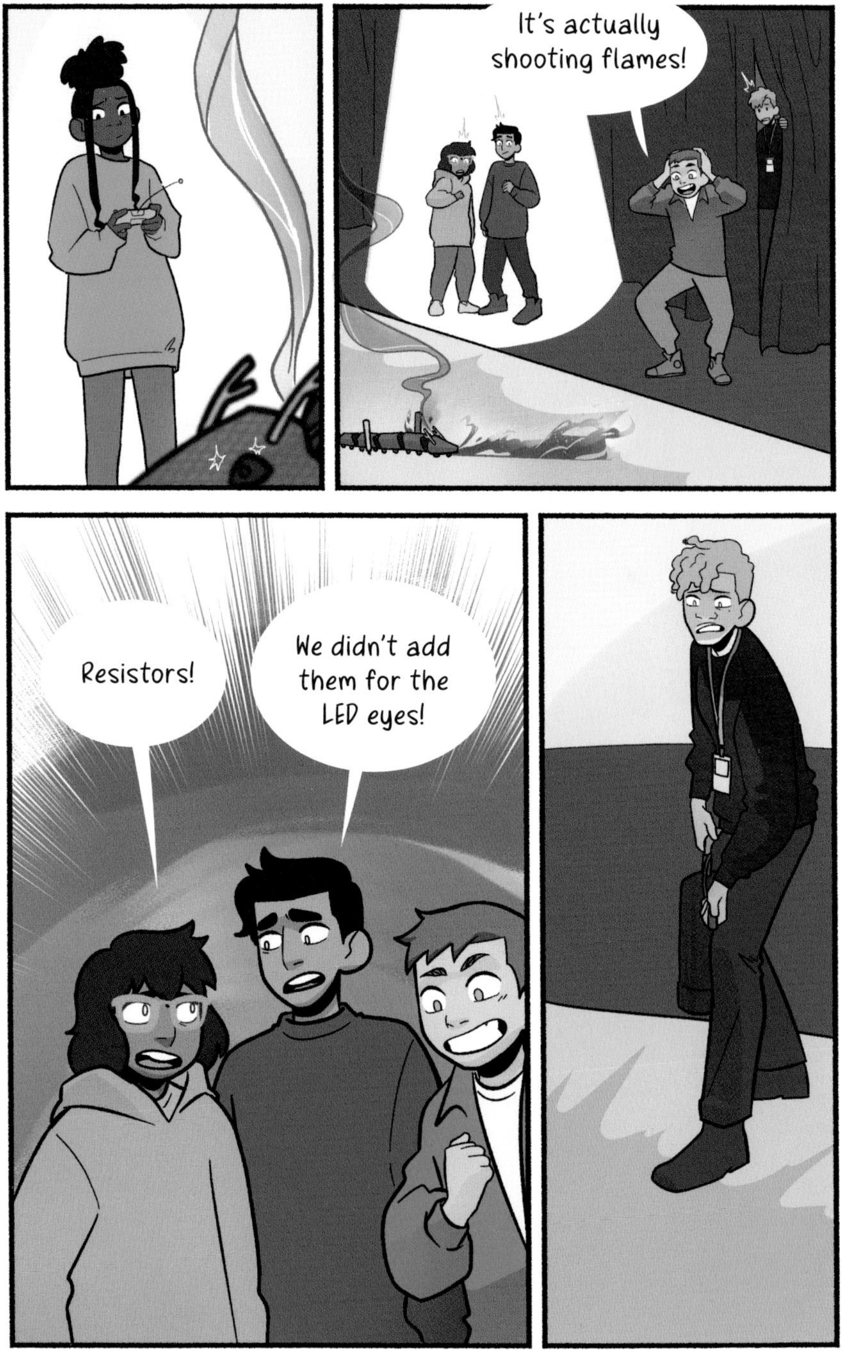
It's actually shooting flames!
Resistors!
We didn't add them for the LED eyes!

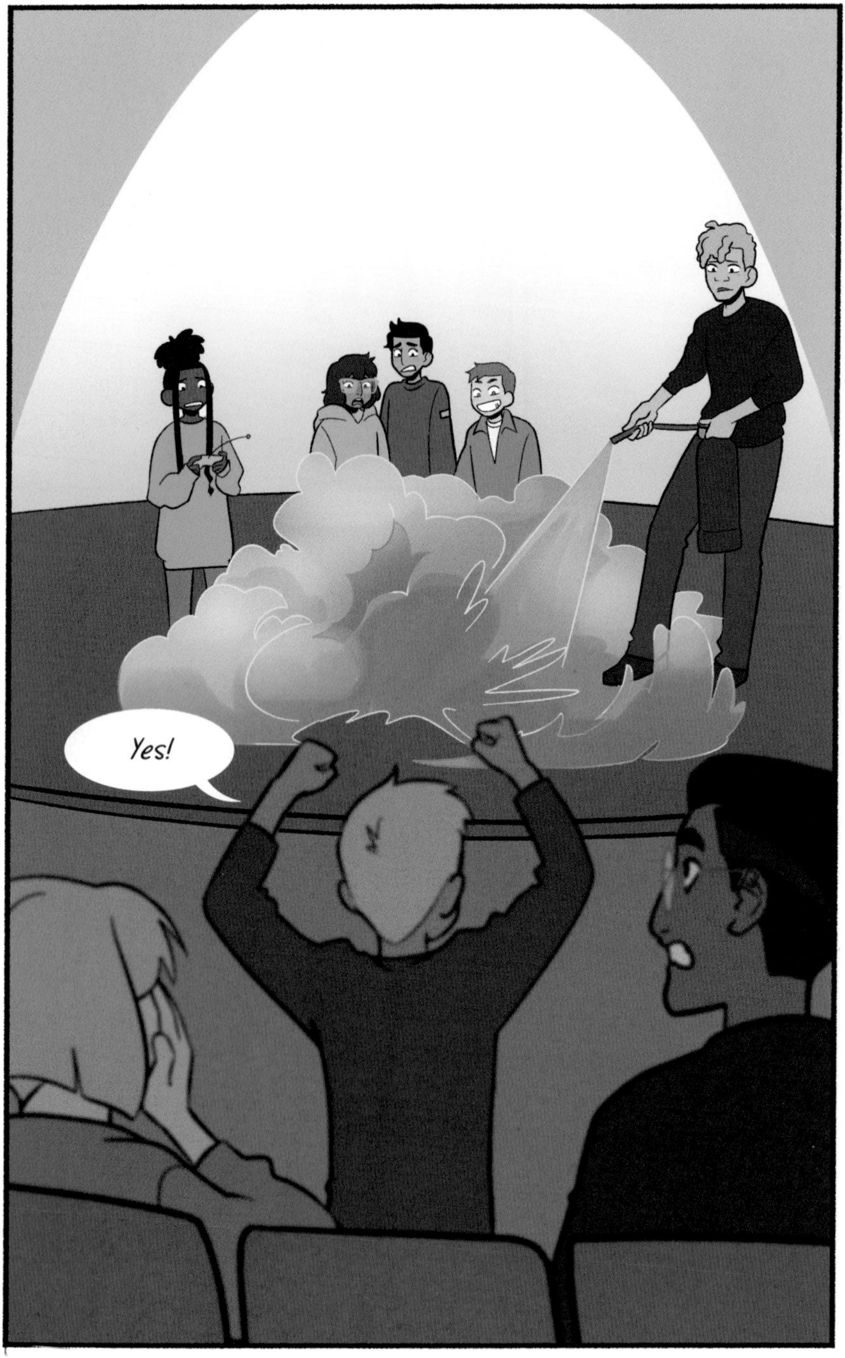
Yes!

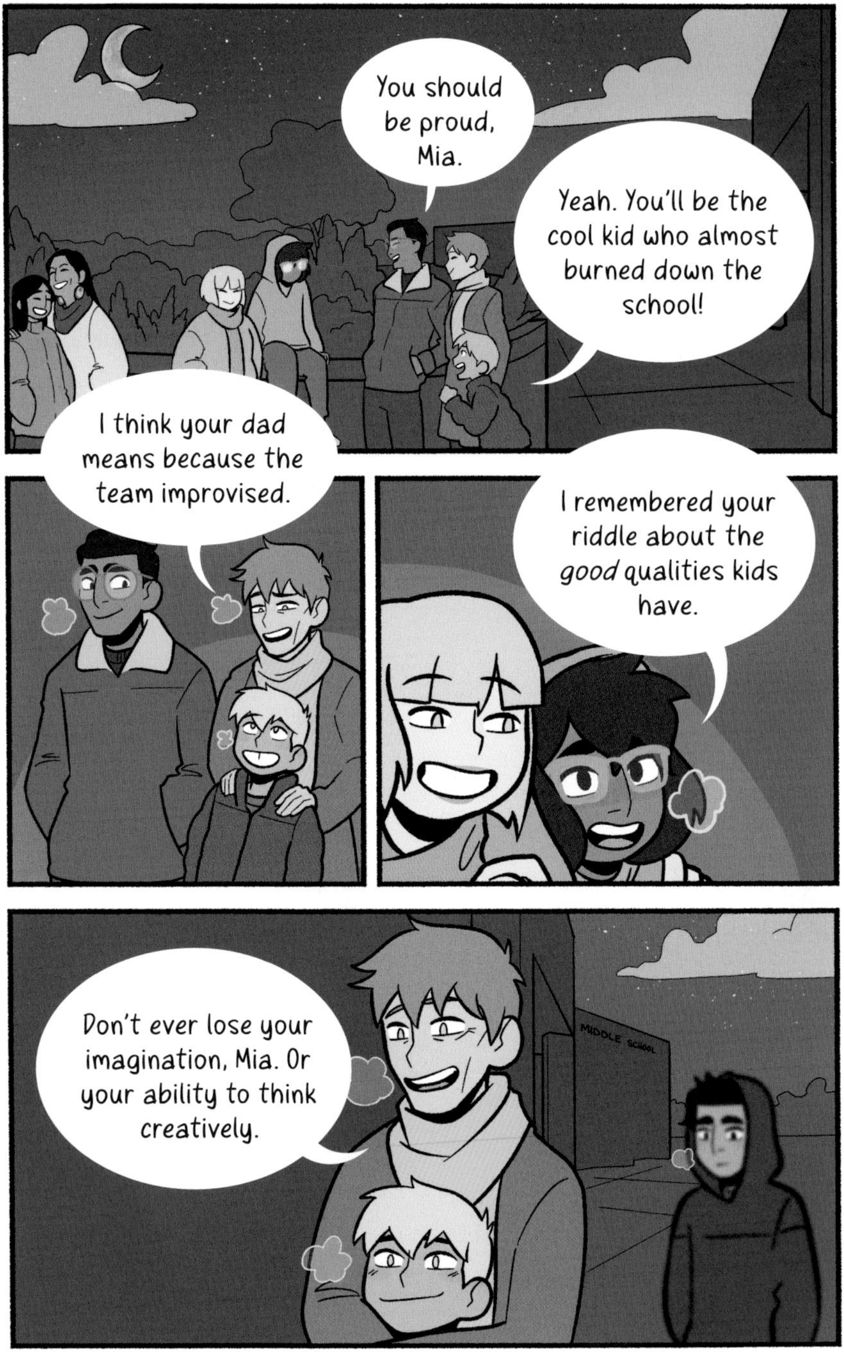
You should be proud, Mia.
Yeah. You'll be the cool kid who almost burned down the school!
I think your dad means because the team improvised.
I remembered your riddle about the *good* qualities kids have.
Don't ever lose your imagination, Mia. Or your ability to think creatively.
MIDDLE SCHOOL

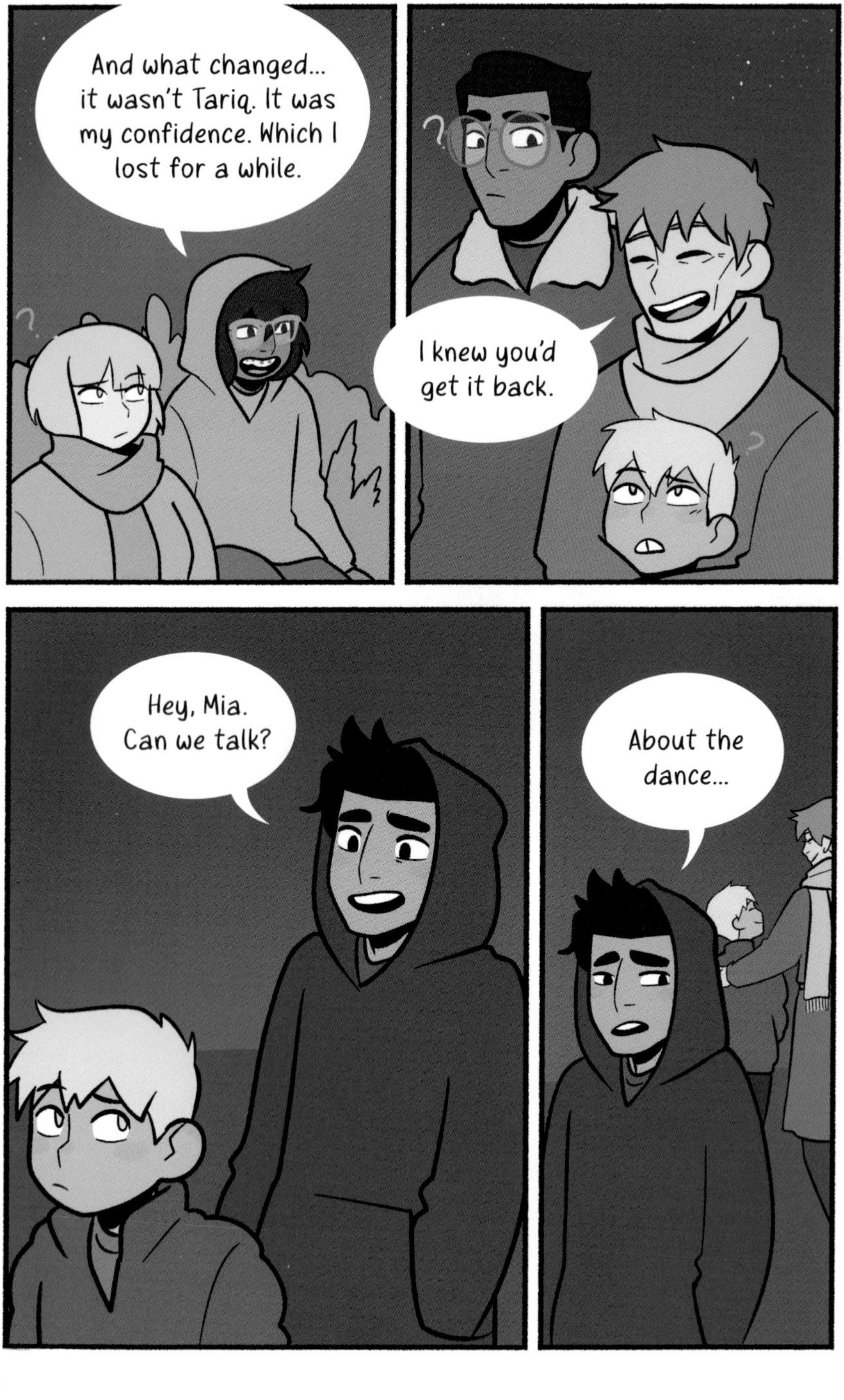
And what changed... it wasn't Tariq. It was my confidence. Which I lost for a while.
?
?
I knew you'd get it back.
?
Hey, Mia. Can we talk?
About the dance...

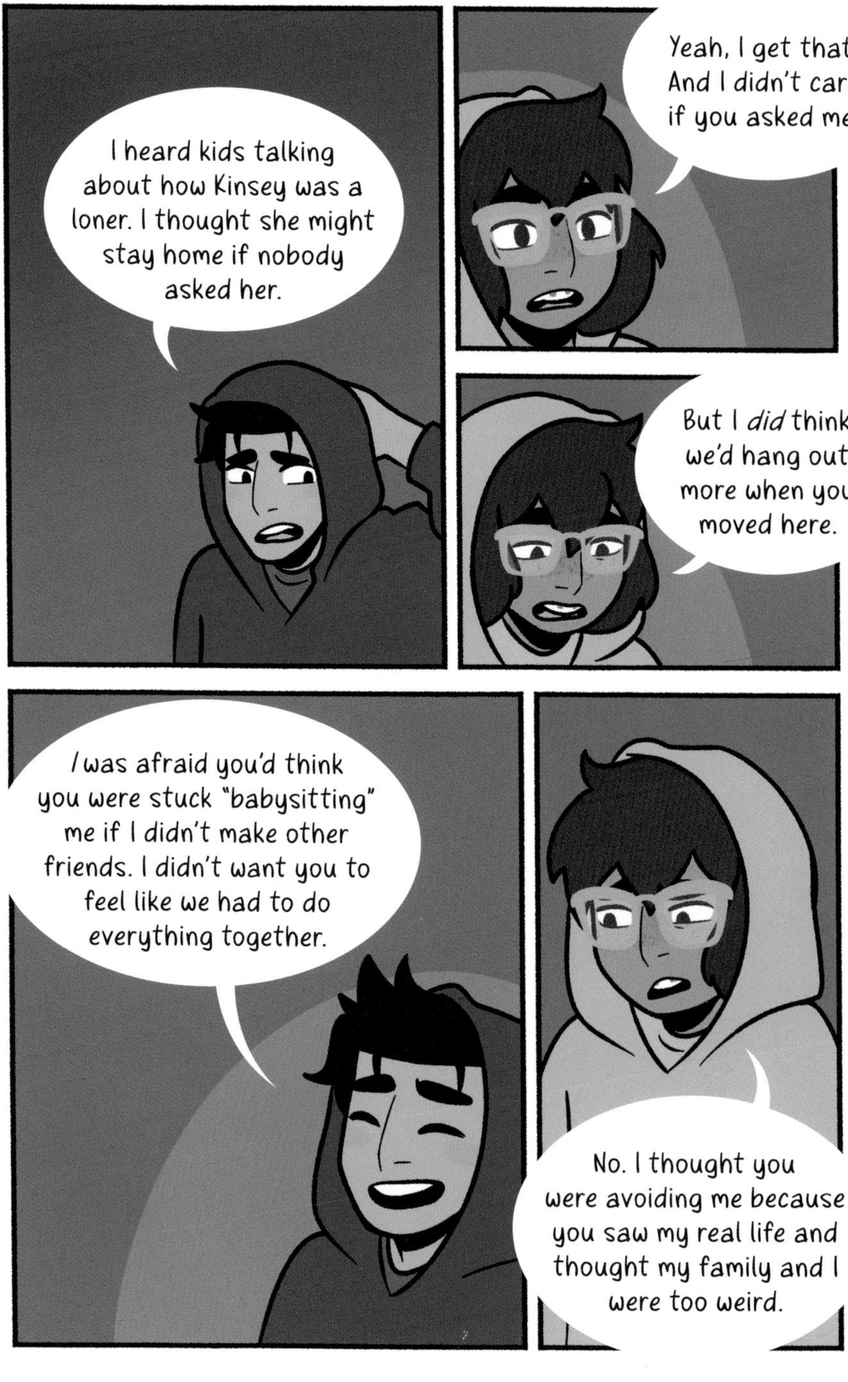
I heard kids talking about how Kinsey was a loner. I thought she might stay home if nobody asked her.
Yeah, I get that. And I didn't care if you asked me.
But I *did* think we'd hang out more when you moved here.
I was afraid you'd think you were stuck "babysitting" me if I didn't make other friends. I didn't want you to feel like we had to do everything together.
No. I thought you were avoiding me because you saw my real life and thought my family and I were too weird.

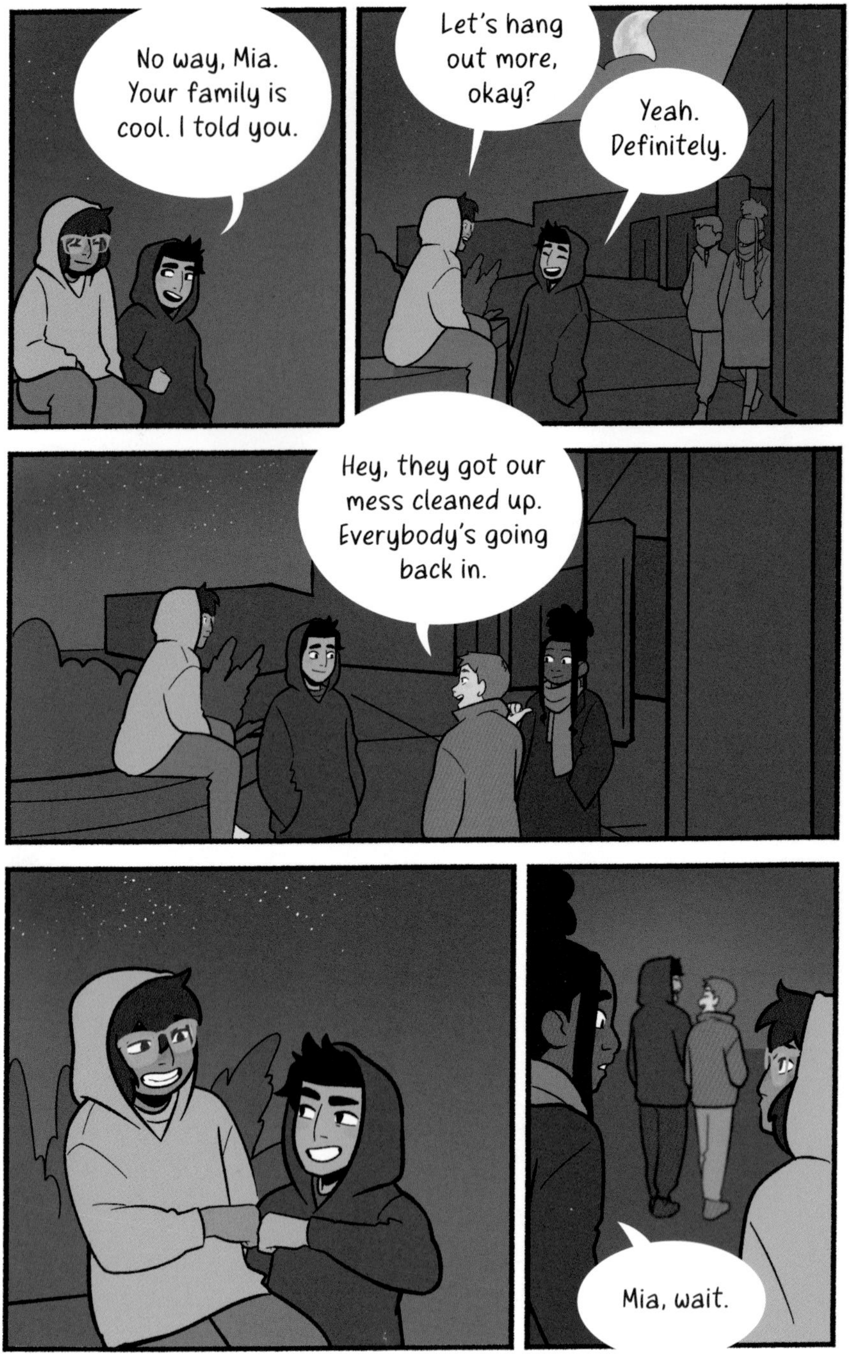
No way, Mia. Your family is cool. I told you.
Let's hang out more, okay?
Yeah. Definitely.
Hey, they got our mess cleaned up. Everybody's going back in.
Mia, wait.

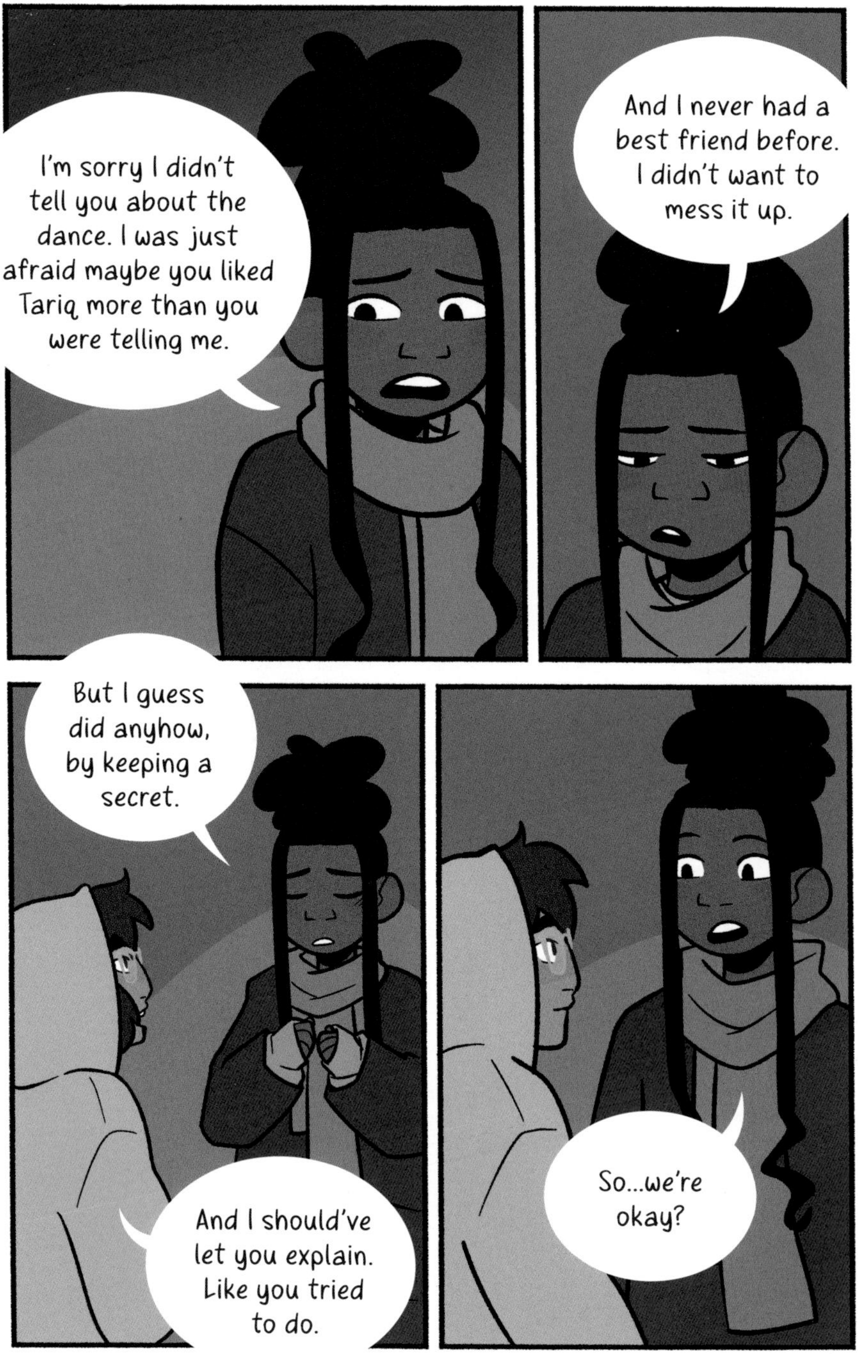
I'm sorry I didn't tell you about the dance. I was just afraid maybe you liked Tariq more than you were telling me.
And I never had a best friend before. I didn't want to mess it up.
But I guess did anyhow, by keeping a secret.
And I should've let you explain. Like you tried to do.
So...we're okay?

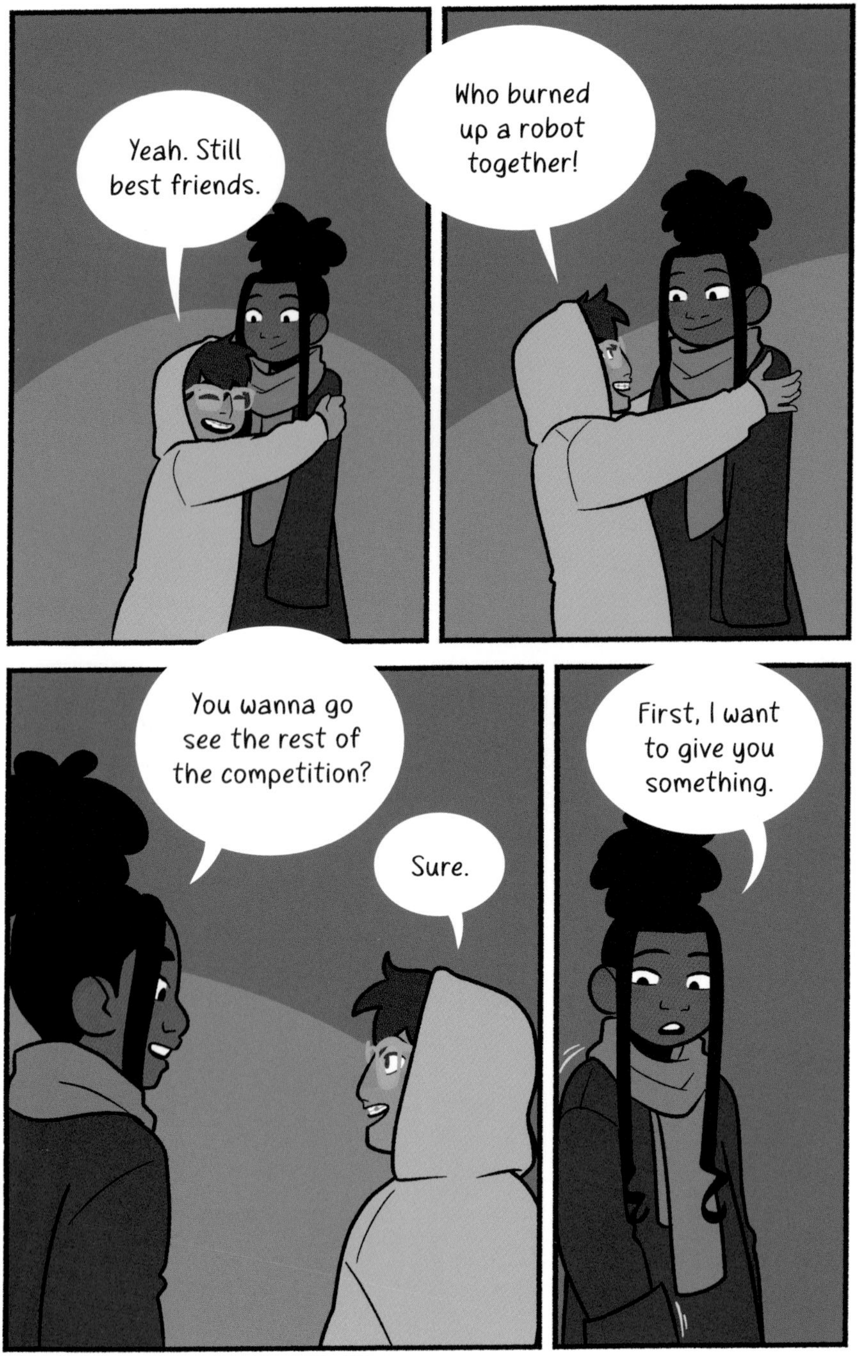
Yeah. Still best friends.
Who burned up a robot together!
You wanna go see the rest of the competition?
Sure.
First, I want to give you something.

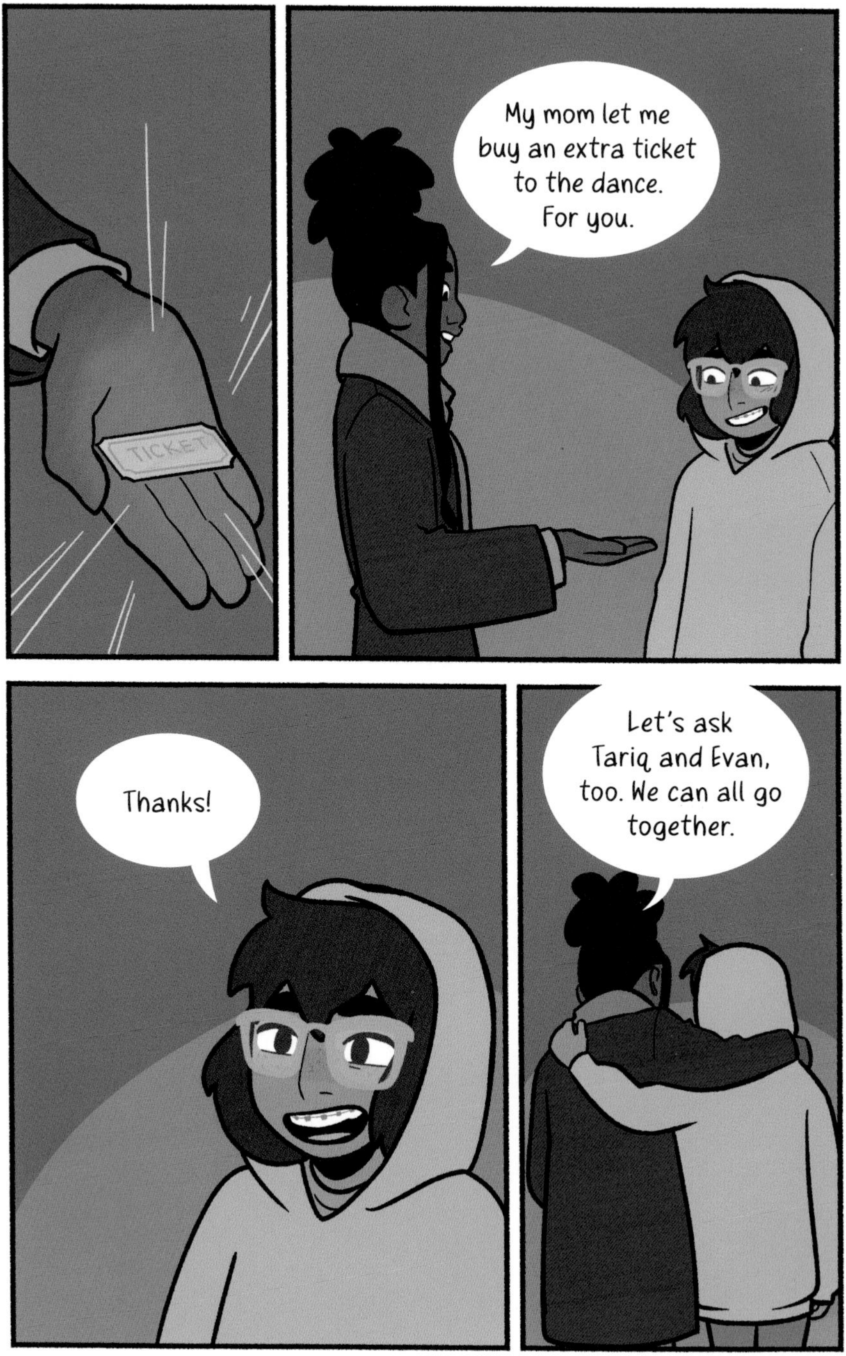
TICKET
My mom let me buy an extra ticket to the dance. For you.
Thanks!
Let's ask Tariq and Evan, too. We can all go together.

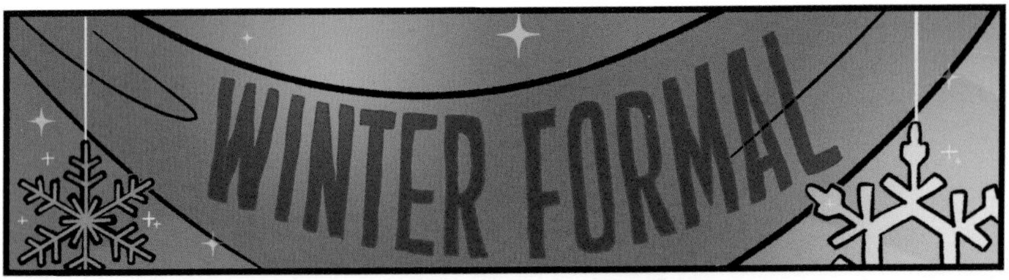
WINTER FORMAL

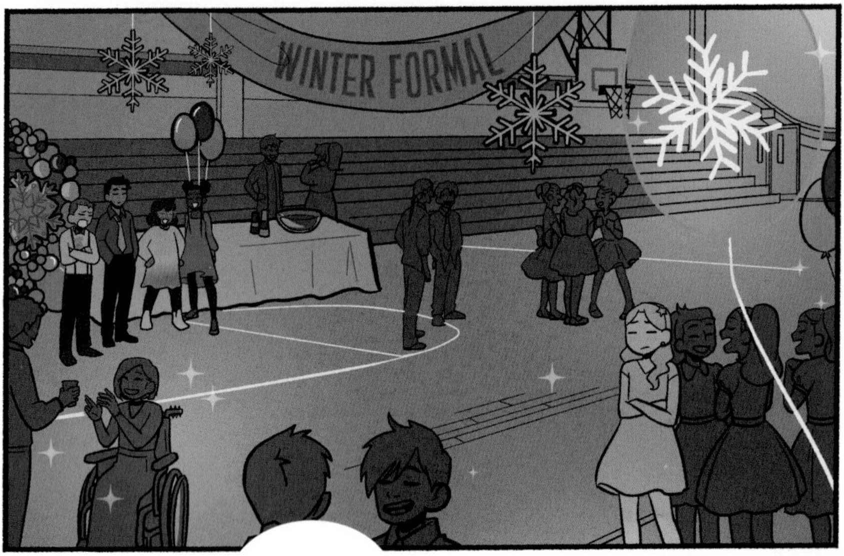
WINTER FORMAL

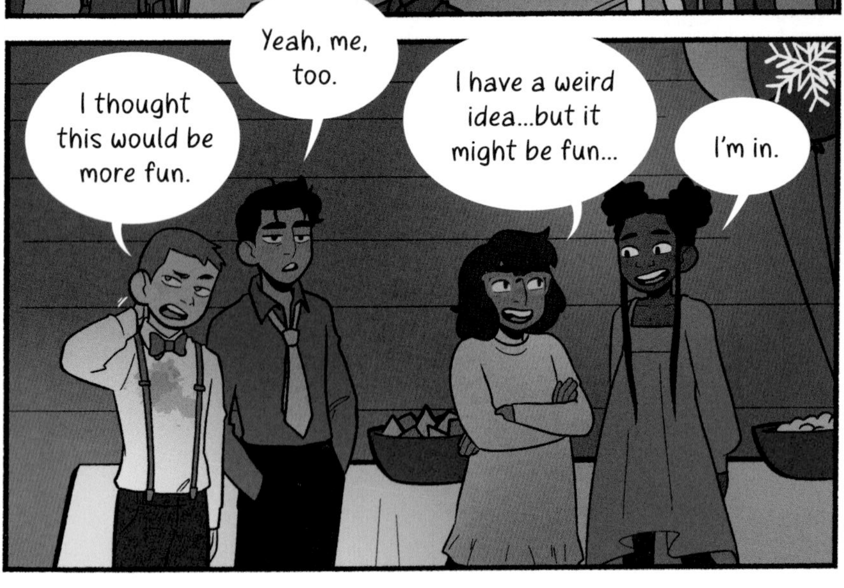
I thought this would be more fun.
Yeah, me, too.
I have a weird idea...but it might be fun...
I'm in.

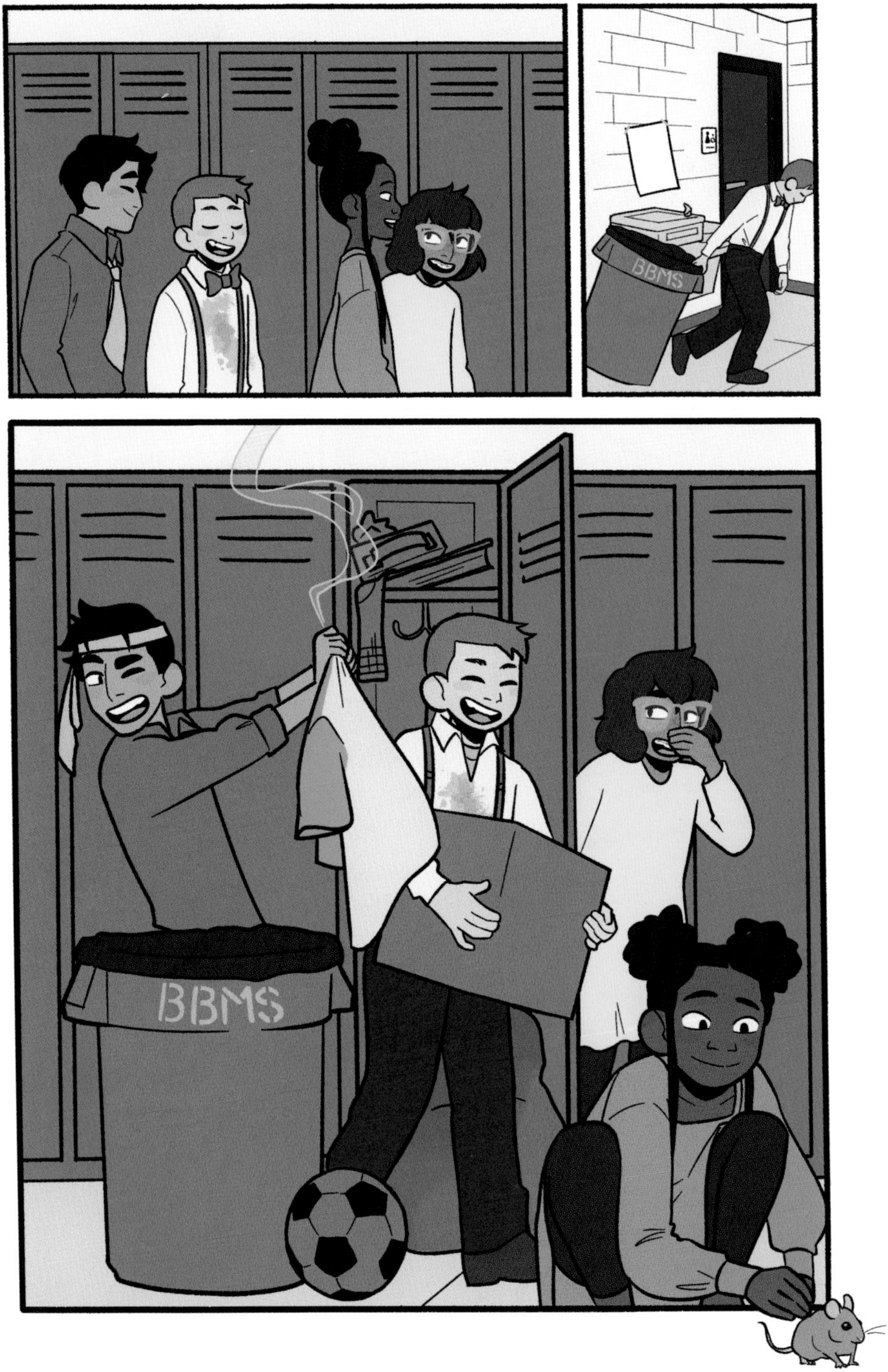
BBMS
BBMS

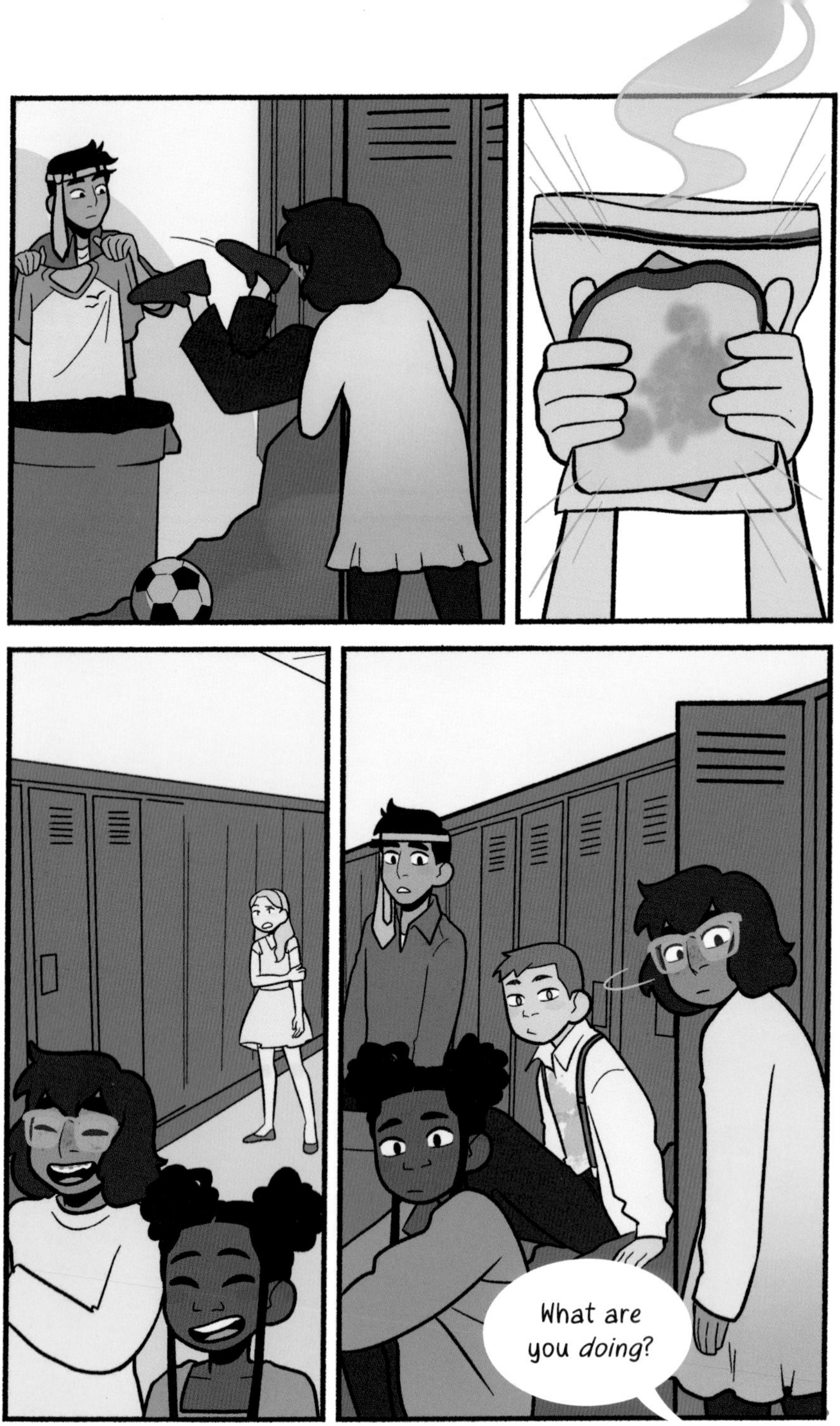
What are you *doing*?

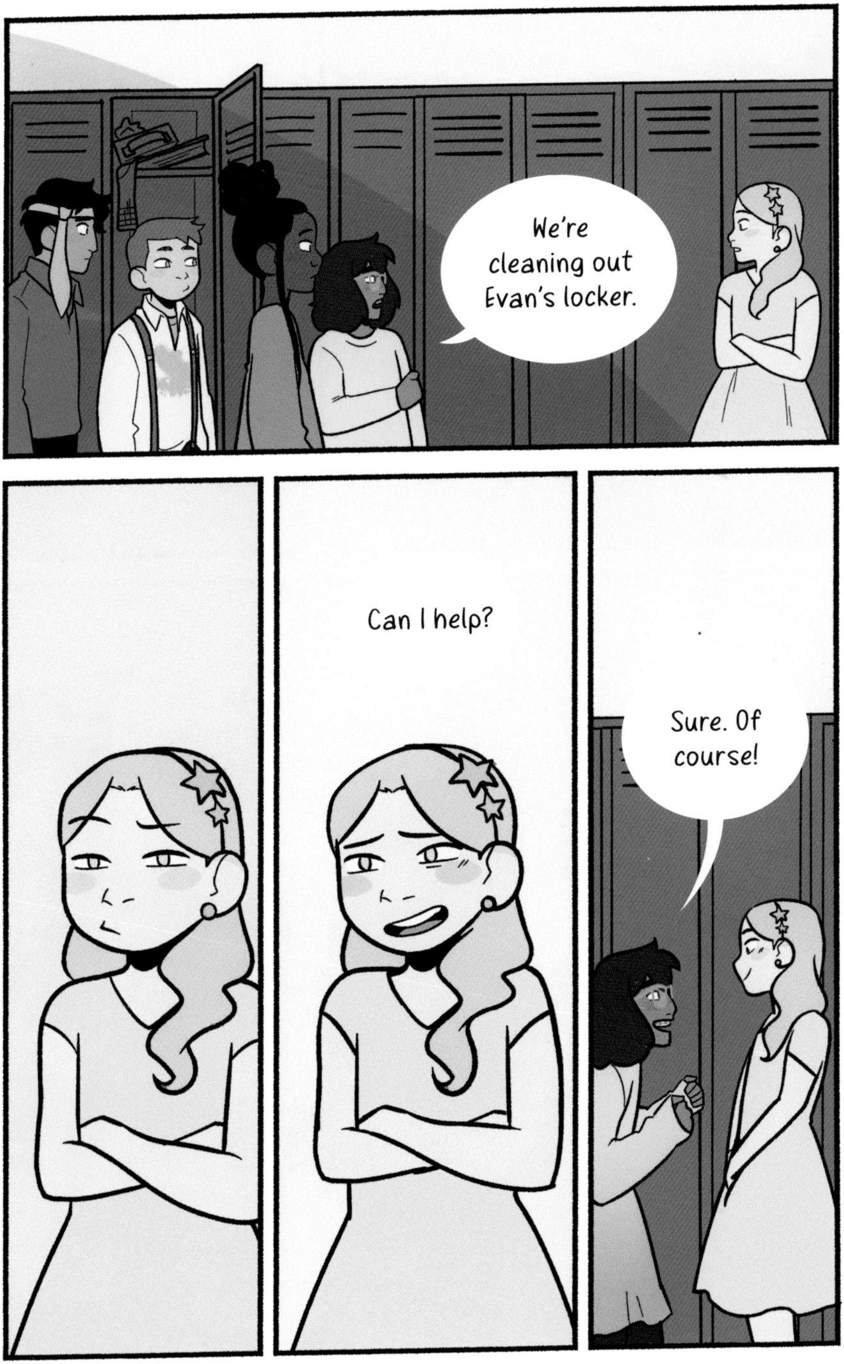
We're cleaning out Evan's locker.
Can I help?
Sure. Of course!

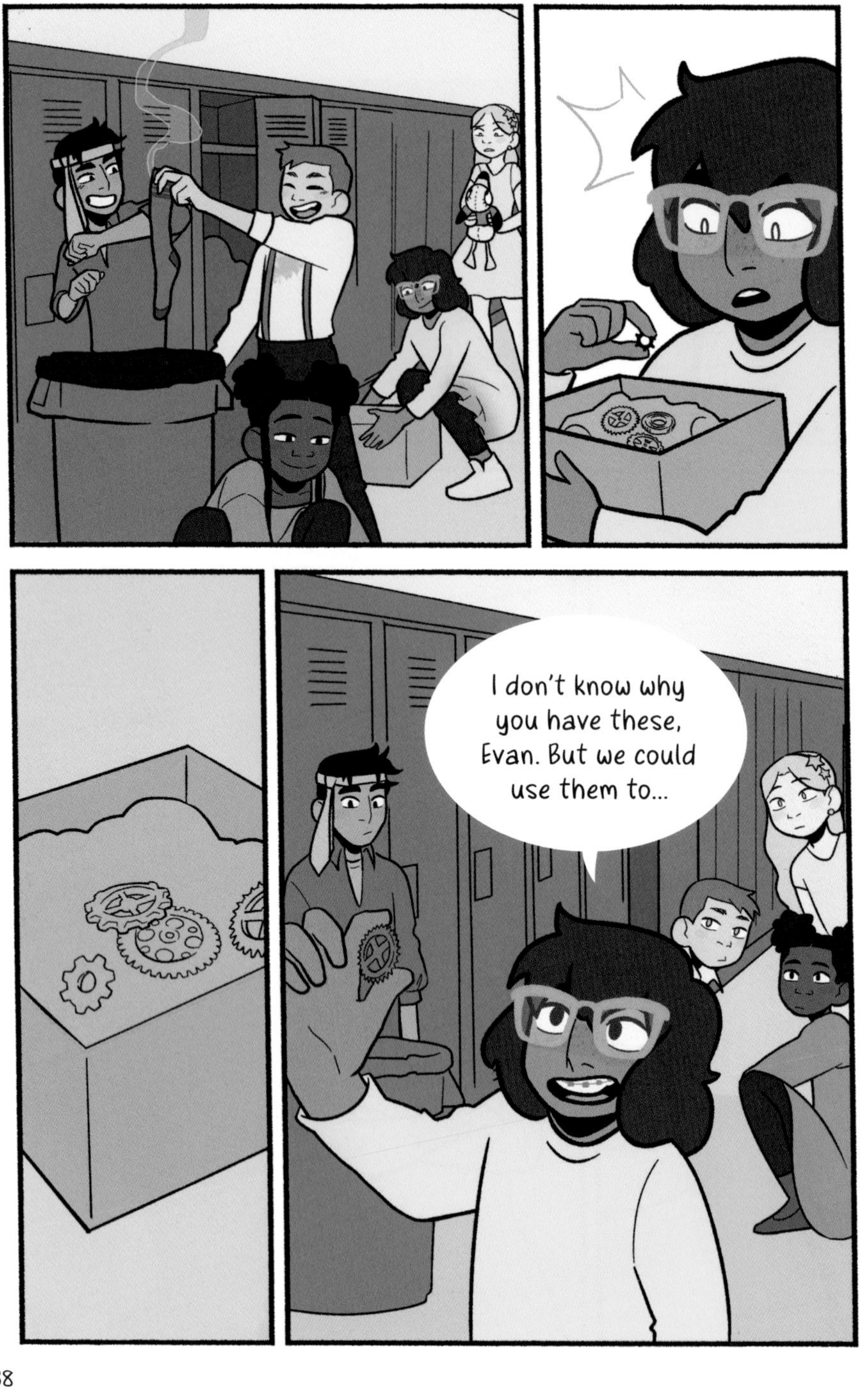
I don't know why you have these, Evan. But we could use them to...

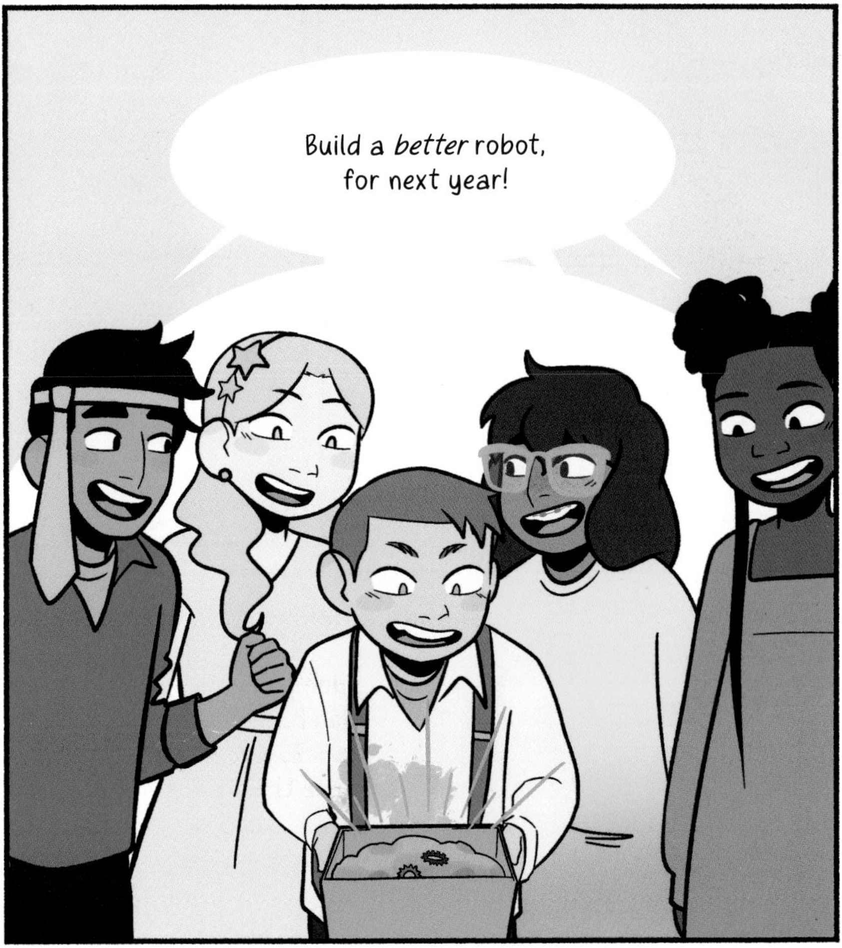
Build a *better* robot, for next year!
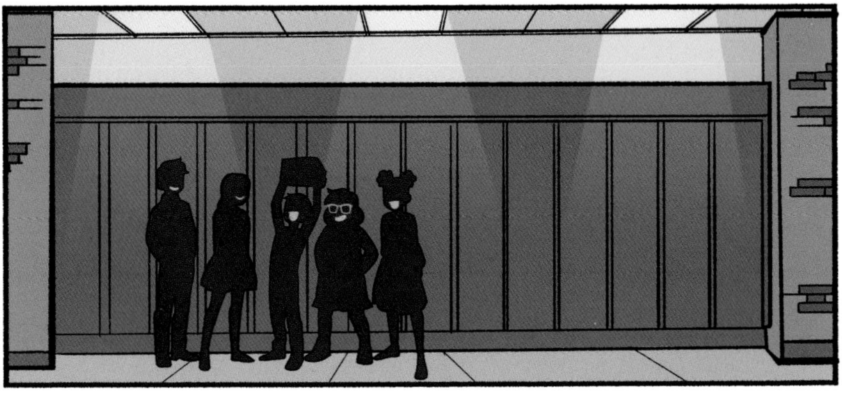